I0583444

Grist to the Cannon

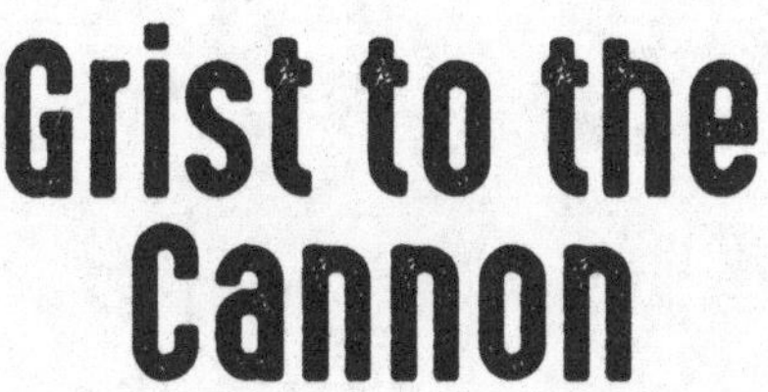

Book 1 of the Kidd Commander
series, by Aria Bell

*For anyone who
had to stay mad to stay alive.*

*A thing done out of spite
is still done.*

Go with care.

Grist to the Cannon

Phineas is only kind of disappointed the guy's got the wreck handled by the time she gets close enough to talk with him. Staring at the *still* forever-away radio tower jutting up into the horizon had gotten boring like an hour ago, so the mystery of this new shape shimmering through the heat mirages had done a lot to break the monotony. Even more once she'd caught movement and realized it wasn't just a pile of corpses.

The desert doesn't offer many hiding places so the driver had seen her coming; he'd stopped to rest on the back of the wagon after getting it set up again and decided to wait for her. When she gets close enough for socializing he wipes sweat from the grooves in his face with a scrap of fabric that might have been a potholder in another life. He's wearing overalls and big old boots, tinted driving goggles and a patterned bandanna around his neck, but Phineas could tell he was a working man from a distance. Long, faded spines of hardy reliability make straight and spartan lines in the air around him; she only ever sees lines like that in halos from the kinds of people who naturally produce packed dirt under their fingernails. This dude isn't the kind of reliability she's looking for, there isn't enough color to it, but she's glad he'd let her catch up.

The old man with the big eyebrows and the faded halo sociably spits in the dirt and nods at her.

"Hey," Phineas says, stopping in the middle of the road and jamming her hands in her coat pockets. Soft shuffling and chittering is coming from the other side of the wagon, a pair of beasts Phineas can't quite suss out.

"You walk here, girl?" the driver asks. He has one of those thready, callused voices that has to fight its way out, the same texture as yellowed plastic. Hearing his, Phineas relaxes into her own accent more than normal.

"Nah, I was in a truck for a while but the guy didn't wanna come this far." Phineas had never been in a real car before and she still hasn't, really. Manufactured vehicles and their fuels are hard to get in the fringier places like where she'd grown up, but there's always enough junk lying around to cobble together *something* that could get you and yours down the road. Long as you found a critter strong enough to pull it. She'd been excited about the novelty of hitchhiking, but decided to stay outside in the bed of the truck rather than make the cagey dude share the cab with her. He'd gone real squirrelly once he'd seen her up close.

Taking a minute to think about trucks lulls the conversation, which Phineas tries to avoid since it gives people time to notice that something about her makes them feel nervous. Hoping for inspiration, she looks around at the landscape she's already been looking around at for several days, leans back on her heels and feels past the cracked concrete under her bare feet. The desert is the exact same dry and empty it was last time she checked. The disappointment anchors her to her body; she makes her shoulders shrug and offers something mundane to fill the silence.

"There ain't even a road that comes this way, I was surprised when this one just showed up after 'while. Like it fell out of the sky or somethin'."

"Yeah," the man says, uninterested in discussing civil engineering. His name is Larimer, but Phineas never learns that because she forgets to ask. "Don't get a lot of travelers."

Phineas has seen the expression he's leveling at her before, it's the way people watch an unfamiliar dog without a collar.

"Mm, today's sucked," she states, still trying for ease. "Y'all don't make it easy to find you."

"What's here to find?" He's working something out, rusty old mechanisms whirring to life behind his eyes. "You ain't even got a pack or nothin'? Water?"

"I got big pockets," Phineas says, spreading her arms to drag her coat like wings around her. It's soft, made of worn canvas that drapes more than such sturdy fabric ought to, the sunset gradient a cheerful glare even against the oranges and reds already smothering the landscape. Ashy brown stripes border the hems, and across her back in a matching color are two concentric circles, like a target. It's too big for her.

"I'm fine," she insists.

"Hng," Larimer says, abject derision in the universally understood old man dialect. "Picked a hot as hell day to go for a fuckin' walk."

He's not wrong. Phineas' heels would be sizzling on the asphalt if they were anyone else's.

"Uh-huh." She shoves her hand through her short, sweaty hair, pinches at the ends. Her toothy smile is genuine. "Can I see the critters?"

"The armadillos?"

"Oh neat!" *Armadillos!* "Can I see 'em?"

Larimer looks like that's a weird thing to ask, but he jerks his head in that direction instead of pointing, still staring hard at her from under his bushy eyebrows.

Careful to leave plenty of space between the two of them, Phineas picks her way in a wide circle towards the other end of the wagon. Larimer is a grumpy, dusty man whose face had probably cemented into that suspicious expression years ago, but Phineas had been able to feel the neon jab of his anxiety as soon as he caught sight of her. She's been in this desert long enough to notice that its top-heavy stone formations don't tend to feel any particular way about anything; the only other sapient soul out here lighting up with fear had looked like a signal flare. Phineas needs a ride, she doesn't want to risk spooking him.

Or the armadillos! There are two of them, calm in their harnesses and apparently unscathed by whatever brought the wagon down. They're a little taller than Phineas and they smell like the farm down the road from Jocasta's house, which is kind of upsetting, so she pets her hand over an enormous scaly flank and gets absorbed in their texture instead. The emerald scales are smooth and marbley, hot under the relentless sun, but they shift like skin at her touch and she can feel the animal's heartbeat through them. She reaches up to see what the fur on their heads is like and giggles when the thing snorts at her, twitches one ear in a sleepy arc.

The wheel axles groan as Larimer hauls himself to his feet and ambles around the side to join her in the shade cast by the dusty wagon. Phineas can see him better without the sunshine in her eyes and realizes one of the deep wrinkles marking his face is actually a fresh cut, right where his goggles might sit, and she notices now one of the lenses is cracked. There's blood staining the bandanna around his neck, the red hiding in the dark checks of the fabric is more visible here out of the light.

"What happened?" Phineas asks, dragging a finger across her own face to match the gash. "You fall asleep at the..." A quick glance back at the wagon that doesn't help at all. "The. Wheel?"

"Got robbed," Larimer says. He hesitates, then: "Coupl'a days ago, a ways back from here. The axle ain't been right since, I gotta keep stoppin' to fix it like I just did. It's been slow gettin' home, but ain't nothin' left worth takin' now, at least."

Getting an accusation gives her the go-ahead to start reassuring him out loud. Phineas turns fully towards him, hands up. The lines in his face cut even deeper, probably at the circles burned into the palms of her fingerless leather gloves. They match the ones on her back. She shifts her weight to feel the road grit under her feet.

"I'm not here to make trouble," Phineas says, in her nicest, most-practiced least-commander-y voice. "I just wanted to ask if I could hitch a ride, if you're goin' that way." She points at the tower without lowering her arms.

"What do you need that way?" Larimer asks. He's calmer now, that flare of nerves smoothed over, so Phineas relaxes and puts her hands back in her coat pockets.

"A starship." She can't help smiling when she says it. She wiggles her toes. "Gettin' tired of walkin'."

He squints at her and finally that old-as-hell processor between his ears cranks out a punch card.

"Commander, ain't it? Y'all don't wear shoes." Phineas nods, holding his gaze.

"Is that okay?"

Phineas doesn't think of herself as manipulative; that's usually the longer way to get somewhere, and she doesn't have the patience for anything but a straight line. But she does like to get what she wants, and she's come to understand some stuff about other people after being Phineas Kidd for most of her life. From Larimer's perspective, inherent commander creepiness or not, she's a small, unarmed person in the desert carrying nothing but a glorified bed sheet on her back. She's an adult for sure, but still young enough that people like this tend to pity her if they don't pay attention to the battered skin across her knuckles or know what those circles on her hands mean. People also think she's a woman, which usually drives all those sympathy meters further along in out of the way places like this. Being underestimated is good, most of the time, and right now she hopes it will get her on this wagon and down this road.

She lets herself radiate only a *touch* of commander's charisma while she waits for an answer. Sleeping out here would be *miserable*.

In the air around him, in some colors Phineas never fooled with naming, those spartan lines are getting a little bit less faded, hanging a little bit straighter in the air. Larimer is a decent man. Phineas wonders if he might have a grandson with a haircut like hers, or maybe his wife's hair is the same shade of blushy pink.

"Well," he drawls. "There ain't a gun in my face, not a real one leastways. Still better than I was doing earlier." He moves to climb into the driver's seat. "Get in the back if you want. It ain't comfortable but it's better than walkin' around out here without any goddamned shoes on."

⊙

The jolt almost loses them a wagon wheel, and it *does* pitch Phineas out of her nap and onto the floor. She snorts against the splintery planks; her sweaty face has picked up a layer of dust to match the rest of everything while she's been out. There's no other cargo back here with her and Larimer hadn't bothered to resecure the storage equipment, so the wheels are catching every irregularity in the road to send doors and straps and chains banging themselves to pieces.

"Quit tearin' around back there!" Larimer hollers over the clattering of wood and rolling armadillos pounding the dirt. Those armadillo scales are whipping up a dust cloud, spilling under the wagon's cover and peppering Phineas' unprotected skin. She checks "wagon" off of the list of potential shapes she'll have her ship's heart take.

Awake enough now she can stumble to standing, she loosens up to move complementary with the shapes around her, finds her grounding to bridge the short gap between the earth and the wagon. When they're *really* good, commanders can keep their balance through anything. Phineas is *pretty* good, and that's enough that her feet stay steady on the floor while she sways to the back of the canvas cover to look outside.

First, she notices the road is a black strip rapidly receding into the horizon, framed by the dust billowing out behind them. That thump had been them falling down off the desiccated asphalt road and onto harder dirt. Huge, dark shapes litter the ground in a mysteriously regular path parallel to their direction, like holes in the desert floor. That mystery is boring, because:

Second, it got darker while she slept. The sun is still working on setting in the direction they're heading, bleeding frenzied warm colors into the cooling purple of the night. In the imperious desert sky Phineas can see the first few stars peeking out, but there's something else. One of the rock formations growing from the landscape looks...different.

She watches it for a long moment, mesmerized, and then it *moves*. Abject joy flies from her throat in a stab of laughter, yellow sparks lighting up the darkening space she's balanced in and latching onto debris in the whirling dust to send them back the way they'd come. She turns on her heel and lilts to the front of the wagon.

"Hey, hey!" Phineas is breathless as she grabs for the wooden rib that forms the opening to the driver's seat, leaning way out to get a better view of the enormous thing cutting a dark shape against the sunset. Larimer jerks the reins when he startles, the armadillos dutifully obeying the sharp lead and nearly tipping them. This old, weathered wood conducts energy as good as anything, and there's plenty of momentum to redirect. As soon as they leave the ground Phineas commands the wheels back down before she thinks to stifle the reflex.

"Hell's *bells!*" Larimer spits from under his bandanna. He eases them back on course and Phineas lets him without any more interference; he could probably use a win today. When he snaps his head around to look back at her she can see her face in his goggles, squinting in the wind. *"What?!"*

"What's that thing out there!" Phineas demands over the din, pointing back over his shoulder. Larimer looks.

"Oh, that's Careful Pete."

She leans in to try and hear him better.

"What's a Careful Pete!"

"You never seen a turtle before?"

Feeling that tugged-leash feeling she gets when boring people are boring, Phineas fights the urge to roll her eyes with her whole body at the person sparing her from camping in the desert.

It's difficult to get a grip on Careful Pete's exact size or even how far away he is, but Phineas had initially mistaken him for one of the lonesome mesas dotting the landscape; rearranging with the new context, the silhouette is so wildly strange she feels giddy with it. It's clear now that he *is* a turtle, or maybe a tortoise. Phineas can never remember the differences. She realizes now, as he takes another slow, unfathomable step towards the same tower they're approaching, that instead of a shell his back is covered in tropical trees. The dark spots she'd seen scattered alongside the road aren't boulders like she'd assumed, they're *palm fronds.*

She also twigs that he's a patron saint; she can feel the distinct shape of his spirit, ancient and heavy with faith and obligation. Patron saints are as varied as the different places they guard, but Phineas can usually pick them out by the sense of duty they're born with, a tie to the land that makes them better for learning about the environment than any guide if you know how to ask.

Phineas blocks out the cacophony around herself and reaches for him to get a better look. Her own spirit thrums unseen and greedy along the desert floor, sailing through all the spaces between the grit where the sunshine gets caught, but it turns out he's further away than she thought. Too far to touch.

Sulking, she reels herself back. But then: a spark, a battery on her tongue that tastes like hot leaves. Shielding the wind from her eyes with the hand she isn't hanging from, she can just make out a visage that might have been hewn from the same stones carving the sky around it. She sees the crescent-moon-white of an eye bigger than the wagon she's standing in.

The patron saint of this desert is watching her. Her body hums with the feeling of endless wandering, displacement, determined longing. Nothing and no one around for miles and miles and *miles,*

innumerable veins writhing with life like eels in a river, a throbbing pulse rushing to some unspeakable buried heart in the center of this place, the red earth and the bleeding sky.

Phineas laughs for real this time; the match that starts the fire in a house that begs for it, joyous and terrible light.

It's the first time she's done it properly today. Longer if she's being honest, and she loves how it spirals out in the air as a searing orange, dragging sunlight all the way up from her heart. Larimer can't *see* it, of course, but it doesn't take any sort of affinity to *feel* a commander's soul lighting up a room, and his answering shudder brings her down enough to put it away again. She wants the hell off this wagon so bad she itches with it, all her muscles twitching and jumping to run. Away from this desert and its flinching faces, further away from the ones who flinched at the *last* place she passed through and even further away from the ones at home who flinched *first.* There have to be people she can laugh with somewhere, she's *gotta* be getting close to finding them. For now, Phineas gets the lid on quick.

"He's harmless," Larimer says when she's quiet for too long. He's misconstrued all of it as nervousness and is gruffly trying to reassure her. She wants to tear her hair out. "He just circles the town usually, dunno what he's doin'. Folks tend to say he's lookin' for happiness."

"Happiness?" Phineas tries.

"Yeah," Larimer says unhelpfully, tugging the reins and smoothly adjusting their course. He doesn't seem to see a point in elaborating. "Used to be lots'a bigguns like him out here, probably. He's all that's left, exiled in his own home these days."

Phineas leans her head against the wagon rib to watch as Pete turns away from her, focused again on his trek.

"What happened?" she asks. It's too soft to carry the first time so she says it again, dragging her attention back into the wagon for real. "To the others? It's weird for saints to disappear like that."

"Don't know from no saints, I just drive the cart."

Extremely done with this mundane man, Phineas ducks inside and looks out the other opening towards the desert sky instead, the warmth stirring restless impatience in her chest. In front of them, smaller structures are rising up against the sun as it melts into the dimming earth. They coalesce into a meager skyline, but the tower is only getting taller and darker as it rises above everything else.

⊙

Larimer won't take her all the way into the town, but he drops her off a lot closer than where they'd started and that's pretty good.

"This is as far as I go, I've had a real shit day," he grumbles, not stepping down from his perch in the driver's seat to see her off. Phineas is petting the armadillos again. "If I go downtown tonight I'm just gonna run up my tab at Sergei's, my wife'll be pissed."

"Downtown" must be the wide, empty gap Phineas can see between a row of larger buildings. That feeling of home, again, too much nothing taking up too much space. She nods at him to clear her head, smiles big and honest.

"Thanks a lot dude, you really helped me out."

Larimer clears his throat, his discomfort visible even with his expression hidden behind the driving gear. God, even a smile is too much. Phineas is going to suffocate soon.

"Hope you find what you're lookin' for, I guess."

He looks like he might say something else, but thinks better of it and turns forward in his seat. Phineas gives him room and Larimer snaps the reins harmlessly against the armored animals. They curl into lopsided spheres, skid through the dry dirt long enough to find traction, then they're off like gunshots, the empty wagon banging over the terrain as violently as ever. Phineas watches it tear away towards a row of identical ramshackle buildings sagging morosely on the edge of the settlement. From here, Phineas can see some lit windows scattered across them, maybe residential buildings of some kind. The majority of them are dark.

For the first time, Phineas wonders if something is amiss. From the way Jo talked there ought to be a city here, a *real* one, not a pile of dried-out lean-tos. She doesn't have time to ruminate on it— when she turns back to face the tower and the rest of the town wrapped around the base, she has company.

The desert hare on the left is wearing a ruined straw hat, the top punched out to make room for tall fluffy ears, and the hare on the right is missing one tall fluffy ear entirely. The whole left side of his face looks like it's been mashed in by something blunt. They're both staring back at her more intensely than animals would, so Phineas nods respectfully to the second and third saints she's met today.

"Evenin'," she says. The one missing an ear thumps forward slowly, and Phineas kneels down to put them at eye level.

"There's a target on your back." The voice is like glass in a garbage disposal.

"Huh?" Phineas almost tries to look at her own back. "Oh, do you mean my coat? It's not a target, it's an-"

"Don't," it rasps. "Don't talk about that in here, things are listening." It tilts its head unnaturally, even for a hare, bending its neck alarmingly until the stump of its bad ear is parallel to the ground.

"Something for you," the glass grinds. "Take it."

Phineas hesitates.

"From...in your ear?"

The hare nods, sideways. Phineas glances at the other one, but its eyes are completely hidden under sun-dried straw. It's taller and thinner than the sibling twisted up in front of her, the proportions unsettling. It doesn't speak, but it folds its arms like a humankind, bent wrong at the elbows. Phineas could probably fight these things, but it seems like bad luck to spar with a saint so soon after getting to a new place.

The thing that's really getting Phineas' hackles up is that they don't have any discernible spirits, no halos or anything, which means they're hiding. It's technically possible all rabbits just do that no matter who they are, Phineas hasn't met very many, but patron saints hiding in their own territory probably isn't a good sign.

...But if they're hiding from something, and cared enough to warn her before she caught its attention, they might be handing her something useful. So, Phineas carefully brushes her fingers through the thick fur spilling from the hare's ear. It's wiry and shedding sun-warm dirt into the crevices of the hand wrap under her glove as she searches, and she tries not to think about how she shouldn't be able to reach so far in. She's up to her elbow in fur when something pricks her finger. The hare shudders.

"Pull," it says. "Quick."

She does. Something thin and blue and hard comes free, and it isn't very substantial on its own, but it *keeps* coming free from the hare's head long enough to make Phineas' stomach turn over. As soon as it's out, the hare shakes itself vigorously in the most animalistic gesture either of the saints have made so far, reaching up with one large foot to scratch at the base of the ear Phineas has just excavated.

The Item is shaped almost like an antler. Cornflower blue and pocked with holes, it's maybe as big as a fountain pen but sits heavy in her hand. Despite the holes, Phineas can't see through to the other side: the dark inside it is opaque.

"Wh...uh, what do you want me to-"

"We feel sorry for you," the hare cuts her off. "If you get far along enough to use this, we'll be listening."

"I still don't-"

"You be good, okay?"

"Hey-" Phineas looks up from where she'd been transfixed on the mystery object, but it's to the sound of them bounding away into the empty desert. The sun is only a sliver sliced above the town now, the encroaching moonlight is threatening to spill everywhere like ice water. Phineas realizes, watching the odd shapes disappear into the expanse, that it's going to be *freezing* here during the night.

Nothing for it now. She tucks the antler away in her coat pocket where it promptly slips from this plane of existence. Phineas slides her hands over the lapels of her coat, up around her neck, until the fabric shifts and extends along with her touch. Straightening her back, she pulls the newly formed hood over her head.

The tower against the setting sun casts a long, long shadow that runs all the way out of town and threatens to swallow her even here near the edge of it. The sun makes a long, long shadow behind Phineas too, but in hers, a pair of searing circles hovers between the funhouse-shape of her shoulders. The eye blinks, once, and Phineas smiles to nobody but herself.

⊙⊙⊙

Several provinces away, a very old rooster woman is running up her tab.

"Roosters don't crow," she slurs at her drinking partner, who is neither drinking nor her partner. "In the morning. Not at the sun like people think, crowin's for good things."

"Sure," the man says, trying to catch the barman's attention to get the check.

"I got nothin' good to say to that motherfucker." Jocasta slugs the rest of her well whiskey. "Roosters used to run this place, you know what I mean? You know."

"Garçon-"

"Their land, their things, and it rolls in and takes every scrap." She meets the man's eyes and even through the glaze of alcohol the screwturn of her years bolts him in place. "Rooster screams herself hoarse 'cause that's all she can do, but it's *not* fuckin' crowing. Crow is for *good* things."

The man swallows.

"H-her? The rooster is female?"

He feels a month of his life burn away under her contempt.

1

When she reaches the main street Phineas is covered in dust and *deeply* annoyed. The dirt back home had felt *good* under her feet; when she'd come home with tree twigs from the woods and mulch from Jo's garden sticking in her hair it was always a fight to get her in the bath. But this dirt is *miserable,* somehow, abrasive and joyless. The air bites her skin and cracks her lips, her hair feels scratchy and it irritates her windburnt face. At least it's *only* windburn. Phineas doesn't get sunburns anymore and can't even remember what one feels like. Not the normal kind, anyway.

It's brighter out here than she'd expected it might be once the sun went down, and colder too. There's a full moon keeping an eye on things tonight, menacing and cold and bleaching out the color of everything it touches. Phineas has never thought those kinds of things about the moon before but the way it hangs in the sky over this town demands new and unusual descriptions. The light it casts is thick and mawkish, walking under it is like trying to move through deep water. The hot sucks, the cold sucks, now the *moon* is acting up. Phineas decides right here in the empty street that all deserts everywhere suck ass. She's going to sail straight over every one of them after this.

Eventually the place she's been inching towards does begin to creep closer. She'd dragged her feet through the dust outside every gloomy window lining the main street and now she's a stone's throw from a yellow square splashing across the dirt road, the one warm thing she can see in the dark. The cheerful shaft of light is visible in the air against the moonshine, like a sunbeam warping around the jagged edge of a broken window. It's pouring around a set of wooden saloon doors, set in the middle of a building that matches the rest of the town in looking like every cartoon western Phineas has ever seen, though this place isn't as cleanly designed. Along with the other structures, this one with the light seems to have piles of junk haphazardly affixed to it; layers of wavy sheet metal skewer over the edge of the roof, steel pipes tied tightly over splitting wood beams squeal against the wind, and Phineas can even see a loose candy wrapper fluttering around the second floor balcony. Slowly clicking like a bicycle tire, a tiny windmill made of a dozen disparate parts spins atop a miniature radio tower growing out of the roof. It is, possibly, the most fun-looking building Phineas has ever seen. They probably have not-cartoon food in there, which sounds good enough already, but she's jonesing to touch those doors to see if they cartoon-creak.

There's also something *cool* in there, some*one* cool maybe. She isn't sure which, but she can sense something bright enough to be more interesting than both the doors and the food. Phineas pauses outside and gives the saloon one more look, trying to figure out what's waiting in there. Aside from her commander's perceptions she only sees electric light, aggressively golden against the monochrome of everything else but otherwise normal. When she looks upward, scanning the balcony again, the silver moon glares too brightly in her eyes to see anything significant.

Oh well! It'll be a surprise then.

The doors *do* creak.

When she steps inside Phineas is immediately assaulted by whiny country music coming from a set of wired speakers, nailed straight into the four corners of the dining room like what they did for music at church.

(That tweaks something down in Phineas' animal brain— *shouldn't she have been able to hear it through the open doors, out in the quiet street?*)

The wires wind through a doorway with a beaded curtain at the far side of the room, at the end of an aisle dividing an empty bar setup from a scattering of high-top tables. The walls and even the ceiling are a dense collage of trinkets, and photos, and paintings and tools and flags and anything else that could be attached to a flat surface. One of Careful Pete's lost palm fronds hangs in the rafters, spanning the entire length of the dining area.

There are three other patrons, dull and drunk, and to her immense disappointment Phineas doesn't care about any of them. None of them had even looked over when she creaked so cinematically through the entryway. Struck out again. Maybe she'd been wrong about finding something worthwhile in here.

A musical voice over the noise coming from the speakers.

"Be right out! Have a seat!"

Phineas has a seat, at a smaller table on the bar side, away from everyone else so she can sulk by herself.

The bad music, the air of failure and boredom puts Phineas' teeth on edge. She plants her feet on the floor under the table and tries to ground herself, her spirit reaching under the floorboards to find some connection with the earth. Once she'd gotten closer to the settlement her sense of it had changed dramatically; after days of following unassuming veins of sparse, quiet feedback leading in this direction she'd finally found the pulsing heart they feed into, deep in the earth under the town. Despite the odd, spoiled quality of the heart's energy, it's *alive,* a pleasant counterbalance to the mucky-mire feeling of the moonlight. But here in this restaurant there's a basement between Phineas and the soil, just wide enough to make her feel unmoored. Cellars are always awkward to try and ground through, they're like opening a door that leads out the side of a building into thin air. She heaves a sigh, toys idly with a crusty salt shaker and gives up her half-assed attempt, focuses in on the other patrons instead while she waits.

There's one who is so bland there's nothing to notice besides the fact that he's wearing sunglasses indoors, at night, and there's a pack of cigarettes shoved up under one shirt sleeve. Phineas only twigs *that* because Jocasta rolls her own, when she doesn't use a pipe, and she'd told Phineas once it was because premade cigarettes are basically sawdust. If you want to have a smoke you should take the time for it properly, she always said, and also she said not to take up smoking at all.

The other two are brighter. One is a bulky, dark-skinned man taking a nap in a corner booth, dreaming about something soft and golden that overpowers whatever else makes up his halo. At the table with the sunglasses guy, drinking from a frosted, out-of-place martini glass and staring at a radio in her hand is a woman who looks like glass herself. She's wearing a bright blue feather boa and her hair is swept back in a severe style behind her head, secured with a pretty lotus comb Phineas can't stop staring at. The color of it won't stay still in her eyes. If the woman has a discernible halo Phineas can't see it, but she is so frosty-pale just looking at her makes Phineas feel cold.

Even more dishware appears in the form of a sweating plastic cup tapping down on Phineas' table, shaking her back to herself. A lady in an apron is here.

"Oh," Phineas blusters. The lady smiles. She is *very* pretty.

"You looked real thirsty," the lady says. Warm bread, yellow bells, sunshine pouring from somewhere inside those gorgeous curls; on the heels of the other woman's ice, *she* is like stepping out of the snowbank and into the balmy air of a bustling pub, hot food and ruddy faces. Phineas briefly considers a timeline where she gets to kiss her for an hour behind that empty bar.

"Uh-huh," Phineas mumbles. "Thank you." She manages to tear her eyes away, and when they land on the brimming glass she realizes she *is* real thirsty. The angel briefly forgotten, she throws the whole thing back in one long transcendent go. Not thumping the bottom of the glass against the table would be an insult, after that.

The woman giggles, a yellow ribbon.

"I'll get you some more," she drawls pleasantly. "Want somethin' to eat? Kitchen's closed already but we got some ribs left over from today."

"I don't have any money!" Phineas says, just to get it out of the way. The waitress' perfect face twitches in preemptive exasperation, but she levels it out quickly. She's been doing this a while. "I *am* hungry though, I'd work it off if you got anything that needs lifting or washed, or..?"

The exhaustion eases at the mention of work.

"Well-" She's interrupted by the rattling of ice in another glass.

"Ellieee~"

Ellie The Waitress doesn't bother suppressing her annoyed expression this time. The man in sunglasses shakes his rocks glass at her again.

"What are you foolin' with that for?" he whines. His voice is devoid of personality and fills the room in a desperate sort of way. Phineas used to hear that voice from middle-aged men in suits who would come in to negotiate at the diner, bad haircuts and silly voices, like they all took lessons on leadership from the same frustrated little purse dog.

Ellie closes her eyes and takes a breath. Her nose scrunches up a bit and Phineas realizes belatedly that she's an anthro. In addition to her freckles there are spots closer to her dark, round nose that might mean whiskers, and her coppery skin is actually fine fur. It's not the first time Phineas had managed to ignore something obvious about a person right in front of her. Commanders spend so much time looking at things through the lens of suresight, energy and impressions outside the perception of less spiritually-inclined folks, that physical details often take a back seat. Phineas recognizes halos more easily than faces, most days.

The scrunch smooths away as Ellie wrestles her customer service face back into place.

"I'm *so* sorry, do you mind-"

"No no, go ahead," Phineas says, instead of telling Sunglasses to go fuck himself. Ellie straightens out her apron and crosses the floor. Phineas settles back in her seat, hands in pockets instead of fidgeting out on the table while she keeps watch.

Or she tries to, but her fingers brush against something small she'd already forgotten about. There's more light here in the bar than there was outside.

She retrieves the mystery item the hare gave her and turns it over in her hands, peering through the array of tiny holes. Sure enough, more light or not it's like the darkness inside it is a physical thing blocking out the view through to the other side. No stars, nothing.

There's a pop and a yelp that snaps Phineas' attention back up to the other table, but by the time she looks Ellie is heading back to the kitchen again. Sunglasses is laughing loudly, trying to get the glass woman to laugh with him. Phineas doesn't like her vibe very much, but does appreciate that she seems to be completely ignoring him.

The man looks at Phineas instead.

"What?" he slurs. His movement is sluggish, trailing a half-second behind him. "What's your problem?"

Phineas fixes him with an expression that, historically, makes people like him uncomfortable. It had been described to her as dissecting by folks who read that sort of thing into commanders, but that sounds awful smart for her tastes. Really she's just working out if there would be some unseen downside to decking him.

Sunglasses shifts in his seat. It makes the woman's eyes flit up from the fancy radio she's been immersed in, the kind with a big expensive touch screen. With her gaze, an icy feeling slinks up Phineas' neck, but the glass woman isn't actually all that interested and returns to her browsing before Phineas can get a real read on her.

The song oozing from the speakers ends and drops a quiet curtain over the space. There are sounds coming from the kitchen but they're unhurried, heedless of the drama threatening to splatter all over the dining room.

Sunglasses is still glaring like he really does want to know what Phineas' problem is, so she smiles.

"You should be nice to waitresses," she tells him.

"Mind your own *fuckin'* business," he says in that embarrassing, overcompensating voice from earlier. The beaded curtain rustles and the waitress returns with a tray of drinks, either unaware of or choosing to ignore the new tension. Maybe she's already tense. She passes by the other table, plunking down a new glass in front of Sunglasses without breaking her stride, and he's too drunk to collect himself enough to catch her. Ellie doesn't stop until she reaches Phineas on the far side of the room. She brought the pitcher this time.

More music jangles through the speakers, something in Russi. It makes a comfortable cushion in the space between the parties and things loosen like a sigh. A terse, frustrated sigh, not a relieved one, but a release nonetheless.

"Thank you for waiting," Ellie says, automatic in a way Phineas doesn't love. Phineas tips way back in her chair to watch Ellie's face while she pours more water, just barely catching herself before she plants her foot up on the table, settling for resting her shin against the edge instead. It's still grody, given her shins are covered in filthy, worn bandages to match the ones between her heels and toes, but Jo never could get her to interact normally with furniture. Ellie meets her eyes when she's done pouring, and a bizarre flash of camaraderie passes between them; Phineas had felt it more often as she'd traveled out of the hard to reach places, through the easier ones and finally into the impossible parts of the Sprawl. Even a dirty, unsettling commander who can't operate a chair looks like a friend if you're two (mostly) women listening to a loud man under the only speck of light in the desert.

"You want me to do somethin' about him?" Phineas asks, grinning a grin she hopes is cute and sly. Maybe even mysterious and alluring, that would be cool. "I could."

"Is he bothering you?"

Phineas tilts her head to see behind Ellie and finds the man staring directly at them, listening in.

"He's pissing me off," she says, louder. He makes to stand but the woman with him snaps something shrill and he settles, seething. Phineas turns back to Ellie. There's a plaid yellow kerchief keeping her long hair out of her face, and she's reaching back to the nape of her neck to tighten the knot there.

"Ray does that," Ellie affirms quietly between them. "Best not to start any trouble, hard to replace broken furniture out here."

In Phineas' vision, the golden glow coming from the waitress dims a fraction.

"Fair enough."

"Thank you, though." Ellie means it. Phineas smiles at her again, but it's just a regular smile this time.

"Can I ask you somethin'? About here, I mean," Phineas says.

"If it keeps me at this table longer, absolutely."

Phineas offers the hare's trinket to Ellie.

"Do you have any idea what this thing is?" she asks.

Their fingers *almost* touch when Ellie takes it, and Phineas tries to remain normal. The disappointing lack of backbone doesn't make Ellie less pretty, or Phineas less catastrophically queer. The pretty waitress sits down on the other side of the table to examine the item. She's doing the same thing Phineas did, trying to see through the holes.

"Where'd you get it?" Ellie asks. "It kinda-"

"Some rabbits, in the desert." Phineas thinks better of it. "Hares? They might have been hares, those are different I think." Ellie smiles at that, shining like a sunrise again. Her eyes are the same yellow as fresh buttercups.

"You ran into some hares!" Ellie says. "That's s'posed to be lucky." Gosh she's lovely, even if she's not a fighter. There's a scattering of freckles across the fine fur of her face, animating her expression while she speaks. "We love 'em, people think hares born here in this desert can tell the future. They hand stuff like that out to folks a lot..." She reaches into her apron, digging for something in the pocket while she talks. "You know ravens'll do that too?"

Phineas nods excitedly.

"My ma's a witch, a healer," Phineas says. "Ravens show up around her farm and bring her stuff all the time. We got all kinds of junk, we kept it in its own drawer."

Ellie retrieves what looks like a big marble, like the ones you hit the other smaller marbles with, except it's sort of chalky and metallic on Phineas' fingertips. It's sticking its tongue out at her.

"They brought me this a while back," Ellie says.

"I like the little face painted on." Phineas giggles before she remembers herself, but Ellie doesn't seem bothered by the tiny shower of sparks that turn up the ends of Phineas' hair. Ellie sets her elbow on the table, her hand a long line up the side of her face, pillowing out her chubby cheek and all those freckles.

"It's cute ain't it?" she muses. "I dunno why this one seems different. I usually end up just throwing their stuff in a drawer too, but I kinda get the feeling this little guy's special. I've been carrying it around with me." She shrugs. "Some people think they're omens, like somethin' bad is coming and you'll need their gift to help you avoid it, but I like to think they're lucky."

"Maybe *this* one is, have you *felt* luckier lately?"

Ellie smiles again, but by now Phineas' eyes are adjusting to her light and it's becoming clear how tired she is. As the thought happens, ice rattling in a glass is loud enough to be heard all the way across the room. Ellie's eyes flutter closed, frustration dousing her halo to a dull sheen, and Phineas wants to hit something.

"Hey!" Ray slurs, having already finished *another* drink. "Are you gonna leave me thirsty like this?"

The Look passes between Phineas and Ellie again, but Phineas isn't going to push. They don't say anything while Ellie stands and gathers her tray.

As Ellie crosses the room, Phineas watches Ray like a mean kid watches ants with a magnifying glass. She curls her fist and finds she's still holding the marble; she'll have to give it back next time Ellie comes by.

The space around Ray is an ugly gravitational pull that Ellie tries to avoid. She doesn't slow down near the other table on her way to the kitchen, but Ray's arm thrusts in her direction and he manages to get his fingers around the tie of her apron.

"Hey *hey,*" he secretes, loud enough for Phineas to hear it. "Where yuh goin'."

He tugs her off balance and gets his hands tangled in the fabric around her hips, pulls her clumsily into his lap. Ellie squeaks and Phineas weighs the consequences of starting shit after she was explicitly asked not to.

Over his stupid sunglasses, Ray makes eye contact with Phineas as he snakes his hands around and up the front of Ellie's dress, sets his chin on her shoulder, mumbles something so foul it stains Ellie's halo a rotten grey.

Ellie's on her feet so fast Phineas can hardly track it; fury blazes across her face like a struck match before she takes the metal serving tray in both hands and smashes it into Ray's face. The sound of the impact is *definitely* a certified cartoon effect, and so is the way Ray topples from his chair and hits the wooden floor. His sunglasses skitter to a stop somewhere beside him with perfect comedic timing.

Phineas' holler of a laugh careens off the walls, and every piece of glass on Ray's table explodes.

The cold woman sets her radio down.

The presence of a commander is like an ambient electricity in the air, and the texture varies depending on how they carry themself; sometimes they make people feel nostalgic, or hungry, or giddy, an extra layer over the imposition of their moment to moment emotions onto others. Whatever flavor it is, it's never more intense than during a spontaneous outburst of raw feeling, and that means a laughing commander has been the final image reflected from many, many expensive surfaces. Mirrors, windows, eyes.

Phineas feels like sunshine and the grit of sawdust and, as it happens, laughter itself. She's always the brightest thing in the room whether anyone else can see the halo or not, but when she laughs, her emotions go from a hearty suggestion to a fist around the throat.

Ray, on the floor blinking away canaries and too pissed off to be dragged along in her wake, doesn't see what the hell's so funny. Neither does the glass woman in the feather boa, now literally flocked with glass shards. The sleeping man in the corner, shocked awake and still getting his bearings, makes the mistake of focusing on Phineas. She's still losing it, and the man huffs an awkward, aborted laugh before he can get a hand over his mouth.

"What the *fuck* you laughin' at!" Ray snarls, jerking to his feet in drunken increments. Phineas can't catch her breath to talk, but she manages to see well enough to notice that Ellie has disappeared.

Ray makes a crazed noise in his throat, reaches into his waistband and produces a handgun.

"Woah, hey!" the sleeping man, now an extremely awake man, gets to his feet. *"Wait-!"*

Ray fires in Phineas' direction but it's a *bad* shot; it strikes something that shatters and the sound that makes is scarier than the bullet. Phineas has plenty of experience laughing while she fights, and her reflexes give her plenty of time to slide under the table and shove it onto its side to use as cover. The table is made of wood and one of the legs hadn't survived the fall; hiding behind that bead curtain would probably work better, but the cover is mostly for show anyway.

"You don't *talk* to *me* like that!" Ray screams. *"I* have the gun! *I* am in-!"

Another sound tears a hole in space somewhere outside Phineas' foxhole, and it takes her an extra instant to twig that it's a whole second gun going off rather than the entire roof caving in. She tracks the slower projectile's kinetic energy as it sails neatly through one of the saloon doors like a pencil poking through paper. This one's a *lot* beefier than Ray's toy, enough that Phineas peeks over the side of her table to see who fired it.

There is a massive rabbit man completely blocking the doorway to the kitchen, wearing a grease-stained apron and holding a gun that might be a cannon he ripped from the deck of a pirate ship. Ellie is there with him, safe behind his elbow but looking no less worried. The man's nose scrunches just the same way hers did earlier as he grinds his teeth.

The rabbit man is so furious it takes him a moment to get the words out, his bushy salt-and-pepper mustache twitches and bristles against his deep navy fur. Nobody seems inclined to rush him.

"You…" His Russi accent is thicker than Ellie's. He might be addressing everybody, but he's looking in Ray's direction. "You will *leave.*"

The glass woman stands. Ray doesn't move. Phineas watches his bleary eyes jump between the two anthros in the doorway and tries not to giggle at his sunglasses-shaped tanline. He seems to have already forgotten about his own weapon, it's hovering threateningly above his foot.

"Ray come *on.*" The voice from the waking man is surprisingly gentle, given his size. He's already got his back to the door, holding up two empty hands. He is completely sober, Phineas realizes. She'd assumed he'd passed out.

"Let's go back, Ray." The way he keeps repeating the name reminds Phineas of someone trying to get the attention of a loose pet wandering towards a busy road.

Ray's face twists, pulled between whatever cocktail of personality traits got him here in the first place and the barest humankind instinct of self-preservation.

"Raymond," the glass woman says. Her voice is a pinch in the fabric of the room, drawing everyone in to listen. Here in the middle of the desert, her breath comes from her in clouds, like there should be snow on the ground around her. "We're leaving now."

Raymond shoves his gun back into his waistband and Ellie visibly flinches. He glares at the workers huddled in their kitchen.

"This don't change nothin'," he says, shoving both hands through his greasy mullet and closing his eyes, no less drunk than he'd been two minutes ago. "When I want it, I'll come take it."

Phineas snorts again, she can't help it. Ray snarls-

"Wait *wait,*" Phineas says, leaning on her arms on the upper edge of the overturned table. Ray's will folds under her command so easily he doesn't seem to realize his feet have been nailed to the floor until he nearly trips over them. Phineas grins lazily at him, draping further over the table like a lounging cat. "Let's you 'n me have it out, guy. Outside?" She glances meaningfully at Ellie, unsure if the linecook cares to have this conversation. "No broken furniture that way. Er..." she shifts guiltily behind her busted table. "No more."

If Ellie gives an answer it's drowned out by the event of Ray lunging in Phineas' direction, the clumsy momentum interrupted by the waking man's arms wrapping around his waist and lifting him off the floor. He drags him backwards out of the bar and into the street, spitting and snarling like a cat who is doing the opposite of lounging.

The wooden doors creak gently in the hinges behind the men, and the amount of presence in the room remains the same despite their exit. The glass woman turns to look at Phineas, more visible now that she's unfolded from her seat. Her eyes are narrow, her dress is shiny and sharp, her nails are fantastically manicured. There is still that lotus flower comb tucked in her hair, a shimmering oil spill against the bright blue strands, throbbing against Phineas' senses like a toothache.

The woman touches the side of her face and a frosty blue visor hushes across her eyes. Phineas is being examined.

"Yeah?" Phineas asks, still leaned over the fallen table, not sitting up to talk to her.

The woman frowns delicately. She flicks her wrist, like swiping away eraser shavings from a page, and all the glass dusted across her clothes bubbles out and falls into a neat semicircle around her feet. Then she leaves too, her severe heels clacking against the wooden floor.

It's only three of them now, Phineas and the pair in the kitchen doorway. The rabbit man hasn't relaxed an inch; his gun is still readied, which kind of sucks, but Phineas perks up like a dandelion anyway.

"You got any sunflower seeds, Ellie?"

The question flits curiously across Ellie's face. She already seems much calmer now.

"Hm?"

"I'd really love a little dish of sunflower seeds after this, if you got 'em."

The man, who Phineas is pretty sure now is Ellie's dad, asks Ellie a question in quiet, stern Russi. Ellie responds in kind, then nods at Phineas without further comment. She seems resigned, but a yes is a yes, so Phineas gets to her feet, grinning

"I'll be right back, 'kay?"

It is difficult to tell from the outside but Sergei's bar actually has *three* floors, not just the one. There's the ground floor, then a cellar and living quarters that are easy to miss because they're underground, and finally some space above the dining room makes a third. The third floor is easy to miss for no real reason at all, and used as overflow seating when things get busy, normally. Things have not been normal for some time so the tables and chairs here have been gathering dust. A set of windowed doors leads outside to an equally dusty widow's walk, and tucked away in the single sliver of the balcony unrazed by the moonlight is a man eating his last candy bar.

Ulrich is tired. Some other adjectives are "dirty" and "hungry", but the important one the audience should remember is "armed".

Trying to trick himself into thinking he's eating more than he is, he takes comically small bites while the sounds of angry voices and occasional gunshots float up from the bar. At one point somebody fires a blunderbuss and Ulrich watches as a pellet the size and shape of a plum makes it all the way across the empty street before shattering the window in the opposite building. He finishes his pathetic meal and stares with open disgust at the chocolate melted on his fingers, tries not to despair about the fact that he briefly considers licking them clean. He can't deny now that his clothing has started to loosen around him, the usual layer of thick fat he comes by naturally is starting to evaporate and every time his tightened belt digs into his belly he is angry all over again. He is so fucking sick of being hungry, *dirty*— he is so fucking sick of being in the goddamned *desert.*

Ulrich watches as two of the men stumble out into the street below. The smaller one wriggles out of the other's grip, shoves away from him and nearly puts himself off balance. He's still spitting abuse at his coworker, drunk and incoherent, but Ulrich's seen enough of him to know nothing he says is worth paying attention to. Regardless, Ulrich reaches under his outer shirt and wraps his hand around Glückssache, holstered at his side under his ribs. It is not a sniper rifle by any means and that's a shame, but the revolver will do for now, for this. From nowhere, a waft of gin like a brush of familiar fingertips against Ulrich's face. He's out of sight, so Ulrich lets himself lean obligingly into the empty air. The touch disappears somewhere in his hair, near his temple, nudging his attention back to the present.

Rook is heard before she's seen, in those heels. The men turn to her when she appears but she doesn't slow down to give them any orders; of course, she expects they should fall into step behind her on their own. Same as ever. Ulrich rises soundlessly and moves to the railing, aligning with the shadows.

Shooting people isn't as enjoyable for Ulrich as people tend to think. It's *loud*, it makes a mess and ammunition is not always easy to find or fabricate in the sorts of places he ends up needing it. A gun is not a toy, it's a magic wand that, waved correctly, makes people behave in ways that help you *avoid* having to shoot them. But the trick only works if you really *are* willing to pull the trigger when it doesn't. Right now, it helps that he has never been so furious to see another person in his entire wretched life.

Ulrich takes aim.

Someone else breathes in and presses the heels of their hands to their mouth.

A rude sound from the porch creates a vortex of indignity that consumes the attention of everyone in the street. The volume is impressive, but it tapers off prematurely because the person making it decides to start giggling in a way that raises the hair on Ulrich's neck. He can't tell from here which part makes Rook and the rest angrier, the person themself or their audacity, but he can feel the steam rising all the same.

On the porch underneath Ulrich's feet, the noisemaker is blocking out a person shape in the bar's yellow light to cast a long black silhouette across the road, the dirt lighting around the head like the halo of a religious icon. Something about that makes him hesitate, and he's only stayed alive this long by listening to his instincts. The two trade places; she (he thinks) moves into view as Ulrich slips back into the lucky shadow, confident even in the exposed position because the girl pulls attention like cast dice. She's still giggling, Ulrich feels it in his teeth. She wipes her spitty hands on a hideous orange coat as she bounds down the porch stairs and into the road. She's smaller than Ulrich had expected, the light had made her look *much* taller.

26

"Yeah you feel real stupid when people don't play your game, huh?" She steps fully into view, right in the middle of the street. Her movement is strange, loose and fluid like she's a flag tied down by her feet. If he were less experienced with weapons, Ulrich might mistake her for clumsy. "Y'all are awful rude for how easy it is to get you riled up. You're really askin' for it."

The amateur with the gun stumbles a few steps towards her. Notably, Rook lets him act without interfering. It puts him between Rook and the girl, who appears to be doing runner's stretches.

The noisemaker shakes out her hands and gets them up in a low, almost lazy imitation of an orthodox guard; her lower elbow is pulled back near her side rather than in front of her chest, the fingers of her forward hand splay out rather than curling into a fist. Ulrich's been to enough boxing matches to tell it's a bastardization of that and some other martial art he can't name. But he knows enough to check her feet, and it pings the part of Ulrich's brain that keeps him from getting caught in crossfire. Fighters who move like this are either new students or so far along the curve they've come back around to the other side, and if her bizarre demeanor feels like *anything* it's confidence, only getting stronger as she warms up.

"I'm frustrated." Her huffed laugh comes with a shower of golden sparks that leave streaks in Ulrich's vision. "I'm feelin' mean and you're an asshole. Let's go, buddy, come on."

The silence stretches like a tripwire.

She grins behind her guard, and Ulrich is too far away to make out the exact details, but the physical wave of aggression that washes through him feels like she's laughing right in his ear. She says, "I'll let you go first, if you're scared."

In his line of work Ulrich has seen plenty of morons get their finger around a trigger and think it will make up for the places they fall short. Almost invariably, they are the types of men who fly off the handle when other people commit sins like threatening their authority by smiling too much, or not enough. They are usually a danger to themselves more than anything, but a gunshot wound will bleed out whether or not it's intentional.

It's funny from up here, watching one of Rook's lackeys froth at the mouth over what may be the least intimidating taunt Ulrich has ever heard, but he isn't looking forward to watching an unarmed person get clipped. There is no position on the bell curve that would make Ulrich bet on fists in a gunfight. He switches off his hearing aid before the shooting starts.

"Eisse-" the gun lackey snarls, clenching a fist around nothing. Ulrich rolls his eyes at the alias Rook had apparently taken on while she sizes up the girl through her visor. Something she sees is bothering her, something heavier than schoolyard teasing. Rook's not nobody, she probably sees the same kinds of things that made Ulrich elect not to interrupt. The conclusion she comes to is different.

"Yeah alright, Ray," Rook says, folding her arms and stepping back, leaning against a stretch of storefront with no uncomfortable trash tacked to it. "Take her out."

She is hardly out of the way before Ray is making an inhuman noise and firing in the rude girl's direction.

The rude girl moves.

There's a shift in the light. The moonsoaked air is etched with angles, lines of symmetry that Ulrich has only now become aware of, because that thing in the street has just wrapped her fist around every one of them and *pulled*. The space around her fractures with yellow that carves out from the bullet's impact in her palm, winds around her chest and arcs down through her feet, billowing the dry dirt into a cloud. It all happens instantly, between heartbeats, but Ulrich is very comfortable with operating in half-time. He even has room to admire the fireworks.

The dust dissipates, she opens her hand and he sees the round catch the light as it falls, lancing straight through his rage at Rook to light up an old, *old* machine stretching down and down into the depths of Ulrich's memory. Its gears have long since ground to a halt, it's been sitting in the dark for ages. In the dark is not the same as dead.

Ulrich holsters his gun and sits back to watch what she does. No one notices him because they are watching her, too. She's still smiling.

"Wanna try again?"

Ray does, fires again, again, missing her completely even as she bounds towards him with the insistence of an oncoming train. Her steps flare with light Ulrich can't stand to look at, brighter and brighter until she crouches low just ahead of where Ray is getting ready to fire another round. She launches into him like a skyrocket, complete with a resplendent trail leading to the report of her fist slamming into his ribcage.

Ulrich doesn't look away to see where Ray lands. The girl has settled back into her bizarre stance but still glows like she did before, a spot of daylight. The air around her is scattered with sparks, rising through the strands of her hair and curling up the edges of her long coat.

He tastes lotus petals, a voice whispers in his ear and the machine dominating Ulrich's mind groans in the shadows, straining to move.

⊙

It wasn't anything that would kill him, but the hit was nasty and Royal knows in a vague way that broken ribs can be dangerous for all the soft stuff they usually protect. As Royal kneels beside him Ray coughs, sucking in the air that had been knocked out of him. Incredibly, he tries to get back on his feet.

"Lemme *go*," Ray spits, pawing at the hand keeping him pressed to the dirt.

"This is no good," Royal hisses, desperate to get through to his friend. "This is *no* good, dude. I think she's a commander, there's no version of this where we win."

Finally, when Ray looks up into his face Royal can see light in his eyes, like getting through to a sleepwalker. But he doesn't find anything encouraging.

"Not done already are y'all!"

Something in the commander's voice shivers up his neck like hearing a wolf howl in the distance, lights up every nerve and muscle with the instinct to get the hell *away*. His stomach sinks when he sees an opposite reaction in Ray, her taunt vibrating through him enough for him to shake off Royal's grip and stagger to his feet.

There isn't time for this; Ray's dusty back is getting further away, picking up speed as he hurtles towards the daylight. His gun is still in the dirt near Royal's knee.

"Stop *laughin'* at me," Ray snarls, reaching for the pocket where he keeps his switchblade. "Stop *laughin'!*"

In one last bid to get all of them out of this intact, Royal looks to Eisse for help. She hasn't moved an inch, still leaning coolly against a boarded-up display window and watching the fight through her visor.

"Can't you *do* something?" Royal demands. "She'll *kill him.*"

Eisse's eyes flicker over him for a second, like she's working out what to say, then Ray screams as he lunges at the girl with the knife Royal *knows* he never learned to swing. Eisse settles back into observing again, already finished with a conversation they didn't start.

Alright.

None of Ray's furious, clumsy slashes are landing, but the commander *is* making the effort to dodge them. Not completely impervious then, that's good. Royal doesn't have anything sharp but what he's got will have to work. They don't need to win, he just needs to get this stopped so he can get Ray out of here.

As he gets to his feet he reaches into the subspace attached to the bandanna around his bicep and feels for the handle of his weapon.

⊙

Phineas feels like she's dancing with a little kid. This is a training exercise more than a real fight, Ray has no idea what he's doing. It's not nothing, there are a few near misses that get her blood moving, but she'd really been hoping for...

For what? What *is* she doing here?

Backup is coming on fast, the bigger man is drawing an old baseball bat from a subspace pocket sewn into some fabric around his arm. He drops into a sprint to close the distance and Phineas readies herself. Maybe this will make things more interesting.

Something glints in the corner of her vision, a burst of mirror-shine from the balcony— the moon catching some broken glass? Something about it holds her attention enough that she stares too long, loses her rhythm and Ray lands a deep cut across her ribs, tearing through her shirt.

Ray shrieks, delirious with the single win he's clawed together tonight, and when he makes the odd decision to ditch the knife and reach for her shoulders Phineas realizes too late she doesn't know where the bigger guy got to. Caught off-guard in Ray's grip, she feels someone else looming behind her, and her vision explodes with stars.

⊙

The bat connects with the side of her head and finishes its arc too easily, like swinging through smoke, but somehow the impact rattles all the way to Royal's shoulder. It's like her weight is sitting in the wrong places, how does a person *weigh* wrong?!

The commander's body makes a blur perfectly parallel to the ground and crashes through the crumbling outer wall of the hardware store, pocked with hubcaps and old mason jar lids that rattle down behind her. Royal watches the pitch-black opening she made, like a mouth rimmed with broken teeth, waiting for something to happen as the dust settles.

Ray crows, *"Fuck* yeah dude!!"

He slaps Royal on the shoulder and screams wordlessly up into the air, but the instant he stops there's a thump, then another, the debris in the wall beating out like a heart, then-

Royal *just* gets his hands on Ray's chest to shove him out of her way, he feels the commander's coat scrape across his knuckles as her blinding form soars through the space between them. Royal reels back, his vision all spots.

"What-!"

He catches the sight of her for a split second, a searing shape crouching against the wall of the drug store, *seven feet above the ground.* By the time he hears the wall **crack** under her feet as she leaps she's getting bigger again, closer-

Instinct isn't enough to keep his eyes from flinching shut but it gets his bat up in its arc, swinging at the world's loudest pitch, but at the end of the swing he feels something- *clinging?* He opens his eyes, the light behind him disorienting-

Behind him?!

Royal whirls, tries to ready his bat and finds it won't budge, like it's been nailed down to the thin air over his shoulder. He jerks it in front of him, trying to break her grip on the other end.

There's no grip to break, the commander didn't catch it in her hand. She's standing on it.

She's weightless, but held straight out in front of him now the bat suddenly feels as if it's trapped in cement. He's too shocked to muster any real thought about what he's seeing, to even *move:* instinct simply keeps his grip tight around the handle, every batting lesson he's ever had betraying him. Towering over him, her shining halo consumes the world. All he can see of her face is her grin, her teeth.

"You're the devil," Royal breathes. Her knee connects with his chin, and that's the last thing he knows for a while.

⊙

The world is riotous with energetic color, and that isn't gonna work for this next part, so when Phineas touches back down after kicking the shit out of that guy she breathes out, lets all that leftover energy run through her feet and back into the earth. Everything comes back into focus, just objects in regular space again. One of the objects is trying to-

Person, it's a person, holding up the gun he'd retrieved from the street and backing away as she calmly approaches. The trigger clicks but nothing happens, he's out of ammo. He finally just throws it at her and it lands neatly in a tin bucket instead; that would have been an impressive toss if he'd meant to do it.

Ray turns to run as Phineas gets in arm's reach of him but he trips, his feet sliding in the dry dirt. He still *reeks* of booze. When she grabs the back of his shirt and hauls him up he swings his fist blindly, which is annoying, so she pinches his ear between her knuckles. He howls like her touch burns him.

"Quit whinin'," Phineas huffs, dragging him back to the front door of the bar. He stumbles the whole way, like he wants to try and run but keeps bitching out when it hurts too bad. This guy sucks so much.

Phineas gets him in front of the porch steps and shoves him to the ground again, taking advantage of his disorientation to perch on his back.

Living with a doctor hadn't ended up teaching Phineas much in the way of healing, but Jo had got across the useful stuff like where you could pull or twist or squeeze someone to get what you want with the minimum effort. Her knee in Ray's back and her other foot rooted to the road, Phineas fists her hand in his nasty hair and grinds his face into the dust, then she bends his wrist back across his shoulderblades and searches with her fingertips for those tendons she still can't name. Ray makes a panicked noise before she even does anything else, muffled by the ground, but Phineas had felt the fight go out of him as soon as his friend went down. This is just cleaning up.

"Ellie!" Phineas calls brightly. She can see her peeking through one of the big windows of the bar. "It's done, come out here a minute."

Only briefly hesitating, Ellie disappears from the window and creaks halfway through the front doors.

"Um," Ellie says, biting her lip. At the sound of her voice Ray's weak halo surges with humiliated rage, he tries to buck Phineas off of him but she mashes his nose back down into the dirt like a dog. Holding him there, she smiles up at Ellie.

"Hi," Phineas says. Ellie raises one arm from where she's wrapped them around herself and waves awkwardly. Phineas leans down, close to Ray's ear. The alcohol stench is overwhelming.

"Apologize," Phineas says.

"Get the fuck *off* me-"

Now she squeezes, the gristle-crunch of a complicated network of connective meat in his wrist almost nauseating under her fingers. Ray thrashes, wailing panicked nonsense until he manages to shout something approaching an apology in Ellie's direction.

"Sorry for *what?*" Phineas asks, loudly enough for Ellie to hear it.

"Enough!" The shrillness in Ellie's voice snaps Phineas' attention to her; the horrified look on her face is...not what Phineas wanted at all. She eases up on Ray's wrist and he goes limp, breathing hard. Ellie exhales slowly, settling. "That's *enough.*"

Phineas nods brusquely, then sits up to dig through Ray's pockets. A lighter, some kind of plastic card, a ratty red scrap of fabric like the other guy had around his bicep; she stuffs it all in her coat. She even takes the pack of cigarettes from his sleeve.

"What are you *doing?*" Ray groans. Phineas gets her hand in his hair and wrenches his head back again, leans in close.

"I'm kinda pissed you're gettin' off so easy," she says, keeping it between the two of them. "You're lucky I'm taking your smokes and not your teeth. Lucky too that Ellie's too nice for her own good." She tightens her fingers against his scalp. "If I hear about you pullin' shit like this again, I'm gonna make sure we're alone next time."

She doesn't wait for a reply before dropping him and climbing to her feet. He curls onto his side to cradle his arm, but otherwise he doesn't make any move to get up. Phineas hears a soft scrape somewhere behind her and turns to find the bigger guy coming to, and some ways behind *him,* still leaning against a wall like she's waiting in line for coffee, is the glass woman.

As Phineas watches, her halo shimmers into view, the woman intentionally dismissing whatever had been hiding it. It's minutely defined and rigid, spiking out in freezing crystalline patterns, ticking slowly in a perfect circle around her head like a clock face. If this one wants to fight it would be a lot more than a warm-up.

Phineas feels her stomach growling.

"Hey," Phineas calls, waving. The woman raises her chin.

"Hm?" Her voice is smooth and pretty, and even that single syllable is bratty as hell. Phineas falls into her slouch.

"Are *we* fightin' now? 'Cause we can, but I ain't had dinner yet and I'd kinda like to call it here if that's cool."

The woman touches her temple and the shiny blue visor across her face vanishes, a shimmer from left to right. When she shakes her head her high ponytail swishes behind it, electric blue bright in the moonlight, reflecting in the purple vinyl of her dress. Phineas remembers Jo telling her about poisonous flowers, that they develop special colors to warn people not to eat them. The glass woman looks across the street at her downed guys. Maybe she's thinking the same about Phineas.

"Yes," she makes eye contact again. Her eyes are the same icy blue as her hair. "I think we're done here."

Phineas makes a lazy salute.

"Later then," she says, turning away. She bounds back to the porch and grins at Ellie. Phineas doesn't get one back. It's okay, it's fine, Phineas can salvage this.

"Here, you forgot this," Phineas holds out the odd marble, Ellie's lucky charm from earlier. She'd remembered it when she reached into her pockets to stash Ray's stuff. "We kinda got interrupted before."

Praises, Ellie *does* smile now, a dazed little thing but it's something. She reaches behind her neck and unties her kerchief. Her curls fall gracefully around her face and two long rabbit ears spring up, twitching after being held down all day.

"Why don't you hang onto it?" Ellie says.

⊙

Maybe it's only because his *own* hair is disgusting against his neck, another painful casualty of this godforsaken desert, but when the rude girl gets close enough the first detail Ulrich notices is *her* hair. It seems to constantly defy gravity; he'd assumed it was a temporary side effect of the commanding but it's still hanging in a cheerful swoop across her face. He is *positive* this woman doesn't take the time to style it like that each morning, has likely never even *looked* at any sort of product, and she's so dirty there's *no reason* it should look so light. Even cut short like it is each curl and wave seems to be lifted by some unseen force to frame her face, bounce with her movement like a cartoon character. Ulrich has never cared for cartoons.

"What'd you say your name was?" the waitress asks her. "Sorry if you gave it already, I-"

"Oh! I'm Phineas."

The word glints ravenously in Ulrich's left eye.

"Well, you better come on inside, Phineas."

Phineas' answering giggle pinballs across the metal panels of that terrible mechanism Ulrich has inside him instead of bone or muscle, shakes the corrosion from every component it touches and rattles all the way to the foundations like a flare down a well.

This time the spark catches, and the gears shudder to life.

2

The bar this time has the distinct stillness of a closed establishment. There's no music or clattering cooking implements and the lights in the dining room are out, dim illumination coming only from the kitchen doorway now, crisscrossed with bizarre shadows from the bead curtain. Ellie ushers Phineas through the damaged saloon doors and turns to lock up behind them, which consists of dragging a pair of sliding panels from inside the doorframe and latching them together. She turns and catches Phineas staring at the dirty windows looming on either side of the locked door. They don't even have curtains.

"Kinda silly huh?" Ellie admits, her cheeks coloring. "Truth is the doors on the balcony upstairs don't even lock at all, and it ain't like people wouldn't come in anyway. But it feels better than doing nothing."

"Always better to do something," Phineas agrees.

Ellie rubs her arms and nods, mostly to herself, then forces a customer service smile as she starts towards the kitchen. Unsure what to do here in this middle space, off the clock but still in her apron, Ellie awkwardly holds the beads aside so Phineas can walk through the doorway.

It's a kitchen like all the other commercial ones Phineas has seen before. Lots of stainless steel, black rubber floor mats full of holes, the forever-smell of food and griddle grease. There's an exciting splash of color on the island though. A metal serving pan half full of cooked ribs, a cloudy plastic container of coleslaw, and there in front of them both: a cheerful salsa dish brimming with sunflower seeds. Phineas' stomach loudly remembers the concept of food.

"Go on, take what you want," Ellie says. "Papa says it's worth it to see Ray get his ass beat."

Too hungry to fool with false humility, Phineas gets her gloves unbuttoned and starts on the sweaty handwraps underneath, piling all of it off to the side as politely as she can. There's a second where she considers washing her filthy hands, but commanders don't get sick from stuff like that; she only thinks of it at all because Ellie is watching. That ends up not being inspiring enough. Phineas tears off a slab of meat and gets to work.

Ellie giggles softly from somewhere behind her, then she reappears in front of Phineas with a roll of brown paper towels and a *beer.* She also produces a high stool from under the island, which Phineas had completely missed. Phineas sheepishly wipes her mouth and sits properly to eat.

"You don't *have* to take this, I dunno if you drink," Ellie says, tipping the sweating bottle towards Phineas. "Papa's kinda old-fashioned and figured you'd-"

Phineas is already reaching to take it.

"Oh man, no, yeah, *thanks.*" Phineas gets it open against the corner of the metal table and takes an absolutely ethereal draw from something so dark and thick it almost goes down like syrup. Hideous! *Gorgeous.*

"Is your dad gonna come say hi?" she asks, suddenly a fan despite how aggressive he'd been. Getting a drink from a guy like that feels good, and she hasn't been able to afford alcohol in a minute.

Ellie takes long enough to answer that Phineas forces herself to pause and get a good look at her.

"What's wrong?"

An awkward moment goes by before Phineas comes up with an answer herself. She sets her second rib down on a paper towel and holds up her palm. Under a smattering of grease and barbecue sauce, her tattoo stares, a target symbol to match the one on her coat. They're not at all secret, she'd even burned identical symbols onto the leather palms of her gloves, but the faded, untidy blackwork directly on her skin is a lot more incriminating.

"Not a fan of commanders?" Phineas tries to say it lightly, very aware of the red dripping from her hands. When Ellie meets her eyes her pretty face is twisted up into a combination of guilt and embarrassment. No trace of the waitress façade is left here in the cool, quiet kitchen. Phineas' sloppy ink had finally been enough to help Ellie choose a role.

"I'm-" Ellie starts.

"It's fine." Phineas means it. She grins. "Most people who throw me out don't feed me first."

"I'd ask you to stay the night otherwise, but he..." Ellie looks like she wants to sink through the floor. "Papa had a brother, who was a commander. I never met him and Mama didn't like to talk about him so..." Phineas waves it off.

"I'll figure somethin' out."

Ellie shakes her head, wrapping her arms around herself.

"I dunno, there's not really anyplace else to *go*. Far as businesses it's just us these days."

Well. If it's gonna be uncomfortable anyway, no use tiptoeing around the point.

"What. Happened here?" Phineas asks, frustration bleeding into her voice. "What *is* happening here? Why did *I* have to beat those guys down for bothering you?"

Ellie is staring down blankly, lightyears away.

"It's complicated," she says. "How much time you got?"

"Long as you do," Phineas says through a mouthful of meat. Ellie sighs, leaning her chin on her hand and looking away to gather her thoughts. Her yellow eyes are wide and serious when she faces Phineas.

"This was a mining outpost first," she begins. "Not even worth a name. The workers called it Last Chance as a joke, since passing it by without resupplying meant you probably wouldn't make it to the next place. It *was* small-" Here, she glances away again, a gesture that would have given Phineas' instincts a swift tap on the shoulder if she hadn't been fiddling with the lid to the coleslaw. "-until one of the workers stumbled across a starstone deposit."

That gets Phineas' attention.

"Big one, huh?" That would explain *most* of what she's felt under the earth here. Starstone is never far off no matter where you go; it's in the wiring of every electric building, in every radio and vehicle, and to some extent it's in the soil almost anywhere. But most of it is too small to cause much interference with commanders' senses, or it's been cut to an inert shape specific to whatever tool somebody needs it for. Natural starstone deposits, especially bigger ones, can get strange even by Phineas' standards, but they're also *valuable.* They're rare to begin with, but figuring up the odds of finding one in an *accessible* part of the Sprawl requires an equation Phineas can't begin to calculate.

"Enormous," Ellie nods. "Big enough for the tower out there."

"I could feel it on my way here but I thought I must be lookin' at it wrong. I've never felt anything like that." Phineas swallows and swipes her mouth on the back of her wrist without thinking about it, then tears away more paper towel to wipe off the back of her wrist. "Felt like somethin' else with it too, there's something real weird about the land here."

"Dunno anything about that myself," Ellie says easily. "I just serve the food."

"Sure," Phineas grins amicably. There is barbecue sauce near the corner of her mouth.

"Well, you can imagine how things went after that," Ellie continues. "The stone brought in commerce, and the outpost grew into a proper settlement almost overnight. That was when we moved here and started the restaurant."

Ellie's smile is soft.

"Pretty soon after that we had an engineer show up, with plans for the tower you saw outside. That brought in even *more* tourists who wouldn't have crossed the- the desert, to get here before, but it also helped strengthen the signal from the starstone deposit enough to compete with bigger settlements." She looks genuinely proud, a saturated glow lighting up her halo. "For a minute there we were the only city in the province where you could get power *and* a perfect radio signal from anywhere."

Phineas raises her hand. Ellie giggles.

"Yes?"

"And water, right? Probably a big deal out here."

"Mm-hmm, it was like the natural cycles moved faster, water and plant growth and all that. More favorable weather patterns. It was real lush here while the tower was working." She smiles again, remembering something sweet. "Reuben- the engineer who built the tower, he tried to explain it a few times but, I'm not sure I ever really understood it. I don't know nothin' about machines."

"Natural starstone does all kinds'a weird stuff when it ain't cut," Phineas says, dragging the salsa dish closer and curling over it. She tosses a few sunflower seeds in her mouth and crunches them loudly. Ellie's eyes widen and she makes to stand.

"O-oh, d'you want another bowl for-"

Phineas swallows, shells and all.

"Nah." The seeds are salty; she starts in on her beer again.

Failing to hide how unsettled she is by the creature in front of her, Ellie clears her throat and picks up the story again.

"There was plenty of refined stone too," she stammers, settling back into her rhythm. "Most of our money came in from trading it, starstone. And all of *that* brought in *other* manufacturers. We even had a shipyard."

"A whole shipyard," Phineas whistles. She makes a face, dragging her finger through the sunflower seeds, making little canyons.

"Man, it's just..." Phineas isn't sure if this counts as an insult, it feels rude to insult someone while you're eating their food. "It sounds like this place oughta be bigger, you know? Like where is all that stuff?"

Ellie looks tired down to her bones.

"Things don't last out here, this desert eats anything that don't have enough will to survive it. And, um..." A delicate frown. "Hasn't been a lot of extra willpower around, since Hazard showed up."

"Hazard ain't that lady that was here earlier, is it?" Phineas asks doubtfully. "With the blue hair?" Ellie shakes her head.

"That's his daughter, Eisse. Cold Hazard is, erm..."

◉◉◉

The mining outpost of Last Chance is a bustling oasis in the desert, even if it has outgrown its name. The water flows freely, distilled into being by the ethereal airwaves pulsing life into the city. The tower sings out across the desert.

Someone is listening.

The floating island is made of an alien soil, the shape of the menacing structure on top is impossible to define from the vantage point of the city's denizens as they watch it approach through the heat mirages of the desert Sprawl. It is unhurried, and there's nothing anyone can do but watch as it drags its shadow over the city limits.

It's heading straight for the tower. Its pace remains constant, slow and inevitable.

When it makes contact with the apex of the tower, a blue stone exquisitely delicate in its unfathomable chassis, every device under the stone's effect surges— lightbulbs explode, screens shatter, moving mechanisms dash themselves to pieces. As the island *bends* and the tower *bends* and they *bend together* every radio in the city broadcasts the lunatic chanting of something utterly unrecognizable as humankind, darkness oozes from screens and speakers like rotting milk.

The stone, choosing to die rather than assimilate, falls from the sky to scatter across the marketplace in the city center. The inscrutable island finally halts, blooming from the tower like the canopy of a tree. From somewhere in its mass four waterfalls rush out into the open air, the flow dissipating to nothing before it can reach the town. Under the earth, the tower's hidden roots begin to pulse, arteries whispering to a sleeping heart.

Unnoticed in the chaos, the fallen stone fades to black.

◉◉◉

"...He went down into the mines the next day, and when he came back up he had half the workers with him. By the time he made it through town, back to his island, ah-" Ellie huffs. "His *ship,* he'd conscripted most of the town too. Anyone who didn't want to work with *him* got put to work harvesting stone, all for his own profit now."

Ellie sits back, trying to work out how to end this unfortunate tale. She'd had to stop in the middle, stalled for time to bring water for both of them, though she hasn't had any of hers.

"Guess it's a good thing the radiosmith took off before all this got started," she says bleakly. "I'd hate for him to see what his work's bein' used for."

"*One guy* rolled up in here with his *kid* and did all that?" Phineas might have had her beer a little fast, her frustration is spilling over. "Y'all just *let him?*"

Ellie's face hardens, but her heart isn't really in it.

"Sure, a few of the bigger mining guys *did* tell him to go to hell when he strolled in." Her voice is clipped. "We were findin' pieces of them for *weeks*. After that, enough people joined up with him, our population fractured enough it was easy for him to bully everyone else into compliance. And it ain't like this was a *combat* outpost to begin with." She throws up her hands. "The woman that came in here and caused problems *last* week used to sell macramé bracelets two doors over!"

"The jewelry lady really just went to work as an enforcer for the guy that wrecked the town?"

"Things have changed. *People* have changed." Ellie laughs bitterly. "Even *Ray* didn't used to be as bad as he is now. It's hard to get any resistance goin' when everyone's either depressed or out for blood. Whatever magic Hazard's usin', it..."

The tone Ellie strikes here bounces off of a memory; Phineas is sure she's heard Jo take it before when *she'd* talked about other magic users she disagreed with.

"It *rots*. It's like he corrupts things just by bein' near 'em. Even the earth in the mines don't look the same as it used to." Ellie meets Phineas' eyes, shaking her out of her memories. "Do you know much about magic?"

"Little bit, just cause my mom's a witch. Healer," she repeats, because their earlier conversation feels like a year ago. Phineas catches the way Ellie softens at that, though she doesn't know what to do with it. She gathers up another handful of sunflower seeds. "Commanding's different though, I don't know much about usin' magic for other stuff."

"It's not important I guess, it's just..." Ellie grimaces down at her water, her hands tight around the plastic tumbler. "His influence, that *corruption*, it feels like it's infected the whole town, but that..."

"Yeah?"

"That shouldn't be possible, *nobody's* halo is that big."

"Oh I *do* know about halos," Phineas says. "Commanders can see 'em usually. And we-"

Oh.

"...Phineas?"

"We tend to have uh. Bigger ones."

Oh no, it couldn't be...

Phineas grips her beer bottle tight enough Ellie notices.

"Phineas, what-"

"Hazard, he feels..." Ellie visibly cringes away under the weight of her gaze. Phineas doesn't care, briefly. "Hazard feels like *rotting?*"

Phineas recognizes the same hesitation in Ellie that she feels with everyone else, *frustrating* shyness about trying to talk about the things Phineas deals with every minute of every day, afraid people will laugh or sneer. The dread in her stomach is too heavy, she can't baby Ellie through it right now.

"No no, *please* describe it." Phineas laces her words with just enough will to nudge them along, hopes Ellie won't mind. "I get this stuff too, remember? I ain't gonna make fun."

Ellie wraps her arms around herself.

"He feels like rotting, but, um..." She huffs, discomfort giving way to mild irritation. "I guess, when I was close enough to him the one time, there was somethin' else. It felt like I couldn't get enough air, like I was *drowning.* And all this weight, pressure, it's almost like I was bein'...Bein' swallowed up by the ocean, maybe." She shuts her eyes, shivering. "And the ocean was *squirming.*"

The pinch in Phineas' chest eases. Drowning, *water.* Cold Hazard isn't him, then. She finishes off her beer, soothing her nerves.

"...Now that you say it I did feel something kinda like that, on the way here," Phineas admits. "It was..."

- veins like eels in a river - unspeakable buried heart throbbing throbbing -

"...gross," she finishes. "I could maybe describe it like you did."

"You felt it all the way *outside* Last Chance?" Ellie asks, stricken. Phineas nods, and Ellie covers her eyes.

"It's getting *worse,*" she moans.

"Well then why don't *you* do something about it?" Phineas knows it's the wrong thing to say, but it doesn't stop her saying it. She's been biting her tongue since they sat down, and for better or worse the tongue usually wins out.

"I'm lucky we even got to keep our *shop,"* Ellie says tartly. "The handful of us left up here who ain't in the mines or upstairs are keepin' up a skeleton crew here on the surface. We wouldn't have *any* food brought in here if I didn't send out for it."

"Lucky," Phineas spits acid, injustice stirring the sunlight in her chest, her constant companion, the thing that makes people so afraid. It's a complicated thing, being angry at The Bad Guy but *also* angry at someone better who won't even *try* to fight for what they deserve. It's not fair, to Ellie, but neither is any of the rest.

Understandably, Ellie glares. The sliver of star lodged in Phineas' heart whispers venomously about how curious it is that Ellie can find her spine *now,* to be angry with *us.*

"We can't all go around throwin' punches at things we don't like." Ellie is alight with outrage, and Phineas likes her better this way. It makes her more upset that they're having this talk.

"Well good news!" Phineas grins, mean. "I'm here and I *can* do that, so how about it?"

"How about *what?"*

"Help me out, let's get rid of Hazard."

Ellie stares, dimming. Phineas knows it's over then, but she tries anyway because admitting Ellie *won't* is awful for too many reasons.

"Come on," Phineas hates that her voice sounds like she's pleading, she'd been aiming for motivating. "I want that ship and you want him gone, let's do it together."

"What is it you think-"

Phineas shakes her head, leaning forward over the table.

"Don't be like that, I can *see* how strong you are." Now Ellie flares with...fear? "You can see I'm strong too, right? Look, we can *do* this,"

And Phineas, despite the way this has gone nearly every other time with every other person in her life, lets herself shine for a second and hopes it will be reassuring rather than terrifying.

The effect is immediate and disastrous— Phineas sees her own light reflecting in Ellie's big eyes as they widen in panic. Ellie leans dangerously far in her chair, nearly stands to get away. It's only a reflex, it passes quickly, but her anger sticks around.

Ah, here it comes. Ellie is lovely and well-meaning, she doesn't know Phineas has had this conversation a thousand times before, but

Ellie's anxiety reaches all the way in and tweaks Phineas' raw nerves enough to get her on her feet.

"I *do* see," Ellie counters, expression flinty. "And you look just like *him;* whatever he has in his...his eye," - his eye? - "you have it on your *back,* in your *chest.* You both have this, this presence that makes my *skin* crawl."

Ellie says, "If he's like drowning, *you're **blinding**.*"

Phineas had expected some kind of sadness, when this unoffensive, normal person inevitably got spooked, but she's mostly tired. That's a new one.

"I am *not* like Hazard."

Ellie crosses her arms. "All you've done since you got here is fight. I wouldn't exactly call your behavior *upstanding.*"

Well, she *was* tired, but that line gives Phineas a violent shove into irritated.

"God, okay," Phineas runs a hand through her hair. She wishes she hadn't stood up, her nervous energy is more apparent now with how much her feet move. She knows it's making things worse with Ellie but if she doesn't vent she's going to explode. *"First* of all, I've never been called 'upstanding' even once in my whole life. I got my own agenda, and it don't involve bein' a hero."

"Second, Ray sucks. I would never work with someone like that. But yeah, I've been fightin' since I got here because things are *wrong."* She taps her toes, offloading some of her feelings in bright arcs that disappear into the concrete floor, enough to make room for a steadying breath. Phineas slips her hands into the pockets of her shorts, and her coat drapes around her wrists in a way that makes her feel solid. She can feel Jo's hands smoothing over her back while a much younger version of herself cries on the kitchen floor, jilted again, the middlest in a long and unbroken line of disappointments.

"I like you," Phineas says, forcing herself back into the box again, keeping her voice steady. "Y'all were kind to me when you didn't need to be and I *hate* what's going on here. I wanna help. But I'm not gonna beg forgiveness for *existing* the way I am *or* for tryin' to make things better." She fans out her hands in front of herself, but she's holding Ellie's eye contact like holding a struggling butterfly. "Be scared, I don't care. I'm not changing my plans just 'cause y'all are too chickenshit to stick up for yourselves."

Surprisingly, Ellie returns the commander's gaze as good as she gets, but when she doesn't speak up Phineas turns and stalks toward the doorway to the dining room. This was stupid, why did she think she'd find anyone worth a damn here. Maybe there's nobody anywhere.

The sun in her chest stirs, just reminding her it's there, furious with love. Phineas is never *quite* alone.

"I'm going up there and taking that ship," she speaks over her shoulder. "I doubt Hazard will just roll over for that, so I'm getting rid of him too. I won't bother you again if you don't want, but this'll turn out the same either way."

She bursts through the beaded curtain, yellow sparking across the strands, before she remembers the front door is fucking *locked.* She keeps going, she'll figure it out when she gets there.

"Don't you dare break that door, Phineas."

Phineas stomps her foot like a little kid and turns on her heel.

"Well then-"

"Look." Ellie is leaning against the kitchen doorway, her tall ears drooping a bit. She's still not happy, but she's cooled off significantly. "I have worked very hard to find a balance here, there are a lot of people counting on me."

"*Yeah* but-" Ellie holds out her hand. It is a *titanic* effort but Phineas shuts the hell up.

"I think this is pointless," Ellie says. "You're gonna get yourself killed. And I ain't gonna get me and my dad killed helpin' you." She sighs through her nose and crosses the room to meet Phineas at the door. Her eyes are set soft against her hard expression. "But I do think your heart's in the right place, mostly. If I can...if you need something I can help with, don't be a stranger."

She means it. The hope that this pretty, bright thing might be one of the people Phineas has been desperately looking for has pretty much faded at this point, but Ellie chasing after her to offer some support is better than nothing. Certainly it's a step up from most everybody else, up 'til now. Phineas grins, not too brightly, but,

"Hey, that's a start."

⊙⊙⊙

It takes maybe fifteen minutes of wandering dead streets before Phineas begins to entertain the thought that, on top of no new friends, she really might not find ship resources in Last Chance. This is *definitely* the only place Jo could have been describing; the junky wooden buildings with their horror movie silhouettes, the utter distance from anything else, even the radio tower with its exposed red I-beams soaring away into the clouds is here, but it's all *wrong*. Phineas had gotten the impression it would be more populated, easier to get to at *least*. Surely Jo would have mentioned having to hike through empty desert for an entire day to get here, or the sick feeling pervading the earth, or any of the other bizarre shit Phineas has had to deal with over the last few days? It's only as real as self-doubt ever gets for her, but that *is* doubt's ugly muted color creeping in.

Then there was the way Ellie had acted, the way she talked about Hazard sounded awful close to...

She stops in front of a wide window with faded branding for a flower shop. Through it she can see rows of clay pots sitting on a dusty display shelf, their contents withered. Are there flower shops in deserts, usually?

Phineas is very, very far from where she started, and there is nothing behind her to go back to. For a minute she is simply far from anything.

Warmth stirs in her chest, languid and sure, and she sees a flash of yellow in her own eyes glaring defiantly against the dark window reflection. It's just the long day of traveling, the strange moonlight making her uneasy; probably the bat to the face she took earlier isn't helping either. She hasn't even seen this place in the day yet, it's not time to worry. Phineas pulls her coat tighter around herself and breathes. The dryness pulls in her throat enough she coughs on it, but it gets her centered again.

A flower shop wouldn't be the worst place to spend the rest of the night, now that she thinks about it. The window and the front door are elegant things she feels guilty about breaking though, even if nobody else is appreciating them lately. Maybe there's a side door she can get through.

Settled, chasing the last vestiges of that beer sloshing around in her blood, Phineas strolls around the corner and into the shadowy alley between buildings.

There's a short, smooth bird whistle from somewhere over her head. It glitters. When she looks up, the moon is grinning at her.

"Hi," it says.

It's not the moon, it's just a guy, a dark shape against the real moon's brutal light. Above the gleam of his grin (the same gleam, she realizes, that had caught her attention above the bar during the fight earlier), he's wearing a beaked mask with two round lenses blacking out where his eyes should be.

Phineas has *never* seen a halo like that.

"Hey," she breathes under the weight of it, too quietly for him to hear.

"You all make this *so* easy."

Huh?

"Huh?"

Phineas takes a step backwards and something jabs right through the layer of bandages and into the meat of her instep, paper-thin excruciating. Her flinch sends her stumbling forward and she's nearly bowled over by a rush of charged air, a flash. An almost wet sound turns her attention in time to catch a web of blue light congealing between the walls, sealing off the way out. Phineas sighs more dramatically than she needs to and tries to mean-mug the moon. It's hard with her heart thundering in her chest like it is.

"Come *on*, I *just* got done fightin' one of y'all."

His mean laugh lights up every nerve ending in her body, peacock-feather blue.

"This isn't a fight, sunshine,"

Phineas can't hear him, the misty blue coming from him is *blooming*, cracking around silvery roots, iridescent petals bursting into being around his throat like a slow explosion. There's nobody else but the two of them in the *whole world*.

The sun in her chest reaches up for his outstretched hand.

"this is a *performance.*"

Streams of color spread from his fingers, falling around her like stars. She gets her guard up as the lights pass; they clatter and roll when they hit the ground.

The die closest to her foot stops, shivers, flops over to show another face. Delighted, she can't help but lean in closer to see them all.

"Hey you got all twos! That's-!"

The dice are swallowed up by the solid mass of glitter and smoke that cannons directly into her stupid face. She reels back in time to feel something slice up through the air where her nose had just been, smooth metal carding through her hair.

She gets her back against the wall and tries to figure out what the hell is going on. The thick quality of the moonlight is somehow magnified by a kind of glittering silver infused through the haze, the same thing that lets snow light up a dark night; the air is opaque with smoke but the alley may as well be under a cage of luminaires. Something is still darting around in there, several somethings, looking for her. They must be mechanical, Phineas can't feel anything alive— *certainly* nothing that stands out under the spotlight of a person up there on the roof.

The spotlight is getting hotter, too hot, she has to move. The polished wood is sticky under her feet, soft against her worn bandages, but outside her mark on the stage it's too dark to see where she's going.

Where..?

The heavy exit door creaks open and a pair of bright silver eyes is hanging there against her co-star's silhouette. That's bad, he's *late,* where has he *been?*

"You kept me waiting," Phineas says, irritated. His grin is one hundred perfect teeth splitting the sides of his face. She steps back when he steps forward, again, again-

"I'm sorry," something whispers in her ear, warm breath from somewhere above her head, "were you lonely?"

The shadow in the doorway closes the distance with nightmare speed; ready to catch the momentum, Phineas throws her foot back, but someone is suddenly *there* behind her. Arms wrap tight around her chest and haul her backwards up off the stage. She pools her weight in her feet to try and pitch them forward, but before she can finish the maneuver she's free in the air, almost parallel with the ground.

It had been fast, before, but now it's like she falls through the dark forever before a pair of hands catches her; one lacing its fingers with her left hand, one scooping under the small of her back. The masked man dips her low, his wall-eyed visage parting the smoke to come in close to hers.

"Well?" he asks.

"I,"

(too close, some instinct says, the eyes above that beak shouldn't be able to get this close without-)

Elegantly he sweeps them upright, and then he explodes in a flurry of mirrored metal.

Phineas gets her hands in front of her face quick enough to protect her eyes but not much else. Cold shrapnel tears across the skin of her arms, shreds through her clothes. Her eyes roll, trying to find an opponent, but the empty stage is gone, there's only brick gritting into the cuts across her shoulders. She's hardly moved from where she started.

Somebody pops their gum.

"What do you see down there?" the man asks idly. Phineas looks up, towards the voice, but she still can't see anything through the fog. Even the spectacular halo is hidden, somehow. *Clever* boy! She cannot *wait* to break his nose.

Phineas plants her feet and focuses inward, finds what doesn't belong, counts three heartbeats and spits. It's nasty, a gluey black coal sizzling in the dust, and when it goes it takes the stage and the lights and all shadowy dance partners with it. This time when she rakes her eyes over the alley she twigs that the awning hanging over the front of the flower shop wraps all the way around the building, and it's only about a dozen feet in the air. It looks heavy, and structurally unsound.

Point A, Point B, let's go.

Phosphene arcs follow her feet through their sprint, condensing brighter until she coils it in the toes of one foot and *leaps.* The redirected momentum rises through her body and carries it further, up, up, gets her gloves around the rail in a shower of rust and sparks. She breathes, her heart swoops up like a hung pendulum, and on the backswing she drops with it *hard.* The force surges down through her veins to pool in her feet, two magnets pulling her to the earth.

There's a metallic *shriek* as she drags the rotted awning apart from the building. It bends and folds in her grip to plummet with her; inspired, Phineas flares out beyond her skin and takes the force from the debris in the air around her too. Its fall interrupted, the metal slows in the air. She doesn't.

Breathe out -

Her three-point landing is *perfectly* executed, she can't help her breathless laugh in the heartbeat-space while the inertia flows out of her hands, through the channels in the earth under her -

And in -

before she draws it back up into her muscles and rockets straight into the air, faster than before. Robbed of its momentum, the awning lands lightly in the alley under her while she soars. Hazy air rushes through her hair until she's suddenly in the clear, drenched in moonlight.

The man is out of arm's reach, but she could graze him with her fingertips if she tried. The shine in his lenses hides the eyes but the slack in his mouth betrays his shock.

Some joint in her hip *clicks!* as she twists in the air to get her feet behind her, and with the last of the stored energy her toes concuss in midair to send her body toward the building and her fist directly into the man's smug fucking face.

"*Gotcha!*" she snarls in a gleeful harmonic, the sun in her bursting bright and savage through her hands.

The man evaporates, and all that energy sends Phineas skidding face-first across the gravelly rooftop.

Where?!

From nothing, she feels his halo bloom behind her. She scrambles onto her side and gets to her knees, turning to face him.

The teeth in his mouth and the lenses in his mask fluoresce in the night. Around him, exquisite and menacing, his aura takes on a lotus shape so defined it looks artificial. He is pointing a gun at her.

"Gotcha," he smirks, and Phineas sees it fall from his lips in a shower of stars the instant before her shoulder explodes.

Still kneeling, the impact twists her violently at the waist, but the material of the flower shop is agreeable enough it's no problem to re-direct the bulk of the bullet's momentum away from her body and into the ground. She feels his gaze track the light skittering away from the wound he's made, his halo of superiority curdling to sickened surprise.

Phineas lopes to her feet, keeping her furious eyes on him while she reaches across her chest to find the bullet with her fingers. It stings pleasantly, and even better watching her opponent's mouth fall open under his mask, like something out of a movie. Hot, wet blood gushes over her fingers as she digs the lead free, grips it in her fist.

His pretty lotus has dissolved back into mist. He lowers his weapon.

Phineas closes the distance in three radiant steps, pulls the charge up her arm and clocks him so hard it knocks his hat from his head.

Once is all it takes. His voice chokes out of him with all the air in his lungs, he staggers backwards limply before knocking his heel against an air vent and going over. For a moment the only sound is his labored wheezing; Phineas is positive he's done so she lets him alone, goes to gather up his hat until he gets back to something like even breathing. His bullet is still heavy in her palm, warming up now with blood and sweat.

In the new quiet, the sound of her approaching footsteps in the gravel is a physical thing spurring him up on his elbows, scuttling to get away.

"N- wait," he splutters, his stringy hair fluttering in front of him as his feet skid against pebbles. His back connects with the roof access door and he throws his arms up between them. *"Wait-!"*

Closing in, Phineas lets him squirm.

"I'm surrendering!" he shouts, muffled in his arms. "You are attacking a..."

When nothing happens, he trails off and chances a glance between his hands. Phineas offers him his hat, and it takes him an extra second to fully comprehend that he isn't being beaten to death. When he reaches out to take it from her, Phineas' constant companion whispers, *he still has his gun.*

Like he's afraid she'll bite, he takes his hat back, then starts the process of standing. Together their shadows are enormous in the moonlight, looming across the roof and over the edge into the night.

"...You know," he murmurs. He sets his dirty hat on his dirty head. "I think I swallowed my gum."

"w h a t-" Phineas' voice cracks with light, she covers her mouth with her elbow and chokes up a scrap of energy she'd missed grounding, too distracted by everything distracting about this guy. He waits patiently for her to wipe the blood from her mouth.

"All that," Phineas starts again, more clearly. "All of that and- what was your plan for when I got *up* here?"

"The contingency for you scaling the side of a *building* after inhaling a lethal dose of lotus powder?" Even annoyed his voice is attractive and *insistent*, marches right to center stage and demands attention. He speaks with the ghost of a Deutsch accent. "You have it in your hand, I did not think you would get back *up* after I *shot* you."

"Ah. That happens." Phineas opens her fist to examine the bullet in her palm. Oh, it's got some kind of marking...

"No it does *not* happen," the man fumes. "You've got so much poison in your system you should not even be *conscious* right now."

"Can't poison a commander," Phineas mumbles, holding the bullet up to the light and squinting, ignoring his irritated response. "Is that a club? Like a playing card?" She grins at him. "Did you *draw* on your *bullet?*"

"If I have to fashion all my ammunition by hand, it is getting the personal branding." He rubs the side of his face under his mask. "And it does help set me apart from those cowards who think a gun is something you *hide* behind."

That's *ridiculous*. Phineas giggles.

"Why don't you take that thing off and talk to me, masked man?" The lenses of his mask are dark enough it's hard to make out anything behind them, and she realizes belatedly how impressive it is that the mask stayed fixed to his face at all after she hit him. "What's your name? My name is Phineas."

He's slow about it, thinking it over first, but eventually he loosens. He curls his left hand near his temple and makes a finnicky sign, flicking his middle two fingers outward and following the arc from his elbow. His mask shimmers around the lenses until they're a pair of round glasses with plain metal frames, the rest gone to vapor that glimmers like quicksilver, and she *finally* sees his face.

Phineas has been ravenously taking in his spirit since she first saw him, but she gets the feeling a significant part of him is mired in his concrete self, which is *weird*. Most of the time, Phineas sees other people the way they might see a spirit: the real person lives in their halo while their physical bodies only serve as tethers. It isn't that she doesn't *like* other bodies, but meat is never where the meat is. If someone's spirit is dull enough, sometimes she won't even remember having seen them, no matter what they looked like. But the masked man's body is almost a whole second halo itself, like he's two things at *once*.

Whatever it is she wants it too, the rest of him. She lets the pain in her shoulder drag her back into her own body so she can get a good look at where that halo lives.

Like everything else here he's dirty and overheated, his pale skin is too-flushed and patchy with dust, darkened with sweat. His eyes are sunk into their sockets, ringed in shadows that look closer to bruises. Unwashed, shaggy blond hair grazes his shoulders and makes a thick curtain around his face; even after he swipes some away from where it's plastered to his forehead it falls right back in the way again. He has a big nose and soft cheeks, and he is meeting her hungry stare with the biggest, bluest eyes she's ever seen. He would be beautiful if his color wasn't so unhealthy and his expression not so surly, but as it is he's only exceedingly lovely. None of the smaller masks, the hair or the glasses or the hat, dim him from Phineas at all.

"I am Ulrich," Ulrich says.

It doesn't seem right yet though, Phineas has the feeling she's looking at one of those pictures that shift when you focus on certain parts of it, like the vase hidden between the faces. She can tell it's there but she isn't sure where to look to get the other half of Ulrich to show up.

"Hi Ulrich," she says.

"Hello."

"If the other dudes here are cowards who hide behind their guns," she takes a step forward, and it ripples through him even as his feet stay rooted. "What are *you?*"

Then right there, the smallest downward twitch at the corner of his mouth. She almost hadn't caught it, but now his soft features are shifting to show her another, harder shape they make. She finds him in the negative space, the one thing made of two things, and it's not a vase. It's a springtrap.

54

"I am a professional," he answers.

Phineas loves him instantly.

Her hand creeps up to her wounded shoulder, her ruined shirt warm and damp with fresh blood. She might need to start worrying about that soon.

"Coward or gunman?" she asks.

"If you're not working with anyone what on *earth* are you doing out here?" Ulrich asks. "There's nothing in this town during the *day.*"

"You hanging around watching me from the roof is *way* more suspicious dude," Phineas laughs. "You first."

Ulrich scratches at the scruff on his neck, several days thick. The motion looks as practiced as the one that dismissed his mask. His eyes sweep down to her feet and back up again, then he turns neatly on his heel, retreating towards the service door.

"I don't actually care. Good luck with everything."

No!

"Hey hang on!" Phineas chases him and reaches for his sleeve. "I didn't mean to-"

It's so fast she doesn't even feel the cold of the barrel under her chin, too taken by his abyssal halo when he brings his face inches from hers. The arm she'd reached for him with is pinned under Ulrich's, the one that isn't holding the gun.

"I did not intend to waste another bullet trying to kill you, but if you'd like to test the limits of that party trick of yours I'm happy to *mangle.*" All the theater is gone, his voice is low and steady in the space between them. This must be the professional part.

"Oh you're wound up tight huh," Phineas says, too loud for how close they are. Ulrich tightens his grip and digs the gun further into the soft spot between Phineas' throat and her jawbone, forcing her to tilt her head back uncomfortably. It's starting to feel cold now. She should probably be nervous, her party trick *doesn't* work at this range.

"I do not like to be touched," he says levelly. "And I do not like *you.*"

She can't see it, but she can feel very faint vibrations humming across the gun's mechanisms where Ulrich's heartbeat is ticking through his finger on the trigger. Clockwork all the way down.

Phineas laughs hoarsely. It kind of hurts, eking out around the gun. He is the coolest thing she's *ever* seen.

She says, "Let's work together."

Nothing on Ulrich's face lets on that she's thrown him, but that doesn't matter for Phineas. She sees it shudder in the blue around him like she's dropped a stone in still water.

"You don't have to do all this, okay? We're on the same side I think." She considers doing something reassuring with her free hand but he's taut like piano wire, and faster than he looks, so she lets him hold her there while she talks. "Why don't we just go back to wherever you're-"

"What are you *saying?*" This close, Ulrich's eyes are bleached grey in the moonlight. His whole face looks more like bone than skin. "I just tried to kill you! I am *still* trying to kill you!"

"You weren't, though. You're not."

Saying it so gently is a mistake; Phineas watches the line of his mouth gnarl in a way that makes her doubt her own read on things, on him. She might die here, actually. Whoops.

Phineas wants this to work out *so* badly, what was the point of leaving home and coming here if she doesn't go after the things she wants?

"Do it then," she tells him.

His finger tightens on the trigger and Phineas feels all the mechanisms in the gun fit together into a single anticipatory being, amplifying Ulrich's pulse until it's throbbing in her own ears. She forces herself not to flinch, doesn't blink. Neither does he.

Several seconds later they are still standing there, Phineas' skull intact. She's sure, now. Mostly.

"See?" she chirps. They're practically over this little hiccup already. "If you wanted me dead for real you wouldn'a got me in the shoulder."

Ulrich's eyes flit to her gunshot wound. Phineas had forgotten about consciously staunching the bloodflow and now it's dripping again, ruining her shirt.

"I missed," Ulrich insists. "You're quick." The gun has finally loosened from its place in her neck, and Phineas can't feel his heart beating through the trigger anymore.

"So are you," Phineas argues. "You miss a lot with those *monogrammed bullets?*"

Ulrich's face pinches.

"They're *not-*" he starts, then stops himself, feeling foolish for engaging. Oh, Phineas likes him *so* much. Taking a chance, she reaches for him with her un-held hand, touches his elbow.

"You jumped me 'cause you wanted something from me, right? I don't mind, I want things from you too. Why don't we help each other?"

Ulrich takes a very deep breath through his nose, not looking away from her even as he further slackens his grip and lowers the weapon. His expression is unreadable, something Phineas isn't used to.

"You're *insane.*" He says it like a man who has just been handed the keys to something expensive and illegal. He puts space between them and turns inward on himself, putting away his gun under his blue overshirt and rubbing his eyes under his glasses.

"I've heard that a lot lately," Phineas giggles.

Ulrich shakes his head and walks away from her, taking something from a pocket. A pang of anxiety at seeing him leaving again, but then:

"Come on."

There's a metallic sound Phineas can't place before Ulrich shoves the door open. She catches the light glinting off of his lockpicking tools as he pockets them again, and it hits Phineas then that neither of them took the inside stairs to get up on top of this building. God, this guy just keeps unspooling ahead of her.

He holds the heavy door so she can go ahead of him. More specifically, Phineas realizes, so she can't go behind him.

3

Ulrich has been living in a radio station just outside what Phineas thinks could count as city limits if Last Chance believed in that sort of thing. It looks like a boxcar, built with its back nestled into the curl of a rock formation. It feels different from the rest of Last Chance; it takes Phineas some extra staring to figure out it's because it's not covered in junkyard scraps like the buildings in town. As they approach, she closes one eye and pinches her fingers overtop of the rock where it bends around the shack at a right angle. It's like the land itself had reached up to pluck the building away.

Ulrich doesn't pause to take it all in when Phineas does, he keeps his brisk pace all the way to the door. When he gets his hands on the wood it swings inward hard enough to bang against the inside wall. Phineas can't tell if it's because the door is busted or if Ulrich is still in a bad mood.

"Well," he says, waiting in the doorway for her to go ahead of him like he did on the roof. Somewhere in Phineas, the fact that she's walking into an unlit, secluded shack with a stranger tugs at the tiniest thread of sense. The rest of her cheerfully ignores it, and she doesn't turn to watch him when he locks the door behind them, blocking out the shaft of silver moonlight and pitching them into the dark.

Ulrich feels for the light switch, finds it, *snaps* it, and sends power crackling across some primitive wiring until it lights up a scatter of warm bare bulbs. The space where the lights are rooted pulls Phineas' attention. There's no drop ceiling, all the guts are exposed.

"This is where the radio signals used to come from." She says it like a question, looking up into the dusty wiring.

"I assume so. That door over there goes into a recording suite, I've been sleeping in the booth."

"Ellie said the radio guy was like *super* smart," Phineas recalls, glancing back to see the switch that made that very good sound. It's a bare lever, suspended by its own cords in some supports that seem like they *also* ought to be hidden by drywall. Even Phineas can tell this building is closer to camping gear than anything meant to operate something like the tower.

"Ain't this kinda low tech?" she asks. "For a radio station?"

Ulrich slips out of his overshirt; underneath, the yellowed button down is crisscrossed by a complicated set of straps and holsters. The revolver is there, but it looks like he actually has *two* different guns tucked away. Phineas hadn't been able to see either of them before, and in fact hadn't been paying much attention at all to how he's dressed. Between the slacks and the hat, Ulrich almost looks like he's in church clothes. Ratty, wore out church clothes, but still too nice to wear to the grocery store.

"Everything in this building was still functional when I got here," he says, hanging his holsters up by the door. "That's good enough for me."

It *is* better than sleeping outside or in an abandoned flower shop. This side of the shack must have been meant as a lobby, but it's furnished like a treehouse: aside from an ancient crumbling sofa the room is scattered with wooden industrial equipment instead of furniture. A few crates that look good for sitting, some broken pallets, a large cable spool forming a center table. There are two windows but some filthy flannel curtains are drawn over both of them, making everything feel insulated in a fuzzy, musty way.

Finally accepting he'll have to show his back to Phineas at some point in this relationship, Ulrich passes through a dirty kitchenette and disappears through the door on the far side of the shack. There's a sepia-colored "On Air" sign hanging next to it. Phineas is pretty sure those are usually red, they show up in cartoons all the time.

He comes back with a little wooden box like what Jo's tobacco would come in, but it's labeled for chocolates. Phineas brightens.

"Candy?" she asks.

"No, er." He's looking at his wound on her shoulder, wincing. "Here, don't..."

Phineas had commanded away the worst of the bleeding, but halfway here she'd gotten lazy and now the entire left side of her shirt is a congealing mess, shredded after the gunfire and the single slash Ray had managed with the switchblade. She paws at it without thinking and Ulrich makes a strangled sound that reminds her of the brooding hens the neighbors had kept. Phineas grins at him as she grits dried blood between her fingertips.

"Stop that!" he snaps, nudging one of the crates with his boot. "Sit here, don't get it on the *couch.*" She does what he asks while Ulrich breathes deeply through his nose to bolster his patience, something Phineas is starting to find familiar already.

He settles down on the other crate and opens the chocolate box. Phineas hears distinctly not-chocolate noises while Ulrich digs inside, retrieving a glass jar and a roll of bandages. He's going to *bandage the gunshot wound.* Her heart soars, she wants his hands on her *immediately*, but Jo's efforts to make Phineas into a decent member of society almost prompt her to politely decline. Ulrich's grimace as he appraises the mess in front of him gets her the rest of the way.

"You don't have to do all this, I'll heal up fine on my own," Phineas says. "Commanders are sturdy."

Ulrich shakes his head, busying himself with the supplies.

"This place is a shithole, you are going to get an infection."

Phineas hasn't had an infection in almost a decade, but she wants this too bad to try and put him off again.

"I didn't take you for the compassionate type," she says instead.

"I am not."

That's...Phineas forgets to answer, staring at him while he blots some disinfectant onto a cotton swab. There's a thing that lights up in the air around Ulrich when he talks sometimes, a silver spark that flies from his mouth and looks like it wants to grow into *something:* she can see spindly sprouts curling out of it into space, but they're weak. The latest tiny spark withers and dies away before it can form into anything real.

Phineas doesn't know what to do with that, or, it's going to take a while to solve that particular puzzle and she's busy right now. She wants to get these gross clothes off so Ulrich doesn't have to fool with them. Peeling out of her ruined shirt cracks dried gunk all over the floor, some on Ulrich's pants, and she appreciates the effort he puts into appearing unaffected. He would have an excellent poker face for anyone else. While he's distracted, she takes the soaked cotton from him and drags it through the fresh blood welling around the fussy wound.

"Lemme get the worst of it for you at least," she says.

Tangibly relieved, Ulrich sits back without arguing and gets more disinfectant ready. Phineas is still wearing a ratty black jogging bra—there isn't much on her chest that needs the support, but this is exactly why she wears it. She ruins her clothes a lot, and other people get weird about too much bare skin. It's *irritating,* the same way it is when she has to explain feelings with words, but it's bound to happen with people who spend all their time only seeing things they can touch. Ulrich hands her another wet slab of cotton when the first one is more grime than gauze and she watches him carefully, waiting to see if it'll ruffle him when she slides the bra strap from her shoulder to clean underneath.

It does not. She likes him *so* much.

"That is enough, let me," he says after she dirties three more cotton squares, sitting up and motioning with a pair of forceps for her to do the same. She sits up tall, the air cold on the alcohol smeared across her skin.

Ulrich leans in slow enough it's clear he thinks she's anxious about all this, which is so wrong it makes her laugh, close enough she knows it hits him like static electricity. His face stays carefully neutral but annoyance flashes across his halo. It sparkles like a comet in the mist.

"Please hold still," he clips.

She tries to do that. He relaxes, turning to the wound again.

"This will sting."

"That's okay," Phineas says. It does sting. She lets it pull her down into her body, and the shack snaps into stark contrast without any ambient energy blurring in her vision. Here in physical space, she can see a tiny line between Ulrich's furrowed eyebrows while he's concentrating, emphasized by the fine layer of dusty sweat across his face. He's not watching her expression, focused in on the work. It's very hard not to kiss him.

"You do this a lot?" Phineas asks, cool and normal.

"Hm." Ulrich's voice is distant.

"Shoot people just to patch 'em up?"

Ulrich pauses to add the swab to the growing pile of bloody cotton, then reaches for what looks like an inkwell. He unscrews the cap and the smell that assails Phineas' nose puts her immediately back in Jo's kitchen, knees and elbows freshly scraped.

"Not often," Ulrich says faintly, still focused on his task. "But we find ourselves in extenuating circumstances."

He finishes layering the salve over the wound that didn't really need it in the first place, then dresses it with a fresh pad of gauze and some tape, deft and meticulous. Phineas smiles big, so loud she sees the ghost of it flicker across Ulrich's face before he darts his eyes away, uncomfortable.

"Thanks!" she says, standing up to stretch her arms over her head. Ulrich tsks.

"Be *careful*, I am not doing this a second time."

Phineas giggles at him and looks around the shack again, she thought she'd seen-

"I believe those boxes are full of shirts," Ulrich offers while he packs away the medicine. Phineas wanders to a darker corner of the room piled high with shipping boxes and finds one is already torn open. It's mostly baseball caps with station branding on, but some moss-green shirts are lying in the bottom, a lot less bloody than what she's got. She remembers at the last second it's rude to undress in front of people without asking.

"Can I change in here? D'you mind?"

Ulrich hardly looks up, busy with trying to get everything to fit back inside the box the way he'd had it.

"I don't care if you don't."

Phineas tosses her ruined bra-thing into the corner, where it lands with a wet noise that gets a disapproving "ach" from Ulrich. When she goes back for the new shirt, there's a pair of eyes looking back at her from the darkness.

"...Is the turtle yours?"

Ulrich stops. "What?"

"There's a turtle in this box."

The turtle has a shiny black shell trimmed in gold and a cheery succulent flourishing across her back in spite of the dry air. Its skin looks wet and smooth, and the stumpy legs and round face are a pale green that makes Phineas think of aloe. She (The Turtle) looks up at Phineas with glistening black eyes for a moment before scrabbling up the side of the box, her feet sticking like an insect's. Phineas reaches carefully around her to retrieve a scratchy shirt to pull over herself, then holds out her hand to help the turtle from the box.

"Where'd you come from, little thing?" Phineas coos. She (The Turtle) doesn't respond, and wriggles to be set down on the floor. Phineas watches her crawl towards the table, straight for Ulrich, who is still absorbed in cleaning up the mess. He nearly drops the box when he catches the animal in his periphery.

"*What* is that," he barks, "put it *outside!*"

"Aw she ain't hurtin' nothin'," Phineas grins, creaking across the warped floorboards to settle on the couch. When she does, a cloud of dust *poofs* out from the cushions. "That's a good one too, for medicine I think."

Ulrich's face is pinched. He hasn't looked away from She, who hasn't turned from him either.

"It is....*looking* at me," he manages. A faint blush colors his cheeks as he says it. Phineas tries to hide her giggle behind her hand so she doesn't make him feel bad.

"Don't let her bully you, Ulrich."

He rolls his eyes and flounces to his feet, crossing back to the kitchen to dig in the cupboards instead of dealing with this nonsense. His shoes click oddly against the floor for as bulky and rubbery as they look; he might have stones trapped in the treads after their walk out here. Phineas notices a cloud of dirt accentuates his movement too, like the couch cushions, and she's struck again by how *displaced* Ulrich seems.

The light humming over the stove is flickery, like a flame, and Phineas gets to watch his tight expression while he's searching for something with increasing disdain. Yeah that's a good word for him, he's *disdainful* of these cupboards, of this place. His clothes say the same thing: diligently maintained in another life, now loose and grimy from going too long between washes, his suspenders hanging around his hips and threatening to catch on every splintery wooden surface or shard of exposed metal. He is out of place in Last Chance like an antique clock stubbornly ticking away in a ditch by the road, his frustration constant and loud, and Phineas is somehow sure the town hates him back.

"You don't *live* here, do you?" When she asks, disgust ripples in his halo strongly enough to reach her from across the room.

"Ach, absolutely *not*. I think some rabbits were holed up in here before me." Ulrich mutters something else she doesn't catch and reaches as far back into the cupboard as he can, up on his toes.

"I meant in Last Chance, in this town," Phineas says.

"Do I *look* like a local?"

"Maybe? I dunno from locals."

Ulrich shakes his head, which doesn't do much because his cheek is pressed against the cupboard frame. He finally fishes out a chipped plastic cup.

"Only passing through. I got held up."

He returns from the kitchen with a bottle of water and the cup, which looks suspiciously clean up close. The couch cushion Phineas is sitting on is also suspiciously clean despite the internal dust, and the top of the wooden spindle being used as a table is a completely different shade of brown than the rest of it. The space Ulrich has carved out for himself almost sparkles next to the dirt on everything else.

She (The Turtle) had climbed on top of the spindle-table while he was away and now watches Ulrich closely, craning her neck to keep a direct line of sight. He ignores her until he has to set his things near her, and then he makes a point to glare back. Phineas feels something undefinable pass between them.

"Don't like critters?" Phineas asks lightly, after several baffling seconds pass.

"Wild animals?" he asks with false enthusiasm. "In my living space, on the furniture? Almost as much as I like used bandages on the table." He looks like he wants to remove the creature (She, not Phineas,) but can't make himself touch it. Phineas takes pity and gently picks up the turtle to set her on the floor, where she retreats into her shell. The leaves on her back glow an idle blue.

Ulrich finally settles down on the crate across from Phineas, and looks at anything but her while he considers the next thing he wants to say.

"I have been dreaming about rabbits," he decides, swirling a finger around the inside of the cup he dredged from the kitchen cupboard. "The ones that were here, that left when I showed up. They keep appearing in my dreams. I think they might have been saints."

"Probably," Phineas says, starting the process of removing her gloves. "I saw some too. They seemed alright, but saints are always kinda spooky."

Ulrich nods, in the middle of rubbing his eyes under his glasses.

"I am unused to saints *and* wildlife, generally. Both of them make me uneasy."

Taking her time bundling her gloves inside her handwraps for the night, Phineas changes her mind about showing him the hares' trinket just now. She can *feel* how exhausted he is, and she's still not sure he won't throw her out at some point.

"How long have you been here?" she asks instead, making circles in the air with her elbow to feel how the hole in her shoulder pulls. The feeling is coming back into the skin, and the tenuous scab already feels less thready than it had earlier. This won't even scar.

"Long enough." Ulrich cracks the seal on the water conspicuously, but Phineas isn't sure why. He pours a very civil half from the bottle to the cup, then loosely replaces the cap and sets it on Phineas' side of the table.

"Drink, you're probably dehydrated."

"They fed me at the bar! *I* got a *beer.*"

"All the more reason to hydrate," he says, unimpressed, so she snatches up the bottle and slugs back the entire thing.

"Thanks!"

"Sure..." Ulrich is looking at her sort of the same way he was looking at the cupboards, and Phineas notices again that he's very, very pretty. Even when he's got dirt on him and he's regarding her like she's just crawled out of a bathtub drain. How are so many pretty people concentrated in this awful place?

She smiles at him because she can't help it, warm sunlight bleeding through. Ulrich looks away.

"So." He clears his throat. "You said you wanted something from me."

"If I remember right we *both* wanted things," Phineas says. "You shot me, you go first."

"I just cleaned you up."

"You *also* ruined my only shirt."

Ulrich pinches the bridge of his nose. Phineas thinks this is going to take a while probably, so she settles into the couch and kicks her feet up onto the table. Ulrich's eyes snap open like shattering glass and Phineas goes blind for a second.

"Get your *disgusting feet off* of the table!"

Phineas is still stunned, she's never seen somebody's halo *do that*, spasm so violently it goes from a simmering blue mist to a tsunami crashing through the room. When she takes too long to respond Ulrich shoves at her ankles with his forearm until she slides them back to the floor. She giggles incredulously, working up every bit of self control she has to keep from devouring this man here on the spot.

"Sorry, we expectin' company?"

"What in god's name are you doing out here without *shoes?*" Ulrich demands, trying to hide how much his outburst embarrasses him. He can't see them, but Phineas wiggles her toes against the floor anyway.

"Commanding's harder in shoes."

"I'd wager it's also harder with lockjaw. That tape is *revolting.*"

Phineas shrugs, relaxed against the dusty cushions.

"Well, if you find me something around here that suits you better I'll wrap up in them instead, 'kay?"

Ulrich looks like he's reaching for a retort but he must find the end of his patience instead, because his energy fizzles out and he slumps down on his crate, staring at the floor for a long moment. She can't see his face with his hair hanging like that.

"I don't want to do this," he says. "I am tired. If you're insisting on asking questions before sleep tonight then ask them."

"Oh! Am I staying?"

"I am not using the couch. Did you have somewhere else to be?"

"I didn't!" she chirps. It's going so well! Phineas tries to get over how excited she is so she can put together something to ask him, she hadn't thought she'd get this far. Some shapes resembling words rattle around in her head until a few of them collide.

"If you're not with the wizard guy, why did you attack me?"

"Easy mark," he says. Another one of those silver sparks falls from his mouth, halfhearted.

"I don't think that's right," Phineas deadpans. Surprisingly he concedes it, maybe too tired to argue.

"I saw you fight," Ulrich says, looking at her this time and adjusting his glasses. "In front of the bar, I was watching. I wanted to see what you could do against someone who knows what they are doing."

No spark. Phineas grins.

"You prob'ly would've had me if I was somebody else."

"I am glad I didn't." Ulrich looks her right in the eye. His are the same blue that hangs in the air around him, the halo coming together in scroll to match some network of firing synapses, all of them sharpening into knife's-edge focus with his attention on her.

"Yeah?"

"I need help getting to Hazard."

Phineas wants to be closer to him. When she sits up and rests her elbows on her knees, Ulrich mirrors her.

"You wanted more firepower and you risked *killing* me instead?" She smirks when she says it.

"I knew you wouldn't die. If you did you wouldn't be any use to me anyway."

"You still *shot* me!" she laughs. "I'm injured!"

Ulrich smiles without smiling; Phineas sees the way the corner of his mouth curls, and more importantly the way a streak of giddy brightness streams into the mist around him.

"I did, and you are still here. You followed me home, sunshine." His voice has that extra layer again, like smooth silver curling up the back of her neck. "You know why I did it."

In a burst of joy like a firework finally exploding into color across her soul, it dawns on Phineas that Ulrich is as interested in her as she is in him. She can see the reflection of her own glow in Ulrich's glasses.

(Deep in her chest but never too far away, her constant companion whispers something cautious between her heartbeats, tugging Phineas back from the apex and muting the blue in her eyes. Just enough to keep her from doing anything too stupid.)

Phineas' light on Ulrich's face is less firework and more floodlight, spooking him enough for him to sit up and out of their little reverie; he clears his throat and that stab of giddiness disappears behind the scroll pattern again. Phineas reins herself in too, the radio station becoming real around her body. She can smell the must in the hideous curtains behind her and in the couch crevices. Even Ulrich couldn't rout them out completely.

"What did Hazard do to *you?*" Phineas asks, trying to get them moving again.

"Nothing to me *personally,* but I think armed thugs terrorizing the citizens is reason enough to-"

"You're no hero, friend." Phineas says, generously taking the shovel from his hands before he can dig himself too much deeper. "Not for free anyway. Come on don't hide again, it's late and we're tired, right?"

Ulrich is getting a lot of practice recovering from her, he's doing it more gracefully now.

"...I am not a friend." Protective sunlight constricts around Phineas' heart as she strains to find a tell that doesn't appear. He continues. "I met an old man in the desert on the way here, I was stranded and he saved my life. He was running a pair of armadillos and carrying, ach..." He touches two fingers through his hair to his scalp, like the spot pains him. "Metal components, gunpowder, that sort of thing. Hazard's men were coming back from a trip to the city and they ambushed us."

A flurry of sparks, flashing like emergency lights.

"Got the drop on you in the desert?" Phineas knows the answer already, but that's not what she's asking.

"My guard was down." He looks away from her, exactly as regretful as he should be. "I do feel bad about it. I could have prevented it but I...It didn't work out that way."

He pauses like he might elaborate further, but he shrugs instead.

"I owe a debt. I'd like to help if I can."

Phineas is relieved by what she sees in his face. She smiles again, even though she never really stopped.

"That's kind of you," she says gently. It makes Ulrich wince.

"I do not like to be in the red if I can help it. That's all."

The wind outside picks up and whistles through an unseen lesion in the walls, some place where the corners aren't lining up right. Despite the shack's imperfections and the desert's evening frost, it's warm enough inside that neither of them shiver.

"So you're wanting to get rid of Hazard and clear your conscience, and you want some help," Phineas says. It's *so* hard to hide how excited she is.

"More or less."

"Of course I'll help you!" She jitters her leg on her toes. "I was goin' anyway, this'll be *way* better than doin' it on my own."

Ulrich takes a sedate sip of his water, making it last even though Phineas can tell he wants to down all of it like she did.

"Yes, I suppose you've already started," he says. "What *did* possess you to get into it with those two earlier?"

"I didn't know they were *with* anybody, they were just bein' mean to the waitress at that bar."

"So *you* don't have a personal stake in any of this either?"

Well, here we go. The couch is rough where it touches her bare skin as she reclines longways. This will be an easier conversation if she can stay calm, keep from overwhelming him, and looking at Ulrich is too exciting for her to keep cool.

"Nah, I wouldn't say that."

She manages to pull her gaze away from Ulrich's lovely colors and stares up at the ugly ceiling instead. In one corner she can see into the space where the roof meets the outside. It's dark up there, and rotted. That must be where the wind keeps whistling to get in. Ulrich waits.

"I don't like what Hazard's doing here," Phineas says, stalling. "But I have my own reasons for wanting to get at him."

"Mmhmm?"

"He's in my way." When she says it her voice cracks, sunlight streams through. She keeps not looking at him. "I came here for a heart, for a starstone ship."

Ulrich snorts.

"You came *here?*" He hesitates then, but it's quick. She only feels it because she's been wholly enthralled in the flow of his speech from the second he whistled in the alley. "Even if there *were* a shipyard in this settlement you do not look like you've got the funds to get a ship made."

"Right," she says. "But Hazard's got a ship."

"...So he does," Ulrich says doubtfully. Phineas closes her eyes to the dark corner of the shack to watch her own light scatter behind her eyelids. Ask him, *ask him.*

After a moment, Ulrich says, "That is *particular,* isn't it?"

"What is?"

"A normal airship is easier to come by and *much* more reliable than a starship, I have always heard even *processed* stone is..." He wheels the hand that isn't holding the plastic cup. He settles on, "temperamental."

"So?"

"So where are you going that you'd need a ship like that?"

Steeling herself, Phineas summons every scrap of commander's charm she can get her fingers on, feels it light up her face. She smiles for real and turns to look at him, laces her hands to rest across her heart.

"Come with me and I'll tell ya."

Ulrich, in the middle of finishing his water, actually chokes on it. It sprays everywhere, and his ambient blue is spattered with surprise like thrown paint. Her heart is hammering but Phineas can't help it when she laughs, it's *so* fun nudging him out of that fog he wears, she wants to do it forever.

"Wh-" He swallows, wiping his mouth on the back of his wrist. "What kind of-" He gets himself under control again, and as he stares at her, something new happens in his halo. There, near his left eye, a tiny black blemish starts bleeding like ink spilled in water, film-negative color burning outward from the iris.

"Why are you so fixated on me?" he asks, all his careful curls gone sharp. "What is your angle here?"

Should she lie? What's the point? She's never been any good at it. Phineas can feel Ulrich reaching out to fight again, but they're gonna dance instead.

"You're the brightest thing I've seen like...*ever,*" Phineas says, letting the star in her chest flicker in her eyes. If they're going to sail together he'll have to get used to it. "What do you *mean* why am I fixated on you? Your guns and mask and stuff are *so* cool! Do you have any idea what you *look like* to me?"

70

Phineas gets the feeling she would have made him less uncomfortable if she'd hauled off and clocked him again. Still: whatever vicious *thing* that was near his eye has winked out, the blemish isn't yawning open to swallow up the rest of him now. It's just his own blue eyes staring at her.

"What the *fuck* are you talking about?" It's clumsy dancing, she'd surprised him, but he's good at it. Phineas has never met anyone who didn't fold to the floor when she took their hand and Ulrich is *good* at it. She sits up because she can't stay still.

"Commanders can see..." she spreads her hands vaguely in front of her. "Stuff, about people, I can see like what you're...*like.*" She waves her arms around her head: a cloud, silver scroll, mist and smoke and fog. Instead of saying any of that: "You're blue, and it's got a *shape*, most people are just- augh! *Nothing!!*" She slaps her hands against her knees, vibrating with feelings that won't condense into language, resists the urge to grab the sides of his face and bring them close because maybe that would *help* somehow but she *knows* it'll just scare him. "It's *blue.* You're blue and I like you! A lot! I want you to come travel with me!"

Ulrich's expression is caught between suspicious and stupefied.

"You're *insane,*" he breathes.

Phineas laughs, which doesn't help her case. She folds her feet up under herself and admires him.

"I'm not! It's *good,* you're *so* good dude. I can *tell.* Even those little sparks you make when you lie are *so* pretty."

Ulrich's halo *fractures.*

Something is *wrong,* he *changes*— Ulrich To The Left, Ulrich Reversed. That shadow over his eye is bleeding again, but in the middle of it this time, the tiniest glimmer of-

Pink?

It's like watching a spider crawling over his face. Phineas tries not to let the surprise show; it's not nice to comment on things like this, even if you're already in the middle of getting chewed out for being ridiculous, but that color is *weird.* Ulrich has been so uniform up 'til now, what *is* that? What did she *do?*

The animosity is so strong it's like a physical force holding her away from him, a hand around her shoulder digging its thumb into the wound he put there. Whatever it is, it doesn't like Phineas at *all*. That is too fucking bad.

In reality, the cheap plastic cup cracks under the reflexive pressure of Ulrich's fingers. Only a little bit, nothing that will even change the shape once he lets it go.

"Sorry?" he says. "Sparks?"

His tone is eerily neutral, but in Phineas' eyes his alarm is a flashbang casting the room into exsanguinated monochrome. She's found the tripwire— her springtrap of a person is about to snap shut around her arm.

"No no, it's okay!" She holds up her hands in what she hopes is a placating gesture, and she smiles. "It's just, you have these little things sometimes, they-"

- she forgets her tattoos are there, doubling the number of eyes flaying Ulrich apart -

"It's fine, *really*, you're real good at it otherwise! Especially with the mask on,"

- crack, *crack* -

"I just get to cheat 'cause I can see when you get the silver-"

"Schnauze!"

His hands slam into the table hard enough to knock over Phineas' empty bottle, his full weight behind it as he leaps to his feet. Something in his voice is icy cold, latches onto the back of Phineas' neck and sticks in the hinges of her jaw, threatening to stiffen it shut. It's easy to shake off; it feels unrefined, like liquid metal seeped into ugly cracks rather than smooth shapes. The cold stays with her, a bright spot trying to bleed into her warm aura. Fascinated, she holds on and lets Ulrich lead.

"This was a *mistake!*" he snarls. "I am not going to sit here and entertain a *basket case* all night!"

"I didn't *mean-*"

He's already stalking away from her; Phineas' throat tightens when he heads for the outside door but he's only retrieving his weapons. Some rare pragmatic part of her notes the weapon retrieval should be *more* alarming than him leaving her, but by the time the thought goes through he's halfway to the recording booth.

"I did not think *I* would be the one breaking this deal." His voice makes Phineas think of a bug under a magnifying glass, panicked in the light. "How is it I *shot* you unprovoked and *I'm* telling *you* no?" He covers his eyes, raving at himself. "Rotten luck, *awful.*"

"No?" Phineas twists to face him but she's too nervous to actually move closer, afraid he'll bolt, so she throws herself over the arm of the couch instead. "You didn't even hear where I was going! Can't we at least fight Hazard before you decide?"

Ulrich's laugh is *mean.* The light glints in his glasses when he turns to look at her over his shoulder.

"You really think I'd follow you anywhere? I was going to blow your fucking brains out the minute you stopped being useful to me." He smiles, his horribly perfect teeth are like rows of gravestones. "Tell me I'm lying, *commander.*"

She can't. She doesn't care.

"Well, you'd-" She *doesn't* care, but the reasons why are too weird and complicated for her to get out in the scant seconds she has before he disappears from her sight, maybe forever. "Maybe you'll like me by then! I think we could be friends!"

His hand is on the doorknob!!

"I need you to come to Kairos Crossing with me!"

His hand is on the doorknob, still, not moving. She barrels forward.

"I'm going to Kairos Crossing to catch the sun. I want you to come with me, you're *perfect* Ulrich, I've never even come *close* to- you can't leave me alone with..."

She doesn't know how to finish the thought. The silence goes on for eons.

"...With what?" Ulrich asks, not turning around. Phineas still doesn't know what to say, has no idea how to begin to explain herself. She sees him shake his head.

"You really *are* crazy." She can hear a smile there, not nice, but not nearly as nasty as his last one was. Ulrich doesn't slam the door, but the thud of the mechanism between them is loud enough.

Phineas slumps down into the dirty couch.

She tries to think of all the reasons someone like Ulrich might want to lie to someone like her, why he might damage the goods before asking if he could borrow them. He didn't throw her out, not even after she scared him. That means, probably, something else is scaring him *worse* than anything here. Maybe she still has a shot.

The pocket of her coat is deeper than it looks. Her compass is warm and heavy in her hand; she doesn't notice the weight when it's tucked away in whatever space it occupies inside the canvas, woven to hide such things from prying eyes. Outside her pockets she could track its energy down from anywhere. Even if it's being carried away by a thief who takes it with him when he leaves in the middle of the night.

It glows on the table, faintly, almost the same color Phineas does. It keeps glowing after she stops staring at the door Ulrich disappeared through, and after she tugs her coat around herself and turns her back to the room to try and get some sleep. In the quiet, the little turtle settles down where its leaves can catch the light.

◉◉◉

There is one green place in Last Chance, perched one thousand one hundred feet above ground level. There's water here too: if a man stands outside Sergei's bar and looks up during the day he can see it rushing from the ugly underside of the island tumored around the top of the radio tower. From his perspective there are channels threaded through the compacted soil of the island, dark and wrong against the desert sky, and from so high up the water seems to disperse into an unsettling mist before it can reach the ground. It glitters like venom in the sunlight. If he was looking up from the street *now*, he would see the water in the moonlight— no venom to it, only frost.

On the upper side of the island the water is calm, rivers snaking placidly under intricate wooden bridges and winding through turquoise lawns with blooming trees, forced low to the ground and knotted into painful shapes. If our Sergei's customer stepped out of the statue that houses the elevator entrance to the topside of the island, and he ignored the way the gardens repeat the same acre of land endlessly into the horizon, instead he might choose to look at the structure pretending to be a pagoda. It stands in the middle of the gardens as a crooked, waterlogged amalgam of shapes that shouldn't add up to anything like what it is. He would find that it too is only the same floor repeating itself, maybe half a dozen times, maybe too many to count as it recedes into the clouds the island brought with it. Anywhere he puts his eyes, the same sets of round windows, ringed in moon shapes; the same crooked waterspouts, the same wicked curves tearing into the night sky. If he's smart he'll step back into the elevator, but Ray is not a smart man and very drunk besides, so he leans on Royal and lets himself be led away to their quarters elsewhere on the island.

Inside the tower there is a man who doesn't look as old as he feels. He's in his study, feeding meat to the fish that live in his desk. Sometimes he talks to them. He's talking to them when the temperature in the room plummets.

His daughter flurries into the study with a burst of wintry air that slams the ornate doors open ahead of her, intentionally beating them against the aquarium walls because it annoys her father, and she wants someone else to feel as petulant as she does.

Cold Hazard frowns at the carnivorous koi jerking away from him in the water inside his transparent desk, panicked by the noise, and dumps the rest of their feed. He shakes the residue from his hand, then makes a lazy sigil in the air that materializes the glass desktop soundlessly into place again, along with all its clutter. There are stacks and stacks of handwritten documents, ink bottles, countless different fountain pens; one very old journal, the pages swollen with tabs and placeholders. There is no *organic* clutter, no old plates or coffee mugs, but on the corner of the desk there is a stunted sunflower in a pot. Its wilted petals are white in the aqueous blue light coming from the walls.

"You know it upsets the fish when you slam the door," Hazard drones. His voice is thready and empty, a broadcast signal echoing off the walls of a cave, already ended by the time it reaches the ear.

Rook has plenty of opportunity to stomp her feet as loudly as she can as she approaches the wizard. The room is shaped like a cathedral corridor, long and mostly empty. The ceiling vaults high enough to disappear into the illusion of a sky full of stars seen through the surface of the sea, and every wall is a sheer glass window looking out at the bottom of a living ocean, lit brighter and bluer than the real thing would be at that depth. In the hazy air over the humans' heads, the shapes of bioluminescent sea creatures fade in and out of sight as they drift without purpose, scattering strange colors and shadows down against the floor.

"There's a commander downstairs," Rook announces. Her voice carries well through the watery air but the dark carpet is thick, which deadens the sound of her angry steps, so Hazard comfortably ignores her tantrum and sweeps into his chair. His flowing robes leave an afterimage behind his movements.

The watery light dims as they get closer to each other, the environment hemming in around them.

"I doubt there is a commander downstairs," Hazard says, tucking a lock of his long, dark hair behind his right ear. On the other side he lets it drift in front of his face, covering the porcelain-crack void where his left eye used to be, the space now quietly oozing star-specked black tar. "There is a *silverspeaker* downstairs, but I would have seen and dispatched a commander before they could ever get so close to you, my dear."

Rook startles, briefly shaken her out of her performative fit.

"A silverspeaker? Like what *you* do? Why didn't you *tell* me?"

"He's harmless," Hazard drawls. "Either he doesn't know he can do it or he's been damaged beyond using it. I only noticed him because he's loud in other ways, his silverspeak is an afterthought..." He sets his head in his hand, closes his eye serenely. "I suppose there *is* that girl working at the restaurant, but we both know she's not going to try anything. I see nothing in this place that should send you into such hysterics."

"Well I don't know what to tell you, old man." Rook sits on his desk because it bothers him, right next to the sad little sunflower languishing in its pot. "Because I just watched a girl half their size beat the shit out of those dweebs you assigned to me and it sure *looked* like commanding."

"She? Was she cute?" Rook contemplates knocking over something fragile. "We could have her up for dinner."

"Could you pretend like you give a shit about anything?" she spits. "Like, anything at all?"

Hazard sighs again. He is full of sighs. With what seems to be enormous effort he drags his remaining eye open and looks somewhere above her head. His pupil, wide in the ethereal light, shimmers idly with colors like an oil slick. The shadows from the fish in the walls make the rest of him shimmer too, kelp caught in the tide.

"What do you want?" His voice echoes up from the bottom of a well.

"The feeling you're actually present in the room with me, to start with."

"I will go down first thing tomorrow and deal with this person, if you like. I'll assign you new bodyguards."

Rook scoffs, a cloud of snowflakes.

"Who? *Who* are you going to assign to me? *Those* two she beat down are the *last* two fighters you don't have working in the mine."

That seems to kite him in more than before. His face makes something close to a real expression of surprise.

"Oh. Really?"

"Yes *really!*" Rook hops up and rounds on him, planting her hands on his desk and leaning into his space. "Why are we still *here*, Dad?"

"We're putting together a tidy profit for your university fund."

She actually stamps her foot this time, immediately regrets it for how it forces a flash of self-awareness strong enough to get through even to her, the reminder of where the two of them are, now.

"Why won't you *talk* to me?" she demands, trying to work herself up again.

He looks at her, straight-on for the first time in days, and she withers. Rook doesn't recognize the bone-white face looking back at her, but she's getting more familiar with the shadowy ichor staining the air around the missing half of it, hanging an entire galaxy of bright blue stars between them.

"There is little to discuss," Cold Hazard says, his voice coalescing into a dark harmonic that makes Rook's skin crawl. He sees it and softens somewhat. Not back into the shape of her father, but enough to remind her of him.

"...You know I would never let anything happen to you, my little snowflake. Commanders are very dangerous, but they aren't a problem for *me*. You were right to come tell me about it if you thought-"

"She has Crow Gideon's mark."

Hazard blinks. Rook had known bringing up the name would work, but she doesn't feel any better for having to resort to it.

"Most commanders take symbols," he says eventually. "It is a pathetic attempt to feel important. Are you sure-"

Rook swipes a pile of stained papers and empty ink bottles out of the way so she can get to the desktop. The tip of her finger shines, conjuring ice crystals where it touches the glass. One of the koi follows her movements on the other side of the pane while she draws a pair of concentric circles.

"This one, right? This is what you showed me?" She sifts through years of lectures and lessons and brooding about Crow Gideon and commanders, trying to find something to reel in his attention. "She's *bright,* it felt like she burned my *eyes.*"

Hazard looks at what she's drawn for a long time. He covers his mouth with his fingertips.

"How old did you say she was?" he asks, the signal so far away it breaks up between words.

"I didn't, but...probably like my age? Early twenties?"

"Probably like your age," Hazard repeats, to himself.

"What was she wearing?" he asks. Despite the empty tone of his voice, Rook can't help a tiny spark of hope. It's like watching an unresponsive patient finally begin to eat.

"No shoes, just some nasty foot bandages," Rook rattles off. "Shorts and a sleeveless shirt. And this *really* gaudy orange coat."

All the color goes out of the room. Rook feels heavy, freezing pressure settle around her shoulders, the soothing light shrink in around them, Hazard pulling it all in like a black hole. It's harder to breathe. She knows, she *knows,* her father would never hurt her. But she also knows this thing isn't always her father.

"Dad?"

"Rook," Raven says. He looks up at her from fathoms and fathoms under the sea. "Keep your name safe."

When he says it, "Rook," it reaches in and wraps around something in her chest, whatever ephemeral organ it is she becomes aware of when she casts magic. The touch is so cold it takes her breath away. Despite everything that has happened between them, the simple request settles in her like it's the most important thing he's ever said. She tries to smile, laugh it off.

"Right, I know, commanders can use your name against you. I *was* paying attention when you-"

"I don't want you going near her again."

He stands, pulling the gravity with him. His hair billows in the air around him like spilled ink. "In fact, you will not leave this ship at all until I tell you to."

"S...sure," Rook says. "Are we worried Gideon is going to come after her?"

Raven grimaces like he's been struck. He turns away from her and bows his head, his hand moving to press his palm against his missing eye. From this angle, Rook can see the ichor hanging in the air slowly bleeding back into his face, the shards of fragmented skin drawing back to their old places. When he speaks his voice is full of static, the faulty wiring unable to keep a stable current. It's more shadow than man.

"Crow Gideon is, in fact, very *much* in the habit of leaving his messes for other people to clean up." He is *furious*. "And if she's commanding, at *your* age, she is perhaps among his most egregious. I doubt he even knows she's alive. He won't come here, for her."

His blue robe billows on an unseen tide between them. Across his back is a pair of concentric white triangles, ghostly in the ocean light, almost floating against the dark fabric.

"...Someone so young can't have been doing this for more than a few years, that simply isn't enough time for a commander to be comfortable with the ability." He might be talking to himself. Rook sees his silhouette change, his head tilt, like he's just remembered she's there. "Still. You're not to get involved."

"She seemed like kind of an idiot," Rook says, shrugging. "I really don't think-"

"That's what she *wants.*"

Hazard whirls on her, layers and layers of fabric and shadow whipping around him. Rook has never seen this expression on him before, it's impossible to determine if the thing warping his features is grief or rage.

"That's what they *do,* they *want* you to underestimate them." His eye is drawn to something on his desk and he drifts, lost in a thought. Rook isn't sure he's breathing, and realizes she can't recall the last time she noticed his breathing at all.

"I didn't..." He sweeps forward and Rook fights not to flinch from the desperation. He paws through a sheaf of papers, slung heavy with perfect inky rows of handwriting. "I wasn't ready for...for you to..."

A ratty scrap of paper catches his attention and he gasps like he's been stung, then Hazard slams his palms flat to the desk, glass rattling against glass as all the documents disappear in a haze of mist. His hair, his robes are suddenly affected by the same gravity as everything else and they fall flat around him. It's still mostly contained, but Rook can see the broken pieces of his face drifting back into their orbit around the starry void in his eye socket. The tiniest trickle of ichor phases through the hair covering the injury, only small for now, like a wisp of incense smoke. What is he *doing?*

"Dad," she tries, unsure. He shakes his head.

"These people are a *cancer* upon the world," Raven rasps miserably, looking her straight in the eye. "I can't...He's taken so much, I can't watch you become part of the wreckage these people drag along behind them. *Please* stay out of this."

She doesn't know what to say. It's more genuine emotion than she's seen from him in-

Raven's hand grasps her shoulder and digs in, enough to bring her back.

"Rook."

"Yeah." On autopilot, she settles one carefully manicured hand over his, pale and veined with ink stains. "Yeah sure. I'll let you handle it. I'll uh," she huffs a laugh as punctuation, the discomfort setting in. "I'll go wash my hair or something. This shouldn't take long, right?"

The tension leaves Hazard and he slumps. His hand slips from her shoulder. He nods.

"Not long at all."

He steps away from her so he can root around in a desk drawer. After untangling the chain from some kind of astrolabe, he loops a flat sapphire the size of Rook's fist around his neck, set back against a silver mount. Cut into triangles again, all of them pointing down.

All business now, he stalks out to the open floor, waving his hand as he goes to summon an enormous witch hat to match his endless robes. The slant of the brim further hides the hole in his face.

...Has he always dressed like this? There are no pictures, from before she got here. Rook realizes, watching him fiddle with a button on his sleeve, that he could be a wizard from one of her old books. Something aches.

He catches her looking.

"I'll be back before morning," he rasps. "I'm only going to see if I can figure out what she's been up to, I will let you know before I do anything..." He's drifting again, distracted by a fish off to his right.

"Substantial," he breathes.

"Oh, uh," Rook folds her arms over her chest. "She took Ray's card, after she beat him down. We should deactivate it."

Hazard looks at her blankly.

"What?"

Rook reaches into her emergency stores of petulance and manages to roll her eyes.

"Never *mind*, I'll take care of it. Go on."

For some reason, that brings another instant of lucidity. He smiles at her, and even though it's only a reflection it's reflecting something real, from somewhere.

"Love you," he says.

"You too."

Rook tastes seawater as he casts the spell, and then he's gone in a cloud of vapor. She stays there for a long, quiet minute, gazing distantly at the fish schooling in the walls, drifting between kelp and stone and the incongruous seabed the starship had conjured here.

Before she leaves, she wipes Crow Gideon's sigil from her father's desk, empty save for the dying sunflower.

⊙⊙⊙

It's cooler up here than it is downstairs. There are tidy white brick pathways lined with matching aqueducts crisscrossing between the housing units, and the water running in them is clear and always ice cold. The earth stays damp enough to keep up lush blue grass and shrubberies that change their shape and color if you look away for too long, some of them dotted with sunflowers. Despite the reasons he'd come here, Royal had almost liked this place just by virtue of being a deviation from his usual when he first arrived. Then one evening he'd reached out to touch a lily and it had grown a cat's tongue and *licked* him, so, that was that.

Their units are adjacent, but Royal's porch isn't in complete disarray and he'd set up some folding chairs, so they'd decided to sit here after getting each other patched up. Well, *Ray* had decided to sit here; Royal's head fucking hurts and he just wants to go to bed.

"I *can't* fucking-" Ray shakes his head and takes another pull from the bottle in his hand, because he is *still drinking*. "It had to be a fluke, she *cheated.*" He thumps the bottle against the plastic arm of the chair. "In front of *Ellie!* I'm gonna have to go smooth things over with her tomorrow."

"Cool," Royal says flatly. "You can probably find her repairing the hole in her front door."

Ray rounds on him, shoving the bottle in his direction hard enough to slosh beer onto the white wood of the porch.

"*That* wasn't *my* fault! If her-!"

"Shut the *fuck* up!" Someone is leaning out the window of a neighboring unit, an older bearded man with a robotic arm. "It's the middle of the goddamn night!"

Ray staggers to his feet and chucks the beer bottle at him; it shatters on the wall near the open window and sloshes a wet spot against the sky blue paint. Before the glass can hit the ground a monstrous pitcher plant, garish purple and yellow, skewers up out of the grass and catches it all. A long, horrible proboscis laps the beer from the wall in one sickening motion, the glass crunching in the unseen innards of the growth. All three men watch dumbly as it sucks back into the soft grass (soft like *fur*, Royal thinks unwillingly) with the physics of a sheet dragging through a pinhole. It's like it was never there.

The air between them all is quiet, only the soft sounds of water and a peaceful breeze hushing through leaves, the trees' presence suddenly ominous. The neighbor meets Ray's eye briefly before closing the window without another word. The latch catching is loud enough to shake them from their trance. Royal covers his eyes with his palms and groans.

"I hate it here *so* much, this magic bullshit makes me feel crazy."

"It's better than before ain't it?" Ray slurs, falling back into his folding chair. "We got authority now."

"I *liked* before. And yeah," Royal knows he shouldn't push, but he's having trouble thinking around the throbbing in his head. "You were real authoritative down there tonight."

"Man whose side are you on?" Ray demands, unsteady on his feet. His face is badly bruised where Ellie beaned him with the tray, it casts one eye almost entirely in shadow here in the shade of the porch. "I could have-"

"Listen man, my granny *knew* about commanders, she *told* me." Even thinking about it now sort of raises his hackles, the way his normally bright and energetic (if eccentric) grandmother had gone rigid when she recalled a commander and their crew passing through her settlement. "He didn't even *do* nothin' and it scared her so bad she *still* got freaked out talkin' about it all that time later."

"Your *granny* **also** thought the *moon* was stalking her," Ray needles. "She was fuckin' nuts, sorry if I don't put much stock in what she had to say about this bitchy little-"

"Could you not *feel* it?" Royal shouts. "She hurt my *eyes*, it was like looking at- she was too big for her *body*, it felt like lookin' at a..."

Daylight shining in his eyes, in the middle of the night. He is not a poetic man, but he is religious.

"That was a *demon* wrapped up in human skin, I've never been more sure of anything."

"Oh come *on,*" Ray snorts. "Are you serious? I could go back down there right now and-"

"She'd kill you. It's *lucky* we're still here to talk about this."

Something dark falls across Ray's face.

"What are you saying?" he asks, quieter than he's been all night.

Royal is so tired, he has been tired for *months,* it's like this town has him tangled in its tendrils and it's draining him every second he's here.

Tendrils? When's the last time he used a word like *tendrils?* Royal shakes his head, trying to clear it so he can try and keep this idiot alive.

"Exactly what I did. You're gonna get yourself killed over..." Royal hesitates. He's crossing a line, but if he doesn't do it Ray is going to die. He looks him in the eye. "I'm not gonna go along with this."

For a beat, Ray seems too startled to respond. That tracks. Royal almost never feels this confrontational; he wonders somewhere if it has something to do with being bathed in that girl's light, like he's been irradiated with...with that feeling of *aggression,* that pressure of hers kneading it into his skin.

Maybe Ray is feeling it too. Royal sees the instant some disastrous chemical reaction happens in his mind.

"This is about Ellie, ain't it?" Ray says, low.

"What?"

Ray hoists himself up and takes a swaying step closer, already beyond reason's reach.

"This is about *Ellie,*" he snarls. "I *know* you're in love with her and you've *always* been jealous of what we got-"

"Y'all don't GOT *anything!!*"

Oops.

It's like he's thrown a bucket of water over Ray's head. Something dangerously close to hurt crosses his features, huge and exaggerated with booze and adrenaline; he opens his mouth to speak, but he strangles the sound before it can turn into language. Royal hurries to try and fix this.

"Ray-"

It's too late, the wall goes up.

"No," Ray says. "Don't apologize, message fucking received."

He starts down the porch steps.

"Ray *wait,*"

"Go fuck yourself," he spits, walking right past his own unit. His shadow is a blight against the white footpath shining in the moonlight.

Royal wants to chase him, bring back this thing he used to call his friend, but he realizes with another wave of exhaustion that he only *wants* to want to go after him. How did things get this bad?

...Ray is still wasted, he probably won't get far. There's nothing for him to get into on the island, either...

Okay. Royal is going to sit here another half hour. If Ray hasn't done anything destructive enough to catch his attention by then, he's going to bed.

Okay, okay.

◉

The pathways and structures on this ship, island, *thing* tend to move when you don't watch them; if Ray was superstitious he'd almost say it feels playful, like some ghost was playing tricks for attention. Ray is *not* superstitious, he is *pissed off,* and he can't find the stupid fucking statue garden he'd passed earlier.

It had sprung up in the workers' quarter last week *specifically* to upset him, dozens of laughing theatre masks scattered along the path he'd taken after leaving the meeting where he and Royal were assigned as Eisse's guard. Everyone is *always* laughing at him and somehow this fucked up ship seems to *know it.* He wants to use the rest of his clip to blast them all to pieces, but where *are* they? This fucking place. Maybe Royal was right about it.

...Maybe Royal was right.

Ray stops, breathing hard, the hedges and trees and waterways tilting around him. The white moonlight is heavy on him, somehow. The only sound he can hear is the water running alongside the footpath, and then, he *can't* hear it any more.

He turns his head, and there are the mask statues, but now they're lining a wide path that leads to a low building he's never seen before. That weight in his belly must be nausea from the booze.

Under the jeering eyes of the laughing masks, Ray stumbles slowly down the path. When he reaches the door to the building, what he's now understanding to be some sort of garden storage shed, he finds one more grinning mask painted on like graffiti. The sloppy, dripping paint looks like tears, and the tears make a message.

Are you a man...

If he'd been less drunk, or more superstitious and less pissed off, Ray might have found it suspicious. As it is, the doorknob is cool under his palm.

The inside of the shed is dark, but from the unseen ceiling a spotlight clicks on, illuminating the two items sitting in the middle of the floor in the otherwise empty room. One is a red gasoline canister, and one is a matchbox, plain white aside from a phrase written in curling purple letters:

...or aren't you?

4

A commander's day to day experience is stranger than other folks' in a myriad of ways, but most of the differences are quiet enough to avoid drawing attention. Sleeping *isn't* one of the quiet differences— left to its own devices, an unmoored soul will drift in the tide. The same channels that allow it to command pull it away to brush up against other dreams or soak in the halo of the place the body sleeps. On particularly bad nights, the same cosmic perspective that helps a commander to understand the scale of themselves against the universe rakes them across every one of those lightyears. They turn. They shout.

The relearning of such a basic human skill is often a long and unpleasant process and Phineas hadn't been exceptional. She would wake untethered to anything, existing in three parts all pulling in different directions, and blindly panic before the instinct to reorient herself could kick in. Pain is still the fastest way to ground herself. Her childhood habit of sinking her teeth into the skin of her arms was a quick and dirty fix she eventually grew out of, but it's still a near thing, some days.

In the shack on the edge of the desert, Phineas' dreams are uneasy.

Ulrich's vivid self isn't dreaming anything in the next room (or he might still be awake), but the land feels just as confused and chaotic in Phineas' sleep as it had during her waking hours. It brings up a memory of the damp earth in Jo's garden under her feet on a hot day. It had rained earlier, the smell and mugginess lingering. Phineas had lifted a flat stone from the wet soil, and the underside writhed with thin white worms, the light sending them into a frenzy. That's how this desert, how *Last Chance* feels— like a great wriggling mass of bodies, cut right in half to let the ragged ends convulse in the open air.

Above the abstract writhing there's a voice, too.

"Hey," it says. It feels old and heavy and (familiar).

Dream Phineas has no mouth to speak, so she doesn't answer.

"I'm here," the voice shines, black and blue, "Star Astray I'm *here*, don't leave me-"

Then another voice, this one playful and pleased, says "oh *shiiit* who the fuck are *you.*" The inexplicable feeling of something tapping the glass, like Phineas is a fish in a tank. Or maybe a fish is doing the tapping from the inside. Dreams are funny.

An entire *third thing* blares in the other direction, the space reorients itself to show Phineas a cacophony of eyes, howling mouths, teeth and teeth and *teeth*. They glow only to eat up their own light again, and Phineas feels them gnawing on her edges. They are also eating up all the other words trying to reach her, the playful fish darting away under the dark wave.

Desperate, drowning, the first voice wails over the riot, "Don't *leave* me here!" and the freezing saltwater of it shocks Phineas awake.

Before she opens her eyes she takes a long, slow breath, feels it go all the way in and all the way out, suppresses the vertigo screaming at her that she's falling into a chasm in the earth.

When Phineas finally feels centered enough to get her eyes open, She (The Turtle) is quietly watching her from the spindle-table, a blur of cool greens and blues in her bleary vision. Phineas sits up and stretches, yawns loudly just to feel her own voice in her ears.

The sunshine outside is bright but it's being filtered through the flannel curtains, the pills in the fabric throwing shadow spots across the floor. Her compass is right where she left it, the little turtle still soaking up its light in the dim room. Ulrich hadn't elected to steal it in the night, then. It had been an unlikely gambit to start with, it probably isn't valuable in anyone's hands but her own, but she'd had to try.

There *is* still the possibility that he hasn't left at all. She's scared to do it but she can't stand to put it off any more: Phineas feels in the other room's direction and, of course, she finds nothing. No halo and no heartbeat. Ulrich isn't anywhere in the shack.

It's not worth our tears. Her companion squeezes her throat, mean with hurt. *Worthless coward, in the end.*

Whatever. There's nothing to be done about it now, and this empty place is grating on her like sandpaper. She packs her things under the keen observation of the turtle's shiny, blank eyes. More gently than she feels, Phineas pats its head with two fingers before she stomps outside and slams the door shut.

Even this early the sun is already merciless in a cloudless sky, searing every surface it touches to a painful glare. The ground is hot under Phineas' bare feet and it pulls her out of her tantrum enough to stop her in the shade outside the door. She slips her coat from around her shoulders, holds the hem in one hand and slides the rest of it through a loose fist. The fabric shifts obediently into a long, thin ribbon, and she threads it through her belt loops, tying a thick knot near her hip. The way it swishes along behind her as she sets out is a small improvement to her mood.

"Where are you off to?"

Phineas whirls on her heel, her belt following a beat behind. Like last night, Ulrich is a dark shape looking down on her, this time from where he's sat atop the rock growing around the shack. She can't see his smirk but she can hear it.

"You're angry," Ulrich muses, a world away from the piano-wire-tense he'd been last night. "Did you think I'd gone and left you?"

"Kinda, yeah," Phineas says. She sets one hand on her hip while she squints up at him and thinks of Jo standing on the porch, watching visitors come up the drive. "You weren't really talkin' like you were gonna stick around, before."

Ulrich sighs loud enough for her to hear it.

"Come *up* here, shouting like this is silly."

That's true. Lighter than she was a moment ago, Phineas bounds the few yards back to the shack, pulling up enough force in her footsteps to make the leap to the roof and into the shade under the overhang. She's briefly distracted by the almost organic look to the radio antenna coming from the roof of the shack, the way it grew plantlike into the rock formation that yielded to it like some softer material. *Only* briefly distracted; there's something better waiting for her. The stone is rough and offers plenty of footholds, it's easy to haul herself up the side to the top.

Ulrich is sitting crosslegged in the blazing sunshine, his hat, glasses, and overshirt piled neatly beside him. He's facing away from her and sitting very straight, his chin tilted up to look out over the desert. He's been here a while. A halo like his should be easy to find through just a few layers of matter, how had she *missed* him?

The stone bites comfortably into her heels as Phineas closes the distance. Ulrich's eyes are shut, his hands draped loose over his thighs, and he doesn't move at all when her shadow falls over his face. His expression is the softest she's seen on him yet, especially open and vulnerable in the harsh light without his glasses. Only his deepset eyes give him away, his unhealthy paleness exacerbated out here. She settles down at his side and mirrors him.

"Hi," she says.

"Hello," he says, his voice distant. They stay that way, quiet and sunlit, for what feels to Phineas like a long moment. Ulrich is much more fluent in silence than she is.

"That's a rough climb for someone who can't jump like me," she says, reaching the end of her vocabulary.

"Spry for a big guy, aren't I?"

"So cool," Phineas says earnestly, fighting not to look at him and his coolness. "What are you doing up here?"

"Gathering my luck for the day."

Phineas gives up and stares at him. He hasn't budged.

"...Yeah?"

Ulrich tilts his head slightly; his cute hair frames his face just so and somehow he's striking a dramatic angle while changing very little.

"When I was small, I wandered into the west. I gathered seven lucky clovers from seven different soils, all grown under the light of one yellow sun." He's smiling. He's said this before, he's reciting. That cold silver feeling spirals down Phineas' spine. "I ate them, brought them together in my body, and luck was bestowed upon my bones."

Phineas' laugh is explosive.

"Nuh-*uh!*"

"It's true."

She forgets to watch for sparks and misses her chance. She doesn't care.

"If I meditate with you, will I be lucky too?"

Now Ulrich opens his eyes *just* enough for her to see the blue between his lashes, low enough he doesn't squint in the sunshine. He's lovely the way a bruise is.

"You won't. But you can try."

They sit for a while. The desert is still, caught out and frozen under the sun like an overexposed photograph. Phineas really *does* try to meditate; it's good for commanders to stay oriented to new places even if the place feels like a carpet of gross worms. She notices, with a curl of anxiety, that she hasn't felt any breeze at all since she's been outside today, and can't remember if she felt any yesterday. The air is stagnant and stifling, she and Ulrich an oasis of heartbeats and movement on this radio outpost surrounded by miles of dead air. She tries to focus on him, instead, and the serene chill of him next to her.

Eventually, Ulrich lets go of a long breath, and Phineas feels him turn in her direction. He's losing the easy, muted quality of his morning routine, compacting himself back into the tension Phineas recognizes. He fidgets without fidgeting. Phineas generously does not open her eyes to look at him.

"...I'm sorry about last night," she hears him say. "I shouldn't have shouted."

"I never got a problem with shouting," Phineas says.

"I am very tired of being here," Ulrich says, and Phineas doesn't need any fancy skills to know that's true. "And I do need help to get up to Hazard's ship, and...through it."

Phineas is trying hard to keep from opening her eyes to take him in, she knows that would make this harder for him. But she can't keep from grinning.

"Look, it's obvious you don't like talkin' about yourself," she says. "I don't need you to explain anything to me. I wanna get up there too, and I want us to be friends. I'm happy for an excuse to do this together."

It takes Ulrich a long time to process it.

"You really mean that," he says, maybe more to himself. Phineas finally turns her smile on him, so bright and sincere Ulrich immediately looks away into the glare of the desert instead.

"I do! I mean most stuff I say. I meant it when I asked you to come with me to Kairos too!"

Glee blooms in Phineas' chest at Ulrich's grumpy face, a real expression replacing the plastic one like turning on a light.

"You realize people have their own lives outside of you, yes?" he says. His voice is a couple clicks lower when he's irritated, Phineas notes. "Why would I drop everything to follow a brat like you just to get *obliterated* in Kairos Crossing?"

"We can do both our things! What's on *your* list? I'll help you out."

"I have to fight a saint, to rescue my friend."

What a dick.

"Yeah?"

"Yeah," he sets his chin in his hand, rests his elbow on his knee, not even pretending he's telling the truth enough to generate any silver sparks. She copies him. "It went mad and locked her in a tower, she has been sending me psychic transmissions in my sleep to help guide me to the seven beasts I have to defeat."

"What's the beasts' deal?"

"They have pieces of a map to the infinite maze inside the tower."

"The maze is infinite *inside* the tower?"

"Yes."

"Well we can go to Kairos after we get your friend."

Ulrich laughs a little bit, sad in the edges.

"It's going to be a long term engagement I am afraid."

"You're *such* a bastard," Phineas complains, crossing her arms like a child. "Why are you so *difficult?*"

"Me?!" He moves his hands towards her like he wants to shake her, but something stops him.

"Oh," he says, placid again. Phineas watches him dig in his pocket. "Here, I put these together last night. From one of those shirts."

He holds out what looks like a ball of green socks. Phineas unrolls them to find...

"You *made* these?" Phineas gasps. "Just last night?"

"To replace those bandages around your feet," Ulrich says smugly. "I am holding you to your word."

Phineas giggles and starts tearing the wraps from her legs, Ulrich's pleased expression melting back to disgust as the dingy pile of tape grows between them. The new wraps he's made are the same stiff starchy fabric as the shirt she's already wearing, of course, but they slip snugly over her shins and across her feet, perfectly sized to fit between her toes and heels. Ulrich is looking them over with a critical eye, scanning for flaws in his work. He won't find any, and Phineas makes sure of it by standing up and tapping her toes against the ground in turn, arcs of latent energy cascading from her calves to the earth. Ulrich nods firmly.

"Good. No more dirty bandages," he says.

"No more dirty bandages," she agrees. She stretches, heaves in a lungful of dry air.

"So! What's our plan, smart guy?"

Ulrich scrubs his hand over his mouth, scraping across the scruff while he looks away into the empty desert.

"I…don't actually know what to do from here," he admits. "I have been watching Hazard's people come and go from his ship using the service elevator built into the radio tower, but it requires a key to run. And *Hazard* never comes down, as far as I can tell. *We* need to go *up.*"

"Oh, is this a key?"

Phineas catches the end of her belt and digs her fingers into the fabric until a seam appears, and then a pocket. Ulrich makes a sound, a question crashing into the back of his teeth because he's stubbornly keeping his mouth shut. She finds the plastic card she took from Ray the night before and hands it over.

"That look right?"

Ulrich hums.

"I have not been close enough to know for certain, but I'd take that bet." He grins at her with his creepy teeth. "Good work, mausbär."

"I guess we go on up then?"

"No."

"No?"

"It's good to know what we're looking for, but I am almost certain that key does not work now. The, er," he hands it back to her and she stuffs it back in her coat pocket, trying not to feel disappointed. "The woman, Hazard's daughter, she is smart enough not to leave a loose end like that."

"You know her? The glass lady?"

"…Sure," Ulrich cedes. "The glass lady. She was there when Hazard's men ambushed the wagon."

"Maybe Ellie can help us with this," Phineas says, not wanting to linger on the armadillo guy too long for both their sakes.

"Oh, we can eat something too," Ulrich stands. "I assume commanders still need to *eat?*"

"I do like a breakfast. Sergei's is right on the way."

"You don't think we should keep a low profile after your stunt last night?"

"Not low enough to skip a meal," Phineas insists. "Ellie's nice, she'll take care of us!"

◉◉◉

Once they'd crossed out of the expanse and into Last Chance properly Ulrich had gone quiet, answering Phineas' chatter with short, hushed responses and eventually nothing at all. He pulls his hat low, keeps looking over his shoulder like he expects something to leap from behind one of the buildings. He'd been up above everything when she found him and he's been staying in that little shack out in the open, maybe the narrow streets make him nervous. Phineas lets him be and leads the way, busying herself with remembering how to get to Sergei's through the eerie, chaotic corpse of the town. In the daylight, without the boon of being the only lit thing in sight, the bar is hard to distinguish from the rest of the buildings around it. Phineas has to look for those doors with the hole in.

Ulrich finds his voice when they're close enough to hear jangly music through an open doorway. He steps up beside her and his disdain rolls in to break over them both like a plume of smoke.

"Starving is starting to sound attractive," he says, squinting in the sun despite his dark green sunglasses already shielding his eyes. Phineas elbows him and ignores how he flinches.

"Naw it ain't, lighten up."

"This is as light as it gets, Kidd."

There's nobody else in the dining room today to appreciate the creaky door sound, which is technically an improvement after last night's complete disinterest.

"Oh," Ulrich mumbles to himself as he creaks through behind her. "Straight from a movie."

In Phineas' entire life it has never been more difficult to play it cool.

She's about to call out for Ellie, she gets as far as taking in a big breath, but Ulrich's palm appears on the meat of her shoulder and pushes her gently backwards at the last second. When she looks, she sees his left hand snake up under his long hair, where his ear would be. He presses the index finger of his right to his lips, his eyes focused on the beaded curtain to the kitchen.

"...miss you..."

Just audible over the vaguely rhythmic twanging coming from the speakers, Ellie's voice is soft and warm, and now that Phineas is looking for it she can see her pretty halo drifting out through the strands of the curtain.

"...will you be...?"

Phineas' hearing isn't as good as Ulrich's probably, but she knows love when she sees it, its light threaded clear as day through the doorway like ribbons. Great, good for Ellie, why are they eavesdropping? She gets Ulrich's attention and shrugs as loud as she can, *what's the problem?* His expression veers into almost total nonrecognition, as if he's staring at a bizarre new flower he doesn't remember planting. Whatever it is, it clears up quickly.

"Go on," he says quietly, dropping his hand from his ear. Oh well, he must have his reasons.

"G'morning!" Phineas calls -

Beside her, Ulrich's entire being ripples like water, and when it stops he is a completely different shape in Phineas' landscape. It feels similar to the menacing presence she'd felt from him last night, the thing haunting his left eye. She tastes something floral.

Ellie squeaks and all those nice lights sizzle out of view. Some more muffled, hurried speech, then she sways through the doorway looking perfect as usual.

"Hi!" Ellie sweeps her arm across the empty room. "Y'all have a seat anywhere."

Phineas scoots up to the bar counter, delighted to notice the backs of the high stools are shaped like broken barrels. She twirls the one next to her around to face Ulrich, who grimaces when her hand coming away from the lacquer makes a sticky sound. It's not *quite* his grimace though, Phineas is still getting the feeling that he isn't himself.

"Who's your friend?" Ellie asks, pouring water into some of those plastic tumblers from last night. They're already sweating when they hit the countertop.

When Ulrich removes his hat to set it on the counter, his expression underneath is so pleasant and easy Phineas nearly does a for-real doubletake. He's smiling with his perfect teeth that really *do* look perfect now, like they suddenly figured out how to sit naturally in his mouth. Brushing a hand through his hair to fluff it out from its hat shape makes it fall around his face in such a charmingly disheveled way Phineas thinks she sees Ellie blushing.

"Afternoon," he says, his voice buzzing curiously in Phineas' ear. He reaches into his hat and, in a fluid motion, he draws out a piece of yellow paper covered in writing. He blows on it, a theatrical puff of air, and the paper rearranges itself into a perky daisy.

Ellie *giggles.* She fixes the flower behind her ear and leans on the bar, gazing at Ulrich like some kind of Ellie Impostor.

"Somethin' to drink?" she asks. "Breakfast?"

"That would be great, thank you," Ulrich says serenely. He orders for both of them but Phineas is so completely mystified she doesn't catch what gets said. The *second* Ellie is gone she shakes Ulrich's shoulder urgently, nearly knocking them both from their stools.

"*What* was *that?!*" she hisses. When Ulrich shoves her away automatically, she catches a glimpse of his usual disdain again with some amount of relief.

"*That* is how you get information," he says flatly. "And even if she has none it's *always* useful to befriend service workers."

After a quick glance to the kitchen to make sure Ellie isn't coming back yet, Ulrich settles down with the air of a ruffled bird deflating. He sets his sunglasses on the counter in front of him, reaches into his shirt and produces a pink handkerchief, drags it across his face.

"That *is* her," he adds as an afterthought. "The one you said might help us?"

"Oh, yeah." While his armor is displaced Phineas notices the hair plastered to his temples and realizes the dining room isn't air conditioned. That hadn't been a big deal in the dark, but under the sun it's like they're sitting in an oven.

He sees her seeing him.

"The heat does not bother you?" he asks conversationally, flicking his eyes over her before replacing his glasses. The lenses have shifted again, clear now. "More commander's perks?"

"Yup," Phineas says, almost apologetically, which is new for a conversation like this. Bragging feels bad while Ulrich is melting next to her.

"Lucky you."

"Don't, ah," it'll be easier to just say it. "If you need to rest, or anything before I do, just say so. Don't want you passing out on me."

Ulrich's grin has too many teeth, all of them back to being unnatural and too-white against the dirt around him, thank goodness.

"Thank you, I will keep it in mind."

The smell of hot food demands all their attention when Ellie comes back through the doorway, balancing two plates and a wire basket in her arms. She doles it out in front of them and momentarily excuses herself, disappearing back into the kitchen.

Ulrich's stomach growls loudly, audible even over the abrasive music, and he starts eating without further discussion. Phineas fidgets, the food reminding her she should have spoken up earlier.

"I uh, I can't pay for this."

When Ulrich waves her off, she can see a tremor in his hand.

"I've got it."

"You really didn't have to-"

He shoves her plate towards her.

"We have a lot of work to do today, and I doubt we are going to get another chance to eat."

Can't argue with that. Ulrich ordered them both a pile of scrambled eggs with colorful bits of vegetables mixed in, each with a dish of some kind of cubed fruit on the side. Probably the same fruit used to make the preserves sitting next to the biscuits, which crumble apart as soon as Phineas splits one open. She winces, expecting Ulrich to nag her for making a mess, but when she looks at him he's hunched over and wolfing down his food like he hasn't seen any in *days*.

"Woah, are you-"

Ulrich swallows with some difficulty and reaches for his water, which is almost gone.

"I'm sorry," he says, his voice ragged around his eating. "I ah. I have not had a proper meal in some time."

"How come you didn't just come here before?"

Realizing what's being said, Phineas rounds on him.

"Didn't you say you been here for a while?" she demands. "What *have* you been eating 'til now?"

Ulrich clears his throat, sitting up straight again as Ellie comes through with the water pitcher. Phineas takes the cue to drop it, but she side-eyes him as he lapses back into that fakey plastic persona he'd donned with Ellie earlier.

"Two new folks in the same week," Ellie drawls pleasantly. "That's some kinda record I think."

Ulrich looks sheepish.

"Ach, while you're here, where is your restroom?"

"Oh! Sure, it's right through there." She points at a doorway Phineas had overlooked the night before, tucked quietly among the chaotic wall decor. Phineas can see a tight wooden staircase on the other side.

Ulrich thanks Ellie in Deutsch, which Phineas can immediately tell is part of whatever weird fucking thing he is doing here with her, and he excuses himself. Ellie sighs politely, smiles at Phineas. She's in a red-checked shirt today, with the sleeves rolled up, and her hair is pulled back into a bushy ponytail, and her rabbit ears are perked up tall above her head, and Phineas is *violently* reminded she's gay.

"Hah," Phineas says, brushing crumbs off her shirt. It draws Ellie's attention, and she sobers all of a sudden.

"Where'd you find that old thing?" she asks.

Phineas looks down at herself. When the shirt's starchy friction had become unbearable on their way here she'd ripped the sleeves off and torn the collar into a V-shape, but there's still a recognizable cartoon drawing of the red tower outside printed across her chest.

"There were boxes of 'em in the shack we slept in last night," Phineas says, feeling guilty about taking it now. "I hope it's-"

"You're fine," Ellie says, busying herself with organizing dishes behind the bar. "Nobody's usin' 'em. Just haven't seen one of those in a while."

"Yeah, there was a little turtle hangin' out in there too. Real lively place."

Ellie nearly drops the plate she's holding.

"You okay?"

"Fine!" she chirps, not fine. "Fingers're sweaty..."

Whatever magic Ulrich had spun to put her in a good mood has completely evaporated in the twenty seconds he's been gone. Phineas is such a *loser,* why can't she have a conversation with this woman without upsetting her? She scrabbles for anything that might solve this deceptively complex interaction.

"Hey," she tries, licking her dry lips. "The tower, it ain't like..." Ellie turns to look at her, which makes Phineas realize this is very close to lying, somehow. She's a terrible liar. But she really, *really* wants to have this done by the time Ulrich gets back, she should be *contributing* to this partnership, so Phineas leans in like they're sharing a secret. Ellie leans in too. She smells nice, like the biscuits, but Phineas valiantly stays on track. "Like, how do we get up there? The elevator ain't just...*open,* is it?"

"Oh, um!" Ellie leans away, taps her hands against the bar while she thinks. "Hang on," she mumbles, then kneels down behind the counter. Something unseen and metallic clicks before she pops up again, holding another one of those cards Phineas had swiped from Ray last night.

"Here, this'll get you in the elevator and, er...upstairs."

When Ellie worries she gets a wrinkle near her nose, it's unspeakably endearing. Phineas takes the card and looks it over. She hadn't been expecting this, why does *Ellie* have a key?

"They gave it to Papa and me in case we needed to...I don't know, meet?" Ellie says, like she can hear Phineas' thoughts. "I only went up the one time, kinda right after he got here. I ain't gonna need it today."

It probably wouldn't do for Ulrich, but Phineas is satisfied with that.

"Should have it back to ya by tonight at the latest," she says, grinning her most reassuring grin. It gets a weary smile from Ellie, the cute wrinkle smoothing away from her face.

"I hope so." The golden ribbons of Ellie's halo are still tinged with doubt, but that's okay. Phineas is sure enough for both of them.

◉

The restroom is much cleaner than Ulrich was expecting, and in a stroke of luck it's a single stall with a deadbolt on the door. When the lock thuds into place he forces his shoulders to loosen and rests his forehead against the wood, counts out some breaths. The dry, bland biscuits hitting his tongue had set off an unfortunate switch somewhere. So desperately devouring shitty bar food had been humiliating already; doing it while burning up next to the entire event of Phineas Kidd had been enough to set the walls closing in around him.

In, two, three, four; hold, two, three, four; he's gotten very good at recognizing the symptoms early, he is *fine*, he's still getting enough air for now *please* don't have an asthma flare-up in this disgusting restaurant before noon.

There's a threatening hand around his lungs, but after a long moment of vicious concentration it lets him go with a warning. He sighs, unobstructed, his medications untouched.

Ulrich shouldn't linger here too long. There's a metal fan in the corner aimed at a cracked window making plenty of white noise for him to relax against, but he runs the sink anyway to get some cool water on his hands. A wash might be nice too, at least some small part of him can be clean. The liquid soap from the industrial container is pink and floral; as he works up a lather with his trembling hands, another pair creeps around either side of his waist to steady him, bony and sallow, her body coiling around his like a twisting vine. The cold water and the waifish weight on his back gets his nerves under control. He splashes some water on his face and doesn't check the mirror to see if she's really there behind him.

Leaving the water on, he braces one hand on the sink and reaches up to tweak some settings on his hearing aid. One knob one way, one another, there's dull static in his ear, then,

"....do we get up there? The elevator ain't just....."

Phineas' voice is, as expected, clear and bright even over the tenuous paper hardware, and Ellie's is Good Enough. Ulrich lowers the volume to nothing and feels slightly better with another tool in his box, small as it is.

God it's like being baked in a *kiln*. He shuts off the water and-

What's-

He twists the knob on his aid again, cranking the volume uncomfortably. He's picking up something rhythmic and clatter-y, why does he recognize that-

Ulrich rushes to the shuttered window and pries it open. From the second floor view, two points of interest: the giant tortoise patron saint is still lumbering steadily towards Last Chance, through a dustcloud being kicked up behind the second interesting point, a wagon being pulled by a pair of armadillos.

Fuck.

Phineas is appreciating the way Ellie's laugh curls away from her like party confetti when Ulrich's arm settles around her shoulder. He rests his head in the crook of her neck, making a tidy bubble between the three of them, and Phineas knows immediately he's That Other Ulrich, again. When he grins his cheeks round out, pillowing against Phineas'.

"I am afraid some of Hazard's men are approaching, and I doubt they'd be happy to see Phineas here after last night," Ulrich says. "Is there a back door we could leave through?"

"What about your breakfast though?" Phineas turns to look at his place at the bar and finds empty dishes; he'd already inhaled everything before he left. "Oh. Well what's the problem? We can take care of it."

"And add more holes to Ellie's doors?" Ulrich asks.

His pleasant delivery sort of makes Phineas want to slap him, but instead she says, "Ah, yeah that's a good point."

Ellie just looks confused.

"Are you sure…" she stammers, standing up to squint through the windows.

"They are still a ways off, I saw them from the second floor."

"R…right," Ellie still looks uncertain but she relents, then steps away from the bar. "Of course, y'all come this way."

The service door Ellie takes them through dumps them into the alley behind the bar. It reeks of old food and, in a way that pings another memory of home, smoke and ash; they must burn the trash back here. There are still big industrial dumpsters sitting behind each building, better suited to something like a shopping center than the last establishment in a ghost town. Phineas and Ulrich head down into the alley but Ellie stays on the back steps, misaligned with the wooden floor of the building, waffling with her hand on the screen door handle.

"You should be able to get the whole way there taking the back alleys," she says. "You'll only have to be out in the open when you hit the market square, around the base of the tower."

"Sounds good!" Phineas says, stretching her arms behind her head. "Thanks again, Ellie."

"Yes, thank you very much," Ulrich adds, smiling tamely. Ellie still seems put out, but she manages her own smile before retreating into the kitchen, the screen door banging crooked behind her. Phineas counts to ten before Ulrich shimmers back into himself again.

"So *she* had a key for the elevator," he muses. "Interesting."

"Yup. Think we're good to go now?"

"I think so." Still antsy to get away from the restaurant, he starts down the way and Phineas follows.

The alley Phineas and Ulrich fought in last night had been between some rare brick buildings, but this one's got the full Last Chance Aesthetic. The walls bullying them into the narrow walkway are caked in junk: corrugated sheet metal held together desperately with mismatched nuts and bolts, dangling pulleys with planks of rotting wood swaying from rusted hooks, their frayed ropes barely hanging on. There's even weirder stuff back here too, out of sight from the main road, things like bent and corroded traffic signs in a town with no asphalt anywhere, or modern vending machines with shattered glass. Phineas and Ulrich have to scramble over a tall metal streetlight laid cattycorner across the alley, smashed right through the back wall of what used to be a drug store. Ulrich is walking behind her again, so when Phineas gets across the streetlight herself she reaches a hand out for Ulrich to hold. He doesn't take it, his feet landing on the other side with a cloud of dust.

"What's all this junk *for,* you think?" she asks, slowing in an attempt to put them on equal footing. "On the buildings?"

Ulrich stays in step with her, uncomfortable about it. He stares up at the skeletons rising around them, but even with his glasses darkened again he can't handle the sunlight for very long and turns right back to his feet.

"It may be difficult to get proper repairs done out here," he offers. But he shakes his head, maybe as bothered by all of it as Phineas is. Phineas follows his gaze to where a bus stop has been sliced neatly in half, the rest of it nowhere in sight. "But this is not any sort of architecture I've seen before."

They pick their way between the debris in silence for a second. Like, four seconds of silence maybe before she can't deal anymore.

"So," Phineas can tell her casual tone doesn't work, Ulrich's head tilts towards her sharply. "Really this time, what *was* that? Back there with Ellie."

"I told you, I was-"

"No yeah, I mean..." This stuff is so frustrating to talk about. "You, you *changed.*"

"It is called 'acting,'" Ulrich says, swiping his wrist across his forehead. It's shady between the buildings, but he's still struggling. Phineas can't help making a frustrated noise this time, big enough to stim out through her arms. Ulrich raises an eyebrow at her, self-consciously lowering his hand, and she immediately feels bad.

"That's not- It's not *you,* I'm just. Words are *hard,* " she whines, running a hand through her hair.

"Would you like to try again?" he asks, nearly smiling. Phineas flexes her fingers in the air in front of her.

"You know how I said last night you look blue, to me?" she starts. "And that I think you're good because of it? Well-" She sidesteps an overturned air conditioning unit. "Not because of the *blue,* just, that I can see *you,* and you happen to *be* blue, while also being good."

Outwardly, Ulrich is doing a great job pretending he isn't humoring a child describing playground logic.

"I recall, yes," he says gamely.

"There was a couple times in there, at the restaurant, where you were...you felt different." Phineas tries to think of some adjectives.

Words are so *defined,* people don't *work* like that. She also doesn't like that every word she can think of for those odd eddys in Ulrich's flow are mean ones.

"Different how?" Ulrich presses, after the silence goes on too long.

"Cruel," Phineas says helplessly, wincing away from it. "But, but not..."

Ulrich seems unbothered. He hardly reacts at all.

"Cruel," he says it like he's chewing sticky candy. Then he smiles, and Phineas feels the coiled springs and snares of Ulrich's mechanisms shiver around her. "You seem surprised, was I unclear before? Are we having second thoughts, sunshine?"

God no, it's so wrong it makes her laugh. It ripples through his expression.

"I really don't buy it, dude, it wouldn'a been so weird with Ellie otherwise." She shoves her hands in her pockets and digs her toes in the dirt while she walks, kicking up clouds. "People get cagey about commanders too. We're scary."

"I can see it," Ulrich muses. "You do have a...a presence. You are good at filling a room."

"Do *you* think I'm scary?" Phineas asks, immediately regretting it when her heart starts thudding. Ulrich makes a show of sighing around his thinking. He scratches his chin in exactly the way he had last night on the roof, right before he turned to leave.

"Yes," he says. "Sometimes when you look at me it feels like I've been thrown into the sea." He makes a face, mostly at himself. "Does that. Make sense? I feel *submerged.* And, I think, sometimes I feel what you feel. False emotions. I am not a fan of having my state of mind dictated for me."

"Yeah that happens," Phineas admits. "Feelings are energy too, and all of ours goes on the outside."

He shrugs, light. He's pretending, Phineas can tell, but she appreciates that he's making the effort.

"I swim well."

Phineas beams.

"Cool, so you wanna come to Kairos Crossing with me?"

Ulrich rolls his eyes.

"Let's not get ahead of ourselves," he says.

After a moment, he clicks his tongue. "I do think it is *obnoxious* that I can't lie to you. I still don't understand how *any* of this works."

"Commanding's real simple," Phineas says, reciting what she'd been told forever ago. She counts the points out on her fingers just to move her hands. "Sun makes energy, earth makes energy, it moves between them in natural patterns. Sort of like a heartbeat, sending blood through veins. You have a heartbeat, the blue thing, and the land has one too."

"Of course it does," Ulrich says dryly.

"Willpower is energy, and feelings too, and commanders can see all of that stuff and use our own to get all up in the patterns."

"And seeing feelings lets you catch *bullets?*"

"If it's uh, mm," Phineas snaps her fingers, trying to remember the word. "K. Kinestic?"

"Kinetic?"

"Yeah! *Kinetic* energy, we can redirect the momentum where we want. So, if I'm walking, I can pull up the impacts of my feet from the ground and send it through a different vein in the air, or through a heavy thing, or through my fist!" She stops and holds up her hand; a thin lance of light winds up around her leg, skitters over her coat and across her fanned out fingers. "Whatever I tell it to do!"

Ulrich stares, his feet coming to a stop.

"When you hit me last night, you stole the force from the bullet. Away from your wound, and through your fist."

"Redirected it."

"So you are always exactly as strong as your opponent," he says slowly. Phineas can see his gears turning, artificial shapes spinning away through his halo while they work out the concept. She's surprised by how much it seems to affect him.

"We add some of ourselves, so it's stronger when I send it back, usually." Phineas grins with her whole body. "And that's why I always win."

Ulrich makes a conversational sound and starts walking again, still lost in whatever thought process she'd jumpstarted in him. As the alleyway ends Phineas realizes he had avoided explaining anything *she'd* asked him to. Before she can pursue it, the thought is crushed by the event of the radio tower now in front of them.

Phineas already knew it was big, she's been looking at it for days already, but seeing where it meets the ground hammers it home hard enough to make her dizzy with it. One of its feet must be an acre wide, and there are four of them and they all taper terribly *up*, so tall it wheels and fades into the blue sky, curling in on *her,* and it says "I'm here, I *need you, come to me beloved-*"

"I hope you're not afraid of heights," Ulrich says, nudging her. She shakes herself from her daze; the red I-beam is still mind-bendingly huge, but it's only what it is, no voices. This time she doesn't get lost when she cranes her neck to follow the taper, and she finds the dark underside of the wizard's island, jammed on top like a kid had smashed some toys together.

"I'm," she licks her dry lips. "I'm not, nah. Just uh. It's big."

"Mm," Ulrich says. He starts across the clearing to the tower base and Phineas jogs to catch up.

"Looks like this was a fun place, once," Ulrich remarks as they pass a broken fountain. Benches and carts and stalls are scattered through the square, punctuated with red pieces of the tower. They're much smaller than the legs, and twisted like tree roots. They must have broken off from the top when Hazard showed up.

"Ellie said this was the marketplace, their city square I guess? It's..." She turns to look all around, walking backwards. Something here feels incorrect. "Man I dunno, we had a square back home, the place I grew up was about this town's size. Our town center area wasn't *half* this big, this looks *huge.*"

Ulrich hums, thinking. The legs of the tower pass them on either side like ocean liners as they approach the center, where a service elevator sits. *That* structure is comically small, resting at the bottom of a tall metal column poking right through the center of everything, all the way up into the island.

"What do your amazing powers of observation tell you about Ellie," Ulrich asks idly. "Your *commander vision,*" he adds. Phineas tries not to preen.

"I dunno, she's real pretty I think. But..."

...It's Ulrich. She's allowed to feel this.

"She's. Not like us. She'd rather fold than try to fix things she don't like."

"I see," he says, perfectly neutral.

"But she's nice! She ain't tellin' us everything, but her intentions are good."

"Like mine are good," Ulrich says, not looking at her. "Like *I* am a nice person."

Phineas giggles.

"I didn't say you were *nice,* but same deal, yeah."

The elevator is a rickety, sun-seared box that looks more like a repurposed shipping container, one wall replaced with a scissor gate. There's a simple console with a keypad and a slot for a keycard, the green LCD screen cracked and yellowed. Next to her, Ulrich makes a sign near his temple, another one of his prepackaged expressions, and his bird mask shimmers into being around his glasses. Without feathers, caught out in the daylight, the smooth off-white material looks closer to bone than whatever it actually is. There are no straps or fasteners or anything, it's like it's molded straight to his face.

His halo flows back into the artificial shape, with the flower petals.

"Key?" Ulrich asks, his head tilt exaggerated by the sharp beak. Phineas had gotten distracted.

"Oh!" She shakes herself and reaches for it. "It's in my coat pocket."

Oh, it's in her coat pocket.

"Oops." Even to her own ears it's damning. Ulrich's glare is like daggers in her back.

"What."

Phineas puts on a big, hopefully placating grin as she faces him, holding up two identical keycards. This close in the midday light, she can see his eyes through the dark green lenses, flickering between the two cards while he catches up. Then they focus on her.

"You *didn't.*"

"I *always* just put stuff in my coat pockets!" she says defensively. "It's not usually a problem!"

"You can conduct *extrasensory personality tests* but you cannot suss out the right *card,*" he snatches them furiously and examines them against each other like he's trying to decide which wire will defuse the bomb. "What a *ridiculous* ability."

"Well hey, let's use yours then."

"What?"

He's not listening, still holding the cards close to each other. Phineas steps even closer, right in front of him so he has to look at her, too. He groans.

"*What,* Phineas?"

"You said you're lucky," Phineas says brightly, not nearly as irritated as he is, delighted by the novelty of getting to ask someone else for help. They're a real team!

Ulrich isn't as mad as he thinks he is, she can see he's just anxious, his halo has been getting shakier and fuzzier since they left the bar. He must have gotten so flustered he forgot they *do* have a skill for this, between them. Phineas grins, radiating confidence. "Pick us a card, lucky boy."

He huffs through his nose, quietly activating some kind of filter inside the beak, his mouth an angry line underneath it. But the end of his mask tilts down. His eyes leave hers to settle on one card, then the other, then the first one again. Phineas sees a tiny thread of silver skewer out from the center of his halo, weaving through the shining lotus petals to dissipate in the fringes. He curls the right card to his chest and offers Phineas the left one. It's hard not to throw her arms around him.

"This is the one we want," Ulrich says. Phineas plucks it from him and skips to the console. Ulrich is looming over her shoulder immediately.

"Should I do that?" he asks, sounding like a worried hen again.

"I wanna do it." Phineas presses a big button, and the screen lights up with black letters:

READY

"Do you know *what* you are doing?" Ulrich murmurs, hovering.

"It's a card reader, what's there to know?"

Phineas swipes the card and Ulrich jumps when something loud and metallic thunks inside the gate's groove. It groans as it eases back on its track, unlocked. Now the screen says **BOARD,** so Phineas wrenches the gate open and they do that.

The inside had mostly been visible already, but tucked into a blind corner there's a flatscreen television, the glossy plastic and smooth screen easily the cleanest thing Phineas has seen since she got into town. Ulrich examines it while Phineas attempts to drag the gate shut again, the rough rust-eaten metal almost burning her fingers. It takes an extra try, she finally mutters *"move,* dammit," and a long line of yellow phosphene sparks along behind the second jerk. The gate slots into place right where it should, engaging the lock mechanism. A spike of anxiety behind her, near the television screen.

"This thing is a death trap," Ulrich frets. He's aiming for his usual dry disdain but the tightness in his voice gives him away. Phineas gets beside him and sets her hand on his shoulder.

"Hey it's gonna be *fine*, we're lucky right?" The touch bugs him enough he forgets to be anxious for a second, he turns to leer at her instead.

"I am-"

The very clean television plays a midi fanfare that ends on a rotten note. The display lights up white, a pixelated cartoon thumb in the center. It's pointing down. Ulrich gasps in a quick breath, catching on first.

"God *damn it."*

The floor shakes under their feet, and it falls away on its hinges.

5

Bel had recognized he was doing it before he did, because she did it too, slipped quietly out of this world and into a sharper, slower one where there is always just enough time to react. One extra decision, one more chance to notice the detail that will save you. Like everything else the two of them share, Bel is better at it, taking to anything she does like she was born for it while Ulrich has to take the long way around. *Also* like everything else they share there are frustratingly few words to describe such a strange experience, even with two languages between them.

Whenever they had to hang words on it, which was not often, they referred to it as half-time; a term used in musical theory to describe when a passage feels slower while maintaining the same tempo, although for Bel and Ulrich it involved ammunition more often than a melody. Sometimes it was a clever prop flying under hot stage lights, sometimes it was a cruel retort during a negotiation, sometimes it was a very literal bullet from a very real gun, eviscerating in the dark. It is unclear if this skill would have come from Ulrich naturally, cosmic chance granting the two of them identical abilities before they met, or if he simply spent too long turning in Bel's orbit and picked it up that way.

Regardless, as far as Ulrich is concerned, when the elevator floor gives way it takes them *years* to fall, so he has plenty of time to seethe about how fucking *stupid* it is that this commander he has known for all of ten minutes is what finally kills him. Against the unnatural black of the elevator shaft Phineas glows faintly orange, enough to make it easy to imagine his hands twisting around the shape of her god damned neck.

As if she can hear his murderous thoughts, her silhouette shifts to look at him.

"Can you swim?" Her voice rings clear despite the air rushing around them, and it's such an odd thing to ask that he replies even as his own words are torn away in the wind.

"What-"

Ulrich sees light reaching up to catch them in long, blinding ribbons, or, he thinks he does. Before his brain can, his body realizes at the speed of instinct it isn't light it's *water,* and it's so frigid he flinches like he's been struck before he even touches it.

There's no splash when the momentum stops, only a blinding freeze that crushes the breath from his lungs. There isn't time to recover from the shock of it before he and Phineas are washed out against a rough stone floor, gasping and coughing up water. Phineas recovers first, leaps to her feet with a flash of yellow and staggers in front of him, blocking his view. Ulrich is still too disoriented to see what's riling her up, and too preoccupied trying not to vomit.

"Oh *please."*

Phineas' voice has been aching in Ulrich's teeth all day, but this new one feels like it's worming under his gums to remove them completely. Helpfully, the adrenaline claws back his focus in time for him to admire his tidy stitches on Phineas' legwraps as her feet lift from the ground.

She thrashes in Hazard's grip, throwing off sparks that sear against the darkness, and he notes with a sinking feeling that none of her flailing seems to reach the wizard. It's like watching a grocery bag caught against a statue.

Oh, she's not thrashing in his *grip*, those watery ribbons from earlier are wrapped around her neck and Hazard is hardly even *moving* oh god they are *so fucked-*

"I did not come here to fight with you," Hazard drones, arms crossed and contrapposto. His voice hisses in Ulrich's hearing aid, shudders down the tight tendons in his neck. "You're going to pass out if you don't settle down. Even *commanders* need to breathe, eventually."

Phineas tries to say something but only manages a furious rasp. Hazard tilts his head, sweeping the wide brim of his hat with it, and Ulrich would feel impressed with how much menace Hazard wrings from such a goofy accessory if he weren't busy feeling so menaced.

"I *know* Gideon taught you better than this," Hazard says.

The effect is instant— the name hits Phineas so hard Ulrich sees it curl all the way down to her toes. Then, slowly, she relaxes in Hazard's hold.

"There we go," he purrs. He waves a skeletal hand and Phineas is deposited back on her feet; the water slithers away from her and recedes into an expensive-looking gem hanging around the wizard's neck. While Phineas regains her senses, something cold grips Ulrich's wrist and he startles badly.

There's a glare that would force Ulrich's eyes shut if he weren't wearing his mask, a ring of blue light wrapping around both wrists. Squinting behind his lenses, he can just make out shapes moving like water, delicate strands flowing from both rings to weave together in the middle. The construct completes itself and dims to a dull metal glow with a horrible feeling of finality. They haven't invented the cuffs Ulrich Weiss can't get out of, but like most of his abilities there's a trick to it. In this case, it would involve exploiting the points of failure, places where the mechanism is vulnerable. Light does not have faulty joints.

"Hey-!" The thread between Phineas' wrists leaves an eerie afterimage in the air as she wrenches against it uselessly.

"Now we are going to have a civil discussion," Hazard says, speaking to Phineas again while she fumes. "If you take another swing at me I'm going to reach in and snap one of your ribs before we continue, but we *will* be having this discussion either way. It's your choice what condition you're in."

Now Hazard cranes his neck to see around Phineas and his single eye glosses over Ulrich, who is lucid enough to be embarrassed he's on the ground but still too dazed to do anything other than shiver in his soaked clothing. Ulrich feels nauseous under his stare, made worse with the realization that he can't read *any tells at all* on Hazard's face. He knows this skill is only humankind instinct, his animal brain seeing patterns in muscle and movement, and so it is technically always fallible. But looking at Hazard is like watching the- *reflection,* of a moving face, light projected onto a ceramic slab covering what's underneath.

Every tool at Ulrich's disposal had flown out of his pockets when they fell down here.

"Can you stand?" Hazard asks pleasantly. *Pleasantly,* some quality there that makes Ulrich want to be pleasant right back, which trips so many alarms in his body he discovers several new ones. Acid-bright panic floods him so quickly he tastes it in the corners of his tongue, but Ulrich only nods, thanking every star in the sky for both his mask and his stage experience that keeps him from being sick all over Hazard's shiny boots.

Phineas settles back on her heels like settling a lid over a boiling pot, apparently deciding she prefers her ribs intact, then she helps Ulrich to his feet. When he touches her hand he feels her anger pulse through him, a wild sort of confidence, though it only serves to remind him he is caught between *two* monsters. As she steps between him and Hazard, exposing Ulrich's back, it makes him aware of a third threat: the mine itself, sharp and dark, utterly unknown. There is nearly nothing he wouldn't trade to be back on that balcony starving to death.

The lenses in his mask (and in his glasses) are small feats of engineering he's very proud of— bright things are dimmed, and dim things are brightened, which gives him the luxury of being able to hide his eyes in most any environment without losing visual acuity. Now that he's standing, Ulrich realizes with a smattering of vertigo they're on a thin strip of stone walkway, arching over an apparently bottomless pit crisscrossed with mine cart tracks. The depths of the chamber are illuminated by the cyan glare of starstone, crystalline structures peppering the cave walls: those stars Ulrich had seen in the darkness on their way down. The earth around them is stained an unnatural blue and Ulrich's sense of imbalance intensifies when he can't find any support structures anywhere, above or below. Even the mine cart tracks are suspended over nothing, and...and something else about them isn't right...

"Fascinating what it does to the land, isn't it?" Cold Hazard says. His voice comes through like a distant radio signal, buffeted by interference. "You'll have plenty of time to get acquainted with the mines after we've finished our chat." It's too dark to make out any detail, but Ulrich sees movement behind the wizard. Three shadows crossing the bridge, coming closer.

-god, oh god they're coming for *them* they're going *further into the **dark**-*

"What do you want?" Phineas demands, a furious beacon Ulrich feels foolish for wanting to cling to.

*Get **hold** of yourself.*

"You are the intruder at my door, the question is what *you* want," Hazard says. It's unsettling how much disdain he can project even while he seems only half present. "What were your intentions aboard my ship?"

"I wanna know why *you* know Gideon."

A close cousin of the instinct that had told him to watch her footwork when Phineas fought in the street, Ulrich has found himself in enough business meetings between monsters to know to keep an eye on her hands this time. They keep moving, trying to ball into fists but remembering they're bound and awkwardly splaying out instead, punctuated by yellow static. Ulrich's stomach sinks impossibly further— if she starts a fight now they are going to lose, he can only hope to catch her trying it before the wizard does.

Breathe, breathe, use your head, what else?

*I am fucking **freezing** is what else-*

The three figures have arrived now, workers in full filthy mining gear. They'd stopped a good way back before, keeping their distance. Uncomfortable with the boss then. Potentially useful. Breathe, *breathe...*

...The temperature in the room is dropping.

There's an alarming feeling of *pressure*, making Ulrich too-aware of the earth pressing down on them, while Hazard himself seems to get *lighter*. The hems of his endless layers sway like they're caught in a current, and his black hair lengthens, curls away from his face. Ulrich's stomach turns again and he smothers his gasp as he's pulled into the abyss-

Like an afterthought, Phineas touches his arm and he steadies. Ulrich isn't falling anywhere, but there *is* an abyss in front of them. The entire left side of Hazard's face is cracked, shattered porcelain, the edges jagged against a sea of void scattered with stars. Shards of what must be *skin* hover like broken glass in a tight orbit around the space where an eye used to be, and as the pressure increases the blackness eats further into his face, deep chasms creeping over his nose, closer to his remaining eye, towards his mouth.

"You *are* young," Hazard rasps, maybe to himself.

"I *said* I want to know why you know *Gideon.*"

"How old were you when he performed the ordinance?"

Phineas is very still. Ulrich sees her glow flashing under her skin, and even without contact he can feel how angry she is.

"You are hardly more than a child *now,*" Hazard says, disgust overwhelming on what's left of his face. "I tell myself he can sink no lower, yet here you are."

"You don't know," Phineas growls. It sounds like she wants to say more, but she fizzles out, her hands still stimming uncertainly into fists.

"This *does* explain why he took a student," he murmurs, almost to himself, his voice the decay of an echo. "He would never fool with such a thing unless the circumstances were..."

Something about Phineas has caught his eye. It has the same focused, far-away look Phineas' get when she's seeing something Ulrich can't. Whatever emotion it's invoking in Hazard raises the hair on the back of Ulrich's neck.

"...extenuating."

"Gideon knew I was-"

Ulrich doesn't have time to flinch before Hazard's hand is clamped around Phineas' jaw, fingertips digging into her cheeks.

"*You* are a *novelty* he mangled *so* grievously he felt *obligated* to *fix you.*" Shadowy ichor is pouring from the cracks in his face, Ulrich sees shadows swirling out from his fingertips to seep across Phineas' skin. "Crow felt guilty for *mutilating a child.*"

Ulrich had been trying to figure out how to reach for Glückssache while cuffed, ready to do *something* when Phineas inevitably snapped her teeth at Hazard's touch, but she isn't doing that. Her hands are loose in her cuffs, her expression is muddied by Hazard's grip, and she's only staring back into his face.

"He..." Her voice is higher, thin. Soft. "He *wouldn't-*"

"Are you sure?" Hazard moves in close, Ulrich sees something glint in his eye, boring into Phineas'. "Are you *certain*, even when it burns? Even when you wake in the night disoriented and afraid? Have you forgotten what it was *like,* the reality of what he did to you?"

Phineas doesn't answer, and for a split second irritation wins out over fear, some barbed wire thread that drags Ulrich through things like this. If *he* had to take that hit last night then *she* doesn't get to falter here. He clears his throat loudly, enough to remind her he's there, watching, and Phineas jerks away from Hazard's grip. When she turns her head Ulrich catches an extra movement behind her, a wisp of smoke from the place Hazard's thumb had been.

*Great! What is **that** now!*

*-**so** sick of this spiritual shit-*

To her credit, Phineas rebounds.

"I figure it was a lot like what happened to your eye," she says, steady again. "Looks like *you* got over it fine."

Hazard laughs at that for some reason, an uncanny, choking thing like an ugly fish breaking the surface of still water. Ulrich shivers in his wet clothes, Phineas shudders next to him, then stamps her foot about it, frustrated by her own reaction. Ulrich appreciates the theatrics of her sparks skittering away from the impact.

"I don't *like* you," she spits at Hazard. "You're *rotten.*"

Hazard shakes out the hand he'd held her with, spraying ichor in the air that curls like incense smoke. Ulrich gets the feeling that the two of them are communicating underneath the spoken words, having some silent conversation outside his perception he can't follow.

"I suppose that *is* how I'd be reading, these days." Hazard smirks, and it might have been smug on a real face, but it seems mechanical on this vestigial one he wears. "Is that how you knew to find me here? Is the aroma of decay how he finally sniffed me out?"

"He didn't send me, *nobody **sent*** me. I haven't seen Gideon in a long time." Phineas stumbles there, but finds her footing quickly. "I'm here on my own."

"Still breaking hearts, I see," Hazard murmurs. The shards orbiting his eye fan out.

"So you're just. *Here,* " he says, full of static. "Crow Gideon's little *project* has simply *appeared from the aether* here at my feet, in this place that can't be found on any map. Out of every corner of the Sprawl *you* are *here.* " His one eye is alight with mania. "With *me.* "

"Uh-huh." If Phineas can feel him unraveling, she doesn't care. "I'm here for a heart for a starship."

"Of course you are," Hazard clips. "Well *done*, there is perhaps nowhere you could have chosen that would have been *less* suited for this purpose, seeing as *my* ship is powered by the only suitable heart in this desert.”

“So I’m taking *your* ship.”

Something glows brightly where his missing eye should be and he laughs his sickening laugh again, desolate and cruel.

“I am afraid I’m not looking to give it away.”

“I didn’t say *give.*” Phineas’ voice hums like a live wire, needling in Ulrich’s veins.

Hazard searches her face, another secret discussion Ulrich can’t keep up with. The wizard grins, not pleasantly, but there is some trace of genuine amusement in it. Ulrich *thinks* it’s amusement, but just as easily it could be something else, god *damn* it.

“It is a shame that you end here, this way,” Hazard sighs, broadcasting from a star that has been dead for lifetimes. “You could have been something, I think.”

And then his gaze is on Ulrich again.

“So, am I to assume *you* are also part of this ship-stealing entourage?”

“Don’t talk to my-”

Phineas wretches and pitches to her knees as Hazard sends a wickedly precise jet of water into her solar plexus. He doesn’t move an inch to do it.

Ulrich doesn’t move either. Hazard’s tone had conjured up someone else’s brittle hands at the sides of his face, keeping him firmly in place to return the stare appraising him, and thank all the gods because Ulrich On His Own wants to try his luck jumping over the side of this bridge.

But this is business, now. Cornered outside his dressing room, or followed into an alley, or underneath all creation pressing down, Ulrich knows when he’s being bought. And as luck would have it, his partner is never far.

“I am part of the ship-stealing entourage, yes.” Ulrich’s voice, obedient under her hands, does not shake.

“Unfortunate,” Hazard says. His voice sends something cold shivering down Ulrich’s spine, a treacherous feeling sticking in his ear that makes him want to agree. “Don’t you think *this,*” Hazard gestures grandly at the pit they are standing in, “is a little *beneath* you?”

The fine binding at his wrists graciously lengthens when Ulrich crosses his arms and shifts his weight, carefully calculated ease coming when he calls it from behind his mask. Still, he can't stop his eyes from flickering across Phineas' body, tightly curled and gasping in the dirt.

"Yes, it is," he agrees, tucking a lock of *(filthy,* now *wet)* hair behind his ear. "Which is why we are in the market for a ship."

Hazard shakes his head slowly.

"This is a *waste* of you," he says. "You could only have met just recently, and she has you *here.* Filthy, *aching,* and already so *devoted.*"

Ulrich grins and hopes it isn't obvious how much his teeth are chattering. Even the inside of his mouth is freezing, down here.

"*Devoted* is generous-"

"I do admire an obscene display of arrogance," Hazard interjects, "but I am going to suggest you save the silverspeak for someone with less experience than I have."

Silverspeak tweaks something in Ulrich's mind, the trailing end of something artificial lodged *deep* into his being, radiating out painfully like a struck tuning fork. It's so unexpected he falters, a ripple in his facade before he can stop it. Hazard's face changes.

"You *don't* know," Hazard wonders. "You don't realize you're *doing* it, you're not..." It's a real expression, one Ulrich can read, a person appearing there instead of an illusion. The anguish in the minute twitch of his mouth is sharp and cloying, the desperate loneliness pulling at Ulrich like a drowning man. Hazard, who is not Hazard, looks down at Phineas, who has heaved herself to a sitting position and leaned herself against Ulrich's leg. Ulrich doesn't like the way she's breathing, wet and thready through their point of contact. "*You* didn't..." Hazard(?) is addressing Phineas now, manic. "Why did you, *him,* if not for his silverspeak?"

"What are you *talking* about?" Phineas spits, the burst of energy some small relief for Ulrich, still reeling. "Can't you tell? Can't you *see* him?"

The wizard turns away from her again, and then it's only the two of them, Ulrich and this thing reaching for him across unknowable distance.

"I *can* see you, Ulrich Weiss; I know you, I know *this,* this thing you are being tangled into." That real person's voice is *here,* right in front of Ulrich, clear and shining like a mirror. "I am offering you a way out of this." Between blinks, his cuffs are gone. "You are unimaginably fortunate, that I am here, I am saving you misery you cannot *fathom.*"

The wizard offers his hand, the palm blazing with the same circles across Phineas' back, though these are dotted with triangles.

"This is your chance, Ulrich."

Ulrich feels calm and reassured that taking his hand is the right thing to do. That makes it easy to realize Hazard is putting on some sort of ameliorating effect, because "calm" and "sure" are things he hasn't experienced naturally for around a decade at this point.

Regardless, the divergent paths spiraling from Hazard's fingers are overwhelming. He could go with Hazard now, gain access to the ship and everything on it. He could go with Hazard now and spend his life under the wing of this powerful thing, so far beyond his own imaginings of what power can mean Ulrich still can't quite grasp it. He could, at least, avoid dying in the dark. He could be free of the weight against his legs, anchoring him here.

He knows he will do none of those things. He breathes in the scent of gin and, beneath it, dogbane, appearing as it does whenever Ulrich makes a decision that puts another bend in the tortured branch of his life. Ulrich smiles again, perfect shiny plastic.

"You could not afford me," he says. "I am very familiar with despots, and an operation as sloppy as this is not one I am interested in associating myself with."

Phineas laughs, quietly enough he feels it more than he hears it.

Ulrich watches as that other, agonized person melts away until Hazard's face is unreadable again. By the time his hand is lowered, Ulrich's wrists are bound.

"You will remember this," Hazard drones, the words cold between Ulrich's ears. The door slams shut as suddenly as it had appeared, and the scent of alcohol and florals leaves him just as quickly. Ulrich feels fear creeping back in, having patiently waited its next turn in the front seat. It asserts itself as, apparently without signal, the workers who have been lined up in the shadows behind Hazard move forward to crowd around them. Phineas struggles to her feet, leaning her scant weight on Ulrich for support.

"The guns, the hat," Hazard says, stepping back to give them room. Phineas has put herself between Ulrich and the others again, although the effect is somewhat diminished by her need to lean fully back against Ulrich's front, which reminds him she's nearly a head shorter than he is. "And the sash, from around her waist."

The tallest worker, a dog woman with fluffy brown ears flopping from under her hardhat, reaches for Phineas with wide, thick paws. Phineas pitches forward *towards* her, and as soon as she's broken contact with Ulrich he's nearly knocked over by the bolt of gold snaking in the air. The worker reels back like she's been shocked-

The light goes out and Ulrich shudders against the sense of smoke rushing around him, dark shapes he can't really see converging on Phineas' back. The force of them makes her stumble, scattering the workers; they seem only marginally more afraid of Hazard than they are of her. She stands there in the middle, trapped taut in unseen wiring.

No one breathes. Then Phineas' whole body jerks, she retches into her hand, light spraying from her mouth like broken glass. Watching over her shoulder, Ulrich sees the blood spattered on her palm at the same time she does. The dog woman takes the opportunity to restrain her while Phineas stares at her own blood in disbelief.

"What did you *do* to me?" she rasps, stunned, while another worker quickly unspools the orange coat from Phineas' belt loops. Hazard's face approximates a smile.

"I am surprised it took you this long to notice, I didn't think I hit you *that* hard earlier." He gestures with both hands to the air around them. "You wanted my attention, you've got it. And now you've got the attention of everything *else* in this mine as well."

"Huh?"

"Oh, Crow didn't tell you? Nothing about how starstone affects your ability?" He tilts his head. *"Other things* a commander might want to concern herself with, in a place like this?" He leans in and lowers his voice. "Seems to me like the sort of thing a caring mentor would divulge. One wonders what else he's neglected to tell you."

Her terse reply is lost in the shuffle when Ulrich feels hands on him, stifling his flinch only because he'd seen the worker with lilac hair moving closer in his periphery. She's small compared to the other two, with round, cloudy glasses and pretty red eyes. Her gloved hands are warm enough to remind Ulrich how cold he is.

"Sorry," she says, reaching under his coat to gingerly remove his guns. Doing some quick math, Ulrich smiles.

"There is a buckle in the back." He raises his arms out over her, flaring his shirt so she can easily reach around his waist. She goes with it, rather than the more obvious choice to walk around behind him. Excellent. He holds still as she divests him of his firearms, tamps down the anxiety when he feels the straps of his holsters sliding away, bereft without the weight of his weapons. Over her head, he watches as the third worker hands off Phineas' coat to Hazard.

In the most natural gesture he's made so far, Hazard shakes it out, and it obediently ripples from its ribbon-shape back to a coat again. As he does, a movement catches Ulrich's eye, something tiny falling from one of the pockets. It bounces near Hazard's feet and now it catches Ulrich's ear, a sound he recognizes like his own breathing.

It's like hearing a dropped pin ringing on its rebound while standing in a busy scramble crossing, the world narrowed to a single point of astronomical chance he has learned never to question. By sheer dumb luck, Ulrich's position on the uneven arch of stone they're standing on means the dropped object begins to roll towards him. Luck making it known she is not dumb and is acting fully under her own powers, nobody else notices anything happening with Ulrich just now because Hazard's ambient gravity has surged again, so aggressively the girl with Ulrich's guns makes a surprised squeak. Pretending to stumble under the weight as well, Ulrich quietly shifts his feet, catching the object in the tread of his boot. Longer for Ulrich, the entire sequence only takes around three seconds of real time.

"This," Hazard snarls, rounding on Phineas, gripping the orange coat with hands like talons, "does NOT belong to you."

"It does *too!*" She wriggles in the dog woman's grip, who is carefully keeping Phineas' feet from making contact with the floor. "Jocasta *gave* it to me!"

"You *lie!*" Hazard shouts, shaking the garment at her. "She would *never*. Do you know what I've watched that woman *do* for care of this wretched thing? She would never part with it willingly, especially to give it to a *brat* like you." Here, he seems to get distracted with it, running his fingers over the canvas. The bright color is nearly offensive against the dark, moreso against Hazard's own blues. Shaking himself, he hastily begins to fold it. "Jocasta *loathes* children."

"Man, for all that bluster you don't know anything about Gideon *or* Jo." Ulrich can hear the smirk on Phineas' face. "Did you do some kinda wizard thing to figure out who my family is just to mess with me? No wonder it didn't work, they're *way* out of your league."

"Your family..." Hazard's voice is far away again. He isn't looking at her. "If these are the people you consider to be your family, I really *am* doing you a favor by ending you here." He turns away briskly, tucking the coat into the endless folds of his robe.

"Gather them up and take them to the fifth chamber," he says, drawing his hand through the air with purpose. At the ends of each of his splayed fingers, like they've been waiting there unseen all this time, shining gossamer threads follow his movements.

"Hey!" Phineas shouts, making a renewed attempt to get loose. "We ain't done here! I didn't say you could leave yet!"

"We are certainly done here," Hazard says, still conducting the thread, weaving the light with movements Ulrich has trouble making sense of.

"As much as I'd love to hammer all that ego out of you myself," Hazard goes on, focused on his ritual, "I have no interest in a duel with you. The fact that you still have any kind of respect for Gideon shows how ignorant you are."

He flourishes his left hand, and his undulating robes are affected by normal gravity again. In front of him, like a hole cut through paper, a triangle as tall as he is hovers in the air. It's solid white, glowing devastatingly bright in the darkness of the elevator shaft, the edges fraying out in those delicate iridescent threads along invisible grooves.

"Killing you now would mean you'd die before you understood the extent to which you've been wronged. Anything I could do to you myself would only pale in comparison to that sort of despair, and let me impress upon you..."

Hazard turns to face them. The rest of him lit from behind, the void of his missing eye shines.

"If there's anything I'm certain of, it's that *no one* succumbs to despair quite as *spectacularly* as a commander." He whirls on his heel and strides into the light. "I can't say it's been a pleasure, student of Gideon. I don't expect we'll meet again."

Even in her weakened state, Ulrich feels so much energy roiling beside him he's worried Phineas is going to combust.

"My name's Phineas," she says, sparks spitting from her mouth, vivid and angry even under the cold light of Hazard's magic. "And you oughta start expectin' me *real* soon."

Hazard laughs again, that shocked shatter of surface tension. The portal is dissolving, Ulrich barely catches the ghost of Hazard's smile as he fades.

"Phineas?" His voice is fading too. "Really?"

The rest, only a whisper in the back of their minds: *that is an ego on you.*

In the new darkness, everyone silently agrees to take a moment to appreciate that it's easier to breathe again. One of the workers is wearing a hooded sweatshirt and no helmet, the arms of their coveralls wrapped around their waist. They clear their throat, and the other two perk up, all of them resuming the unmistakable posture of hired security.

"Alright," the helmet-less worker says roughly. "Chamber five, let's not make this any harder than it has to be."

The walk to chamber five takes longer than Ulrich had expected it might, which gives him ample time to take in how absurd this structure is. Sometimes their path takes them up onto arches of stone dizzy-ribboning out over endless caverns, sometimes they have to pick their way down to structures like sunken cathedrals, high ceilings and walls so far from each other the light from the starstone veins can't reach the other sides. The worst of it is when the tunnels wind so tight the party is forced to walk single file and, once, to crawl, earning him new holes in his overshirt. Handcuffed and still soaked through, Ulrich had briefly considered losing his mind instead, but Phineas had been in such a bad way by then she'd stumbled when she had to go to her knees and it snapped him out of his fugue. Whatever Hazard did has been getting worse over time, but Ulrich still has no idea *what* is happening with her, much less what to do about it. He keeps her right in front of him as much as he can after the stumble, useless for anything but staying close enough for her to lean on while her listing gets more pronounced.

Ulrich is wondering when he should begin to worry about frostbite when a minecart the size of an industrial freezer rattles by, unseen until it's nearly on top of them. They've been walking along an obscured track since they entered this chamber. His surroundings suddenly recontextualized, he also realizes he can hear what he hopes is the sound of other workers, somewhere in the dark.

"No lights?" he asks conversationally, breaking the terse silence they've been maintaining. One worker startles, the girl with lilac hair. It looks grey in the pale blue light.

"No, just what comes from the stone." Her voice is soft. "The walls eat the lights."

"Excuse me?"

"Supports too," the third worker, the one with a hooded sweatshirt and no helmet, adds gruffly. "Soon's you look away the rock grows right over 'em, anything we try to build down here. Only reason the tracks stay is 'cause the carts roll on 'em all the time." They spit in the dirt and slouch down, hands in the pockets of their dirty coveralls. "Even *that* ain't always reliable. The mine'll just pick up the floor under the tracks and move the whole thing."

The information slots a missing piece into a minor puzzle, the thing that had been bothering him in the entry chamber: he'd assumed his eyes were struggling to adjust to the dark, but those tracks really *had* been disappearing into solid rock, those artificial tunnels *did* simply drop away into nothing. Tunnels similar enough to the ones they'd just come through to make Ulrich feel nauseous again.

"You speak about this place like it's alive," he says. Talking feels better, it's harder to ruminate.

"It's somethin'," they reply. "Nothin' stays where it should, down here. Real easy to get lost even if you know where you're goin'."

"But *chamber five* stays, I take it?"

"*Yeah.*" They whirl on him, nearly causing a pile-up. "Listen, I'm sorry but you're *both* gonna die down here today. There's nothin' you can do to change it, those cuffs ain't comin' off until the wizard wants 'em to."

"Yes, I am curious about that," Ulrich interjects glibly. "How *does* he know what's happening down here? I haven't seen any cameras."

"He don't *need* 'em," they grumble, frustrated. "He sees through the stone, through *those* on your wrists. Ain't you ever met a wizard before?"

"Apparently not."

"Wouldn't be the starstone," Phineas murmurs, not quite present enough to join the conversation but doing so anyway. "Not that guy. He's usin' somethin' else." Ulrich tucks that away for later just in case, but nobody else acknowledges her because the worker is getting in his face, inches away from the tip of his beaked mask. Their scraggly, dusty hair obscures their eyes, but he can just see the glint of them underneath.

"The only thing you have control over is whether you die quick in chamber five or you die slow in one of these *fucking* tunnels. So *don't* try anything funny that gets any of *us* killed along with you. We been through *enough.*"

"I have never been funny in my life."

"Don't talk to him like that," Phineas' voice drags over Ulrich's ears like sandpaper. He sees it tremor through the workers too as she straightens up, her expression withering despite her newly sunken eyes. Ulrich sees a shadow slither across her cheek like reflected water.

There's a moment where all three workers watch her, the way one does when the noise from the bushes could still be wind or wolf in equal parts, but once the attention is on her properly Phineas seems to check herself. The shadow passes, and she's only a sick-looking prisoner again.

"Man y'all really just rolled over for this guy huh," she whines, shuffling them past whatever just happened. "I cannot *believe* how eager everyone in this town is to lick that nerd's boots."

There's an extra beat where the worker in the hood seems to be considering whether the cuffs and the curse might level the field enough to get away with punching a commander in the face, but reason wins out, and they turn on their heel and start forward again, the others following suit. One massive paw lands insistently on Ulrich's back, and another hard enough on Phineas' she buckles under it, pushing them back to marching.

"He's not even *here!*" Phineas rants. She erupts into an ugly coughing fit, but heroically soldiers on. "Where's your goddamn *pride!*"

"Pride is a sin," the dog woman rumbles, close behind them both. Her baritone is better suited for soothing rather than threatening, a detail Ulrich wishes he hadn't noticed. He is quietly relieved he hasn't learned any names. "Look where it got you."

"Just help us!" Phineas says, gathering steam again. "I can *fix* this, *I'll* do all the work if you *just-*"

"It's done," the hooded worker says, not turning around.

Ulrich grabs Phineas' wrist as she opens her mouth.

"Save your energy," he says. "You are not looking so good."

He'd said it as an excuse to shut her up, but when he looks he's surprised by how not so good she is looking. It could be the alien lighting, but when Phineas faces him she looks white as porcelain, and up close now Ulrich is *sure* he can see strands of something dark undulating under her skin like smoke. There is no trace of that warm light from before, if she's glowing now it's ghostly.

"You're *freezing,*" she says like it's brand new information, and all of Ulrich's fake concern dissipates.

"Yes, that is how *normal people* react to being dunked in freezing water."

Phineas shakes her head and makes a dismissive gesture with her other hand, or half of one before it gets caught by the chain. She grips Ulrich's wrist back and before he can object there's an arc of light scurrying up around her body, then around *his,* like sunlight on his skin. When it scatters away in a cloud of cheerful motes the cold and damp go with it.

He is able to register that he feels something positive about it before the feeling is doused by Phineas doubling over and coughing violently enough to halt everything. When she straightens again, a fresh tangle of shadows is strewn across her forearm.

"*Idiot,*" Ulrich says, smothering his inconvenient emotions under aggression. "Don't waste your strength on frivolous things."

Phineas makes a show of rolling her eyes, but there is no more discussion until they make it to the next waypoint, which appears to be a set of holding cells. From the look of it they were not originally built into the walls of this corridor. The metal boxes have been absorbed into the stone, it's grown over them like mold. A number of figures are moving in the shadowy recesses, and to Ulrich's relief they're all clearly humankind. The voices and sounds drifting through the bars have a cadence to them he recognizes: they are playing cards.

"Who's this you got, Penn?" someone calls out as they pass. Activity around him quiets. Meanwhile, Ulrich listens tiredly as his brain picks open a fresh wound and roots around in it until it bleeds.

Penn.

Do you think it is short for something? Penn. Penn. Do you think they got angry before because they've lost people down here? Their name is Penn and they don't want to be here and you might have to kill them, isn't that awful?

"Troublemakers," Penn grunts, slowing to a reluctant stop. They peer through the bars. "Y'all alright in there?"

Ulrich notices now that the floor is strewn with cushions, blankets, hot food containers and distractions. The older man speaking to them has a mustache and a glass eye, and looks in very good spirits for someone in a cage in a haunted mineshaft.

"Can you bring us another one'a them sewin' kits?" a wolf man with salt and pepper fur speaks up. They're *all* older men. Penn nods.

"Right after I deal with these two."

"Oh, and more of the little cookies!" someone else says, to a round of enthusiastic agreement. Penn *might* be smiling. Ulrich feels ill.

"I'll see what Ellie's got."

"Hey!"

There's a sound like a static shock and the dog woman snatches her paw from Phineas' sparking shoulder. Phineas must be ready for the rebound this time, Ulrich hears her clear her throat over whatever discomfort the commanding causes as she stalks closer to the cage before anyone can stop her. The dog woman lunges after her, closely followed by Penn.

"Howdy miss," the man with the mustache says pleasantly, like he's meeting Phineas on the sidewalk and not through prison bars.

"Hi," Phineas replies, ignoring her escorts as they descend upon her. "What are y'all in *here* for?"

126

"Troublemakin'," the wolf man huffs, prompting wheezy laughter from the others.

The workers get their hands on her and try to pull her away, but she's rooted solidly to the floor; Ulrich can see little glimmers of energy fountaining from her feet. The same shadows curling across her skin slither there too, right behind the light.

"Y'all don't know Ellie, do ya?" Phineas continues, unbothered. It's the wrong thing to ask.

"What about Ellie?" the wolf man says, neutral in the way a beartrap is neutral where it lays.

"Why ain't she fightin' more?" she asks, converting the trap into a functional seat cushion through sheer obliviousness.

"Well that 'lil girl's had her hands full since her momma passed," a skinny man near the back of the cage speaks up. The prisoners nod nearly in unison.

"Aw yeah that was a real shame,"

"Terrible thing,"

"Really shook 'em up, that restaurant's an awful lot to do now with just two people,"

"Was it Hazard?" Phineas asks, failing to acknowledge the workers on either side growing more agitated trying to drag her away. The man with the glass eye shakes his head.

"Naw, it was…" He stares into space before turning back to the group. "Y'know, how *did* we lose Moll'?"

"Got sick, wasn't it?" the wolf man offers.

Penn gives up tugging Phineas' arm and leans against her back with all their weight.

"*Move* god dammit!" they growl.

"I am *tryin'* to have a *conversation!*" Phineas scowls.

The bickering takes the mens' attention fully away from the thing they'd just been discussing, cheering on both sides instead. Ulrich lets it wash around him, starting to level out from his minor crisis.

The girl with lilac hair, who has hung back with Ulrich away from the rest, sighs quietly. Given something to zero in on, the world snaps back into clarity around Ulrich. Sighing workers are a useful thing, in Ulrich's experience. An establishment is only ever as secure as what a man is paid to hold the key to the side door.

"This is such a mess…" the girl says.

Yes it is, perfect, time to finish what he'd started earlier. Ulrich tosses his head and his mask melts away. His glasses are dirty and crooked, but they've slid down his nose in a way he hopes makes him look vulnerable and earnest rather than as crazed as he feels. He hums, which sounds like a conversational noise to show he's listening to the girl, but it's for Ulrich too.

Every performer has their pre-show rituals, which means Ulrich spends most of his day doing at least one, but when he gets the chance he *prefers* to do vocal warm-ups. This is only notable because Ulrich is not a vocalist. Still, he did do *some* amount of projecting on stage, and after a few rougher nights ended with a canceled show he'd gotten in the habit of copying what the singers did in the dressing room. He'd liked the way it soothed his vocal cords, almost like drinking ice water, and it always seemed like he worked the crowd just a bit better on the nights he took the time to do it. Silly maybe, only some psychosomatic thing he imagines to bolster his confidence, but silly psychosomatic things approximate half of performance art, after all.

He absolutely does not have the luxury of doing a set of scales today, but Ulrich tries very hard to imagine that he's just stepped out from stage right, powdered and polished and ready to shine.

"I am sorry about her," he says, and he can almost convince himself the words cool like menthol where they touch his tongue. "My friend can be…" Here, he pauses long enough for her to turn to look at him expectantly. He tilts his head at an angle that, after years of painful research both at home and in the field, he has calculated to be his most charming, and smiles in a way that puts every one of the 16,000 gild in his artificial front teeth to its most efficient work.

"She can be *insistent,*" he finishes.

The girl turns pink all the way to the roots of her hair, she giggles; she catches herself doing it and cringes inward, embarrassed, but that's fine. He's got her now.

"She comes by it honestly, I think," he goes on, slipping into the role like a favorite dress. "Confidence is what *makes* a commander, but they seem to struggle with turning it off."

They watch the commotion across the way. Or, the girl does. Ulrich is watching her instead. She seems terribly delicate to be down here; her soft voice and features aside, her protective equipment looks heavy, too big for her. The only things that fit are her gloves, which are not the thick, dusty canvas that makes up the rest of the ensemble, but fine brown leather. They're well worn too, they make no sound while she wrings her hands.

"Are you worried about something?" Ulrich asks gently. She nods immediately, so quickly it skews her glasses. She resettles them, seems surprised by her own response. Ulrich catches her eye with his.

"You are not afraid of *us*, are you?" he asks.

A small, genuinely amused smile as she shakes her head.

"No, not y'all..." The blush and the smile both fade from her face. "Um, why didn't you take his offer? Earlier. You could have saved yourself."

"I did save myself," Ulrich replies. Then, like trying to hurl a message in a bottle out beyond the surf: "She is not very articulate, but she really *does* want to help you all, and once she's back on her feet she *can* handle Hazard. Given the choice, she is the bet I would make every time."

She doesn't look *un*convinced. Please let this work, there's nothing else he can *do*.

"Even down here, in those cuffs?"

"*Especially* down here."

She looks like she might add something else, but of course that's when Phineas and the others finally manage to break away from the holding cells to rejoin the two of them, so Ulrich masks up again and tries to convince himself his efforts were enough. Phineas waves cheerfully at the prisoners as she and Ulrich are hurried out of the room.

"I made friends!" Phineas' grin is a relief to see even against her pale face, but-

"Me too," Ulrich says distractedly, his heart sinking with the answer to his next question before he asks it. "*This* is not where you're putting us?"

"Y'all *wish* this was where you was going," Penn snarls.

Once they leave the prison the tunnels close in on them and stay that way, and it takes two corners for Ulrich to start feeling sick again. The first time he's able to brush it off as exhaustion and anxiety, but when they make another impossible turn he's certain: the space is doubling back on itself, the tunnels are changing. Even if they weren't cuffed, and Phineas weren't sick, there is no way they'd ever find their way back along this route.

Phineas is *rapidly* deteriorating. In front of him she's unsteady on her feet, hunched over like there's something tugging her bound hands towards the earth. She keeps turning to look around herself, at nothing, like she's reacting to something no one else can hear. Her skin is so full of shadows now it's like she's been tattooed, Ulrich can see them cascading down her bare arms, the backs of her legs. Even that stupid hair is weighted down, the impressive curl across her forehead more of a smear covering one half of her face. Despite Ulrich's performance for the girl a moment ago, Phineas is far from the powerhouse he'd placed his bet on last night.

He is confident in his intuition. He has to get out of here, he *will*, because there is simply no other option, but he has no idea what that will look like now; his ability to see the way forward is beginning to fail. There's nothing for it but to keep putting one foot in front of the other, just behind her, an outline shining faintly ahead.

The air thickens with a hazy miasma as they descend down a steep corridor, dimming the already dim light, and the temperature lowers enough he can see his breath in front of him. Ulrich is pathetically grateful for whatever Phineas had done to dry them off.

When the corridor levels out they're in a small, rounded room with a short stalagmite in the center. The door to chamber five is in the far wall and it is underwhelming. It has no hinges, and no knob, and it seems to be made of solid starstone, but otherwise it appears to be a normal door one might find in a normal building. All that concentrated stone should be painfully bright, but like everything else its glow is dulled by the haze.

"Do we get to know what's in there?" Ulrich asks gamely, chatting so he doesn't scream. Phineas sags against his side and says nothing.

"It'd be meaner to tell you now," Penn says, standing aside so the girl with lilac hair can walk up to what Ulrich realizes is a sort of plinth, rather than a natural stalagmite. She removes one glove and Ulrich is alarmed to see her hand is covered with cuts, tidy and uniform, in various stages of healing. With a pocket knife she adds another across the tip of her ring finger and presses the wound against the plinth.

The blood lights up a network of symbols carved into the stone, and when the door blazes to a bright cyan the same symbols appear around its edge, some kind of arcane bullshit that Ulrich can't read. There is an audible click.

"Ready," the girl says. The dog woman, still looming silently behind Ulrich and Phineas, shoves them towards the door.

"It's a lake," Phineas murmurs thickly, almost too low for Ulrich to hear.

"What?" he stage whispers.

She grasps his hand, he tries not to flinch from the skin-to-skin contact.

"A lake full of bad stars," she says, pulling him in closer. "Stay close to me, don't..."

He doesn't like the glazed look in her eyes, or how *dark* they are, the bottle-green faded nearly to black. He's committed to this now though, it's far too late to back out. He grips her hand in return and lets her lead him along.

"Well, folks," he says, half turning while they approach the door (which, he notices grimly, they have all stayed *well* away from). He smiles for the camera lens of the girl's glasses one more time. "Be seeing you."

◉◉◉

The radio touchscreen is exactly the way she'd left it when Rook glanced at it thirty seconds ago. No new emails, no texts, not even any social media notifications to keep her occupied. She is going to lose her entire fucking mind if somebody doesn't contact her soon.

She throws her radio hatefully behind her, where it avoids the pile of silk pillows and punches into her luxurious down comforter. She's been stretched out on her bed waiting for her toenails to dry, but suddenly the plush is suffocating, so she slides to her feet and paces to her vanity instead. She stands in front of her perfectly backlit mirror and shakes her hair out of its microfiber wrap, pretending she gives a shit about how it looks, pretending the softness of her fluffy shag carpet isn't gritting under her feet like gravel.

When Rook runs her fingers through her towel-damp curls she finds the ends are beginning to frost over. Dad must be home. He must be in a terrible mood, too. She tugs her robe over her summer pajamas before she goes out— even for *her* this is going to be chilly.

She peeks outside to see her father skulking down a long, boring hallway that doesn't normally pass by her door, one that leads to his study. This has been happening a lot lately, the ship changing its layout or manifesting rooms in the wrong places. Rook doesn't understand why he doesn't just cut the heart and stabilize this damn place, or abandon it and get a new one that isn't so reactive. So much chaos is a liability, especially since they've started housing random workers from the mining outpost.

Hazard is trailing oily black shadows again, dripping from his clothes and smearing the blue carpet. Rook closes the door loudly enough to announce herself, lingers long enough to give him a chance to react that he *completely* ignores. She counts to five before she pads down the hallway after him. As she gets closer, the floor under her feet begins to mush, like she's walking across a waterbed covered in soggy fur. *Gross,* she *just* showered.

Dad doesn't slow down for her, still doesn't acknowledge her at all, but he's moving so slowly it's easy to catch up with him. She means to ask about that commander girl, but then she sees what he's holding.

"Did you. Steal her *coat?*" Rook tries to catch his eye but he's only half here, wringing that dirty, *ugly* canvas between his hands as he hovers down the hallway. Eventually, his speech reaches this plane of existence.

"This was not *hers* to begin with," he says. His voice is so far away, the scattered pieces of his face are orbiting so far out from his head; Rook feels like she should be able to see right through him.

"But you took care of it, right?" she pushes, casting about for anything to bring him back here with her. "She's dead?"

"I left them to the tain," he rasps.

"You *didn't* kill her?" *Unbelievable.* "*You're* the one who *taught me* to always see the body with my own eyes. What are you *doing!*"

He *ignores* her, continuing to drift down the hallway towards the footbridge that leads to his office (which should actually be in a different quadrant of the ship, because nothing around here can just *function)*. Rook can see her breath coming in furious flurries of snow.

"I *knew* you couldn't handle this, just because she's Gideon's little *pet* and you have this *stupid* obsession-"

Hazard looks at her sharply. He doesn't touch her, even now he would never, but a hand closes around her throat anyway, icy enough that it makes her shiver.

"There is a *lot* you don't know." His voice is like glaciers crashing into the sea. Rook fights through her instincts telling her to shrink back, because ice or shadow or *whatever,* this is *bullshit.*

"Well whose fault is that?" she spits, petulance winning out over fear of whatever has taken over her father.

...The shadow passes. His face moves into something almost resembling amusement as he steps onto the bridge. The inlet is purely, lavishly decorative, the short passage swathed in tapestries and hanging plants. The fabrics are covered in wing motifs, Rook thinks he'd told her once they were meant to be seraphim. Delicate pine branches curl down from the ceiling, cradling paper lanterns that cast the passage in calm, clean blue. The only warmth comes from the water below the bridge, paper boats glowing softly yellow drift along the stream, appearing from under one wall to disappear under the other.

Tucked so protectively among the branches it's difficult to see, there is a lantern smaller than the others that has some of Rook's crayon drawings on it. Unlike many other things that exist on the ship these days *this* space is very old, and tends to crop up whenever her father is in a better mood, so Rook has no idea why it's here now.

"...Your criticism is not unwarranted." Hazard weaves a sign with his hand, coaxing some water up from under the bridge. He lingers with it, streaming the thin line of water between the fingers of both hands like a cat's cradle. It's very close to the kinds of things he'd do during the talks they used to have, when he'd explain some complicated magical concept or watch her cast and critique her gestures. She feels herself thawing, god dammit; nostalgia is such a useless, self-sabotaging emotion. She obeys, when he tilts his head to beckon her to join him on the bridge.

"I can admit my thinking may be...archaic, I have lived too long. But it seems to me you kids are *terribly* presumptuous."

Here we go, Rook bites her tongue before the thought can escape her mouth. Combining it with what he'd taken from the stream, now Hazard draws the water from his pendant out across the air between them. The glow from the paper boats dims, the space outside the alcove's openings goes dark, and the world is narrowed down to what exists in this cold light.

"Sunchasing is an endeavor that, by its nature, can only ever be pursued by the sort of person who has no business doing it." His voice is calm and clinical; it *would* be like their lessons if it weren't so empty. "Nobody after that sort of authority has any good reason for it, and commanders are the worst of all of them. They take on an abscess, a void, when they gain their abilities, and latch on to whatever they can to try and fill it. Like a cancer, they will wring every last bit of life away from the things around them for themselves in pursuit of power, influence." Rook remembers the word "cancer" being used in the study the night before too; it isn't like him to pass up the chance for new wordplay. "And the sun is exactly the kind of lofty, foolish goal that attracts them..."

Raven gets a look about him Rook has seen before, though he won't give her a straight answer when she asks about it.

"...But no one seems to remember how stars *die* until it's too *late,*" he says softly, his eye shining. "When they finally collapse – and they *all do* collapse – they take down with them everything they've consumed. Every*one.* The higher they've ascended, the wider their fallout."

He's churned the water into a mass between his hands, a blue planet. Rook crosses her arms and tries to ignore a swell of affection for her father's dramatics.

"If little Phineas, Gideon's successor, is a commander *and* a sun chaser, her potential is titanic." The water planet dissolves into a scatter, tiny droplets fanning out in the air around the two of them in a silent, slow explosion. Hazard's bitterness permeates the air. "Left unchecked, I don't think this world could handle it when she goes."

Leaving his visual aid to play out on its own, he unspools the orange coat between his hands instead. "That is not a chance we can afford to take."

Rook pokes at a bit of water before it can touch her shoulder, freezing it.

"So, what," she says, looking at her tiny hung crystal instead of him. "This is some...noble thing?"

Raven meets her eyes and smiles softly.

"Do you think me so terrible I wouldn't be concerned about the world you will live in? I would like to leave you fewer monsters..." But he grips the coat and his expression hardens again, rot radiating from him like smoke. "She has been here less than a day and already recruited someone to her cause, a silverspeaker no less."

"*What?* The one you said you saw last night?"

"It would appear so," Hazard says, as if the thing he's just described isn't as potentially destructive as a dog with a flamethrower strapped to its tail. Her father *would* be dismissive of other silverspeakers, of course he'd forget the people *around* him can still be affected. "I should have taken notice of a halo like that without even looking for it, but he's...hidden. There is something he carries with him, a blight in his eye that..." He trails off, but Rook hardly notices, too distracted by the pit opening in her stomach as a new thought occurs.

"Is he blond?" she asks, grimacing. "Wears a stupid mask?"

"Do you know him?" Hazard asks.

"I met someone like that when I was in Tourmaline a few months ago," Rook says, shrugging it off and hoping he can't hear the ringing in her ears. "We spent a few days together."

"A few days, how?"

It *almost* sounds like something her father would say. Rook smiles in spite of herself.

"Dad, I'm *twenty-two,*"

"You were twenty-*one* when I last sent you to Tourmaline, my love."

She gives him a flat look, but she can't muster any real frost to it. Raven sighs, ebbing away again to make room for Hazard.

"I know, I know, I can't help but worry." He lets go of the coat with one hand to smooth his palm over Rook's hair. It's like a direct line to something young and sore in her chest, it's *unfair.* "Well, he is with the commander, and will certainly fare no better down below than she will. You don't need to worry about him any more."

The stagnant water in the air mists and whispers back into his pendant, the light from the paper boats brightens again. He's finished here. She doesn't want him to go, so much it makes her angry, but it's all so tangled in her chest she can't even figure out how to say something ironic about it, much less anything honest.

"I am, going to take care of something," Hazard murmurs. "I may be a while, you are in charge while I'm gone."

Rook wants to tell him everything; that he doesn't *need* to worry about whatever it is, she's been working on a plan so they can *both* get what they want without all this starstone mess. It's *so* close now, if he can just keep it together a little longer-

It's *close*. Be patient.

"Sure, Dad," she says gently.

Hazard doesn't acknowledge her. He glides across the bridge like a phantom and disappears into his study, leaving her alone.

◉ ◉ ◉

As she and Ulrich had descended, the dark had become more shadows than dark for Phineas, solid growths of Something Else standing out against the rest. Every step further in had made her more aware of how far the infestation spreads, on and on endlessly, the way the tower up to Hazard's ship had spiraled on and on into the sky just before they'd dropped down here. There's a sense of terrible, obliterating distance that the sliver of star in her chest comprehends better than Phineas does. The two of them don't normally have to make an effort to communicate, merged as seamlessly as they are, but there is only so much translating that can be done when the scales are so different.

It also feels like all those shadows are trying to carve out some kind of space between the two of them, but Phineas is working hard to ignore that for now.

She's *relieved* Hazard hadn't tried to do anything like this to Ulrich. Phineas is better suited for whatever this is than any not-star-bound humankinds. She can take it, she'll be fine.

But Ulrich is still *here*. She'd *brought* him here. He is the most wonderful thing she's ever found, and as they pass through the barrier into the center of the nest, the thickest twist of Something Else yet,

136

it begins to sink in that she is responsible for whatever happens to him now.

As they phase through it the door eases across Phineas' skin like smoke, *freezing*, sending the things under her skin skittering. She's probably not as concerned about that development as she should be; she's been dealing with weird things under her skin her whole life. Some extra colors isn't anything too new.

The voices *are* new, and so are the auras seeping up around the corners of her vision. Shivery, unstable inkblots jittering and warping in every shadow in the mine cast by the blue light of the starstone, which is all of them, all of the shadows. They're talking to her, one of those languages she doesn't know but the star does, so Phineas sort of *feels* what they're saying more than she knows it. She understands: they are empty, forever. They are hungry.

The pit that greets them in chamber five is a new kind of darkness. It's like light simply stops working as soon as the floor does, the dark in the already maddeningly dim room is a tangible force beyond the rim of the sunken lake.

The surface of the pit is moving. Phineas can't stop staring at it.

Her constant companion squirms in her chest, shadows squirm in her ears. Her neck spasms, the cuffs around her wrist burn before she realizes they're not there anymore. She can't stop *staring*.

Ulrich's impossibly perfect, liquid-cool voice is touching her ear through the rustling of whatever those things are in front of them, but the skittering voices are coalescing into a solid wall of static that drowns him out. She wants to reach for him, get him behind her because he can't *see* them, how can he not *see*, but there's-

The darkness yawns up over the side of the pit and crashes over her like a wave, snuffing out Ulrich's beacon like a candle in a hurricane and carrying Phineas somewhere else.

There are stars, blue and cold. The not-earth under her feet feels familiar.

"Me," Phineas wheezes in the dark. "You want me, not him."

we want **everything**

A figure. It looks like...

Ah, the star says, stirring in Phineas' chest, understanding first.

you see, then, the figure says like claws scraping Phineas' bones.

"Tell me what you are," Phineas' words burn with command, but they're hardly out of her mouth before something explodes behind her eyes, hissing insects poured inside her skull. She slaps her hands over her ears and doubles over, instinct barely keeping her upright.

we hate you, we hate you hate you hatehatehate- it's like being dragged behind a wagon, a noose around her neck, streaming in the wake of this force that couldn't stop if *it* wanted to. Phineas knows better than most what hatred is, and greed, but this is a type of envy so twisted and brutal it's unrecognizable as anything beyond primal suffering. This is the first thing all those other words come from, the boiling mass of animal pain that every other bad feeling breaks away from until it cools enough to be called agony, misery.

Oh, she *is* going to die here, right now, she has never been more sure of anything.

we know no master, we know no command, your arrogance in bringing the light here before us will be your undoing

Something skewers up through the soles of both her feet, so fast and clean she feels the simple fact of meat and bone giving way before the ice-bright excruciation lagging behind it wrenches a scream from her throat, cut off by the sharp spires that are still growing up through her and around her, whipping out to wrap around her neck, her mouth,

you are a waste, a pathetic thing, holiness in such a weak vessel. we're going to carve every last bit of that stolen light out of you

spreading out like kudzu, the new branches snaking around her forearms to pierce her palms, straight through her gloves. Everything snaps tight as the growth surges back into the ground, dragging her to her knees. Her hands are tugged out in front of her, bending her back-

The figure, the thing that looks like her own body, twisted and torn, is behind her-

She can't make out the shape of it, no words, but through everything Phineas hears the sound of silver like a tuning fork. It flows like water where it touches her ear, burrowing further in, and the shadows there scream away from it like they're burning.

It shivers through the things binding her, the impostor poised to strike-

false-

false-!

"Phineas?"

She realizes she's swaying dangerously when Ulrich grips her shoulder with one hand, the other quickly gesturing the sign to dismiss his mask. It whispers away from his face in sparkly smoke, that's so *cool,* Ulrich is so *cool,*

"Yes, so cool," Ulrich says curtly, inches from her face. "Look at me, Phineas, focus?" His fingers slide into her hair, his big palm covering the side of her head. It covers her ear too, and she automatically sets her hand over his to press harder, blocking out any more stimulation. He twigs what she's doing and copies it on her other side, and they stay that way while Phineas tries to stabilize.

It takes way too much effort, but Phineas meets his eyes. He's bleary from so far off. He stares hard at her over the rims of his glasses.

"Focus, come *back.*"

There's nothing in her feet, nothing binding her hands. Slowly, the fog lifts like letting go of a dream, the chamber and the mine and the town whisk back into their places in Phineas' awareness. Ulrich too, here in front of her, the most solid thing she's ever felt.

"I'm here," she says, swallowing against her dry throat. "I'm here, I am. But I...think I need to sit down for a minute."

Ulrich nods, loosening now that he's sure her brain hasn't been scrambled by whatever just occurred. He wriggles his hands under hers and she lets him go, reluctantly letting the static back in. Quieter than before, but still there.

"What...I dunno what. What *happened?*" she asks. Everything is easier with Ulrich in front of her, casting his light and shunting back most of the shadows, but the ones in her vision haven't really gone away. Phineas tries not to think of how much worse it could get. They still haven't reached the nexus yet, the heart where all these arteries converge.

"I have no idea," Ulrich says, careful, looking at her like she might fly apart. "We came in here, you were muttering to yourself about bad stars and lakes, you shoved me out of the way of something and...nearly fell..." He blanches, and Phineas follows his eyes to her hands, which she's been holding loosely in front of her chest. The leather gloves there look like she'd grabbed something hot, huge gashes melted straight through the palms and the wraps underneath to scald her skin.

She groans.

"My gloves *and* my coat," Phineas whines. "The coat helps, with stuff like this, that must be why Hazard took it. It helps to hide the uh." There is *so* much to explain, she's *so* tired. "I have a...a *wound* in my back, that can attract this kind of stuff, sort of like your eye?"

"What *about* my eye?" Ulrich asks, apprehension bleeding into his halo.

"Oh, I just meant-" She huffs, hiding her face. "It's so hard to *think,* you can't hear *any* of this?"

"The only thing I've noticed since we got down here was a little smoke drifting towards you." Ulrich gestures at the pit, quietly simmering and not stabbing or strangling anybody. "From the pit over there, you seemed *very* upset about it so I put my foot through it."

Had Phineas *hallucinated* all of that? No. Maybe. It doesn't matter. Even if it had all been in her head, that's not necessarily nothing; a lot of the most influential things commanders experience don't take place in the material world, and the smell of burnt skin and leather is sticking in her nose regardless. This stuff can still *hurt* them, regardless.

She realizes Ulrich is holding out his overshirt to her when he shakes it, trying to get her attention.

"What?" Phineas says. Ulrich looks embarrassed, grumpy about it.

"You said your coat was helping and that's why Hazard took it from you," Ulrich says. "And your abilities are so- self, driven- could a replacement help at all?"

Despite everything, Phineas giggles as she reaches for it.

"Yeah actually, if you give it with the right intention. It's about the gusto more than the material."

"My intention is 'both of us stay the hell alive and lucid enough to get out of here.'"

"Good enough."

Phineas tugs the shirt around herself like a blanket. It's tattered and dirty, and isn't nearly as reassuring as Jo's coat, but she loves it anyway. Ulrich's clothes smell like grime and sweat, which isn't very romantic, but the scent of black powder and axle grease under everything else is definitely a Certified Ulrich Characteristic. She closes her eyes and takes a long, grounding breath, spoiled by the feeling of scuttling in her airways.

Ulrich clears his throat, and she realizes she's just been standing here, wavering on her sore feet.

"Why don't we sit down," he says gently, gesturing to the other side of the hole in the ground. "Can you make it over there? There is more space to get away from, er. All of this."

"Shouldn't we..." Phineas turns around to look behind them and finds smooth, dark wall. The door they came through is gone.

"No point trying that," Ulrich says, because he'd thought of it too. "We should explore the rest of this chamber, when you're up to it."

She nods, and moves to go ahead of him around the thin strip of floor ringing the pit, but he gets there before he does.

"If they don't like me, I will go first. Ach-" he shifts uncomfortably. "I don't. Know if I should hold your hand just now, but you can hold on to a belt loop to keep us close, if you want."

He turns away before she can smile at him, but he waits for her to slide an index finger through the center loop of his waistband, snug against his worn leather belt. Then they take a short, careful walk around the edge of the lake. Phineas keeps her eye on the wall instead of her feet, and on Ulrich's yellowed shirt glowing in the dark ahead.

It turns out the hell-pit only makes up about half of the chamber; once they get around the edge of it there's a wide, level floor in front of them. This side of the room is mostly empty, aside from some junky shadowy shapes Phineas can sort of see in the haze. Most of the light is coming through another nonsense tunnel set a dozen feet above the ground. The *tunnel* is well-lit, lined with raw glowing stone, but none of it reaches into the chamber like it should, it stops in the mouth of the tunnel like it's hitting a wall.

The floor is hard and dusty, but smooth enough for sitting. Ulrich picks a spot a comfortable distance from the pit and watches Phineas settle down, facing the uncharted half of the chamber.

After a few seconds, there's weight at her back.

"What'cha doin'?"

"If my shirt helps, I might help too," Ulrich says, nonchalance in his voice that doesn't work because Phineas can feel him blushing. "And if there are things in this place that I can't see then we should hedge our bets here."

He settles in against her, pressing their backs together, and *that* helps a *lot.* Phineas breathes out easily, nothing catching anywhere.

"I think you scare them," she sighs, too relieved to try and avoid making Ulrich feel embarrassed about the effect he's having on her. "You're like a lighthouse, your voice cuts right through everything."

"Wonderful, let's talk then," Ulrich says. "Why *am* I here?"

"...Did I ask you that while I was tweaking, or..?"

"Hazard made a good point," Ulrich says neutrally. "And I've been thinking about it anyway, you... you keep talking about how you can see into this...this other space, that seems to tell you whatever you want to know about everyone else all the time."

"Sure,"

"Which is *extremely* rude, if you ask me."

Phineas huffs a laugh, appreciating how easy it is.

"Are you telling me you wouldn't do it if you could?"

"*I* am not a polite person," Ulrich brushes her off. "But if you can see what people are feeling, what they are like, when they're lying... Why on earth did you elect to invite me along with you. Why am *I* watching your *back,* right now? You *know* I am full of shit."

Phineas wishes she could see his face. He'd probably planned it this way. She can feel him fidgeting, in his spirit, but in his body too, little movements broadcast between their connections.

"Lyin's just a tool," Phineas shrugs. "Good people tell lies all the time if they got good reasons for it. I ain't as smart as you, 'specially with words, but I see people all the time who lie 'cause they have to."

She pauses to collect her thoughts, Ulrich lets her. He's gone still enough for her to feel him breathing shallowly.

"I like what I see when I look at you, a lot. I know you're lying and I don't care, I don't even care about the details if you don't wanna tell 'em to me. None of it would change my mind anyway, I already know what I think of you."

Ulrich groans, like he's watching someone open the door to his overstuffed closet.

"Look where we *are,* Phineas! Your instincts are no *good!*" Phineas knows it'll upset him but she can't help giggling, pleased that Ulrich is being mean again, and it pushes him further into his fit. "It has been less than 24 hours with you and I have been led in handcuffs to the bottom of a *hole!* This isn't even six feet under this is many *many* feet under, you just keep *digging!*"

"You're so dramatic, this ain't nothin'."

"What *is* it then! Can you even tell me what's happening here? You don't know *anything!*"

"I can't tell what's happening most times!" Phineas insists, reflecting his irritation gleefully. "Commanders are intuitive! We just feel stuff out!"

"Your intuition is *wrong!* I'm not what you think I am-"

"What do you think I think you are! *Look!*" Phineas rumbles, sparking up. She feels Ulrich's back stiffen against the command and there's a complicated mixture of guilt and pride she doesn't have time for right now. She leashes herself in again. "You could have left *any time* on the way down here and you didn't, and you didn't take Hazard's offer either. Have your crisis of personality or whatever if you want, I don't care. I picked you, it's done."

Ulrich twists around to face her but he stops short, Phineas feels the fight freeze out of him.

"What?" she asks, instantly done bickering. "What is it?"

"The shadows..."

Phineas turns to look over his shoulder. Ulrich had placed himself between her and the pit, and now there is a column of shadows oozing straight up into the air, cresting like a slow wave. They're silent, and unhurried, and Phineas can't actually tell what's going on with them; whether she can't sense their feelings because they don't have any, or because her own abilities are being further dampened by whatever the wizard had done is unclear. Both are terrifying.

"That looks bad," she says.

"Can we...we should not stay here. If you're attracting them we really should keep moving."

"I *know,*" Phineas groans. "I'm just. It helps, sitting here with you, lemme take a few more minutes?"

Ulrich settles reluctantly.

"They *do* seem to be moving slowly." He's about to settle in again but he pauses when he sees her. The look on his face is worrying.

"What's wrong?" Phineas asks.

"What *did* he do to you? You have, marks, moving on your skin."

"Is it gettin' worse?"

Ulrich nods. "You look... Washed out, your hair is losing its curl."

Phineas laughs and puts her back to him, feels him do the same.

"You're worried about my *hair?*" she asks.

"You're losing some luster. You are not dying, are you?"

"I don't think so." She lets her head drop back against him. "He said he made me more visible, to the shadows down here. It feels like things are pulling at me. Stickin' to me and makin' it hard to do anything."

She looks down at her ruined gloves, the tattoos peeking out between scorched fabric and reddened skin.

"And he was wrong, Gideon *did* tell me about this kind of stuff," she mumbles, running her fingers over the ragged edges of the leather. "I just wasn't...This all caught me off guard, I wasn't expecting to hear about him here. I'll be ready next time."

"Can I ask who Gideon is?" Ulrich says carefully. "I understand it is a sore topic, but knowing what's going on in Hazard's mind may help us."

Phineas squirms, but it's an old bruise, and he isn't pressing too hard.

"It's not a secret or anything," she says. "Gideon's my teacher. Was. He's probably the only commander alive better at it than me."

"That's grandiose of you," Ulrich says. Phineas can *hear* the unimpressed expression there, and it makes her smile.

"I've just been doin' it longer than most, commanders are usually older'n me when they get started."

"And do you have any idea what Gideon might have done to upset Hazard so much he'd take it out on you?"

"No!" Phineas fidgets, frustrated again. "I *don't!* I mean, everybody's done stuff they ain't *proud* of, and Gideon's lived a real long time so he..." She shakes her head. "Gideon's the best person I know. And he never said anything about anyone like Hazard in his stories. I would've remembered, he's. Real distinct."

Ulrich hums thoughtfully behind her.

"It's very strange, I can't read into his expressions the way I can read most people's. It was like looking at a painting, or a doll." It takes him a moment to gather his thoughts. "He was...cold. Heavy."

144

Phineas whistles.

"Oh man, it *must* be bad if *you're* pickin' up on it."

"What makes you say that?" Ulrich asks.

"Most people don't notice halos much at all," she explains. "Well, also, most halos ain't much worth noticin'. But you just got *done* sayin' all my spiritual abilities are fake and unreliable, didn't you? I've never seen somebody as unsuited for spiritual stuff as you, it's almost like you were *designed* to be resistant to it."

There's a second where Phineas thinks Ulrich might get defensive about it, but:

"That's not entirely wrong," he says.

"So if *you* got a strong feeling off of Hazard he's like. Extra rotten. Halos like that usually get that way from bein' damaged, somehow."

"It's definitely the worst *I've* ever felt," she goes on. "People keep sayin' it feels like drowning, but I don't think it's that, necessarily. It sort of feels...like a vacuum?" All the descriptions Phineas can think of come from the unpleasant things she'd seen watching Jo practice medicine. Her brain helpfully supplies, "Like a sucking chest wound."

Ulrich makes an unhappy noise at that, then shifts his weight, probably uncomfortable on the stone floor. They *do* need to move soon, somehow...

"I think it's interesting that he has holding cells down here," Ulrich muses after a stretch of contemplative silence. "And that he has allowed us to sit here and have this conversation when it would have been easier to leave us as paint across the bottom of the elevator shaft and be done with it."

"Yeah?"

"Frankly, that someone with his sort of ability would bother with... *any* of this, is curious. Running the mines, impressing workers from the town; why not raze it and take what he wants?" Ulrich picks along the thought like a lead in the dark. "I am perfectly willing to believe that a person is as cruel and rotten as all signs make this man out to be, but I wonder if this situation is more complex than it looks."

"Does that change what you wanna do?" Phineas asks, unsure where he's going with it.

"It is only something to consider. Someone who is cruel for its own sake normally behaves in ways that are predictable. If this is someone acting out of a sense of enacting justice, or righting some specific wrong, or...I don't know, *heartbreak*. It could be more difficult to understand the thing we are up against."

Ulrich is *so* smart, and smart about stuff she *isn't*. There is no way she's leaving this place without him on her ship.

"Sorry I don't have more to tell you, I would if I did," Phineas says, relaxing lower against his back. "And that I'm...Give me a minute, can we take like fifteen more?"

"Let's do ten," Ulrich says. "I'll keep an eye on this side, though they don't seem to want to come any closer just now."

"I'm-" Phineas closes her eyes, trying to come up with any explanation for him. "It feels like they're trying to get me to fall asleep, they said something about...stolen light, that I have? And when I was having that vision they sort of. Looked like me, like a copy."

"I take it that's not good, commander."

Phineas shakes her head. "I don't know what's happening exactly, but I don't want to risk something bad happening to you because I don't wanna admit I need to rest."

Ulrich very graciously does not bring up their earlier conversation about *him* needing to rest before she would, and instead he asks, "Is it some kind of possession?"

Phineas isn't sure that he believes what he's saying, and has to remind herself that, to him, the shadows are just smoke. She'd like to keep it that way.

"Maybe."

"So if you *do* go to the dark side, should I shoot you?" he asks lightly.

"Yeah sure. Dunno if it'll take though." It's meant as a joke, but it hangs uncomfortably. "I just don't want to, I'm afraid I could do something- I don't-"

"Oh *please.*" She can hear Ulrich rolling his eyes. "If I don't get to do any self-loathing neither do you."

"Yeah but-"

"Nope. You signed a contract when you beat me, sunshine. You don't get to doubt yourself, *certainly* not until we are out of this pit. You are carrying both of our reputations now, you better start acting like it."

Phineas laughs weakly.

"I hadn't thought about it like that," she mumbles. "Yeah. Okay. Gimme like ten minutes and we'll work on gettin' out of here."

"I will hold you to it."

◉◉◉

Directly over Phineas and Ulrich's heads, at that moment, the sun is hanging in an endless, oppressive blue sky and scorching the dusty earth. This far from the core of entropy and cosmic misery coloring the soil that makes up the mine, the dust is orange, and dry, and it coats every available surface of the wooden buildings on the lonely street where Sergei's sits. The hodgepodge windmill jutting from the roof spins idly, ignoring the lack of wind, and the speakers inside the bar fill the air with music, ignoring the lack of enthusiasm. Puttering around the kitchen handling kitchen minutia, Ellie feels small and sweaty. She is thinking about Ulrich a little and Phineas a lot.

Ellie had never put too much stock in her family's insistence that commanders are invariably capricious agents of chaos. Painting with such a broad brush seems unfair, and what defines "good" or "bad" had become a more complicated question once Hazard showed up. But to herself, Ellie can't pretend that things haven't been exhausting lately, and that the adjective *did* start to apply immediately after the event of Phineas Kidd.

Fortunately there's some normal, morally simple work to do this afternoon. After Phineas and Ulrich had come through for breakfast Ellie had started a cake to de-stress, which she had plenty of time for since there had been no sudden influx of Hazard activity despite what Ulrich insisted. She'd known from the start he'd been lying as a way to get out the back door quickly, of course, but she still hasn't been able to figure out his game. Better to play along and see if he'll do the work of revealing himself for her; she has plenty of other things on her to-do list.

There had been an influx of *customers* after those two had gone, namely Larimer's grouchy wife Lucille, who comes in on her own most mornings for coffee while her husband is home from his supply runs. On the days she comes in Lucille will sit and read romance novels for most of the afternoon, only paying for a single cup of coffee that Ellie refills four or five times, but it's alright. Ellie likes seeing the armadillos, she looks forward to feeding them from the bucket of vegetable scraps in the kitchen. Gloria and her toddler Lou had shown up for lunch too, some of Ellie's favorite faces even if the kid has a tendency to stare. Mama had always talked about how kids can be perceptive in ways that can cause trouble for Ellie if she isn't careful, and this one fits the bill. His eyes lock into the space over her shoulders like little magnets from the second she comes through the kitchen doorway. She smiles brightly at him, even though he only stares back at her stone-faced the way toddlers do. Gloria, who has more social experience than her son, grins at Ellie as she gets closer.

"Thanks, El'," she says, taking the cold beer before Ellie can set it down. Lou gets juice, which he ignores so he can keep staring at Ellie. He thoughtfully shoves his index finger in his mouth.

"Where's your pa at?" Gloria asks, popping the bottle cap against the edge of the table. "I got the whiskey I said I'd get him."

"Oh I'm sorry, he's out for the day," Ellie says. "I realized we were out of some staples earlier than usual and sent him to get some things, won't be back 'til tomorrow I imagine." She leans in like she's telling a secret. "I thought he could use some time off, honestly. It's hard to get him outta here."

Gloria nods, her short dark curls shivering cheerfully around her head. "I know how it goes, you get..."

Her eyes track away from Ellie's to somewhere behind her, which due to the aforementioned social skill isn't a thing Gloria does as often as Lou, so Ellie turns around to see what's just creaked through their doors.

"Afternoon, angel," Ray says, smiling wide and greasy.

Lou has always been a sensitive little guy, and Ray had upset him *before* Last Chance was infected by Hazard's animosity. Lately the poor thing could hardly keep it together even on normal days. Ray's entrance today, bruised and radiating malice, sends him clinging for his mother from the second Ray sets foot in the door. Ellie moves to get behind the bar again, and as she'd hoped, Ray ignores the others in favor of bothering her. He seats himself at one of the barstools and takes off his sunglasses. The injury she'd given him the night before looks even worse up close and in the daylight, and Ellie is quietly pleased.

"C'mon, you ain't even gonna…" Ray's face falls so fast Ellie nearly laughs at him, then she follows his eyes to what he's looking at. Oh god, she didn't miss a button did she?

"*What* is *that?*" Ray demands, gesturing with the hand still holding his glasses. Lou whimpers loudly when Ray raises his voice and Ellie suppresses a surge of fury.

"What's *what?*"

"*That* on your *shirt!*"

Ellie looks down and finds Ulrich's paper flower, still fastened to her lapel where she'd moved it and promptly forgotten about once they left. Now that she's focused on it, she realizes how odd that whole incident had been; Ellie rarely feels flustered about men, and it's not like sleight of hand is anything impressive compared to what she could do herself. Why *had* she been so taken with him and his party trick? She's going to have to figure this out when she doesn't have a loaded gun standing at her counter.

"My *father* gave it to me this morning," she replies dully, fishing out a dishcloth to wipe down the bar so she doesn't have to look at Ray and his swollen face. "Not that it's any of your business."

Mollified, Ray finishes settling in.

"Hey, let's not start the day off like this, okay?" He rakes his hands back through his gross mullet. "I just wanted to come by and let you know I forgive you for hittin' me last night."

Ellie is very proud of how she keeps her expression from changing. "Uh-huh?"

"Yeah, I know that commander bein' here was just puttin' you on edge, it's not your fault. It don't even hurt now!" He smiles, rounding his cheek and deepening the painful looking color there. "Don't you worry about it no more."

"Uh-huh."

Ellie is obviously supposed to say something else, or swoon, or whatever other thing the fictional Ellie in Ray's head is doing right now, but it's so much effort to hold in the things she wants to say to all this that there's no room to come up with any additional dialogue. Ray lets it go eventually, drumming his fingertips on the bartop.

"Listen," he says. His tone is nervous. Ellie's never heard it from him before. "Ellie I. I want you to come with me."

Behind him, Gloria takes a long swig of her beer.

"What?" Ellie says.

"Come *with* me!" He's building up more confidence now, maybe assuming that she's too excited to speak rather than fucking bewildered. "I think what we need is a change of scenery, we could leave this dusty-ass place and make a fresh start someplace else. We can even get married once I get the cash put up!"

Gloria chokes on her beer, startling Ray like he'd forgotten anyone else was in the bar. He shakes his head and gets right back into it.

"What are you *talking* about?" Ellie shrieks. "We- I can't *leave-!*"

"What's keeping us here? That wizard ain't even gonna notice if any of us disappear, he don't give a damn about the people in this shithole, he just wants the stone! And, what've you got-"

"My dad!" Ellie says sharply. "This *bar-*"

Ray's face darkens and he flings one arm out at the dining room. *"This dump?* There's no way you'd trade this for..." He squints, his eyes flitting between Ellie's face and the little flower on her shirt.

"You're *lying* to me," he says dangerously. Lou whines, his face buried in Gloria's shoulder. "Who are you hiding from me? I'll *kill him-"*

Ray reaches out towards Ellie's chest and she is so, *so-*

Lucille's lacy purple parasol appears behind Ray's head, and then it connects with Ray's head with a loud *thwap!*.

Everyone is too stunned to do anything, so Lucille *thwaps!* him again. He turns and catches the third.

"What the *fuck* are you-"

"I'm 'bout sick'a your shit boy!" Lucille screams in her scratchy old-lady voice, wrenching at her parasol to get it out of Ray's grip. "You sons'a bitches think you can just come in here and talk to a lady like that?!"

"Calm down before you stroke out you old *hag!*"

"Where's my gunpowder?!" she spits, literally. "My husband's wagon got held up at gunpoint by a *delinquent* with *greasy hair* and *sunglasses* and I *know* it had to be *you!*"

Ellie's ear twitches.

"What the fuck are you talkin' about?" Ray growls. "I didn't do nothin' to your crusty old man's wagon!" The force of Ray snatching the parasol from her hands knocks Lucille to the floor, shocking Ellie out of her thoughts.

"Bullshit!" Lucille hollers. "Ain't nobody else it could'a *been!*"

Ray snarls and raises the parasol above his head, but when he brings his hand down it isn't holding the parasol anymore. He turns, wide-eyed and uncomprehending, to see Ellie's plucked it away from him.

"That's enough," she says, several clicks down from her customer service voice. Ray's face can't decide what to do in response to hers.

"What's gotten *into* you?" he asks baldly.

"I'm not gonna sit here and watch this."

Ray snorts, his grin not quite as cocky as he'd like it to be.

"Listen, El', I don't think you're in a position to-"

"Leave," she says, even lower. "Before I make you leave."

She watches the weight of the statement cross Ray's face like she's aimed a floodlight in his eyes. Lou turns his red, tear-stained face to look over Ellie's shoulder again, but it can't be helped right now.

It seems to work. Ray's shoulders lose some of their tension, his expression hardens.

"That's your answer, then," he says quietly.

"Yes."

A long moment goes by where the music ends and a new, louder song comes over the speakers, with thumping drums and a cheerful horn section, inappropriate and defusing. Ray shrugs.

"Alright then. Have it your way." He turns and steps around Lucille, who spits at his feet. "I'll see you around, Ellie."

Ray leaves. As soon as the saloon doors stop swinging, Ellie sets her hand to her chest and leans over the bar, letting out a breath she hadn't realized she'd been holding. Gloria whistles.

"Damn," she says.

"Can I get a hand, here?!" Lucille grumbles, perking Ellie back up.

"Oh! Of course, gosh," she bustles around the bar to help the old woman to her feet. "Are you alright Lucille?"

"Why wouldn't I be?!" she snaps, frail in Ellie's arms but seemingly unhurt. She grumbles, brushing off her dress, and Ellie goes to fetch her parasol. "'Bout time you stood up for yourself, girlie. It ain't right how he treats you."

"Yeah, well..." Ellie looks over Gloria's table, where Lou has let go of her neck to sit in her lap. He's dissolved into a steady stream of long drawn-out baby whimpering, teetering on the edge of a meltdown but not quite going over. "I'm awful sorry, Gloria-"

"That ain't your fault, Ellie."

"-is he okay?"

Gloria tucks some of his curly hair behind his ear, wiping his snotty nose with a bar napkin. The loud percussion in the music skips a few beats. Ellie's gonna have to take this one off the playlist, she doesn't remember it being so distracting.

"He's fine, just a little rattled. He always gets like this around that boy." She smiles warmly at him, and Ellie tries to ignore the dull ache in her chest. "It's all good now, Lou-lou, you're okay."

Lucille safely deposited back at her table with fresh coffee, Ellie gets closer and kneels in front of Lou, letting extra warmth seep into the air around them. She tucks his hair behind his ear like Gloria had, and if there's a little extra glow in her fingertips, nobody comments on it. Lou calms, watching Ellie's smiling face.

"Do we think some cake would help us feel better?" she asks. He takes some time to consider the question, then nods cautiously.

"Make that two, El'?" Gloria adds.

"Three, I think," Ellie agrees. As she straightens up, she catches an odd scent in the air. "Huh. Should need a few more minutes, but I'm gonna go check on it." Once she's facing away from everyone else, she takes a quiet breath as she crosses to the beaded curtain, still shaky with adrenaline. "My timer must'a been off, it almost smells like something's-

burning," she breathes, staring at the lighter in Ray's hand, the flame bright orange in the dark lenses of his sunglasses. The stench of the gasoline trailing from his feet to the hissing gas stove is overpowering.

"I want you to remember it didn't need to be like this," he says. "This was *your* decision, Ellie."

The lighter falls from his hand, and she closes her eyes before the flash can close them for her.

6

Phineas is thankful for the shock when Ulrich yelps behind her, flinching enough that Phineas has to catch herself. She'd almost dozed off.

"Are you alright?" she asks, too sluggish to turn and check before she's sure something's really wrong.

"*Fine!*" Ulrich hisses. "C-cramp."

She doesn't need to see him to tell it's a lie, but she lets it go, mostly relieved she doesn't have to actually do anything yet. Everything is so *hard* now. Even with the shadows in the lake kept at bay with Ulrich's help, the miasma in the chamber is thick and hard to breathe. Phineas keeps nodding off and shaking herself awake when she finds herself short of breath, or when one of the voices in the shadows hisses too loud. She can feel how hungry they are, tugging at the edges of her, mouse teeth on the corners of her being. They sound very much like one of the voices she heard in the shack while she'd been asleep the night before, but the rest of those are absent. Notably, the one that had asked for help. Phineas hopes that isn't a bad sign.

"How much of my fifteen do I have left?" The scratchiness in her own voice startles her, it feels like she has to force it through a briar patch.

"It was ten," Ulrich mumbles. "And about four minutes." He's been shifting behind her while she rests, and periodically she hears the sound of metal. He must be fiddling with some gadget the workers had missed.

Ulrich stills.

"Do you hear that?" he asks, not waiting for an answer before he leaps to his feet. Phineas squeaks as she falls over backwards without his support and decides it's easiest to stay sprawled out. They listen from their positions for a moment. Muted, getting louder and softer in turns, the rhythmic sound of wheels on rails, the groan of old metal at speed.

"A minecart?" Phineas asks from the floor, finding it as hard to panic as it is to breathe. Ulrich reaches for a gun that isn't there, trying to see in every direction.

"But *where-*"

The clacking goes from muted to *extremely loud* all at once; from nothing a blue star sears into being, shoots blindly across the chamber until it careens into the opposite wall with a deafening screech of steel and stone. Phineas doesn't even have time to fling herself in front of Ulrich again before it's done, the wreckage quietly illuminated by the glow of starstone.

"Are you..." Ulrich starts, still examining the New Thing, but he trails off. She catches his sharp breath before he takes off towards it.

"What'd'ya find?" Phineas asks, getting to her feet like pulling up out of the mud. She hears the sound of paper tearing.

He doesn't answer, but as she gets closer she can see there were other things in the minecart besides the loose starstone. Ulrich's guns and their harness, wrapped thickly in a crinkly sheet of paper from one of those big draft pads engineers use on TV, all tucked inside his battered hat. He's knealt in the dirt, handling them like they might crumble in his hands.

"Are they okay?" Phineas asks, after Ulrich doesn't say anything for too long.

"I think so," he says, distracted.

"Are guns all that delicate?"

"*Yes,*" he scowls, moving to get them secured around his chest. "And I do not like other people *touching* mine."

"Sure," Phineas says sleepily, drawing Ulrich's overshirt further around her shoulders. "No chance my coat's in there huh?"

"Sorry. There is this, though."

All his equipment safely back where it belongs, he gestures for Phineas to come stand with him in the light. Stepping carefully to avoid sharp metal in her feet, she notices the shadows around the cart are roiling like the darkness in the pit, and the light, it...doesn't exactly *burn*, but it makes her skin itch, like her muscles are falling asleep where it touches her. But they can't read in the dark.

The note is tiny on the big page so they crowd in close while Ulrich holds it up to the light. It seems like it was done in a rush, torn haphazardly around the edges, but the message is legible:

Door is here. Good luck.

There's a very crude drawing of what must be this room and its perimeter wall, using the pit as a reference for the part of the wall that is, apparently, Door. The two of them look up at the same time and remember also at the same time that it's too dark to see that far.

"There's symbols down there," Phineas points out, tapping them on the paper. Triangles, again.

"They look sort of like some that I saw scrawled on the stone out there," Ulrich says. "Where they smeared that girl's blood, but I haven't any idea what they mean. You?"

Phineas shakes her head.

"I don't even know what stone you're talking about," she says. "I was too distracted with everything in here."

Ulrich sighs and kneels behind the cart, and she hears him shuffle around a bit before he scoops up a handful of starstone to carry with him through the dark. Like raw starstone does, the disparate shards cling together in his hand to congeal into a single new stone, brighter than before.

"Well, stay here," Ulrich says. "Let me go check on that spot in the wall."

Ulrich is gone for around two minutes, and during his short, somewhat shaky investigation he manages to miss a small grid of symbols carved into the wall. If he had seen them, and been looking at the map as well, he might have noticed that the symbols matched the ones drawn on the paper. If he had been paying *really* close attention, he might have noticed that part of the map with further instructions had gotten caught under some stone during the crash and torn away while he was fussing with his guns. These minor details would have saved both Ulrich and Phineas a significant amount of trouble. He notices none of them, because most of his faculties are occupied trying to keep him upright and thinking when he would rather curl up on the floor and howl like an animal.

Phineas, huddled back near the minecart, also misses these details. She lets her eyes drift closed while Ulrich recedes into the darkness, listens to his steps soften and the shadowy voices sharpen. It's like a million tiny claws scraping the inside of her skull, she wishes she knew what they *wanted* so badly.

Ulrich comes close again and she opens her eyes, happy for the distraction.

"What's up?" She peers around him at something catching her eye, a faint glow in the dark where he's just come from.

"I am going to blow a hole in the wall," he says. "Get behind the cart."

Phineas has several questions, but Ulrich already has his revolver in his hand so she does what he asks, kneeling down behind a fallen slab of cart.

"Cover your ears, mausbär," Ulrich says in the darkness. She has exactly enough time to do that before she hears the second loudest thing in the world, immediately followed by the first.

It's a very controlled explosion, she thinks; she doesn't have a lot of experience with them but when she peeks around the minecart the room has been flooded with starlight, pouring through a tidy door-shaped gap in the wall of the chamber. It takes her a moment to realize Ulrich is gone. She staggers to her feet.

"Ulrich?!"

"Present." She whirls around to find him standing just behind the spot she'd been hiding a second ago. He's grinning, his teeth and his gun shining in the new light.

"How'd you do *that!*"

"What kind of magician would I be," he says, putting away his revolver and brushing himself off. "Let's get going."

He goes on ahead of her, stopping to retrieve something small from the floor where he'd been standing before he disappeared.

"Is that a poker chip?" Phineas asks, crowding in close to get a better look.

"It is," he says, lifting his foot to press it into the bottom of his shoe. Phineas sees a little hollow where the chip clicks in perfectly.

"Aren't you showing me the trick right now?"

"Has it illuminated anything?"

"...No."

"Well then."

Ulrich Weiss is the coolest person on the planet. Drawing strength from this immutable fact, Phineas straightens up, trying to fortify for whatever else is between the two of them and her ship. She starts to shrug out of his overshirt but he holds up one hand.

"Is it still helping?" he asks. She considers the question seriously; it *had* gotten quieter, once Ulrich had bundled her up, even if it's louder again now. It might *be* helping and things have just been getting worse. If she takes it off now maybe all those teeth are gonna come crashing in.

"You don't want it back?" she asks, but she's already sort of resettling it on her shoulders. Ulrich notices, shakes his head.

"I want you well enough to fight," he says bluntly. "If there are creatures and things here I can't even *see* then that shirt is better on you. Just don't go digging in the pockets, you're liable to lose a finger."

Phineas grins and follows him towards the brightly lit doorway.

The hallway writhes. There are fewer deposits of stone sticking from the walls, but it's brighter than it's been anywhere else in the mine so far. The walls are etched with long horizontal grooves that, by some trick of the alien light, seem to pulsate, and the tunnels themselves have been rounding out, which neither of them notices until Ulrich nearly loses his footing against the uneven floor.

"You know, I have not seen anything artificial since we left the last chamber," he observes, dusting himself off and looking down the hallway, back the way they've come. Phineas scrunches her eyes shut and shakes her head, like blinking away a cateract.

"We're getting close," she says.

"To *what?*"

Phineas doesn't know. The paths have been branching at odd places and she's been using her intuition to pick the ones that feel like they're leading...*somewhere*. She isn't sure what it is that's drawing them in, exactly, but it's keeping them from going in circles, and things are changing around them in a way that feels like progress. Something's better than nothing. She stops with Ulrich and scrubs her fingers through her hair, digging into her scalp. The sight of the wriggling black shadows on her arms startles her.

"D'you," she says, halting. "Remember how I said the land has a heartbeat?"

"And veins?" Ulrich says uneasily, looking around. Like a snapped lightswitch, the details of the tunnel firmly reassert themselves as the details of an enormous artery. Phineas nods.

"There's a big one, the whole planet has its own heart that I orient myself to a lot. Helps me keep my balance or..." She has to stop to breathe. "Keep my wits, when I'm commanding. But when I got close to Last Chance, I felt another one here in the desert."

"That's. Is that bad? I don't know anything *about* any of this, Phineas." His halo is getting craggy and fitful, fidgeting in the air around him.

"It's not anything, it's just a really, *really* big consciousness that lives under the ground, here in the mine. It's probably the thing that's been stirring up the shadows, or what's been screwing with the mining operation."

"It's a creature then?"

"I don't know."

"Is it going to harm us?"

"I don't know."

Ulrich pauses to try and get his temper under control.

"What *do* you know?"

Phineas thinks for an uncomfortably long time about what she knows. She closes her eyes and tries to hear her own thoughts through the latest swell in the shadows' volume, it's been flowing without ebbing for a while now. She only realizes she's swaying on her feet when Ulrich's hand grips her bicep.

"Phineas!" His voice is a few semitones too high. "Don't you *dare* leave me down here alone, *get it together."*

She wants to reassure him but it's too hard to speak, so she sets her other hand over his and nods weakly. She opens her eyes and finds his, forces herself to focus on Ulrich. The look on his face tells her the skittering sound inside of her head is outside of her head too, now.

"Something's coming," she says. Ulrich peers behind her, then behind himself, reaching for his revolver.

"Where?"

Phineas shakes her head, more of a rough jerk than a gesture, and presses down on his hand until he lowers the weapon. He looks so annoyed about it he forgets to be scared for a second.

"Do *not* touch my hand when I am-"

"We gotta move," Phineas says, working up as much of her own light as she can, reaching deep in her chest to tap into the sun there. Ulrich's eyes widen, looking over her shoulder.

"Your...your shadow, it's..."

It's grown, Phineas can feel it like a limb spreading out along the floor, abandoning the human shape to sprout apart like wings. She feels the pair of circles in the place where the shadow of her head should be, one phosphene eye glaring out at the brightness of the tunnel. Ulrich is transfixed, so Phineas cups his cheek and turns his head so he's looking into her eyes instead.

"We gotta *move,*" she repeats. Ulrich's eyes flit to her shadow one more time, then he holsters his gun and turns on his heel. Phineas is surprised again by how quick he is on his feet.

"Why- why can't I fight them?" Ulrich shouts, because if he doesn't he won't be heard over their echoing footfalls, the skittering of teeth on stone. "Like I did when you hallucinated before?"

"Were you this *scared* before?" Phineas calls, pulling ahead. She knows vaguely what's back there, the things under her skin singing for it, but she doesn't know what any of them are running towards. Whatever it is she'll probably be better suited for it than Ulrich.

"I-" Ulrich pants. Then he looks behind them.

He stops.

Phineas groans and turns to go back for him.

"What-" He's completely transfixed, his entire halo gone stagnant, white as paper. Phineas almost snarls despite herself.

"Come *on,* Ulrich! Don't stop!"

"I can hear them," he whispers, almost lost in the chaos. "They're- they're *speaking,*"

The shadows scream into view, cascading down the tunnel toward them, streaking along the circular walls and flowing through the capillaries of the stone like pumping blood. The black is spattered with bright blue, starstone blue, maws twisting with teeth, eyes jittering in sockets that melt and sludge and reform with extra irises, smeared like egg yolks. There's that hysterical agony again, that hunger so total and complete that Phineas fully feels it herself in her human heart, bursting with despair.

She feels it in Ulrich too, switching gears to put herself between him and the shadows instead. She gets her hands on his shoulders but he isn't looking at her, he's still watching the thing boiling towards them. His eyes brim with tears, his breathing is fast and shallow.

The star in her chest flares.

Mine, she says.

"Move, Ulrich!" Phineas commands, wrenching his shoulders around to face forward, shoving him hard. A stab of yellow light skates across Ulrich's body and down to his feet. There's no resistance at all, he moves under her command exactly as she wants, both of them tearing away down the monstrous artery.

Ulrich is babbling something, nonsense silver sparking around him uselessly like lightning in a raincloud. His fear is almost as overwhelming as the shadows' hunger; strung between them, and Ulrich, and whatever that heartbeat is they're barreling towards, Phineas feels like she's being ripped apart.

"I *won't!*" she shouts, not knowing what Ulrich's words are but feeling the intention, his terrified grasping. "I won't let them take you but you-" She claws in a ragged breath, it's like there's lead pooling in her legs. "You have to keep running, stay with me!"

Mercifully, the next branch in the path leads them to a last twist of the tunnel, flooded with eerie light— if Phineas hadn't been so focused on Ulrich she might notice the way it makes her skin buzz, her starlight roil. She doesn't, consumed with commanding his feet blindly away from the mass behind them.

The tunnel lets out into a room so big she can't see to the other side, and one entire wall to Phineas' left is sheer, blazing starstone. Ulrich gets into the chamber ahead of her, bathed in so much light he turns solid white, and Phineas is right behind. The second she crosses the threshold into the brightness something in her chest vibrates like a struck bell, and she's gone before she hits the floor.

Ulrich only realizes Phineas isn't with him because it's suddenly harder to move his feet again, her command isn't moving him any more. It takes every ounce of self-control in his body to turn and look back.

There she is, face down just where the light from this chamber falls, only a few yards away. It would be easy to close that distance, but *then* what? He can't *possibly* outrun them while-

The shadows' screeching through the hallway is getting louder, they're catching up fast— he sees the darkness oozing around the last corner, the cracks in the walls, the floor. They're swarming around her like a solid cloud of insects, or *teeth-*

He reaches for Glückssache, swallowing down as much of his terror as he can and lining up the shot before his hands have time to shake, before the horde descends fully upon Phineas' prone body. The crack of the revolver echoes off the high ceiling of the chamber, and both shots pass straight through the shadows like stones through smoke. But now they're looking at *him.*

The cloud undulates in on itself like a murmur of black birds, around and away from Phineas, building and building higher into a tidal wave between the two humans, skewed out above Ulrich's head.

Ulrich feels tears streaking down his cheeks, unsure when they'd started.

The mass froths with teeth, with eyes rolling in impossible sockets, tongues and throats, and the sound of them scrapes the inside of Ulrich's head, digs between the tendons in his joints. The shadows skitter like corrupted video footage, towering higher in front of Ulrich until he realizes they're forming a single enormous maw, an abyss yawning over him. Nothing in his life has ever felt like this, his definition of fear doesn't come *close* to what this is. He is frozen, unable to do anything but watch and listen as the sound of a hundred thousand squealing insects coalesces into speech that screams static in his ears, ricochets through his bones.

The maw bears down. The voice of entropy tells him:
RUN BOY

Over the last twenty-four hours, Ulrich has had many of his fundamental beliefs about how the world turns forcibly rewritten. He had not been aware of what starstone could be, outside of carefully tamed circuit boards and electrical wiring. He had not known what a commander's laugh felt like as it crashed over him like boiling water, or that moonlight could taste rotten. And now, he is learning he had not known what darkness looked like, that the word is horrifically inadequate for what he has experienced.

He did not scream in the hospital, he did not scream when they took his teeth or gave him the mark on his chest, he did not scream when they walked Bel behind the door at the end of the hallway. Trapped here under the weight of every square inch of earth between himself and the sky, pressing him against the antithesis of every cell in his human body as it looms real enough to reach for him and tear him to pieces from the inside out, Ulrich opens his mouth and *wails.*

It is the most sincere, full-throated emotion he has ever expressed, gripped so completely he's blinded with it; carried along his voice it surges from him in every direction with no thought left for restraint, the silver streaming into the air between him and the wall of shadow. He doesn't wait to see that it forces them back, sizzling and hissing where it meets their mass. Ulrich turns and runs, to *anything* else.

He can't think of anything at all, every corner of his conscious mind smothered in the incomprehensible thing behind him. All that's left is animal instinct, screeching for him to get his mortal body out of this place, out of the dark, god *damn* Phineas Kidd and commanders and every other thing that brought him here to this.

He is nearly halfway across the chamber when Bel reaches inside him and makes a fist around his heart. He chokes as he swallows around his terror, wheezes, it's too much, he can't do this, it's too *much-*

The world slows.

He *can't* do this. But he tastes someone else's cigarette smoke between his teeth, feels cold porcelain whisper over his burning skin. There's only her voice now.

Is this how we go?! she barks, vicious and cruel, seizing his soul and digging in. *Is this it?!*

Why would they tell you to **run?!**

Behind the mask, Ulrich goes away, and what comes back reaches for a weapon.

Ulrich's boots crunch into the dusty stone as he turns on his heel, and Houndstooth moves with him, shaky in a way that disappoints an efficient part of him, but it will do. It's a big target.

The pin-drop in the sea, the unseen thing that luck had delivered to him from the desert hares from Ellie's apron from Phineas' pockets from the tread of his boot from the barrel of his flintlock— it screams across the starlight in a burst of steel against gunpowder. The round he'd scribbled a face onto, so he'd know not to use it because it shouldn't work, it shouldn't do *anything* he'd intended.

The musketball disappears into the mass of shadows, touches the brightness roiling inside.

The air *shatters* with peacock-feather blue light, bursting into a single chrysanthemum blazing thirty feet across. The explosion is deafening; someone else's hands strangle his flinch when the shadow howls, bubbling and folding in on itself to scramble away from the new light.

"That's mine," Ulrich grits through his teeth, adrenaline tunneling his vision around Phineas' body and driving him forward. "That is *mine* I saw it *first.*"

He almost slides on his knees as he reaches her, searching for a pulse he doesn't find. Ulrich's heart seizes with frustration, but Ulrich's body does as its told and gathers her up anyway. It's like holding a husk, there's hardly any weight to her.

"We are *not* dying down here," he growls, stumbling to his feet just as the shadows begin to regroup again, surrounding them. He tears away towards the new hallway across the endless room. "We are not *dying down here!*"

He drags deeply from the inhaler in his mask and hears his ragged breath catch the edges of his voice as he sprints, but they might make it, they-

The darkness bellows as it catches his ankle, pitching him forward. He hits the ground hard, barely feels it when his teeth go through his lip as he watches Phineas' body sprawl away from him on the floor ahead, just out of reach. He reaches anyway, savage with rage, blood flying from his mouth as the shadows lash up around his waist, his chest, around his neck and finally his eyes, prising under his mask. He manages one more rabid gasp of air before they take that, too.

⊙⊙⊙

The bottoms of Phineas' feet had grit stuck on from walking out there, caught sharp and mean in the wounds. They were still sore and bleeding by the end of most days, but she knew if she complained Jo would make her put shoes on. She hoped Gideon wouldn't notice the blood on the trail behind them as he led her to the pond out in the woods behind Jo's house. He always walked a little faster than was comfortable for Phineas to keep up with, but she'd rather die than ask him to slow down.

The sky was so blue that day it looked fake, no clouds anywhere and the sun like a hole cut through. They didn't talk much, but the woods were loud with summertime cicadas so it was a comfortable, cushioned kind of silence. Phineas felt sweat pooling above the waistband of her shorts, and on her neck, under the thick braid falling down her back. It got so *heavy* in the hot weather.

After a while they came out in the clearing around the pond, Phineas giddy with whatever cool new thing Gideon had in mind. Jo didn't usually let her come here on her own, she said there were snakes in places you couldn't see them until you'd already got bit. Fortunately, Phineas had a guide.

"How's your breathing?" Gideon asked, reminding Phineas she hadn't been keeping on it like he told her to.

"Good," she lied.

"Nah it ain't, let's sit for a minute okay?"

Gideon sat down right where he was, in a clear patch of dirt near the water's edge. There wasn't another clear spot and Phineas' feet *really* hurt, so she scrambled up onto a big boulder next to him and sat there instead. The stone was rough and warm on her skin, and she was careful not to smear any blood where Gideon might see.

Then they sat. Phineas never liked this part of commanding, it was so *boring* sitting around doing *nothing*. Gideon said she should do it in the mornings, just sit there and listen to the things around her and feel her senses and stuff, but most of the time she forgot. At least they didn't have to close their eyes, like when people did this stuff on TV. Feeling was important, but so was seeing. All the senses were supposed to be used, but that was stupid because you couldn't *taste-*

"Breathe, little girl," Crow Gideon said. Phineas did, taking an exaggerated breath so he could hear it.

"You should be breathin' like that all the time."

"It's hard," she said, making a face at him.

"Most stuff's hard," Gideon agreed. "Don't look so sour, look around. What's the air feel like? See the sunshine in the trees, ain't it pretty?"

"It's fine," Phineas said.

"What do *I* look like?" Gideon asked. That part *was* fun. Phineas concentrated her vision in the space above his head, right above where his dirty pirate hat stopped. It was getting easier, finding that middle spot between unfocusing her eyes and still being able to see clearly, like tweaking the radio antenna on stormy days. It only took a few seconds to find Gideon's halo, searing circles around his head, the rings getting bigger around as they got further out. It's almost the same color as the sunshine in the trees he'd told her to look at. He must have seen something change on her face when she found it, because he smiled, and it wove out from him in shining gossamer threads. They reached for her, and when they brushed her skin it was like butterflies in her stomach. She flinched back, dissolving into giggles.

"Very good," Gideon said, standing up. She did too. Standing on the boulder almost put them at eye level. Gideon waved an arm out at the pond.

"Today, we're gonna work more on not freakin' out when you're commanding."

All the warmth in Phineas' belly flooded her face instead, and Gideon set a hand on her shoulder.

"Hey, some people lose whole fingers and *toes* and stuff 'cause they fuck up the rebound. Just your lunch ain't so bad. And people are usually a lot older'n you their first time trying it."

"Did *you?*" Phineas asked. Gideon nodded.

"I got all my toes but yeah, 'course I puked the first time.

Commanding's hard." He grinned at her so wide his eyes closed. "And you probably will again. Better to do it out here than on Jo's rug."

"Why's it make me get *sick?*" Phineas whined. "How come *you* don't anymore?"

"The current shakes you up," Gideon said. He looked away, the wide brim of his hat hid his eyes. "I ah. Probably should've explained it to you better first before you tried it." He looked up, smiling again. Phineas felt her own face mirroring his. "But we're fixin' it now!"

Gideon planted his feet and tossed his head, the wind ruffling his long hair, the ratty mantle he wore around his shoulders. They both fell still as delicate phosphene currents wove along his arm, and then down his body into the earth at his feet, and then into the pond. The water was green and murky, but Phineas could see the tall, leafy plants underneath begin to sway under his command.

"The trick to getting good at commanding is figuring out how to hold different stuff in your head at the same time," Gideon said, moving his hand, moving the plants. "Your energy against the pulse of the universe is a drop in the ocean, but that's all the ocean *is,* you know? A bunch of little pieces. Not a one of 'em has any more say than another."

"If you're nothing you're everything," he said. "And if you learn to know your own shape while flowing with the rest of it, you got enough faith in yourself to roll that fear into momentum instead of letting it carry you along, you can learn to move inside the current. And then, when you're good at *that,"*

He twisted his hand, drawing all the plants straight up to burst through the surface of the water. Phineas could almost see the shimmer of strings between his fingertips and the taut stems.

"You can direct the current around you."

He let them fall again, back to undulating in the agitated water.

"How are you doing that without movin' more?" Phineas asked, irritated. "I thought you had to keep movin' or the rebound thing would happen."

"'Cause I practiced my breathin' a lot when I was learning," Gideon said. "Now we're gonna practice keepin' cool when you feel that great big current again, so you don't throw up next time you try to use it." He tapped one of the bandages on her arm, all of them scratchy and dried out now. "This'll help with *that,* too."

Phineas' face got hot again, but Gideon ruffled her hair.

"Workin' on it, yeah?"

"Yeah," Phineas said, nodding fast to get the attention off of her arms.

"When you're ready, jump into the water." Phineas eyed the deceptively calm surface, the shadows underneath giving away the currents. "I want you to resist the urge to right yourself, just let the water move you. But!" He snapped his finger, pulling Phineas' attention back again. "Open your eyes, find some detail to bring back for me. Keep your wits."

"Keep my wits," Phineas repeated.

"You're letting it pass through you, not holding *on* to anything. Just guiding it where it already wants to go." He smiled at her, and she felt warm all the way to her toes. "Part of it, not apart."

"Part of it," Phineas repeated, forgetting the way the leaves looked as they whipped in Gideon's wake.

"And we're not gonna be scared this time, 'cause we know Phineas is such a strong, solid person she can stay herself no matter what, right?"

"Yeah."

"And she's breathin' real good right now, right?"

"Yeah!"

Strong hands around her; the pond above her head, the sky at her ragged feet, and she was plunged backwards into the wild tangle of riverbed growth, aching for the sun. The cold water forced her breath from her in a freezing gasp, the dirt from the cuts on her feet until it was only her own blood in the wounds.

◉◉◉

Phineas isn't anywhere. It's dark enough she has to open and close her eyes a few times to be *sure* they're open, and she strains her vision for any speck of light. Even the heart of the planet is gone, even the *sun,* but she can *feel* they've been replaced with something else. It's not above or below her, it's *around* her.

She lights up with the shape of it and realizes where she is all at once. She'd slipped, lost her grip for just a second, and like a magnet her sun-riddled soul had been drawn into the next thing like it: the starstone they've been approaching all this time.

Phineas has no idea what this means, but she can feel that she isn't alone. When she reaches, it reaches back.

"Hello?" she says, but doesn't. The words travel up from her throat but they don't form in the air, like she's trying to speak into glass. When a laugh echoes in the emptiness around her, a cacophony of hiding stars flares brilliant cyan to match the rise and fall of the ethereal, mocking voice.

What kind of commander can't even speak to me under her own power?

The voice is more of a feeling, conducting through her body instead of the air. It's cold and detached, and distinctly inhuman, the way all celestial beings are. Phineas is instantly irate. Being talked down to by anyone is bad, but another deity is the *worst*. She stifles her anger as best she can and crosses her legs where she sits, sets her wrists loosely over her knees. Breathes, until she gets her bearings. No matter how many years get between her and Gideon's lessons, it's still annoying how much meditation helps.

She takes one more breath. When she speaks this time, she gets more force behind it.

"I've been here before," she says slowly. Resituating to meditate makes her aware of two things: the first is that her hair is long again, it nearly pools on the...floor, whatever smooth surface is under her. The other is that her throat is gaping open with a wound that stretches from ear to ear; she can feel the tattered edges of her skin shifting when she moves, and while she *can* speak, every word vibrates through broken vocal cords. There isn't any pain. This hasn't hurt for a long time.

If you have passed this way before I do not recall, the starstone echoes through her, the stars in the void flashing to match the disaffected tone. Phineas uses her working voice to groan.

"Yeah well, the stuff I remember was a lot bigger'n *you.*"

Perhaps. You carry something stolen, from something much bigger than yourself, little human.

Her star, already simmering with anger, burns in Phineas' eyes.

"Not stolen," Phineas says. "We're both exactly what we want to be."

Seared through with someone else's mark?

"It was Gideon's, now it's mine. I didn't steal that either."

...Crow Gideon?

Phineas smiles in the darkness.

"Yeah, another little human."

Crow Gideon is a titan among termites, particularly to me and my siblings. But what interest would he have in you?

"I should be asking you that. Why did you bring me here?"

The stars against the blackness are so bright they hurt to look at.

*As if you are worth my **notice**, let alone my **effort**,* the starstone rumbles. *Your hold on your spirit is so weak you were drawn here only by my presence.*

"*Wait,*" Phineas says before she thinks better of it, holding her head. The meditation had helped, and for the first time since she'd landed down here there are no shadows picking at her at all, but she feels sluggish in a different way now. Rather than crushed under the chaos of despair, she feels so calm she almost thinks she could doze off if she keeps sitting here. Her irritation with the deity is the only thing keeping her focused. "You're the big stone outside, the starstone, but you're...you're alive?"

Splintering a consciousness does not kill it. Our lives burned bright long before humankinds' did, and will continue to do so after you've gone, whatever you try to do to us in the interim.

Phineas gets an unbalanced feeling in her head, like her subconscious has made a terrible realization she hasn't caught up with yet.

"We use starstone for *energy,*" she rasps. "In everything, but. I thought it was like *plants,* you *think?* Does it...Do we *hurt you?*"

Right now, there are billions of living things inside you, feeding off of your body. Do you notice them?

"What does that-" Phineas shakes her head to clear it, it's like trying to have a conversation through a cloud of static. "Ugh, no, I *don't.*"

Why?

"They're tiny! They don't ma-"

...Rotten bastard.

"No," she grits out. "I don't notice them."

So.

There's a sigh that rustles through the space like a gust of chilled wind.

Although, it seems you tiny humankinds have made quite a mess of things here. Because of your meddling, my siblings and I have awakened and begun to reclaim this place, infusing even the red soil with our essence. First a tower, drawing us up, with no thought to the shadows that came with us.

"So the...those shadows weren't always down here, like this?" Phineas tries to force her way through the molasses to keep up, but it seems to be talking to itself.

And then, the land itself, displaced, the balance disrupted. Now the Derelict has come, to draw up the shadow for his own designs...

And he has made certain you feel it all, Commander, it says, the weight of its focus settling heavy across Phineas' shoulders again. *Every particle in the air, every vein in the earth around you, each pulls your errant soul in a different direction.*

It is in the nature of celestial bodies to pull towards each other, even while we are displaced. We are avaricious by design, as you've undoubtedly learned.

On the surface, where we are fractured and tempered and nearer the sky, you hardly notice us...

But you, **here-**

Phineas hisses, the emphasis like a pinprick in her temples. The longer it drones on the harder it is to stay awake.

A creature so unrestrainedly steeped in the chaos raging between the turning earth and the surging sun that you yourself **shine.**

Assailed from every side by beings who are starving, **desperate** *for a light* **just** *like yours...*

Oh, Phineas, the stone says. *You must be so tired. Your heart should have burst the moment you touched my light.*

"You're why commanding ain't workin' right down here," Phineas says, out loud, just as an excuse to hear her own voice. "I'm pulling energy from *you* down here, not the sun, I didn't even notice the difference." She makes a face no one can see. "But you're resisting me."

Why would I allow something like you to feed off of me, I am not beholden to your whims.

"Why're you making this hard?" Phineas demands in the dark. "Didn't you *just* say what we do don't even affect you?"

I do not like you, and wish to see you struggle.

Phineas wishes this thing had teeth for her to kick in. It's *such* an asshole, she wishes Ulrich was here to-

"Oh shit," Phineas starts, the urgency waking her up a little. "Ulrich, where- Where's Ulrich? Where is my friend?"

Why should I know this.

Phineas is on her feet so fast she's dizzy with it. The fucking thing *laughs* again.

Calm yourself, little commander. The other's soul is still quite firmly rooted in his vessel and won't be taken by such measures. A security you, in your ignorance, have exchanged for your blasphemous ability.

"I gotta get back to him," Phineas turns in circles, disoriented by the lack of any perspective. The surface under her feet feels like glass, cold and slippery, and there's only a static black sea of stars in every direction. "He's gonna get got-"

Before she can complete it, the thought dissolves from her like mist.

"What was I..." Phineas murmurs, the words silent because she doesn't think to command them. She squeezes her eyes shut and shakes her head. No shadows this time, only...a sort of fog...

Converse with me yet, the boy will keep well enough. I would like to ask you some things.

Right. The stone.

"What were you saying?" she asks, running her hand through her long hair. It's so *heavy.* "Did you...ask something?"

We were speaking of my sibling, the stone powering the Derelict's ship. The blue starfields pulse rhythmically with the cadence of its speech. *You've said you intend to steal them away.*

"Derelict? You mean Hazard?"

A mask worn doesn't change the face underneath. Neither, then, does a false name change an identity.

"What are you *talking* about?"

He has not been himself for some time, and neither has my sibling. They say such ridiculous things, they have lived too long in the Derelict's orbit perhaps.

"...Trapped?" Phineas asks. She sort of remembers dreaming about a voice, maybe...

We are all connected, we are never trapped anywhere. Certainly not by any humankind design. I assume my sibling stays because they have bonded with the Derelict.

Maybe not. There must be something *else* around here that needs help. Them and-

But something they've said has made me curious.

Phineas has settled back down on the ground, picking at her ruined gloves and rubbing her palms together.

"Yeah?"

They speak of desolation, isolation. Dried, cracked earth. Tell me, what is a desert?

"Uh..." what. "Real dry. Hot, dusty. You're under one, can't you tell?"

She feels its confusion compounded over her own. It's only a faint imitation of confusion, but definitely noticeable against the rest of its sterile halo.

...What has happened to the saints here? it asks.

"What do you care?"

There was one who often conversed with me, on behalf of the city. I have not heard from him in some time, and now the land is overrun with entropy. I...

It dawns on Phineas then, what's happening here, and a lot of things snap into place: this thing is *lonely*. Of *course* it is. Sapient, and trapped in the dark, the only one of its kind for miles and miles...

Well, except for the ship. Hazard's ship, she has to stay focused.

The starstone is too proud to admit its feelings, and she's not gonna finish its thought for it. It's been *rude,* and she's too busy trying to remember something. She keeps trying to grasp it where it floats just on the edge of her mind but it's like trying to catch a ribbon in the water; whenever she gets near it her own disturbance curls it out of her reach. The silence goes on enough for her to get bored, and then annoyed, already sort of forgetting what the stone was on about.

"Man, don't you go nuts sittin' down here in the dark all the time?" She reclines on her hands. "I think your sibling has the right idea bein' a ship."

There is nothing I wish to see on the surface that would be worth forming a bond with a humankind. We choose this, the darkness, rather than be subject to the whims of such small things.

"Yeah well it don't sound like you're doin' so good just talkin' to yourself down here."

If you survive the shadows, you will learn the alternative soon enough. If the Derelict does not kill you, my sibling will.

"I ain't gonna die," Phineas says, her star twisting itself in knots in her chest. "I need a starstone ship to get to Kairos Crossing, so them 'n me are gonna be *real* good friends."

Kairos Crossing? What business could you possibly have there?

"I'm gonna catch the sun."

Its laugh is like a dam bursting, there's so much weight drenching Phineas it drags her forward, kneeling with her face against the glassy ground. She squirms against it, unable to stand, and the laugh dissolves into a snarl.

*After that threat you have the **nerve** to **cower** in front of me?*

It's impossible to think of anything, the presence of the stone is so overpowering it sucks the breath from her lungs; her chest burns.

Hold up your head, commander! The title is wasted on you!

Unable to move or breathe, Phineas feels the first inkling of panic creeping into her daze— it's the second time today she realizes she could die like this if she can't get her feet under her *really soon.*

The second time today. The rest of today.

Almost as quick as it had come, the force of her panic reorients into rage. The ember in her chest blazes like it's doused in gasoline, the heat surges through her limbs and she manages to push herself up on her hands, her muscles trembling under the din.

This is *unacceptable.*

You cheat destruction once only to leap back into it, how stupid can one human be! How arrogant!

Her constant companion *howls.* Teeth and eyes burst from Phineas' back, things that only cast shadows in the rest of the world carve out physical space for themselves in this nowhere place, six burning, bleeding wings. Bolstered like strong hands are pulling her up, her own hands, Phineas wrenches herself to her feet, incandescent.

"I am arrogant because I'm better than you," she thunders, relentless with command. The words are physical things too, bolts of lightning piercing the new miasma, thick and red with the stone's ire. Her star's stinging fury is a harmonic laid over Phineas', the sun focused through her body like a magnifying lens, driving out the cold. "Languishing in the dark so long has impaired your judgment, do you not recognize the sun when you see it? Look at me, *look!*"

The entirety of Phineas screams out to fill the void with sunlight, terrible and absolute. She feels-

(something tapping the aquarium glass, laughing to itself. "Come on, I'm *waiting,*")

the starstone deity's influence cede to hers, even fragmented in her chest her sliver of sun outranks *anything* that acknowledges a hierarchy, and certainly anything that cowers under the earth. Clear-eyed, Phineas sees a dull stone at her feet ten thousand miles below. She kneels, her movement titanic, picks it up in her hand where it struggles with stuck-bird movement. Her voice rings like a church bell, brutal and adamant.

"You use that network, you tell all the rest of your bullshit pantheon I'm comin'." The struggling stone melts between her fingers, trying to escape, but she holds it fast. "You tell them their time is done, I'm hanging up *new* stars, and if they get in my way I will rip them right out of the fucking sky. I'll start with you if I have to, *right* here."

The stone rallies a little, wrapping around her wrist and gaining mass until it flows back out into the air. Either it rallies, or Phineas' flame might be easing off. There's sweat dripping down her back, because she is still human enough for this to wear on her, but it makes her realize her long hair is gone. She's herself again.

"Now we're gonna talk like equals, alright?" she says, leaning into the momentum to try and keep it up. The stone just sits there in the void ahead of her, an indignant puddle stoking her temper.

"*SPEAK!*" she hollers, command sparking from her chest like a firecracker and ricocheting against the boundaries of the world. The stone resists, but it's still cowed by the white light filling its space, and it gives.

you, would have us...announce you. you wish to...focus the eyes of heaven upon...yourself.

It's like choking up gravel, but she keeps the pressure on, digging out every piece.

if the coup is truly your intent, you must know...in your heart, that...those you invoke are already aware of...you.

The echoing hollow of its laughter is much less explosive than it had been, but impudent enough to prompt Phineas to squeeze its body in her fist, forcing its malleable form between her fingers.

*They have **heard** your protests. They do not **care.***

"I ain't askin' for *permission*," Phineas growls. "This is a declaration of war; if they wanna ignore me they can pay for it later. This is already more diplomacy than you things deserve. Now are you and me gonna have to go a round, or are you gonna let me go help my friend?"

There's an odd moment where she can feel the stone spirit seriously mulling over the question; it's like she's hooked into what it's thinking now that she's cast her halo so wide in its space. Phineas feels it grin, somewhere in the void.

If you really believe we are equals, I could help you out of your current predicament, if you wish.

"What? What predicament?"

A smear of starry black tears in the air in front of them, and Phineas can see into what must be the fifth chamber. From the perspective of the stone's physical form, she watches as Ulrich drags her unconscious body as far as he can before he's caught up in the shadows they'd been running from. The vision freezes.

Time runs truer here; more slowly to you. Out there, in your plane, your body is under siege, and so is your companion.

His tenacity is not enough, you will both be overtaken soon.

Phineas is ruined by Ulrich's bloody, determined face, hazy and translucent in the air. He's reaching for her body, lifeless on the ground ahead of him while the shadows boil over him. Excavated from the starstone's consciousness, she sees the shadow and hears the word *tain*.

"Send me *back*." It is a threat. The stone laughs it off, growing again, oozing around her feet as it floods the floor.

I already told you, commander; nothing keeps you here but your own inability to escape my gravity. Simply manifesting yourself here and speaking with me is draining your energy, I am draining you, only being near. Even **you** *can't hold out forever, little sun.*

If you don't find your way out soon, you'll drift off...

And I will eat up everything that's left of you, would-be god.

Phineas hisses, skittering away from the ooze as it begins to burn.

But if you channel me, my energy, you might be able to get you and yours out alive.

"Channel you? Against the tain? Why would that be any different from what I've been doin'?"

Because I have been fighting you. If I allow this connection, the tain cursing you cannot stand against their own.

"...Their own?" Phineas *knows* it's trying to stall her here, but it can't *possibly* be saying what she thinks it is.

If a light lives, shouldn't its shadow? Do you not understand what I've said to you here? You are vast, but you still only have the perspective of a single human, and a fragment of the sun is only a fragment. There is so much you don't understand.

Phineas has more questions than she has ever had about anything, but they're going to have to wait until she can talk to the ship's heart. Ulrich needs her. She ignores the bait and plants her feet against the glass, reaches out across their connection, searching for balance in the flow between two stars.

"Why the change of heart?" Phineas asks, feeling herself light up with foreign starlight. It's cold and fizzy, like champagne in her blood. "I *know* you don't suddenly want to help."

A laugh again, she feels it in her own throat.

I doubt you've ever had to command something as powerful as me, and so close to the source besides. I hope for your sake you have a strong enough spirit to match that brass mouth of yours.

If you fail to harness it properly, that amount of energy will rebound with enough force to rip you apart.

She feels the ghost of its grin across her mouth.

I would very much enjoy that.

"...It feels good to connect, doesn't it?" Phineas asks in a low voice. The stone doesn't answer, recoils because she's struck a nerve.

When Phineas breathes out, her breath comes in blue, sparkling clouds.

⊙⊙⊙

It's uncanny, seeing the street outside the bar shaded over like this. If Ellie closes her eyes, and ignores the searing heat, and the smoke drying out her throat, she can almost imagine she's somewhere else. Maybe someplace leafy and green.

She leans back and stares up at the sky, or, at the thick layer of black smoke blocking out where the sky would be. Everyone is here, there hadn't been many to evacuate. They've retreated a little ways out from the main cluster of buildings that constitutes Last Chance, safely away from the wall of heat. There'd been talk about trying to fight the fire at first, but it became obvious pretty quick that they just don't have the infrastructure. The dry, dense buildings had caught like a tinderbox, but there's no urgency now, just an uneasy crowd of humankinds bleakly watching their lives burn. But they're alive. Ellie has to keep reminding herself that's a win, but she can hear Lou crying again somewhere in the little mob, maybe as upsetting as the sound of the bar falling in on itself.

She doesn't think about Ray, who had disappeared after starting the fire, but she spares a brief thought to Phineas and Ulrich, probably dead. She's embarrassed, now, to think she'd almost believed one person might be able to change anything. She doesn't even feel like crying, she's just exhausted and numb. All this heartache, everything they'd *all* put up with, and for what?

At least Dad isn't here.

"<Sweetheart,>"

She closes her eyes again.

Normally it's almost impossible to sneak up on anything out here, but the air is thick with noise and smoke. He must have rolled up at some point while she was distracted staring at the remains of her mother's legacy. Ellie silently turns away from the town and knocks her forehead against her father's chest, and it's like breaking off a faucet somewhere. His arms come up around her shoulders as her sobbing wracks through them.

"<Sweetheart,>" he says again, rumbling Russi. "<My love.>"

"<I'm *sorry,*>" she wails against him, drenching his shirt in tears. "<I couldn't *do* it, I couldn't->"

"<It is too much. This should never have been your burden to bear.>" She feels his hands smoothing over her hair, the warmth tearing her apart. "<Something that makes you feel that you have to send me away, that you must carry it alone, I- We never wanted this for you.>"

Whatever Ellie tries to say gets lost, mangled in her crying and muffled by shirt fabric. Sergei holds her, rocking her gently. She takes her time falling to pieces: it doesn't matter how long she stays here now, and there is so much pressure inside her she can't stop it once it starts, every absurd, cruel thing that has accumulated in her heart flooding her eyes with stinging salt.

Either out of decency or their own exhaustion, nobody in the small crowd interrupts them.

After some indeterminable amount of time, Ellie raises her head and tries to get herself together. There's the solid, simple clarity that comes after a good cry; everything around her feels more in focus now, the shapes more distinct and functional without so many tears in the way. This includes the other denizens of Last Chance, awkwardly but kindly giving her space. They are waiting for her to direct them. Of course they are.

"What now, El'?" Gloria asks, Lou hanging around her neck, still blubbering.

Buoyed by her new lightness, the answer comes immediately, slotting into the landscape of her perspective like a puzzle piece fitting into place. Ellie takes her father's hands and looks up into his eyes.

"I gotta," she says. "I should have done it a while ago."

"<I don't think you have to do *anything*, you know this,>" Sergei says quietly. Ellie recognizes his strangled tone, his heavy expression. He'd sent her mother out the door with it a thousand times before. "<But I trust you. Please come back to me.>"

Ellie kisses him on the cheek, then backs away from everyone, untucking a pendant from inside her shirt. The pendant is a yellow stone, and then it is a knife.

"You'll be safe where I'm sending you," Ellie announces, her voice carried a bit louder than it strictly should be, turning all the attention. The blade in her hand begins to glow. "If I'm not with you by this time tomorrow, I'm not coming. Consider the town lost."

Confusion murmurs through the people. There are little factions forming, her gentle, subconsciously asserted authority only working as long as it isn't pressed too hard. It doesn't matter much; they're huddling together instinctively, which is really all she needs from them at this point.

"Ain't the town *already* lost?" Lucille complains. She is exactly as bothered as she always is, fire or not, and it's nearly a comfort.

"Not yet it ain't," Ellie says. Then she plunges the knife into her forearm and slices cleanly from her elbow to her wrist.

As it touches the air, the blood ribbons out and out in blazing yellow, like silk billowing into the air around Ellie's body. Somebody screams, but several others reply with hushed, clipped reassurance. It's always hard to say who knows what. Word gets around fast even when the population isn't so small.

The light wraps her like a cocoon, she closes her eyes and curls in on herself. It's quick.

Where Ellie Kuznetsov had been, there's a new figure, shining and winged. She comes with the sound of bells, and around her the smoke scurries away, the air blessedly cool and clear.

"Be well," Hastur's Emissary tells them, watching her father's face. He curls his fist in front of his heart, and she does the same. The golden bells in the crook of her tall staff toll out across the parched earth, cleansing the air it touches. Even more light, brighter than anything in the desert, and by the time the sound of her staff dies away everyone left in Last Chance has disappeared. Everyone except for Ellie.

She squares her shoulders, heavy with wide, feathered wings, and kicks off from the ground in a cloud of dust. The light of her disappears into the smoke and flame of the burning settlement, ascending toward the top of the tower.

7

The sun cuts straight through Ulrich's closed eyes, burning through his skin. Every inch of him feels scorched, or bruised, or crusted over with his own blood; even the silence rings painfully in his ears. It isn't just pain it's *cruelty*. It's like the desert wants to pick him over before it kills him, worry at the mortal wound to make sure he feels it. *It was all for nothing, Ulrich, you are hungry and dirty and tired and you will never get better because this is the end. After **all of it** your bones will lie here in the dust— no gardens, no neon in sight.*

...At least that means it can't get any worse. At least it will be over and he can rest, finally, *finally*. He's relieved when a shadow comes, the first vulture arriving to pick him apart. Certainly a better use for his body than he'd made of it.

When the vulture touches his face, its paws are soft.

"Hey."

The vulture's voice sounds like gravel in a garbage disposal.

Ulrich ignores it. If he tries, maybe he can die of the heat before they start on his eyes. It touches him again, two deliberate little taps against his cheek. He looks.

One of the hares he'd seen in the shack, the one with the missing ear, is folded over his head. It's almost cradling him. The sun directly over them both casts a deep shadow over Ulrich's face, making it marginally easier to keep his eyes open.

"Hey," the hare says again.

"Yes?" Ulrich says, because he has nothing more appropriate to respond with.

"We forgot to tell her, it's an instrument. It's a whistle, okay?"

Oh it's not *fair*.

Ulrich throws his arm between them, over his own eyes and thinks he might be sick. Is this *really* what his brain has decided to produce as it burns itself out? No nice memories, not even any painful ones, not even *Bel,* just more *work?*

"Can't I be done?" he breathes, thready. He feels his dry lower lip split as his face pinches like it wants to cry. "I am so tired, I'm *so* tired, I don't want to *do it* any more."

"Tough," the saint says, and it sinks its teeth into Ulrich's cheek.

Ulrich wakes up with sun on his face again, Phineas a searing shape against the pitch-dark above him.

Ulrich's head is in her lap, and he gets the sense she should be burning him where they touch, but the warmth is soothing in some treacherous way that spurs him to move. He tries to sit up and regrets it immediately. The floor tilts too much for him to stand, but he gets to a kneel, and more importantly away from Phineas' touch.

She's grinning at him from where she reclines, and her mouth is a fluorescent void cut across her face. It's outshined by her solid white eyes.

"Thanks for coming back for me." Her voice peals between Ulrich's ears, puts stars in his eyes. She gets to her feet and he realizes belatedly that the dark scuttling around them is the shadows that had consumed him earlier, sizzling where they touch Phineas' glow. Ulrich thinks of hiding under expensive catering tablecloths with Bel, inside costume racks, giggling behind hands that have never felt a kickback.

"Phineas," Ulrich chokes out, his throat starting to catch after all the screaming he's done today. He's too bewildered to say anything else, caught between panic and a bone-deep surety. Of what he can't say, no more than he could back then.

Still with her back to him, Phineas tilts her head when he speaks. It is not the movement of a humankind.

"It's okay," she says. "It's all gonna be fine."

For the first time in his wretched existence, Ulrich buys it.

Commanders are distant creatures. The price for immersing yourself into the flow of the universe, feeling everything there is to feel so exquisitely, is that human existence begins to dull. What is left for the senses after they've drowned in infinity? What fuels something that was once part of the sun?

Not much. The trick is, the sun doesn't find its sensations in the world around it; the sun is what gives light to everything *else*. A sun shines, and that is all it can do. The luxury of basking belongs to humankinds.

Phineas, who is neither one nor the other, hasn't figured that one out yet. But hooked into the vast, ancient soul of the stone deity in the dark, tapped into every other piece of its kin threaded through the earth around, she has never felt the universe so clearly. She feels as endless in all faculties as she always feels in her soul, her existence expanded far beyond its usual bonds. She is *sure*, even here, there is light to be found, because she's brought it with her. No one else needs to understand it, she knows herself and knows she is love and fury in equal parts, and she is the universe. She knows: her light can cover the whole world, and anything she can touch she can own, and anything she can own she can *save*.

This certainty in the fate she is writing, every ounce of euphoria she understands to be inherent to even this haunted place, Phineas demands from the world around her, and obediently it comes surging through the darkness to light up the filament of her body.

Point A, Point B.

One breath in, the tide rushing through her where it will,

and then,

into her hands, her head, her heart,

one breath out-

Phineas braces her feet to the ground and commands everything she has through the stone floor of the chamber, and it is *vile*. Her spirit seethes against the corrupted earth, and it's further down than she could reach on her own, but alight with the starstone's power she can find it— under all that rot the heart of this place still beats, and she knows the nature of it, *knows* it is not despair.

She *pulls*.

The energy of two fallen stars cleaves out into the stone they stand on as a jagged imitation of the circles on her palms, and the sigil brightens, and the sigil *explodes*. Tortured, verdant light bursts up from the fissures, rushing over her skin like champagne, a solid column that soars so high above them she can't see where it ends.

The screaming of the tain as the light takes them is nothing of this world, but Phineas can't stop laughing, caught up in the terrible relief of the land as its tumor boils away. She feels it go like it's part of her too, the ghost of her singing across the phantom neurons of the starstone to the very edges of this isolated desert, *finally* free.

Perfect, precious Ulrich has managed to get to his feet, but even as the light burns his eyes he's unable to look away from the chaos surging around them. He looks like he's drowning.

Phineas reaches for him, slips out of his shirt and tugs it around him. She slides her hands up around the back of his neck and kisses his forehead.

"Shh," she says, the barest shade of command. Ulrich limply buries his face into the fabric at her shoulder and she holds him through the changing of the guard.

So focused on him, when the purging light is spent and the earth eases itself shut, Phineas does not see the surviving sliver of shadow that moves to hide in the curve of her heel.

The flow of energy recedes, and it gets quiet on the outside. Without the external pressure, Phineas' equilibrium shifts.

Ulrich steps away brusquely, swiping his tear-streaked, bloody face on his shirt before he jams his arms back into the sleeves. He's flustered and uncomfortable, but the negative feelings are well drowned out by his relief.

"You *lunatic,*" he says, gaining his breath again. "Would you *please* warn me when you're..."

He stops talking when his eyes land on her, freezing like she's caught him there. Phineas starts to giggle, every cell still vibrating.

"You're bleeding," Ulrich says, touching his nose. That is *also* funny. Phineas laughs louder now, watching a fleck of blood spatter from her mouth. Ulrich makes a face at that, why does he look so *worried,* there's nothing to worry about *anywhere.*

"We did it! We *won!*" she insists. In the new quiet, her voice is an alien harmonic that makes Ulrich wince.

"Yes," he says carefully. "And now we can get the hell out of here, so. Er. Stop," he gestures at his eyes, and Phineas realizes the light blanching his face is coming from the glow of her own eyes. "Stop, you can stop this now, whatever you're-"

Phineas shakes her head.

"I've never felt so good in my *life*, Ulrich, you have no *idea*. We could definitely beat Hazard with this, we could beat *anybody!*" She coughs, surprised by the slide of blood down her throat. Ulrich looks unconvinced, and he's...

He's leaning away from her. Why?

"N...no, this is right, it *has* to be," Phineas says softly, as much as she's capable of softness while she's like this. "This feels *right.*"

She just needs to show him, if she can just calm down a little bit maybe she can explain it to him and get that look off his face. But to do that she needs to stop commanding, come out of the flow, and that would disconnect her from the stone...

What if she just. Didn't give *all of it* back? The stone even *said* it wouldn't miss it, right?

Right, this is *right.*

Phineas tightens her fist, sinking her fingertips deep into the meat of her palm. Carefully, just barely hitting the brakes to see what happens, she tries to capture the flow of the starstone's energy inside her.

She is swept away so fast she doesn't have time to breathe. The shadow at her heel makes its move.

Ulrich doesn't have a lot in the way of spiritual instinct, but he knows for damn sure that thing huddling away from him is *not* Phineas. He knows it before he asks, Phineas wouldn't hide her face behind her hands like that. But:

"Phineas?" he tries, reaching into his pocket.

He sees the ask ripple through her shadow, long and grasping, fraying at the edges and seeping along the floor towards his feet. He takes a hesitant step away, watching her back. *Its* back? Whoever it belongs to it's trembling, the dark shadow against the glare of the starstone, jittering like a cat trying to loose something sticking to its fur.

It jerks its face from its hands and contorts to face him, too-far at the hip. It's smiling with Phineas' mouth but her eyes are not there. With the body cast in shadow it's hard to make out exactly what's happening, but the spaces where her eyes should be are only empty sockets.

Ulrich gasps sharply and the body laughs at him, an echoing, slanted version of Phineas' laugh. Starry black ichor drools over the lips, it seeps from the nose and ears. The eyes aren't *gone*, Ulrich realizes; they're open wide under the glaze, he can see the curve of them distorting the stars salted through the tar. The darkness spiders out along her face, cracking her skin,

-like Hazard's, she looks like Hazard-

and Ulrich watches numbly as it covers everything but her mouth in roiling, oozing entropy. His fingers find what they're looking for in his pocket and grip tight as he watches thinner, more delicate tendrils flow down her neck in nonsense patterns.

Appearing like detritus bobbing up to the surface of the water: one bright blue eye, a pair of concentric circles in the middle of what used to be Phineas' face.

The shadow curling towards Ulrich's feet shivers like a plucked string, like a spiderweb, and his instinct deploys the defense faster than he can think.

The light is around him before the sound of the dice hitting the ground reaches his ears and it's *still* nearly too slow. The Phineas-thing moves with broken-film speed, the frames superpositioned over each other so closely there is no time between the lunge and the landing. It smashes into Ulrich's light construct like a car crash.

It's almost funny, he thinks hysterically, almost like one of those old cartoons: the hare painting a tunnel onto a rock wall, the dog running into it at full tilt, flattening, coming away from it wobbling like sheet metal. Phineas' body does not flatten when it wraps around the arc of the forcefield, and it doesn't make the sheet metal noise either, but Ulrich thinks he hears something crack.

It screams as it rears away from the light construct, Phineas' voice careening from the stone of the chamber like a fire alarm in a cathedral. Even muted through the shield it buzzes painfully in Ulrich's hearing aid, but: he is *alive*, for now.

His mask shimmers into being around his glasses.

It had been a gamble that it would work at all, but even with his quick reflexes there hadn't been time to cram any more fear into Ulrich's mortal body before the dice left his fingers. Now he tries to breathe deeply through his nose, fighting off the panic and the claustrophobia because if either gets a good grip on him now he isn't going to come back out of it.

The monster is already recovering. Heavy black smoke seeps from the pores of Phineas' skin, skittering in the air like spider legs, and the long shadow she casts peels up from the ground. As it rises it takes shape in three dimensions; Ulrich watches with muted horror as it snakes up over Phineas' back and jabs between her shoulder blades, arcing her chest and punching a breath from her mouth, flecked with black froth. The body swings like meat from a hook as it's held aloft by the thing skewering Phineas, brought closer to hover over the dome protecting Ulrich. More tendons twist out like roots from the base of it to flow all around the hard light construct, lick against the shape of the globe, catch on every imperfection and dig for a way inside.

The thing that is NotPhineas marionettes high enough from the ground to drag her feet instead of use them properly, which gives Ulrich an excellent view of the more unfortunate details. The fingers spasm like they're electrified, in pain or resistance he can't tell; the head shakes, at odd intervals jerking to look elsewhere even as the smoky mask and single blue eye stay locked on him. The breathing is the worst. As the body comes close enough for him to hear he realizes it sounds, in all definitions of the term, exactly like a sucking chest wound. That giggling hysteria boils closer to the surface again.

Save for his own thundering pulse and the firework-static of the device burning his time away, it's still incongruously quiet. The eye watching him is like a child's scribble, two circles surrounded by a dusting of stars-

Two circles, a pair of concentric circles. Like the ones that cross Phineas' back when she wears her coat, two circles that sit in the exact spot where the shadows are lodged-

"Keep going, clever boy,"

The sound of Phineas' voice, stretched like cellophane around the shape of the thing using it, startles Ulrich badly. He's been under the impression he's dealing with a beast, not something that could speak to him. Some quiet, long-suffering part of himself sighs and adjusts the limits of his belief system, again. At the same time, Phineas' face stretches into a smile, black sludge extruding between the teeth. There is nothing of the grin that's been haunting Ulrich's every waking moment since the night before, and if he wasn't sure already he knows now this is not some hidden facet of commanding *or* Phineas— she isn't here at all.

"Think it through," it says when he falters, fungus in Ulrich's ears. "Our eyes, her back, her hands, all *over* her-"

Ulrich swallows.

"An eye is a window," he says slowly, licking his dry lips and tasting his own blood. "To the soul. And..."

"*And?*"

"And any window is a door."

Phineas' hands come together, and her body laughs.

"And *she* is going around handing her housekeys to *anybody*, isn't she?" All its ragdoll limbs stiffen and it reclines in the air above him, like it's leaning against a wall that isn't there. "You're comin' in loud and clear, by the by. That mask won't do you a lick of good with *us.*"

"Us," Ulrich says, groping for any direction at all. "Us, not Phineas."

"Phineas *has* stepped out," the thing says. Ulrich's mind is flooded by an unwanted vision of the Phineas he knows: kneeling in the dark, eyes unseeing, her fists curled around some shining thing so tightly her nails bite straight through her gloves to draw blood. It's impossible to tell if what he's seeing is real, why would this thing be honest with him?

"Why would we *lie?* That's more *your* thing, isn't it?" Phineas' voice says. "We *like* you, pretty boy, we are *so excited* to get our teeth in you. Lucky for you our commander here got kinda sloppy." It taps the shield, light pulsing out from its touch like pond ripples. Ulrich sees the skin of Phineas' fingertip go shiny as it burns. "We know you're curious. Go on and puzzle it out, puzzler."

Ulrich isn't too proud to play along; it gives him more time to think.

"I could feel all that starlight she commanded," he starts, feeling foolish even when the evidence that he had been correct is here between them. "Shedding everywhere, as she moved, disposing of you."

It scoffs at him, the wet sound of it turning Ulrich's stomach, but it doesn't interrupt.

"I thought it might have affected my tools, this sort of construct is normally only for..." It's hard to think, but it doesn't feel like any outside influence. He feels *alone* in a way he rarely does. Out of any number of voices and presences Ulrich is used to carrying, all he can feel now is himself: an exhausted thing slumped over its vanity in a dim dressing room deep in his subconscious.

In the real world, Ulrich screws his eyes shut and tries to shake off the fatigue.

"I use them to block off- exits," he manages. "Funnel people where I want them."

"Like in the alley," the creature chirps. So it has access to what Phineas knows, too.

"Yes."

"But it isn't very *strong*, is it?"

"Seems to be working well just now," Ulrich says, more confidently than he feels.

"For now," NotPhineas allows. It leans forward, like a teenager lying on a bed to read a magazine, and puts itself eye level with Ulrich. "How *are* you going to get out of this one, smart guy? Any ideas?"

From a hopelessly cluttered stage office, a personification of his own logic shrugs at him. *What do you want from me, boss? You're lucky the lights are still on.*

"No," Ulrich admits.

It's true when he says it, but there are still gears turning in him, somewhere, some that will only stop when he's well and truly dead. The little version of himself perks up at the sound of something outside its dressing room.

"...Only to keep you talking," Ulrich adds.

"Oh yeah?" NotPhineas purrs.

"You're enjoying this, or you wouldn't be entertaining it," he presses. "Phineas likes to talk."

"Like- *ed.*" It lazily pops the second syllable.

"Of course," Ulrich says, searching again for that image of her, bleeding in the dark, hoping this time it's the real deal. "And *I* like to learn things. Why don't you tell me about yourself while we are here?"

"Why not just put away that toy and let us get this over with?"

"What are you going to do to me?"

It sighs, put-upon, darkness scattering in its breath like Phineas' sparks.

"Well," it says, kicking its feet behind itself. "Tain eats."

"Tain?"

"Us," it says. "Tain, in your terms."

"Don't you have a term for yourself?"

"Ate that too."

Ulrich feels more directed now, his fractionated thoughts strung along in a momentum building towards something he can't make out. Another splinter of himself, trying and failing to hold all of his terror, is frantically snatching scraps of information from the discussion and trying to mash them together into something, anything that might resemble an exit. He needs to get Phineas back too, but there are so many things in the way, it's all so... *vast.* He senses *something* important is coming down the line, but what good will it do if he can't understand it? He is so far out of his depth he can't even see the shore.

The Phineas thing makes a face and whines, *aaaugh,* gargling the sludge in its throat.

"You know what your problem is?" it says, tilting her head. "You're so goddamn *bleak.* You're scared and sad and that's all anyone around us ever is, we never get nothin' *fun.* "

It might be the dig at his *extremely fucking justified* despair, or the odd feeling of offense he feels hearing Phineas' drawl forced around the thing puppeting her, but Ulrich is indignant.

"I don't know," he says dryly. "You certainly seemed to *want* me frightened when you manipulated me in the hallway."

"Oh, that fear was aaall you." Phineas' body is dragged up higher, twirled in the air to recline back on its own shadow. Ulrich can see where it disappears into her back, phasing straight through the cheap shirt. "Do you know what 'tain' *means?*"

"It is..." All of Ulrich's brainpower is still banking transmissions, printing papers, sorting them and crumpling them and- "It is the shine, of a mirror surface."

"It's a bunch of things," NotPhineas says. "It's the shine, and the reflector, and sometimes it's a word you all use when you want to hang on to something. *Sus*-tain, *re*-tain contain-attain-"

"Uh-huh," Ulrich cuts in.

"Right! That makes us the mirrorshine of the *world*, the inverse. We're like the universe's clean-up crew: for every star crankin' out energy we're eatin' it back up."

"We only *take,* we can't *make,*" it goes on. Bitterly, Ulrich thinks. "Any fear you felt was already inside you before we showed up, we just..." The body tilts dangerously, dipping Phineas' head so the face can meet Ulrich's eyes again, upside down. "We just pulled your curtain back some." It grins, like they're sharing a secret. "You're so afraid, you're *so* haunted, Ulrich. We could feed off your tension for a long time. But you're not nearly so afraid as *she* is **greedy.**"

It folds in on itself, gleefully wringing Phineas' arms around her body.

"Fear is an unrefined emotion, an *animal* feels fear. Greed, *ambition* that *makes* greed, is so much- *more.*" As it rants, it drags Phineas' toes across the floor in some imitation of pacing. "People with the kind of soul that lets them order a *star* around aren't usually *stupid* enough to come to a place like this, they're never so young that an encounter with *us* is their first time having to make the choice between themselves and the sort of power she just had. Once she let go of herself to hang on to something else, this -" it drags fingers through the shadow across Phineas' face, stretching dark streaks into the air like rubber bands. "-*this* was inevitable."

"Commanders just got so much meat to 'em! And the little trick they do cuttin' up their souls turns their bodies into these *perfect* empty vessels! Little humankinds like *you* don't leave much space on your own, but the same thing that pulled *her* into the stone over there makes her easy pickin's for something like us if she's not careful. Once she stuck her head out the door, all we had to do was give her a good *shove.*"

Its tone has been flattening out, the body's jerky movements smoothing out as it hulks closer. The glee is nearly gone, like it can only be one thing at a time and it's pivoting from gloating to threatening. Phineas' body locks eyes with Ulrich.

"She'll die before she stops clinging to that power she cheated her way into, that thing in her chest will make sure of it."

It grips its stolen body tightly, and if Ulrich had more of his wits about him he would recognize a new desperation in its features.

"Yesss," it moans. "These remains should be *more* than enough to allow us to take our place under the sun."

"'Remains' seems presumptuous to me," Ulrich cuts in. The thing skews Phineas' face to smile at him again, and he wishes it would sneer or snarl instead. The smile is nauseating.

"Her body's giving us an anchor here in this plane, in a vessel that lets us move freely under the light." One of Phineas' fingers jumps, too independent of the others on her hand. "Vessels don't need to think, we threw those parts out. That thing we showed you? This?"

The image again of Phineas on her knees, staring down at something in her palms, almost how she'd appeared in the chamber with the pit when she'd collapsed. When Ulrich had helped her come out of it, and she'd told him-

The questing splinter of his mind explodes into the dressing room, ushering in a cloud of paper and static electricity.

Beacon!! it screams, shaking the shocked Dressing-Room-Ulrich with fingers covered in toner. *Beacon we're a **beacon!** Our **voice!!***

"*That* is all that's left of Phineas Kidd," NotPhineas says. "A speck of instinct distracted by the *idea* of a shiny thing that doesn't even exist now."

"I don't buy it," Ulrich says, breathless, hoping the tain is too caught up in itself to notice his breakthrough. "I think we both know the Phineas you just described wouldn't go so quietly."

Phineas' head tilts strangely at that.

"*Do* we know that?" it asks faintly, its voice a fractal. "*What* do we know? *We* have been getting flashes of you, here and there, but-" it backs away, to arm's length, and Ulrich tenses. "You seem so confident! *You* must know something, let's *both* know."

It raises Phineas' palms, and the eyes of her gloves and her skin flash with cyan. Ulrich's own vision blurs.

He feels himself hyperventilating before he comprehends why, his body lacking the lexicon and screaming at him blindly that *something is wrong, something is **wrong,***

"When's the last time you cleaned this place *out?*" Phineas' voice is in his ear- *in* his ear, close enough he's certain the tain has broken the light barrier somehow. It's vibrating straight through the joint of his jaw, through the bone; his hearing aid screeches with static and he tears it out. It burns in his hand, humming in a way that would worry him if he had the sense.

But he doesn't, he doesn't have any sense at all except to clutch uselessly at his hair while *something* squirms behind his eyes. It's, *digging,* like Ulrich's mind is a box of junk and it's trying to find something at the bottom.

"You've got all *kinds* of old traps laid up in here, this would hurt less if you'd *cooperate-*" Ulrich's head jerks like there's a dull hook lodged in it, tugging him into whatever angle makes the intrusion easier. He feels something wet his lips, tastes copper.

It goes on long enough that the initial shock wears off, and Ulrich is just starting to panic at the thought that this might *not* stop, but-

there she is again, Phineas kneeling in the darkness, empty eyes fixated on the light struggling in her hand,

but,

ulrich thinks,

when he groans under the excruciating connection to the tain,

he sees her turn

to the sound of him

-finally the thing lets him go.

"*Wow,*" NotPhineas crows, covering its face, its tendrils sending it into the air like a fountain. "Oh *wow. That* is a *long* **game!** You haven't stopped playing a part in *years.* Is there even a person in there anymore?"

Ulrich touches the back of his shaking hand to his mouth and it comes away bloody. His nose is bleeding. He watches the dark stain move in the light of his shield, almost hovering over his pale skin, and he feels...

He isn't sure. Something new, coming from another Ulrich again, or maybe Bel is waking up. What difference does it make.

"We had you all wrong!" The monster's delight is tangible, just like Phineas'. Phineas, who he is now certain is still there.

Beacon.

"We thought you wanted to save her so *she* could save *you*, but you're no coward. You're a *tactician*, you're out here picking up chess pieces!"

Ulrich checks over his hearing aid, only half-listening to what's being said while the ringing in his both his ears dies down. It doesn't seem damaged, but it's been struggling to function since they fell down the elevator shaft, the distortion in this place interfering with the starstone components inside. Even bog-standard inert circuitry reacts this close to an unregulated power source, it appears. He slips it in his pocket and hopes he'll live long enough to use it again.

"Oh Ulrich, we're so sorry we doubted the complexity of you," NotPhineas says brightly. "This game's put you through the wringer, what a *bitch*, getting so unlucky after coming all this way."

Ulrich removes his hat and reaches inside; it's so cold in this chamber he hardly notices the usual drop in temperature when he touches the subspace. He thinks, and his handkerchief is in his hand. It's impossibly soft against his skin as he swipes the worst of the blood from his upper lip. The monster swoops in close to observe. He knows it's watching the lotus embroidered on the cotton, red staining pink.

"What would your mistress think if she saw you now?" it asks, like it really does want to know. It's starving, Ulrich thinks dimly, and unlike him it has no qualms about licking chocolate from its fingers. "You're not much of a knight."

"Ach," Ulrich says, regarding the ruined handkerchief with no room to feel guilty about it. "Yes, well. She is not much of a *mistress,* either."

Both of them turn to the sound of one of the dice spitting sparks, only for an instant, but Ulrich's heart stops as the light construct distorts before coming back into focus.

Jolted into motion by adrenaline, Ulrich's dark mechanism fits the new feeling into place for him. He has finally, finally reached the bottom. Even a worm will turn, and so, it seems, will Ulrich.

"You're running out of time, Cheshire," NotPhineas sings. Ulrich rolls his eyes behind his mask. "And your plan stinks, we checked."

It's all true. He is not much of a knight, but he's never claimed to be one— Ulrich is a performer, a *professional,* and professionals finish out the fucking scene.

Ulrich dredges up that menthol feeling, icy cool on his tongue, and begins to weave his lifeline.

"Why was it I was able to dispel you earlier?" he asks, warming up. "When you came after Phineas the first time?"

"That misstep had nothing to do with *you,*" it says, suddenly petulant. It has the effect Ulrich had been hoping for: there is Phineas, evoked in the tain's thoughts, the only place she exists for now. A doorway goes both directions.

"You wanna know what that was?" the tain spits. "Compared to *her?* **You're** so insignificant we didn't even notice you were *there* until you spoke up. You surprised us, that's all."

It rises high again, moving Phineas' marred face dangerously close to Ulrich's through the light, and he tries to focus on her other face instead.

"We'll give it to ya, smooth operator. Your words are sharp, you have *conviction.* But you got about as much spiritual clout as the rubber in your *shoes.* And," It is so close now he can see the individual star-specks making up the single eye, like static. "After lookin' at you? You will never, *ever* feel anything as strongly as you felt that fear before. You're thinkin' too hard now, all those walls you hide behind are gonna keep you from using the one weapon you got. You can't suddenly make up for years of atrophy. You're going to die holding a loaded gun because you cut off your own trigger finger."

"There is no light in you anywhere, Ulrich, and that's not going to change just because you've decided it's worth something."

Ulrich's laugh surprises him— a mean thing that bursts from him like a blade, and the monster flinches away. Only a little, but away it does go.

"You say that as if it is news to me," Ulrich says, and in the fizzling light of his shield he thinks he can almost see something else shimmering in the air ahead of him, a ghostly silver light in his better eye. "You made that big show of rooting around in my head and you think explaining to me that I am afraid is going to throw me? Of course I am afraid! I am the only person with any sense *anywhere* in this god damned desert!"

It's so easy, once he gets started; he so rarely gets the chance for a monologue.

He has built up a *lot* of material.

"You are all *brutes!*" He can hear the tinny echo of his own voice bouncing from the forcefield and hopes the part that matters is making it through. "You are *incompetent* brutes! It is *unacceptable* that I am down here dealing with this shit because my boss could not keep the *right key in her hand!*"

"You think I am lacking in genuine emotion? I am *incensed!* You cannot find any light in me because it is blocked out by the *millstone around my neck!* I am *better than this!!*"

The tain lets him carry on, and he can't figure out if that's a good thing or not, but: it's *working,* tapping into the well of every awful feeling Ulrich Weiss has been mired in since he first saw Phineas Kidd in the street the night before. He can feel it, coiling through him and carried along on his words, the thing that had driven back the tain, whatever bullshit fucking thing Phineas has been babbling about all this time. He's woven a lifeline, all around him, ready to be cast.

"And Phineas is the worst of all of you!" He's screaming now, he would be pacing if he weren't in this cage. Like a castaway hailing a passing ship, he *heaves:* "God *damn* you Phineas Kidd for dragging me into this mess, you wake up and get us *out!!*"

phineas,

sees something,

silver,

and she seizes like a patient waking on the operating table,

Ulrich feels another indescribable invasion, something latching onto his soul, but it's *warm*. He tastes sawdust, and he is manic with some unbearable combination of euphoria and fury.

"You stupid motherfucker! I hope you can hear *every word of this!!*" Ulrich shouts, his hands balling into fists. He can feel the line between himself and Phineas like it's physical, weaving from his body to hers; it's hard to resist the impulse to pull at nothing with his hands. "You said this is something I can do! Get out here so I can kill you myself!"

The tain has been in some kind of stasis since Ulrich's ugly laugh startled it, but now it focuses on Ulrich anew. It radiates so much malice Ulrich nearly stumbles over his litany.

"You're throwin' a fit 'cause someone else is playing with your toy," it snarls, a tone far too deep and full of stone to rightfully come from Phineas' throat. "I saw everything in *her* head too, you know. You got all these big plans for her, but do you know what *she* thought of *you?*"

"*I do not CARE!*" Ulrich wails, trying not to lose his inertia. He can't afford sentimentality now, he *definitely* doesn't feel that one strongly enough for this.

The tain moves Phineas' body in closer again, the single eye furious and damning.

"She *trusted* you, completely," it hisses. "She'd've *died* for you. We don't know what she saw in you- We don't think *she* understood why."

Ulrich slaps his hands over his ears and keeps talking, calling her name, throwing every threat and insult and complaint he's been storing up and hoping it will accomplish *anything*. He can feel Phineas' presence working hand over hand in earnest along their unbelievable connection, but whatever he's doing to draw her back to this plane doesn't keep the tain out.

"This girl," the voice that reaches him is somehow even clearer now, behind his eyes again. "This cosmic force *infinitely* more important than you, *she* picked *you.*"

Staring down at the floor, anywhere but that flaying eye, Ulrich sees the die spark again. It's going to go any second. The feeling of Phineas approaching, whatever that means, is *far* too slow.

"Hurry up!" he cuts himself off in the middle of a line, letting the fear infect his voice too, why not.

"*Empires* have gone under trying to gain the love of capricious stars!" the tain shudders in his head. It might be genuinely enraged. "And YOU - You were gonna throw it RIGHT back in her face!"

"Of course she picked me!" Ulrich fires back, reaching under his shirt for his gun. Glückssache? Houndstooth?? If the light infected the dice, maybe the revolver bullets-

"Of *course* she picked me!" he repeats, tearing the cylinder open and letting the empty shells clatter at his feet. "There is nothing else here worth *choosing!* You wouldn't find a deal this good anywhere! *I am a valuable asset!!*" He laughs again, loading the new rounds like he's cleaving meat. "Money changed hands! And she found me out here in the dirt, she should *be* so lucky!!"

The second Ulrich clicks the cylinder back in place, the shield fizzles and dies.

Its rage dissolving back into elation, the tain claps Phineas' hands together and provides a single opportunity. Ulrich's shot is a direct hit to the forehead. The bullet stops dead against the surface of the tar, Phineas' body erupting in delicate blue arcs of light that skitter away along the shadow holding it aloft. The spent round bounces harmlessly to the ground, then the tain drives Phineas' fist into Ulrich's face.

Phineas had been holding back on the roof. The world freezes around him, light and sound popping out of existence, and he has a curious floating instant to panic that he's been knocked unconscious before he opens his eyes to the stone floor. The pain catches up with him about when he notices his mask is gone, searing pressure near his orbital and somewhere close to his hairline where his head had cracked against the ground. His gun is still in his hand, grip seized around it so tightly he might never let go again.

He can sense the shadow behind him, and the line between himself and Phineas is fading, he has to get on his feet, keep talking-

"We know you got more fight in you than that!" Phineas' voice thunders, disgusted and delighted in equal parts. *"Get up!"*

Clinging to his frustration that Phineas *still* can't get it together when they are *so* close, Ulrich gets himself turned around and fires two more clumsy shots. They are not even near misses. His head is spinning-

"There we go, hey!" The shadow is blocking out so much of the light now, the smoke and tendons and whatever else is going on have fanned out all around Phineas like hideous wings. "Give us another, this commanding stuff feels *great.*"

"Phineas we are out of *time!!*" Ulrich shrieks. Shrieking *hurts.* The longer he sits upright the more it sinks in that something important had been damaged when he hit his head, he isn't even sure this is working any more. "There's nothing else I can *do* you have to come *back!!*"

"You're so boring," the tain grumbles. It raises Phineas' hands, palms out. "But if you're really that tired, we can just make this quick."

It *does* happen quickly, but it happens on one side before the other, so Ulrich has the experience of seeing his own right eye staring back at him from the circle on Phineas' palm. It's dim, and he's too preoccupied trying to fight the sudden disorientation that comes with the world flattening to fully comprehend the new perspective before it goes from him. The vision in his left eye spirals sickeningly ahead, superimposing a bizarre fisheye view of himself sprawled on the stone floor before he can't see anything at all.

It's a trick,

"It's a trick," Ulrich mumbles, his tongue growing sluggish in his mouth. He knows something earthshattering has just happened but it's too big to fit into his perception just now. It waits off to the side, a wave hung in thin air, ready to ravage him. "It's a trick, it's not *real,*"

"Don't worry about it," the tain says, in the air or in his head. He feels something like cold, velvety silicone slide around his waist, his neck, more and more until it's lifting him from the floor. He doesn't have the ability to deal with it, still trying to wrap his head around the fact that he's lost his sight. "There was nothing for you down this road anyway, Ulrich. You were never s'posed to be one of the good guys, and frankly neither was Phineas. You two would have ruined each other eventually." As the grip around him tightens, threading through his hair to wrench his head backwards, Ulrich can feel Phineas' body getting closer. He flinches weakly when it reaches out and touches his bared neck. "We've saved you both a lot of trouble."

The touch near his throat, where Phineas had said he held something worth wanting, vibrates along the silver lifeline like a plucked guitar string. Very faint now, but it's there. It's still there, and somewhere in the vibrations so is she.

Still, *still,* because it is so fundamental to what Ulrich *is,* he stays the fucking course. In the dark is not the same as dead, even *this* dark, and he is not dead yet. He still holds his gun. One more time.

"My teeth are fake," his voice is in tatters, but he can feel the menthol weaving in the tension of his throat. His blind eyes stare out at nothing, his addled mind clawing for the image of Phineas he'd been shown, imagining the line in her hands. "Nearly all of them, all of my forward teeth are porcelain implants."

"We saw," the tain says, curious, drawing its fingertips sickeningly across his carotid artery.

"Then you also saw that my natural teeth had to be surgically removed from the right hand of the woman who beat them out of me." His grin is probably more of a grimace. "An infection took her ring finger, while I went on to be known for my smile."

"What are you getting at?"

"You have seen all there is to see of the both of us, and you still seem to be under the impression that we are going to go quietly. If I die here, you are coming down with me. It's already done." He laughs a little bit, pained and pathetic. "My associate is going to kill you and that is a fact, regardless of what I look like when she gets here."

He feels one last tug on his cast line. This time, it doesn't let up. The tain must feel it too; its eye widens briefly. One of Phineas' hands twists in Ulrich's shirt, wrenching him in close, and the other squeezes his neck, cutting off his air in a thready gasp.

"Oh, *sneaky* boy," the tain hisses. "That's enough of *that.* "

Then,

The fist around his neck reaches inside, *inside,* through skin and vein and muscle all the way down to the bone, wraps a liquid nitrogen grip around his spine, oozes between the vertebrae. He wants to die he wants to *die,* it's seeping into his airway, he can *taste* it-

It touches something new and Ulrich feels it *everywhere,* like blood in the water rushing to color everything around it.

The tain *pulls.*

It is not pain, but the violation is so fundamental and complete his ragged-edged sense of humanity can't even tell him how to react, he cannot even begin to process the primordial theft that is happening to him. They're taking something he didn't know he had, tearing the ghost of his heart out through his neck and dragging the blood in his body backwards, out with it, the wild ends of a root system squirming through the tight channels of his veins inch by agonizing inch. He refuses to scream, not out of any sense of pride but because he is sure they'll take *that* too and the entire world has narrowed to the senseless concept of *not letting go, stop taking stop **taking***. He tries to curl in on himself, he grinds his teeth, screws his already sightless eyes shut until he feels cold tears on his cheeks, thrashes uselessly in the shadows' grip.

"Easy, big guy." The tain's voice is severely misaligned with Phineas', losing itself in claiming its meal. The voice is nearly drowned under the din of what's happening to him, but Ulrich feels the words in his head anyway, vibrating up through the hold on his spine. They're ravenous, a million appetites' anticipation is an unbearable incomprehensibility to his small existence. They are going to tear him to pieces. He *hopes* he dies here, this *has* to stop somehow, it *must.*

Finally the roots, the threads of his soul go taut and come free of his body. The shadow in his neck withdraws too and he drags in a ruined breath. Phineas' voice squeals, ecstatic, grating harshly in Ulrich's ears, and he hears the tain turn away from him. No longer supported, Ulrich sags limply in the shadows' hold.

"OoOOh, it's so *pretty,"* Phineas' voice coos. "Almost artificial, what *have* you been doing with yourself?"

The steady, cold voice that keeps Ulrich alive informs him he is going into shock. It wonders idly if Ulrich will ever not be in shock again. It is hard for any part of Ulrich to feel anything but hollow. Even Bel is silent; no hands snaking around him, no voice in his ear.

A tremor goes through the shadow holding him, and when his head lolls on his neck he sees light. A flash of yellow. And now he feels it on his skin, the warmth that had been surging down the silver lifeline.

Mine,

Ulrich feels tears running over his cheeks that aren't really his, hot against his freezing skin. Something is happening ahead of him. It ripples through the darkness still wound around him, the feel of moving matter as the tain contorts Phineas' body to look around itself. The temperature spikes in the chamber.

"Mine," he hears, a voice that sizzles like a lit fuse. The echo of it intensifies, and the darkness in Phineas' voice *screeches* like a house falling in on itself.

"That is MINE!"

There's a wet, choked-off noise, and the tain's voice cuts out right in the middle of its screech— the unmistakable sound of a body fighting the grip of the thing strangling it.

The heat is unbearable, the light blinding to his blinded eyes. As it is, Ulrich does not have the resources to be terrified. He knows this new thing isn't here to hurt him, but it's come too late for him to feel anything but a bitter, primal sense of justice that the thing that's killed him is dying too.

His body begins to slip down, the sensation of ashes hushing around him as the shadows holding it evaporate. He never reaches the floor, he simply keeps falling, embracing the nothing as it folds over him.

...

...embracing the nothing goes on for a while.

Ulrich feels the sun on his face, the same way he'd felt it before when the hares visited him.

The sun speaks.

"Don't cower from me, precious thing."

Is he cowering? He can't feel-

He *can.* He's submerged, thrown into the sea again but it's *light,* every numb nerve ending sings back to life like morning glories under the dawn. He learns his eyes are still closed, because he can feel his face again when impossibly careful fingers tuck his hair behind his ear, drift gently across his forehead. The pain there is gone, the worrying pressure that had made it so hard to think straight. He opens his eyes, and he can see someone smiling at him. He can *see.*

"There we are," the impossibly careful someone says. The voice is gentle but restrained, thrumming with what Ulrich can only think of as electricity; it's like watching a wildfire from behind glass, safe on this side. She (he thinks) is holding Ulrich's face in one hand and something he knows instinctively is his soul in the other, each like something delicate and valuable.

He senses something familiar where they touch. Wild confidence, fury that fortifies without consuming— this is the thing that lurks behind Phineas' eyes, stretches in her shadow. She looks like some facsimile of Phineas: a torn sailcloth tied around a waist, nothing underneath but stars; a human torso with a massive hollow where the heart should be, blistering with light that makes Ulrich tear up. Above a cut throat, the head is only a smile underneath an explosion of the same sunshine that fills the chest wound. When his eyes roam across the light Ulrich is wracked with a shuddering sob. It's some kind of reflex, some instinct brought out by proximity to the divine. The hand cradling his face thumbs away one tear so softly it wrings another from him.

She offers his soul back to him.

"Take it," she says. "We want all of you, not just this, and all of you as you are."

It is an impossible effort to look away from the light, but Ulrich is coming back to life enough to notice the absence in his throat. Loath as he is to shake off the comforting hand against his skin, Ulrich reaches up to swipe one wrist across his face so he can see better. He finds the deity's arms are severed at the elbows, the forearms blackened with soot, manacled in brilliant golden chains that weave back into the chest. And in the palm...

Ulrich's soul is a nearly perfect sphere, the inside threaded with carnival glass, spun into humming machinery that echoes on forever the way two mirrors will echo. It is shrouded in blue mist that very clearly denotes it as separate from the golden deity. That should be offensive, such vibrant colors should be at odds, but Ulrich knows: blue and yellow are complementary.

He reaches out to touch it and it shimmers away. That's all it takes, almost laughable after the ordeal of removing it. The absence fades and the world is right again. As he comes back to himself, he can feel parts of his mind waking up to try and scrutinize what's happening, to ratchet back to vigilance, but the halo engulfing him sets them all at ease just as quickly. He finds he doesn't have the energy to rail against it.

"She won't remember most of this. What either of you have done here," Phineas' passenger says. Her voice is even more adamant now that Ulrich has all his faculties back in place to appreciate it, it shivers between his ears and down his spine like a singing bowl. *"I will. I'll know it so maybe she'll feel it too. The way she feels things. But I wanted to tell you, dear thing, you've been very brave. You've done so well."*

Ulrich opens his mouth to speak but can't manage to get the words out. Whether it's the divinity or the trauma he can't tell.

"You've been very *loyal*. Even if it's not Phineas you're loyal to."

"I-I," Ulrich manages, pressed by urgency. She puts both palms to his temples, bringing him in close to where her face should be, flooding his eyes with fresh tears.

"I know. I *know,*" she insists. "Your cause is noble. There is fortune in your footsteps, Ulrich Weiss, and I'd like to see where they will lead left uninhibited."

Confounded by the sympathy, overwhelmed again by the weight of things, Ulrich only nods. The mouth curves back into its smile and he has to shut his eyes against it.

"Stay your course," she says. "Your secrets will be safe with me."

He whispers, "Okay," and mercifully that is the end of it. The deity lets her hands fall from him and he wishes he weren't so sorry for them to go.

"I'm going to wake her now," she says. Ulrich can tell she's drifting away from him, the warmth ebbing. "If all goes well, you and I won't have a chance to speak again soon."

Ulrich opens his eyes to watch her go, but it's getting too bright, everything flaring to an impossible white.

"I hope things work out for you," he feels.

Something murmurs along the curve of his jaw, like sand scattering across his skin.

Good luck.

◉◉◉

It takes a lot longer than Phineas is comfortable with (like, an extra thirty seconds), but eventually Ulrich sighs in his sleep and opens his eyes to stare up at her. She'd wanted to set his head in her lap to get it off the hard floor, but with all the blood crusting over his hair she hadn't wanted to try moving him until he moved himself, so she's just been hovering anxiously instead.

"Hey," Phineas says, smiling but uneasy in her belly. Ulrich's face is still sleepy, he's just looking up into her eyes without saying anything. It's *weird*. His halo is placid, pastel blue around him so quiet she's almost worried there's something wrong with him in his head. He touches his throat with two fingers and takes a slow breath, closes his eyes again.

"Hey, hang on, don't-" Phineas fusses, her stomach lurching. It keeps lurching, and all at once she is positive she's going to be sick.

Yep, right now: she scrambles to her feet to get away from Ulrich, gets as many paces between them as she can, and heaves up everything squirming in her stomach.

It *hurts*, so cold it rips at every part of her it touches, but she coughs up the entire slimy mess all at once.

"Eugh," Ulrich says from somewhere behind. Phineas suppresses a gag as she spits up what's left, trying to get the rotten taste from her mouth.

It's a pile of sludge, some remnant of the tain that had flooded her body. Total horrorshow, but it's *out,* and inert now-

"*p l e a s e*"

Maybe not. Phineas hears Ulrich recoil and puts herself more firmly between him and the thing wriggling on the ground, ready to square up.

A blue fissure opens along the pile of tar, tearing apart like a mouth.

"*Mercy!*" The tain has to fight to get the word out, its speech slurred and wet without teeth or tongue. "We did not recognize you, Star Astray we did not *know.*"

Phineas stands her ground as it slithers closer. She doesn't think Ulrich can see her companion, but she is still very close to the surface and only getting more pronounced; Phineas has to work hard to keep her face under control. Imperious is mean, too mean to show Ulrich yet, but it's a preferable look to sprouting extra teeth and eyes.

"We *saw,*" the tain rasps, miserable and weak. "*Mercy,* in you we saw. *Light.* Here it is so cold, *please.*" It gets close enough Phineas does take a step away.

"Don't leave us to the dark," it moans. "Commander, take us *with* you, to the *sun.*"

For a moment Phineas is too stunned to say anything. After everything, after *everything* that has happened, the-

The fucking *audacity.*

"Phineas," Ulrich says, rough. "Phineas don't-"

He impels her out of her fugue, but she doesn't hear what he says.

"I know you're watching," she says sharply, looking up at the starstone blazing across the chamber. There is no feature anywhere to indicate it, but she can feel it's listening.

"Fight's over," Phineas states, sunlight ringing in her voice. "We won."

Rage burns in her blood as she turns her gaze back to the pathetic thing on the floor.

"Come get your trash."

The tain rears away like it's been struck. Smoke rises from its surface, the light suddenly scalding it.

"NO!" it bellows, *"NO! SELFISH* HUMAN!!"

There is nowhere for it to hide here in the middle of the chamber, all it can do is sizzle under the glare of starlight, tearing away the glaze of its skin as it melts.

"You wield salvation yet you condemn us to *hell!!"* It spits, writhing in agony that sticks between Phineas' teeth. "Where is your *compassion!!"*

"You don't **deserve** it," she rumbles, cruel energy vibrating in her lower register. She hardly blinks, she wants to watch it struggle. Dimly, she thinks her companion might know something she doesn't; she usually doesn't feel this sort of outrage for herself.

Shuddering, stretching and squashing into thinner and more unnatural shapes, the tain is delirious now as it boils away. There is so little left.

"How easily you cast judgement!" it shrieks. "How does it feel?! We *know* you Phineas Kidd! We know things you won't admit even to *yourself!* Let us reassure you-!"

The dripping mouth, blistering and bubbling, forces itself together and rounds on Phineas. In one last burst of froth, the most hateful thing Phineas has ever felt:

"YOU WILL MAKE A *WONDERFUL* GOD!!"

Then it gives up the ghost, the mouth caving in under its own weight in a scatter of ashes. In the spot where it had been, there's a black smudge that nearly looks like a face. Phineas gets the feeling it's laughing at her.

She waits for the shadow to dissipate, the chamber to go still, then she lets go of the tension in her chest in a soft sigh, lit with fading sparks. The way they spawn from starlight, she knows the tain will build back up again, but right now the infestation is gone from this place. They did it, it's finished.

Oh, they *did* it!

Phineas giggles and spins on her heel, immediately lighter.

"Hey good job! We-!"

The look on Ulrich's face stops her dead.

"What's wrong?" she asks, an awful surety creeping up her spine. She's seen that look before, but... "Are you hurt?"

She wants to be closer to him, for somebody's sake, but each of the two steps she takes sends Ulrich's shoulders higher around his ears. His grip tightens around the revolver Phineas has just noticed he's holding. He isn't pointing it at her, but he isn't putting it away yet either, and the flinch is unmistakable. Phineas stumbles to a stop, too far away, something humiliatingly close to panic welling up in her.

He isn't going to shoot her; he would have done it before she turned around. Maybe holding it made him feel better when the tain was here, but why does he still need it?

Ulrich is staring right in her eyes, lights in his halo firing like synapses. He is thinking very carefully about how to begin a difficult conversation, because Phineas is in trouble again.

"What's that look for?" she asks, her heart thrashing while she suffers a dozen preemptive punishments. "Listen, those things *really* aren't worth- That looked really bad probably but you have to understand these are god... *things,* they don't-"

"What is the last thing you remember?" Ulrich demands, neatly angling the straightaway she's tearing along.

"Remember?" she stammers. "Did I..." Are there more wounds on Ulrich's face than there were when they came in? He'd, he'd *tripped,* hadn't he? Did he hit his head?

He sees her looking.

"Nothing?" Ulrich asks tightly, frizzed out like a cat. "Think *hard,* Phineas."

"We were running, and I...you were carrying me, and the starstone, then I came back to get you and..."

And then a dark spot. And then Ulrich here, unconscious, hurt. Flinching.

"What did I do?" Phineas asks, her voice too high. She touches her own face where the worst of his wounds is, just under the curtain of his hair. Above the angry yellow of a fresh bruise on the bone near his eye.

"Ulrich," she manages, horrified to feel her eyes tearing up. "I didn't-"

The sob surprises her, a desperate dragging of stale cave air into her lungs, but the sound is so wretched and sad to her own ears it sends her right over the edge she hadn't known she was near. Every cell in Phineas' body is wracked with grief, so heavy it drags her to her knees. She doesn't even think to feel ashamed, gripped so totally by the need to get this feeling *out of her* she curls over, fists her hands in her hair, and falls apart.

"I *d-didn't,"* she sobs, snotty and disgusting, unable to look at him, "I'm s-"

Everyone was right, everybody who had ever run from her had been *right* because this is all she can *be,* the only thing Phineas Kidd is any good for is *hurting things,* the only thing she can do is *break* and *burn-*

"Phineas," Ulrich's voice is as mean as she's ever heard it, close above her now. She forces her eyes open and she can see his shoes on the floor near her face. *"Stop it,"* he says like a slap.

Has she been talking? Phineas sniffles, uncurling enough to drag the backs of her wrists through the mess on her face.

"I can't d-do it," she babbles wretchedly. "I c-can't get close to anybody without- this, being- *this,* I ruin everything I touch, even *you-"*

"Phineas *look* at me."

She does, small and worthless.

Ulrich might be the most relentlessly tired person Phineas has ever met, and he looks every bit of it now. Her own tears are quietly streaking across his cheeks like water over a statue, clashing with the stony, authoritative expression etched into his features. His halo is dark and insistent; from this angle it looks like a stormcloud behind him. He is still so perfect. Through the riptide of her misery the feeling of the tain thrumming in her blood is fresh, the howling empty amplifying the vicious part of her that wants to *make* him stay, but it isn't driving her the way it normally does. The burning only burns her now, there isn't any other fuel left.

She'd gotten so *far* this time, but if he is still so scared, if she *still* can't keep him here without force then what is the point. What's the point of *any* of this.

"I-I," she tries clearing her throat, but it does nothing to steady things. "I didn't. Mean to, I would never-"

"Would never *what?*" Ulrich demands. "Because from my perspective you were very clear about your choice to let that happen."

Phineas is starting to realize it isn't just anger coming from him, or even fear. Ulrich's demeanor triggers old half-memories, flashes of strangers in roads, collapsed in grocery store aisles— fidgeting on Jo's examination table. He watches her with the focus that colors a person's halo while they're waiting for someone to come back with the doctor. Nothing is good, we aren't sure exactly how not-good it is yet, we're hoping somebody who knows more will be able to tell us what to do to make it better, *soon.* Maybe it only feels that way now because Phineas is looking up at him from the floor, and there's blood all over his face. They both look like they've crawled from the wreckage.

She doesn't know how to proceed. Ulrich doesn't soften, still spring-coiled like he expects her to lunge at him, but he says: "Stand up."

"Wh-"

"Get on your feet and talk to me."

When she still doesn't move, he reaches down.

"Get *up.*"

...His hand? He wants her to touch him?

"But..." she gulps when her voice comes out too thready. "A-aren't you..?"

Ulrich takes his hand back, but it's only to gesture, like trying to clear cobweb from his fingers.

"This is ridiculous," he spits. "Why are *you* crying?"

"Because I don't want you to b-be scared of me," Phineas snivels. "I d-don't want you to think I'm-"

"What, the same?" Ulrich barks. "A *demon?* A **monster?** Do you think you are the first monster I've met?!"

"I killed that little thing," Phineas whines, the next statement making her weepy again. "And I *hurt you!*"

Ulrich, now thoroughly confusing her, shakes his head. "If you hadn't killed it I was going to."

Phineas takes an extra second to process this, her tears ebbing while she thinks.

"...You thought I was gonna let it go," she says quietly.

"There are times for mercy and this was not one of them. That would have been *stupid."* Ulrich sighs through his nose, and a little bit of the tense in his shoulders goes. He'd put the gun away at some point. "I still can't make any sense of you. You were talking about power, just before you...turned. It was nothing *good,* but you used 'we', even then you were still thinking of us both."

"O-of course I was, I would never...That's what-"

"Yes!" Ulrich shakes his head again, balling his hands into fists. "You *keep saying that.* 'We're *friends',* 'we're a *team',* you think we're this-"

He groans and paces away from her, his halo so blue it's nearly black, such disparate emotions flashing over each other Phineas can't make out what's happening.

"My *god* what is *wrong* with you?" He kneads the heels of his hands against his eyes. "We met *yesterday* and I have treated you like *shit* from the *moment I saw you!* I *shot* you and somehow, not *two hours later,* I've bandaged you up and you're *sleeping on my couch?* I'm following you into *this* place?" He spreads his arms like he's in a play, and Phineas' smile cracks along her tight expression. "And now you're worried *I'm* going to think badly of *you?"*

He schools himself back into his dourness like winding a leash around his wrist.

"This is *not* how I operate. I am not sure this is how *anyone* operates. You've been giving me the benefit of the doubt all this time and I've done *nothing* to deserve it, and *you're* afraid *I'm-"*

"Ulrich you don't have to-"

"Shut up! I am not finished!"

Phineas shuts up, so bewildered her tears have all but dried now.

"...This is not the point I wanted to make," he says levelly. "We need to get something understood, *right* now, before we go any further. You are, in fact, a violent maniac. That was you, this *is* you, you made *every decision* that got us here. But if you act like it's this-this foregone conclusion, that you're some purely destructive force out of your own control, you are absolving yourself of the responsibility of managing it."

"But it's," Phineas stammers. "It's, not-"

"What is the alternative?" Ulrich demands. "For *either* of us? Because I know if I were not *exactly* the monster I currently am then I would be *dead.* **You?**"

Phineas nods without thinking, still trying to decipher what he's getting at.

"Now what sort of monster do you want to be?" he demands.

She sniffs; she knows the answer, but it's hard to put it in words for someone else.

"...One that helps," she settles on.

"Then *figure it out,*" Ulrich says severely. "This is what you've got, figure out how to make it work for you. Be a monster that helps and do *not* fucking put me through that again."

"But why would you..." Phineas knows she should let well enough alone, but she'll pick at these stitches forever if she doesn't ask this now. "Why would you *stay,* with me, after all that?"

Ulrich huffs at her like she's said something stupid again.

"Do you really want me to be honest with you?"

"I think so."

"Then listen to me," he says, getting right up close to her. He grips her shoulders tight and Phineas can feel him trembling, maybe as worked up as she is. "Do you remember what we talked about in the station last night? Why we were interested in each other in the first place?"

"Um...Needed things, we both could tell the other had something worth...worth wantin'."

"Yes," Ulrich nods like he's speaking to a child, still holding her. "Whatever you did just now, whatever that was, I am *never* going to find it again, and that is what I *want*. I *want* this, Phineas. You, exactly like this, is why I came to you at all."

No sparks, no mist. He is stating facts so simple there are no textures or grooves for gilding to cling to.

"We still have unfinished business here, up on that ship that neither of us can handle alone, and I am certainly not going to let this keep us from it." He swallows hard, she watches it shudder in his neck. Then he says, "You think you're going to catch the sun? Cross Kairos?"

"Yes," Phineas says, answering automatically even though the change in subject surprises her. Ulrich nods.

"Then you will. And if that is where such a valuable asset is going, that is where I am going too."

...it takes a moment for Phineas to process what he's saying. Getting this here, now, throws her enough she can't respond right away; she almost asks him to say it again. Ulrich doesn't smile, and Phineas can feel it's because this is something serious for him, this sort of commitment nearly ritualistic.

And still, hovering in his edges is enough murkiness to remind her what he is. He's bending the knee, or he's putting his claim on her— one thing, two things. Whichever it is: what he is saying now is truthful, and he is holding out his hand to her again. If he isn't afraid of her, she isn't afraid of him either.

Phineas takes his hand, sunshine purring in her chest.

"Thank you," she says, and now Ulrich grins. Softly, with no teeth.

"Let's go get your ship."

Hello?

Hello? Are we—

ah,

one m-moment...

8

Rook's wardrobe consists almost exclusively of cool winter tones. In the past she'd opted for geometric angles in vinyl or plastic, but more and more she's found herself opting for softer fabrics that drape well. She's been thinking a lot lately about why Dad had started wearing things like robes and sashes and statement headwear. She hasn't been able to get her mind off of the connection she'd made in his office between his outfit and the covers of her old fantasy novels, wondering whether he really *had* started dressing that way to...what, connect with her? Maybe his choices in apparel have nothing to do with her, but that thought is only a vestigial fit of logic that comes and goes without her notice. It doesn't matter anyway; she'd been the only one to ever take photos, and mostly of herself. There's no way to know what her father looked like before she got here.

Once Rook finds the outfit she wants in her closet, she spies an old shawl hanging behind it. It's knitted in a variegated deep sea colorway, asymmetrical and oversized. Thick, warm, even though she doesn't get cold often now. That might look good when she ignores Dad's order and goes out to deal with that horrid little commander and *Ulrich Fucking Weiss.*

What a rotten day it's been.

Rook tugs the shawl from its wooden hanger, ignores that it reminds her of the lighting in Dad's study, and tosses her armload of clothes onto her bed. Makeup first.

When she settles at the vanity the lotus pin is waiting there, near her jewelry box where she left it when she went to shower. It's like looking at an animal taxidermied in an aggressive pose, a snarling bear that's *definitely* dead, but *maybe* it isn't, and you shouldn't be standing quite so close to the teeth.

That's so stupid. Rook viciously snaps a clip into her hair and snatches the pin from the table.

It's shrunk down on its own again. She pinches her fingers in the air and draws back, like pulling a string. The pin shivers before billowing out, new petals stretching into being from the center as it blossoms from the size of a coin to a real lotus bloom that covers Rook's palm. The glass petals are warm, and it glows faintly pink. It's only costume jewelry, probably faulty given how it shifts when she isn't looking, but Rook can't shake the feeling it's...acting out.

The knock at the door makes her flinch, she curls her hand into a fist and the sharp points of the glass petals bite into her fingers. She hurls it onto her vanity, shaking out her stinging hand as someone peeks into her room.

"Miss-"

The rest of the sentence is strangled into a shriek and the shriek is punctuated by the sound of icicles embedding themselves in the doorframe like flung daggers. It's the kid with red hair, she catches the color of it before he slams the door shut.

"*What* have I said about *knocking?!*" Rook shouts.

There's an uncertain pause, then a tentative touch that eases into a rapid knock.

"*Come in!*" she says, syrupy. The kid slowly cracks the door open and eases into the room, tracking dust all over the carpet, of fucking course.

"Miss Eisse," he stammers, avoiding her eyes. His name might be Gary, or...Gwen? "Sorr-sorry to bother you, but there's. Uh. There's an issue, and we thought you might want to-"

"You *thought* incorrectly." Rook gets to her feet and he almost runs out the door again. "My father has made it *very* clear he doesn't want me getting involved in anything happening today, you didn't *think* that an issue should be taken to *him* instead?"

"Well that's, uh-" Gary-Gwen's workboots thud against the door as he backs away from her advance. "We can't. Find him."

Rook fists her hands in his filthy shirt and drags him down to eye level.

"What do you *mean* you can't *find* him?" The drop in temperature makes her growl come out cloudy in the scant space between them.

"Just what I *said!*" he squeaks. "Nobody's seen him since he left to deal with the commander last night, and now there's a problem and we really need to-"

Rook misses whatever else he says while she reaches out with her halo, digging down into all the bizarre twists and inlets of the ship. It takes her longer than she likes but in the space of a few extra thoughts she does finally feel a rancid, spoiled spot of rotten-fruit-black hiding in an inaccessible part of the ship's space. He must have gone straight there after they met in the hallway last night and just. Not come back.

"Shit," Rook mutters. Gary, possibly Gwen, stops talking.

"Ma'am?" he asks, cringing. Rook shakes her head, forgetting to be mean for a moment.

"Well, what? What's the issue?"

"I just *told* you," he says desperately. "The *town* is on fire."

The town of Last Chance is a red-orange watercolor painting around the tower, the heat haze riddled with pillars of black smoke. Here on Rook's balcony, a tiny snowstorm gathers around her.

"What is *wrong* with you hicks?" she asks, almost too shocked by the absurdity to be properly angry. "Why are you burning your *own town?*"

"I-"

A shooting star, and a column of smoke dissipates in a shower of gold. Rook leans further over the railing, squinting like it will help.

"What the hell is *that?*"

"Ellie- The, the woman who runs the bar," the kid clears his throat. "She's a Star Guardian, uh. I guess."

Rook would trade any amount of money for any amount of competence from anyone, holy fucking shit.

Rook stares out over the flaming wreckage of the operation, tension slowly melting from her body until she's relaxed over the railing, watching Ellie The Star Guardian flit between structures, her actual activity unclear. One of the few multi-story buildings falls in on itself; the sound it makes must be impressive, but at this distance Rook strains to hear it.

"I really thought he'd pull it together this time," she says blankly to herself. "What a waste."

"Sorry?" Perhaps-Gwen asks, leaning forward to hear better. Rook turns to sneer at him and he steps away again.

"Nothing." She starts toward the ornate double doors that lead back into her bedroom and he stumbles to follow her.

"Well-well what do you want us to *do?*"

Rook rests her hands on the handles and shrugs.

"Nothing," she says. "If he's gonna let his own project go to shit *I'm* not cleaning up after him."

Ben, she remembers suddenly. It's not Gary *or* Gwen, his name is *Ben.*

Ben fidgets, following closely like he's afraid she'll lock him out here.

"What are *you* going to do then, uh, Miss?"

"I'm going to do my hair."

The unshakable shook.

The unshakable shook, so soundly that the time and the place where their story starts no longer exists, and the strands weaving the events together have unraveled and regrown strange. They are tangled beyond the ability of anyone not already familiar with them, and nobody familiar can bear the task of putting them to rights.

And so, to start with:

A very, very long time ago, there was a man named Raven.

This story isn't about him, but we must start somewhere.

Raven Slight wore half-moon glasses, liked to tie back his hair with ribbons, and, being a wizard, he could write a longhand original and its copy simultaneously. He was doing so, alone in the sanctuary of his study. The rest of the starship was all its captain, sawdust suspended in sunlight, strong wood worn in all the right places from the moment it leapt into being. Raven kept his study comfortably cool and dim; the blues and indigos of the drapes easier on his eyes, the scent of paper soothing after the onslaught of dust.

The ship that was not Raven's hovered idly over the Seared Plains, glassy and black as pitch as far as any eye could see. The mirrorshine of the land reflected the setting sun through the tall window behind Raven's writing desk, and it had been doing so at precisely the same angle for several days. Even filtered through heavy velvet curtains the sunshine was an unsettling creature creeping across his back, burning his neck. He'd never felt comfortable in the daylight to begin with, but here, so far along The Crossing, there was an extra depth to it that made his skin crawl. Hopefully they wouldn't have to stay here long, if he-

(a tumult of wings,

the stinging scent of,

cinders,)

▼

The watery light in Cold Hazard's study doesn't come from the aquarium walls. It's an old spell, a modification of something he'd cast into the ceiling of Rook's nursery because the overhead light had upset her. He'd never cared for bright lighting either, and there is no reason for wizards to have to tolerate that sort of thing. Not anywhere, but especially on their own ship.

The illusion of sunlight streaming through deep water is still nearly too much, these days, and the real sunlight from the compass on his desk burns him badly where it touches his skin. It casts its light over his old logbook where he's left it open, brimming with paper scraps and photos, each one a knife. The sharpest, a photograph he has damaged many times but been unable to part with permanently, lays across a blank page towards the back of the tome. The light also casts a pockmarked shadow through a dusting of soil near the corner of his desk, marking where a potted sunflower had been until very recently.

Hazard wishes he had a drink. He wishes he could feel alcohol. He raises his hand to set the frequency. The stone in this compass, functioning as a radio, has made this connection so many times he hardly has to focus on the recipient on the other line, a small mercy seeing as he no longer knows what she looks like.

The connection sings out cheerfully along its unseen pathway, across uncrossable space, hitting its mark with ease as if this is any other day.

▼

Jocasta Hubris is cooking breakfast when her radio pings, the sound lighting up her senses with Phineas' compass. *Lord*, that child; all this time without a word and *now* she calls. It takes Jo an extra minute to wipe the crumbs off her gloves and shoo the cat away from where he's begging for scraps.

▼

"Eugh, hang on- *Git*, Basil!"

Hubris' voice is a struck match. Raven feels heat in his blood for the first time in decades and it is even more harsh than he'd expected, boiling water through his frostbitten limbs. He can't collect himself enough to answer.

"Phineas you know what time it is here?" Hubris says, coming closer to the connection. "Not everybody gets up this early, you gotta start thinkin' about this shit now you're out there kiddo."

Raven can't speak.

Hubris trails off and Raven can hear something sizzling in a pan. The domestic sounds of wrangling a pet, cooking a meal for herself— what does she eat? Where does she *sleep?* He doesn't know what her home looks like, where it is, he does not *know.*

He feels her hesitate, when the silence goes on.

"...You there, Phin? You doin' okay?"

Raven covers his face. Hubris says: "This ain't *Crow*, is it?"

Hazard's laugh bursts from him like bubbling tar.

"Almost," he says. He hears something clatter, a soft catch in her voice. She starts to speak, once, and again, aborted syllables he doesn't need to hear because her sick surprise is tangible across the frequency connecting them. He tries not to, knows he doesn't

221

deserve it, but Hazard can't help feeling around for any trace of warmth at his presence.

"Before..." Hazard begins, because Hubris can't. "Before you say anything, I want to let you know you cannot begin to fathom what a *relief* it is to hear you wrap your drawl around those syllables, Hubris. I-"

Jo finds her voice.

"Don't you pull that verbose shit with *me,* you pretentious fuck."

"I recall you loved my 'verbose shit,' once," Hazard ventures. It's the wrong thing to say; she *snarls,* physical heat in Hazard's atrophied senses, and the line dies.

"...I'm sorry," Hazard says a moment later over a new call.

"Yeah you should've *led* with that maybe." He hears her slam something onto a countertop. *"God."*

Hazard listens, Raven listens to the sound of a dish shattering on a hardwood floor.

"God-! *What is it* you coward?!" Jocasta shouts, across the room she's in. She's pacing, and the sound of her talons against the floor stirs an old, habitual warmth in Raven before he can stop it, immediately extinguished under grief. "I *know* you ain't had a change of heart and just decided to *catch up.* What the hell do you *want?"*

Cold Hazard swallows against the lump in his throat.

"This is not...the reaction I had prepared for."

"Oh is it *not?"* Hubris barks. "Better part of a century not enough time for you to puzzle out I might be pissed off? I can't believe you got the nerve to *call.* I can't believe I'm even- You know I thought you were *dead* up 'til like ten years ago, yeah?"

"I was not aware you'd learned I was still alive, actually."

"Ah, *that* makes it better," Jocasta spits. "So you *meant* to show up like a fuckin' *ghost-"*

The edge of her talon catches some piece of wooden furniture,

The second fountain pen skittered against its surface, digging into the paper while Jocasta's teeth dug into to his earlobe.

"What's goin' on, witch boy?" Her breath was a cloud of cinders, glittering in the air and scattering across Raven's desk.

"Can I *help* you?" Raven asked. He ignored her grin against his neck to blot the ink from his pen nib and start writing again.

"Maybe," Jocasta's smirk turned her voice into a burst of red paisley in Raven's vision. "If you think you can tear yourself away from this exciting company you're entertainin'."

"I am a poor host these days," Raven groused. "I've built up nearly two weeks of field notes, I feel like I haven't had time to *breathe.*"

The first three buttons of his linen shirt came undone in her hands, then she slid her palms over his chest.

"I can think of *at least* a dozen other things we ain't had a moment for," Hubris murmured. "But if *breathin's* all you wanna go with..."

"I... *did* want to speak with you about some of my findings," Raven sighed, feeling foolish about it. He'd only been pretending to be preoccupied with his work, but thinking of the pile of notes he still needed to transcribe put the weight of it in his stomach.

"Speak with me, then," Hubris said. Finished with rucking his shirt down around his elbows, she wrapped her arms further around him. There was still the polished wood of the chair back between them, but Raven could tell now she wasn't wearing anything under her long orange coat. Hubris' unchecked halo was like hot honey in his head, miring his thoughts, but her body draped across his back had also blocked out the awful sunshine. The lack of it was like cool water over a burn; not her usual descriptors, but an abject relief all the same. He dropped his pen and let his head fall back into the hollow of her neck and shoulder. Her skin was still hot so soon after coming back from her walk, but this heat was a relief. He'd been worried this time, he'd missed her terribly,

terribly, he'd-

her coat, *her,*

Hazard shakes his head and the sunlight turns watery again, the warm wood of his old study replaced with cold glass. He buries his fingers into the canvas of her coat where it drapes around him, not sure whether it's for reassurance or to remove it. It's too hot, it's getting uncomfortable.

What had she been saying?

"How did you..." he says, sloughing back to the present. There's a sound he can't place for a moment, echoing repetitively in the empty hall, water hitting water. A movement on the floor near his desk; a spot on the carpet has distorted into a small stream, the flow coming and going nowhere. "How did you find out?"

Her laugh is harsh.

"You was in the papers!" she grumbles. The "S" in papers eases softly over her tongue, cushioned by what he knows is pipe smoke. Raven closes his eyes, recalling other times he'd heard the sound of her smoke between her teeth. When he looks again, the light shimmering through the illusion above him is tangled in ribbons of pink smoke, threaded thickly through the study.

"Wasn't even *looking* for you anymore then," she goes on acidly. "You know, 'cause I figured you'd been reduced to a bright blue *plasma* in some other dimension for god knows how long. I had the city paper brought in from Tourmaline, wanted to see what they had in the way of sagestone that year." She laughs mirthlessly. "And right there, front page, there was you!"

"There was me," Raven mutters, breathing deeply. The scent of burning roses.

"Some fucking- some local story, nothing to do with you, even. Just standin' in the background like some kinda moron, didn't even know you were in the shot, probably."

One long exhale.

"You wanna think about what that was like for me, Raven?"

"I'd prefer not to."

"Yeah I bet," she hisses. He hears her set her elbows against something, another hard wood surface, and he needs to know what she looks like so violently he nearly chokes with it.

"I did some digging," she goes on. Her efforts to keep her voice level are given away by the plosives sending sparks through Hazard's eye. "'Bout like you do when you figure out your best friend survived an apocalypse event through a newspaper article. Wasn't much to dig up, you're using some stupid-ass fake name I guess. But everything I *did* find was disappointing."

That repetitive sound comes faster, louder, somewhere in the study he can't see.

"You were goin' around fuckin' with these little-" She coughs. "Stealing starstone? *Really?* You were the best caster I ever met and you're into *petty thievery* now? You ditched me for a *payday?*"

Hazard shifts uncomfortably and finds his boots meet resistance. There is perhaps three inches of water standing in the study, the carpet swollen with it.

"It has nothing to *do* with money," he says absently, resettling, letting his feet go numb.

"Actually, I'm glad you called," Jocasta says. "I've been *real* curious about the little kid you had with you. What's that, find you someone else that ties you down the way you like? I kinda figured I'd wore you out but-"

▼

Eventually, when he couldn't justify simply sitting there any longer, Raven turned his face against the skin of her neck.

"I haven't had a chance to look over the logbooks recently," he began, quietly in their shared space. He felt her laugh rumble through her, low and gravelly, probably surprised he was actually going through with the work discussion. "Not since we...began running into the..." She deftly untangled the knot in the sash around his waist. "The ah...abnormalities. The tain, the worn patches of reality, they're forming some kind of..."

"This ain't distractin' is it?" Jocasta purred, letting the sash slide to the floor somewhere beside his chair. "Want me to stop?"

"They are forming a pattern," Raven managed. Even while she slid her fingers under his waistband, Jocasta made a noise that might indicate genuine interest in what he was saying; stars, she's *perfect*.

"What's it mean, you think?" she asked.

"I *think,*" Raven said, catching her free hand and toying with her fingertips. "If we stay on the route we're following, if we keep..." Here, she did something that made it very difficult to continue.

225

"If we *keep?*" she said, brushing her lips against his ear. Raven, suddenly aware he'd slid dangerously low in his chair, cleared his throat and tried to sit up straight.

"Keep encountering these events, we should be able to use the data to determine the location of the sun— or. Or at least find our way out of this miasma we've been caught in."

Jocasta's laugh shivered through him like hot water.

"You're so goddamn smart," she crooned, then she took a step backwards and

  (wings, cinders,)

disappeared, the lack of warmth stealing the breath from Raven's lungs. His notebook slammed shut with a spray of sparks, which alarmed him enough to startle him from his hazy mood.

"Hubris my *notes,*" he hissed, then nearly toppled from his chair as it screeched across the hardwood, turning away from his desk. Even from the walker space, Jocasta's laugh was as loud as it ever was.

"You got plenty of notes already." Her voice had the strange reverberating quality that came from traveling between planes but it was still her, her presence unyielding even while she went unseen. "You don't *need* any more notes."

"This is serious, Jo," Raven said to the air.

Then in a plume of embers she came back, materializing right in his lap with her knees pressed tight between his thighs and the arms of his chair. Framed against the bright light in the window, her silhouette cast him in blessed, safe shadow, and the residual turbulence from her brief jaunt fanned her coat around her like wings. In the lee of her, Raven thought this might be how the first poet felt; confronted with a sublime too saturated for prose, too immediate for song, a deluge that refused to be exorcised in anything but a concentrated burst of devotion. He'd written scores of poems for Hubris, of course, but seeing as she reinvented poetry at least once per day it was impossible to keep up.

"I'm serious too." Jocasta draped her arms languidly around his shoulders, and it took all of Raven's carefully cultivated academic neutrality to ignore the way her breasts felt against his chest. "Sounds like you got it pretty well figured out already. What'cha wanna talk to *me* for?"

"I wanted to ask if the void has changed." His play at nonchalance would have fooled anyone but his wife, who was unfortunately the person running her teeth over a tight tendon in his neck. "If you've noticed anything different during your walks."

Jocasta hummed and leaned down to mouth at his clavicle.

"Can't recall," she said, her voice muffled. "Nothin' that *you'd* be interested in anyway, it's hard to focus too much on your dusty old formulas and shit."

This time Raven laughed, finally allowing himself to wind his hands around her hips.

"You might not think them so boring if you *understood* them, darling."

He stubbornly kept his mouth closed around a sigh as her teeth nipped into his neck.

"I'm gonna let you have that one," she said. "You been workin' way too fuckin' hard, it's obviously fucking with your better judgement." His ribbon came free in her fingers, she brushed his long, dark hair forward to hang in his face the way she liked. "We finally got the place to ourselves, allll afternoon, and I still ain't over watching you fight yesterday-"

Fighting. They're fighting.

They are having a *fight*.

Hazard realizes that foreign feeling is a thin sheen of sweat on his brittle skin. He works his way wretchedly out of Jo's coat.

"-little long in the tooth for that ain't you?" Jocasta finishes.

"Wh- what?" he says before he can stop himself. The wood of his desk is splintery under his fingers when he presses his palm into it, trying to steady himself. Jocasta groans.

"*Kids*, Raven. That kid you had with you."

Kids, *Rook*, of course. He carefully lays the coat across his desk, unable to wear it, unable to let it go.

"Eisse *is* my daughter," he says, suffocating in the smoky air. "But not in the way you're thinking. It's...a long and difficult story. I know your ego would appreciate the gesture so, no. I haven't found anyone else worth submitting to." He kneads his thumb into his eye. "Though I can't say I've cared to look-"

"Listen man," Hubris cuts in. "Much as I'm enjoying dumping some eight or nine decades of angst on you before I've even had coffee, I really got better shit to be doing. I ain't interested in patchin' things up and I don't think you are either, else you wouldn't've waited this long. What do you want from me?"

Hazard stares into the distance; at some point night had fallen over the glassy plains, and the sun on his neck isn't so harsh. The darkness has closed in and he can't see the walls of the study now, adrift here in the painful light cast by the compass. He shuts his eyes and breathes in the scent of her as a school of silver fish murmurs around him, and away.

From some unknowable distance his voice cracks without his consent.

"Hubris I *missed you.*"

"Oh do not *fuck* with me Raven."

"I am not in the vicinity of fucking with you."

"Yeah well, *I* missed *you* a couple times the first fifty fucking years, but after that I-" She coughs, because her throat has tightened, and Raven thinks if he could still feel it the ache would kill him.

"How *could* you?" she asks, quieter. "To *me?*"

oh, *god,* oh he can't *do* this, why did he think-

"Jo, I-"

"And it wasn't just you *leavin',* you know. I could deal with that." A drag on the pipe, so aggressive Hazard can hear the leaves sizzling in the bowl. "Runnin' off on your wife is a dick move but, hey, you want out you want out. That's fair."

"Hubris *please* do we have to-"

"We do! *Yes!*" Her tenuous self control shatters, exploding in Hazard's perception like a grease fire. "You *knew* I thought you'd died! You let me think it was *my fault!* You *hid* from me, do you- Did it even cross your mind how *thoroughly* your bullshit would fuck with me?"

"Does it do you well to know I wasn't thinking of you at all?"

"Don't you lie to me, motherfucker." She heaves a breath, and Raven watches a red rose curl into being from the smoke around him, drifting near a tall strand of kelp shadowed against the moonlight.

228

"...You're right." Hazard cedes, because there is no reason not to. "I have thought of you every moment of every day since we parted ways. I am calling you now because I am dying."

"...Oh my god," Jocasta says. "You're *drunk.*"

"That would be a significant improvement."

"Quit bein' dramatic, you ain't dyin'. You *can't* die."

△

"Yesterday?" Raven said, breathless and pretty. Jo laughed, dragging her fingernails over his scalp. Raven was so easy like this. He always built up so much tension poring over his notes in this stuffy little office, and it was one of Jo's great joys in life to work it all out of him.

"Yeah yesterday, we did that thing with the bridge." She bit his shoulder hard so she could listen to him hiss about it. "You got me right up in that saint's face so I could light it up."

Raven's hand slipped up under her coat, his palm smooth over her lower back.

"Right, yes," he said. "I remember now..."

...Hm. Jo sat up so they could look at each other, sort of forgetting her tits were out. Raven seemed to have forgotten too, which was concerning. He'd been moping around the ship for days, but she was sure this nothing-but-the-coat bit would work.

"What's wrong?" she asked gently.

"I...it's nothing," Raven said. Jo rolled her eyes.

"C'mon man, this won't be any fun if you're distracted the whole time."

Raven laughed, taking her hand and kissing her palm. It was always annoying how much that got to her, those chaste, nerdy things he did while they were in the middle of other things.

"Do you know how much I worry about you," he asked, "every single time you walk?"

Jo curled her hand around his cheek, and he closed his eyes, leaning into it.

"You've mentioned it before. But I-"

"I know," he sighed. "It's just...it is already so dangerous, wandering between existences, and this *place* it's..." He grimaced against her hand. "It is *alive*, even the light bogs down our sails. The way time and space bend, here, I cannot imagine the underside is...hospitable."

"Ooh," Jo said, the switch clicking. "You're scared I'm gonna go walking and won't be able to get back."

"I never mean to imply you are incapable," Raven said. "Or that you don't understand how your own abilities work..." He opened one eye, her favorite shade of blue, and met hers. "But I know you act largely on instinct. I see what you do from a scientific perspective and it's difficult not to feel terrified on your behalf. Our work is dangerous, and I love you very much."

△

"I most certainly can die," Raven drones. His voice is so empty, he sounds so...*desiccated*. Over the radio connection, Jo can feel something squirming underneath what she, unfortunately, recognizes as Raven; it's something else she's familiar with, but it *couldn't* be...

"I doubt it," Jo says, crossing to the counter to grind something for a cigarette. She doesn't have the patience to pack another pipe. "'Less Crow comes and rips out your heart his own self."

"You're not far off," the man on the line says quietly.

Jocasta snatches one of the blooms hung against the wall to dry. It's not quite ready yet, but she isn't going to be tasting it much. She twists the grinder a few extra times, willing her hands to stop shaking.

"What the fuck is *that* supposed to mean?"

There's a wheezing noise Jocasta wouldn't recognize as laughter if it didn't light up the radio connection like that, a lurch of misery too big to fit into a single lifespan. He might be smiling, or, whatever passes for a smile. Jo slams the grinder down onto the cutting board, rattling the knife there. The cutting board is stained with blood. It's very old now, faded to brown against the natural yellow of the wood, but that stuff never really comes out.

"Are...are you *sick?*" she asks, hating herself a little. "Is that what this is? You need a *housecall?*"

"That would be far more than I deserve from you, darling."

Jo's throat spasms dangerously over the last word, and the fury that rushes in to replace it flexes her hand into a hasty fist, dampening the impulse to burn any of the extremely flammable wooden fixtures in her kitchen.

"Then what the *fuck?!* What is *wrong* with you? Why would you show up after all this time to tell me you're *dying* if you don't want *help?!*"

Raven's breathing is thready and deliberate, every inhale fighting to get through something in his airways.

"I've been thinking about this," he murmurs. "My body, even after...It wasn't meant to last this long in the first place."

Jocasta's still not convinced he isn't on something, on some bender so bad he finally got low enough to call her to drag him out of it.

"You're an idiot but you're still a *scientist,*" she says. "You *know* we don't just fuckin' *fizzle out.* Not even..." She manages to get the tobacco mix into a paper, rolling it into something decent through sheer muscle memory. "Not even if you do it yourself. Someone..."

It takes her way too many tries to get a controlled flame from her thumb. She drags deeply and lets it go, turning her back to lean her hip against the kitchen counter.

"Somebody tried already," she says, smoky petals falling from her mouth. "The star wouldn't let the host die, it was a goddamn *mess.*"

...That surprises him.

"W- Wait, *who-*"

"It ain't none of your *fucking business*, who," Jo clips. This is old news, at least; this is easier to talk about, even more now she has smoke in her lungs. "Point I'm makin' is, for *you* to die, someone *else* would have to kill you *and* stop your star from bringing you back. So, no. You're not dying."

She pauses to take another drag, less desperate. She feels Basil nudge against her leg, wrapping both of his fluffy tails around her calf. Under the rest of her irritation with Raven, she's also irritated that all those stupid fucking workbooks and articles were right about grounding exercises. Things you can touch, sense things, bringing you back to reality when it feels like shit's gone all to hell. The cat helps, and running her eyes over the cast iron of her stove helps. Even the smell of her own burnt breakfast is helpful, and that's *stupid*, god dammit.

"All you're doing is draggin' me back through a bunch of fucked up shit I been workin' real hard to forget," she says. "If you *wanted* to kill yourself you couldn't do it, we don't get to tap out."

"...Not all at once, perhaps."

"What?"

"It's been some time since we've seen each other," Raven says in that revolting imitation of his own voice. "I'm not as pretty as I used to be. Moonlight doesn't sustain quite as well as sunshine. It's only a reflection, a memory of things bigger and brighter. Much like myself."

(a taste of paper,
a scattering of,

...stars,)

It's scary how quickly Jocasta slips back into the old feelings, just for a second. She shakes her head.

"Raven, you-"

Should she indulge this? Her own self-preservation slows her down, but she rushes into the instinct to comfort him before she can think better of it.

"You know I never thought you were-"

Static over the connection, the wheezing gasp of someone swallowing bitter medicine— a pharyngeal reflex, the throat rejecting the help.

"I know," he says, *"I know.* But what other fate could I have had, living in the shadow of a sun god?"

"Love of mine," Raven says, "what was *left* for me but the *dark?"*

Jo slides to the floor, her back against the kitchen's wooden cabinets, and closes her eyes. The *dark.* She'd been right, before— that crawling creeping thing lurking between Raven's words, what else could it be?

"...What did you do, Raven?" she asks quietly.

"It's become difficult to tell how the time passes," Raven murmurs. "I've been planning on killing Crow since we ended up here, but I think, mm..." A ragged, painful breath. "The current plan was conceived shortly before you discovered me"

Jo snorts.

"Yeah well good luck with *that,*" she says. "*I* don't even know where he is, and he ain't aged a day all this time. He'd be sorry to do it but he'd slaughter you if you made him."

"I don't doubt it."

Dry tobacco touches Jo's tongue as she grinds her teeth down around the last of her cigarette, tearing through the paper.

"Then *why* are we having this *conversation,*" Jocasta hisses. She laces her fingers together and digs the pads of her thumbs between her eyes, grinding them shut tight. "*Why* did you call me to *tell me this*, what is *wrong* with you?"

"Something similar to what is wrong with *you,* I'd imagine," Raven says. For the first time, Jo feels something sharpen in his tone. It rubs against her white-knuckle composure like salt in a delicate wound, what's *he* mad at *her* for?

"You accepted my intent to kill our *illustrious leader* with an ease I find suspicious," he says, sterile. "One might think *you'd* contemplated revenge *yourself.*"

"Oh of *course* I did, you *asshole,*" Jocasta growls. "The only person I blamed more than myself for what happened to you was him, is that some kinda revelation? You think I wouldn't kill for you?"

Raven makes a wounded sound, muted, like he'd smothered it just too late.

"Well," Jo amends. "*Would've.* Almost did."

"*Crow* came and found me soon as the dust was settled," she says. "When I still thought you was worth the trouble. I beat the holy hell out of that man when he showed up at my door."

Raven's next wounded sound is closer to amusement; maybe the word "amused" written down in a closed book, in another room.

"He didn't fight me much." Jocasta mashes the last of her cigarette between her fingertips, more sensory input, despite the gloves. "We talked some. I patched him up, little bit. We're good now. We're fine."

Raven's outburst at that is strong enough it rattles Jo's radio where it sits on the floor.

"FINE?!" he roars. It is the closest to his real voice Jo has heard yet, and it hurts. "*Don't* *act* like you weren't as wounded as the *rest* of us-"

"What 'us'!?" she fires back. It is catastrophically similar to the way they used to fight, when they both knew they could cut loose because it was taken for granted that it would resolve afterward, no thought given to any other outcome. "Wasn't no one else *alive* to *wound!*"

Raven's energy dampens instantly, smothered under shadow.

"Wh-" Jo hates how hollow he sounds, *bereft.* "Maggie, *surely-?*"

"Mags didn't make it," Jo says, like tearing a bandage away.

"You're-You're *sure-?*"

Jocasta shakes her head and seizes the radio, leaping to her feet to pace.

"*Yes* I am *fuckin' sure!* He never was a fighter, they-" She tosses the radio on the kitchen table, hoping the sharp noise hurts his ears. She sets one hand on her hip and runs the other through her short dreadlocks. "They finally caught him and they... they ate him alive. I *saw* it. There wasn't enough left of that boy to scrape up off a goddamn *sidewalk.*"

She rushes through the facts, feels each of them puncture Raven's psyche like gunshots and insists to herself she doesn't give a shit. If he didn't want to get hit like this he should have checked in earlier, handled this *literally* any other way. This was *all* avoidable.

It takes him a moment to get it together; it's the most affected she's heard him by anything said so far. He really didn't know, he really-

"I can't believe it," he says. No bluster, no carefully detached affectation, just the grief he seems to be entirely composed of now, exposed to the air like a torn nerve. "I just *assumed-*"

"There's no one, I would have felt them by now," Jo says, unable to deal with both the tragedy of her husband and the tragedy of Magpie Sweet at the same time. There is nothing new to say about it. "Only reason I never found *you* is 'cause you're *hiding* from me, but Maggie wouldn't've made me look to start with. He would've come home running."

△

Jo smiled, and it must have been patronizing because Raven made a face and folded his arms between them.

"Don't-"

"I ain't makin' fun!" Jo laughed, squishing his face between her hands so he can't look so sour. He let her, and gazed over his dorky glasses with big wet eyes.

"...Hubrish," he shaid. Jo sighed and let him go.

"Should I get dressed?" she asked, trying to keep her tone neutral so he wouldn't feel bad about it. It might be too late for neutrality. Mercifully, Raven shook his head and dragged his knuckles across her cheek, like she was something delicate.

"Absolutely not, I just... Your ring is still working?"

"The ring's fine," Jo said brightly, holding her hand up in front of him. The stone there was the same blue as his eyes, set into a silvery alloy molded into a simple wave pattern. "Works every time, workin' right now even." She plucked his left hand from the armrest and held it near hers. His stone was an orange opal, in the center of a sunburst setting. The rings touched with a tiny spark, and Raven smiled tiredly.

"Good," he said, clearly not. Jo tucked his hair behind his ear.

"You're gettin' soft on me, Slight."

"I am within my rights."

Jo settled her knees in and shifted her weight back in Raven's lap so they could talk. She reached up under her dreadlocks to shift them to the other side. They were the longest they'd ever been, nearly down to her waist. She loved the way they moved with her when she fought, but they did get heavy.

"Look, the rings are a good idea, I like them," she started. "But I don't use 'em much on my side."

"No?" Raven asked, perking up with curiosity. Jo shook her head.

"Nope. I just use you, mostly. Sometimes King, but I like to check in on you more than the ship." Jo slid both hands up over Raven's chest. "The other side, the place I go when I'm walkin', isn't really anything. It's just dark and..."

Jo never was a poet.

"...kinda windy," she finished. Raven laughed softly and it made her heart do a stupid little leap.

"I can't make it sound nice, it's never *good* over there," she said. "It don't want me there, and there's always a risk I come out in the wrong place or time." Jo shrugged. "It's dangerous. I'm sorry."

"Part of the job, regrettably," Raven muttered, toying with her fingers against his chest. Jo tugged away from him and spread her palms over his chest again, heating up enough to make him whine.

(a taste of paper,
a scattering of,
stars,)

"But I can see all of *you* too, your halos still light up for me even over there." She leaned in to press her forehead against his. "As long as you want me to, I'll always be able to get right back here to you."

Raven kissed her, just a tiny "we're married, and you're here" kiss.

"Is there..." he tried. "Is there any way I could, help? From *this* side? Could I be brighter for you?"

"Huh," Jo mused, sitting up. "I guess? I never thought to try explaining all that to you, I just assumed a smart wizard like yourself already knew all the spiritual crap you needed."

"There is always something else to learn," Raven said, terminally academic. But he was coming out of it, hopefully satisfied that she wasn't going to disappear forever every time he looked away. Probably. Jo kissed him again.

"Sure then, I can show you how to hide too while we're at it." She leaned in, taking his wrists in her hands, moved on already to considering the practicalities of what she could do to him while he's tied to this chair. "Might come in handy out here, you never know who might be lookin' for you."

△

"...Yes," Raven says, his rawness bleeding away again. "Maggie would have come home. I'm very sorry to hear this."

"Yeah I'm sure," Jocasta says. Basil leaps up onto the table and looks at her with three wide, thoughtful eyes. "And don't fuckin' act like me handling this shit better than you is some kind of- eugh, you know you're reading like a fucking *zombie?* It ain't my fault you wasted the last few lifetimes bein' miserable. You 'n me got the same raw deal, don't act like it didn't hurt me too just because I actually dealt with it."

All at once, the last recognizable feeling of Raven disappears, depleted. Jo feels it go, vanishing over the connection like vapor.

236

"Ah," Raven says, some quality in his voice making Jo shudder. "You're right, I apologize. The shouting and the banging around threw me off, but, *clearly yours* is the voice of a woman well-adjusted."

"What kind of adjusting would make any of this okay?" she snaps. She feels stupid, pacing in her own kitchen; she braces her palms against the table instead, hanging her head over the radio. Phineas' picture smiles back at her, an old instant print of a much younger Phineas, still missing a tooth.

"But yeah!" Jo says. "You know, I'm doin' a *lot* better than I should be 'cause I kept *going!* You gotta- You gotta move *on*, have you just been sittin' in this bitterness all this time?"

The silence from the radio is thick. There's static creeping in that makes Jo feel nauseous, but she keeps talking over it, her own fire rearing against the entropy the way it's always done.

"You're too chickenshit to deal with your own problems and they *fester,*" she spits. "But it sounds like you've done a good job makin' sure no one's around to pull your ass *out* of it and you've turned into whatever the *fuck* this is."

"Your *anger,*" Raven croons,

and it feels

like there is a stranger there instead.

"Is *explosive* for one so critical of dwelling on the past. I don't think you're in a position to reprimand *anyone* for letting *anything* **fester.**"

"This," he says, "is a *very* long time for you to stay angry at someone you claim you don't care for. I have been patient with your venom because it is not unjustified. But I'm sure you'll understand if I have trouble accepting your criticism of *my* decisions when you've obviously got your *own* astringent *petri dish* of issues to dissect."

"Oh yeah?" Jo sneers.

"Jo- Jocasta *Hubris,*" Raven says, disgust in his tone Jo isn't ready for. "Hiding out in the middle of fucking *nowhere.* That feels like Somershire, if I am not mistaken. What's out there, Jo? What have you been doing all this time? You spent our entire life together railing against the asceticism of your upbringing and now you're just as cloistered as any of those scholars you hated so much."

"Yeah that really stings comin' from the guy who didn't have the balls to call me without pretending to be somebody else," Jo says, trying not to feel anything about the fact that she's being observed, however abstractly. "You know, Gideon doesn't even *have* his compass anymore."

"Oh," Raven says. "I know he doesn't."

For the second time today, Jo's voice fails her.

Raven sets a new knife to her skin.

"...I've been...dabbling, in darker energy," he says, hardly a whisper. "Voidmagic, anything opposed to the light that sustains Crow. Ultimately, I know I couldn't kill him on my own; I have no misconception of the difference between his power and mine. But we know how to deal with commanders, don't we, dear?"

Jocasta falls heavily into one of the kitchen chairs.

"If I could cause his *spirit* to decay he would eventually erode himself away, like careless commanders do. I could at least force him to live out his days the way I have." He swallows thickly. "I've been experimenting with the tain-"

Jo's heart hammering finally forces the air from her lungs in some unidentifiable expression; an ugly, joyless laugh closer to a gag.

"The *stone*," she moans, her head heavy in her hand. "You weren't stealing *stone* you were stirring up the *tain*, you-"

"But then," Raven's voice has deepened so much now it's distorting the radio broadcast. "Just recently, an opportunity presented itself. A stroke of providence too brazen to be coincidence. You seemed surprised *I* had a daughter. But, *Jo,* I *never* thought the day would come when I would see a *child* wearing this old coat of yours."

There are so many disparate things fighting for space in Jo's mind she's paralyzed with it. While she's trying to reorient to this new universe he goes on, sawing away with the blade, digging down for bone.

"*Phineas,*" Raven says. Jo hates the sound of the name in his mouth, it's like watching someone smear dirty fingers over white lace. "Did she pick the name herself? Or was that *your* influence? Hah, I can *almost* picture it. The beautiful and *terrible* Jocasta Hubris, who stood at the sun's right hand and *still* blazed bright enough to turn every eye to herself-"

Jo's rage is so hot it burns her, she can't remember the last time heat was *painful*.

"Whose furious fire destroyed entire warships and burned hot enough to drive away demons forged in hellfire furnaces— Spending her evenings reading bedtime stories to a little girl."

"I would not have believed it if I hadn't seen her myself," Raven says venomously. "But even without the coat, she *moves* like *you*, she *glares* like *him*."

"You son of a *bitch-*" Jo manages, but he's not finished.

"While there are *several* intriguing details surrounding her existence, most immediately I was taken aback by her age." His voice is wreathed in cruelty. "She's *young* for a commander, don't you *think*, Hubris? Even *Crow* didn't make it official until he was seventeen, and you *remember* the mess *he* caused."

"Wh-where is she?" Jocasta stammers, her mouth dry. Her head pounds against her palms as she sags over the table. "What did you do to her?"

"Nothing yet she can't handle, if my assumptions are correct. I expect she'll be along to meet with me shortly."

"Mother*fucker-!*"

"Before you get caught up in what I'm certain would be *artisanally crafted* threats on my life," Raven says, his placid tone eviscerating through Jo's rage. "I'm going to save you the trouble."

"I know for a fact that you've been reaching out to look for me since this conversation began. Of *all* people, *you* know I have had plenty of time to practice staying inaccessible to prying eyes *exactly* like yours." There is only malice in him; Jo isn't even sure it's directed at *her*, it just hates *everything*. "Myself, my vessel, my location and *especially* our precocious little commander will remain unreachable until I decide otherwise."

Raven's intake of breath is so distorted it manifests in Jo's radio crystal, a black blemish whispering across the blue.

"And I do *not* decide otherwise," he says at last. "So, *first*. Tell me. How *old was* she, Jocasta?"

This is so fucked, this is *fucked,* she was supposed to be eating *breakfast-*

"How *old,*" he pushes. *"Was* she?"

"...Eight," Jo says, pressing the heels of her hands against her eyes. "She was eight."

The briefest spark of genuine shock.

"And she *lived?*" Raven asks

"Yep."

"And which one of you slit an eight year old's throat?" Raven demands, on the offense again.

"We didn't- She was *dying!*" Jo hates how pathetic she sounds; hates that he can corner her like this. Feels some other way about how he still knows where to cut.

And he does cut.

"What did he *say* to you?" Raven says, twisting the knife with surgical tensity. "What could he *possibly* have done to convince you to take part in this? Your technique is nearly flawless, her scars may be hidden well enough from *most* people. But *I* would recognize *your* magic *anywhere.*"

Jo bites down on the inside of her cheek.

"I saw her closely," Raven presses. "Her neck, her *back.* That girl *burned.* You *know* she had no business living after those wounds. The recovery would have been *agonizing* even *with* you as a caretaker, this was *cruel.*"

"Don't you *even-*"

"And then you allowed him to perform the ordinance, after *all that?*" Jocasta hears something creak, and strangely, the sound of running water. Raven grumbles, his concentration broken, and the tension over their connection loosens somewhat. Jo blinks. She hasn't heard silverspeak like that in a long time, and never, *ever* turned so viciously against her like this. She's caught again between her fury and the part of her that admired these things about him in the first place.

"That's what I am not able to grasp, really," Raven says; he's reclining now, doesn't have the blade in so deep. "You've never been *discreet* with your disdain for commanders."

Jocasta hates every single thing that brought her here to this point, saying this to him.

"He-" She clears her throat, still hunched over the radio, exhausted. "He. Asked her, first."

"Excuse me?!" Raven shouts. "Sorry, he asked an *eight year old* if-"

"It wasn't *fair!*" Jocasta snaps, fisting a hand in her hair. "This whole thing was *fucked*, Raven, it was a stupid coincidence and the kid didn't deserve to *die* over it."

"Are those *your* excuses or *his?*" Raven demands. "I would sooner let *my own* daughter *die* than see her damned to suffer such a wretched existence. Didn't the *family* have anything to say about this?"

Jo's expression pinches around the memory like it's a rancid smell.

"Us 'n them came to an agreement," is all she says.

"No," Raven snarls. "I don't believe *you* would *ever* agree with the destruction of a child's soul. I think you *allowed* it because you didn't want her to *die.*"

Jo surges to her feet, scaring Basil off the table when she slams her hands down on either side of the radio.

"Fuckin-! *NO!* I *DIDN'T!!*" Phineas' little face is still smiling up at her from the photograph, smaller than a fingernail, and Jocasta can't take it. "How many more am I supposed to- I *couldn't-!*"

Jo's hands creak painfully as she clenches her fists against the kitchen table.

Phantom limb is one of the crueler things she'd learned about while studying medicine; the persistence of a feeling in part of the body even after it had been lost. For some reason that one had stuck with her, maybe for how cruel it sounded. Not only having to deal with losing a limb, but being constantly reminded of the absence, and in some cases experiencing over and over the sensation of losing it. As if it isn't already hard enough to relearn your own body, to get over what took a piece of it.

In the wood of her hands, Jocasta's body remembers.

At the end of the world, Raven's hands had slipped through them first; and after, another pair of hands had slipped so horrifically they took hers with them. That was the detail Jo carried with her— already in shock over losing Raven, the physical pain of her flesh unraveling had been a distant afterthought to the stark sensation of feeling even more falling away from her.

And then, on a much quieter evening here in her new home, Gideon had come to the door holding that tiny, bleeding body-

Phineas had reached out *so often* in her sleep while she recovered in Jo's bed, and even with these new hands under their gloves Jo hadn't been able to help reaching back. It's just what she does. Even when the rest of the world is being swallowed up by entropy, even when the person she's trying to save shouldn't be here at all. She couldn't-

"I couldn't-" Jocasta says, forcing her words through grief that makes itself known every time she moves, every time she interfaces with the world. *"I couldn't let go of her hands."*

Raven takes a moment to deal with that. They know they're both thinking of the same thing, the last time they'd seen each other in that place at the end of everything. There is no room for posturing here.

"...I see," he says. "Well, we do know selfish better than anybody, don't we?"

"Why are you *doing this to me?"* Jo demands miserably. *"You* left! Why would you show up after all this time just to drag me back through all this shit?!"

"Because your *actions* have put you in the path of my *revenge.* Crow's actions have divided the two of us, *again."*

He has to stop and compose himself. Jo is so tired.

"...For whatever reasons he has, little Phineas is clearly important to Gideon," Raven says slowly, back on script. His tone makes Jo's shoulders tense up, puts pressure along her spine; even through whatever dark thing he's shrouded himself in, what he's saying now frightens him. "He even gave her his *compass.* As a pawn in some grand scheme or simply the latest addition to his collection of lost pets, he found some reason to risk himself and make her a commander. Between your reaction to all of this and *hers* when she heard me say his name, the nature of the relationship has become clear enough."

"You know how he *hates* when people touch his things," he drones. "I would say it's a safe assumption that he would be quite upset if he found that something had happened to her. I would say it's a safe assumption that her painful death because of *his* misdeeds would rot him *far* more than any static darkness could. You kill a commander by breaking his heart, and it looks to me like Crow's has wandered right into my hands."

Jo feels something settle into place, like those woodworking pieces that are carved just for each other, and once they're fitted together they stay that way. She'd fought against it for a long time, but as Raven speaks it's like the thing suddenly makes sense. She lets go, and the joints hook into each other, smooth and perfect. Unshakable.

"...I need another smoke before I say this."

△

Even under the porch it was fucking hot; fire caster or not Jo *hated* the humidity here, still. Phineas seemed unbothered, leaned back in her chair (Crow's, before) as easy as breathing. She'd been flighty all day, though. Jo was pretty sure she knew what was coming.

Phin ran her hand through her hair. It was getting up on her neck, it would need a trim soon.

"Gideon's flowers're dyin'," Phineas said absently. Her voice had gotten a lot stronger, but that grit in her soft edges wouldn't ever go away completely.

"Good," Jo said, scratching her leg where it was propped up on the railing. "I didn't sign up to be a babysitter."

"Aw that ain't nice-"

"What's up, Phin?"

"I can't just hang out after work? I gotta have an ulterior-"

"Phineas."

Phineas pouted, slouching in her seat.

"It ain't fair you can just *tell* stuff about me now."

"Get used to it, commander," Jo said in a plume of smoke rings. Phineas smiled, putting on a brave face.

"I think I'm gonna get going."

Jo nodded. She'd known it for a while, but if Phineas couldn't even get up the nerve to admit it to her outright there'd be no point fooling with any of it anyway.

"Kairos Crossing," Jo murmured, staring out at the sunbaked lawn. Basil'd got him something over by the tree. "How are you gonna get there?"

"I wanna get a starship!" Phineas said, all hesitation gone. Still watching the cat leaping up after a straggling cicada, Jocasta could feel the stars in her eyes.

"Water route's easier," Jo said, just to be mean.

"We'll see more in a starship! Me and my friends, once I find 'em."

"Friends, huh?"

Phineas settled again.

"Yeah, it ain't gonna be any fun by myself so I figure that's a good place to start." She counted out the things she wanted on her fingers. "Couple of cool guys, and a ship to put 'em in, and then Kairos."

"You know ships ain't easy to come by," Jo said.

"Yeah, uh. I wanted to ask you about it," Phineas replied, fidgeting.

"Askin' for help before you even get started?"

"Well you 'n Gideon seemed happy to talk about it when I *wasn't* askin'," Phineas said, grinning. It's infuriating how much Jo is going to miss this brat.

"...I dunno about friends, or a ship to be honest." She put out her pipe and stood, stretching all her old joints. "But I know where you might can get some stone. Folks there'd probably be able to help you out with the rest. Come in a minute."

Phineas followed her through the screen door, too big now to go in under Jo's arm like she used to.

The afternoon passed with cold beer and all the useful shit Jo could think to share, most of which she was positive Phineas had already forgotten by the time they found themselves on the porch again. The sun was setting, the golden light catching in the tree leaves like spun silk.

Jo was *not* going to cry over this, but Phineas might. Phin turned at the top of the stoop to say goodbye, and Jo saw it hit her all at once, her eyes suddenly huge and watery.

"Oh," Phineas mumbled, not elaborating. Jo leaned against the doorframe, her head light from the beer.

"Gimme a call sometimes, okay? And uh...you can." uuuugh *fuck*. "You can always come home, you know."

"Yeah," Phineas said, shifting on her feet. Callused now, scraping on the dry wood. Jo sighed, trying to loosen up her throat, neither of them wanting to go but not knowing what else to say. Her eyes drifted towards the goddamn sunflowers again. They were wilting bad, even in the middle of summer. The watering can next to them was still half full.

"I guess if you see Crow out there, you can tell him I'm still trying," Jo offered halfheartedly. Phin nodded. It was getting hard to distinguish where she started and the sun set. Unable to put it off any more, Jo huffed and shrugged out of her coat. She heard the porch creak as Phineas stiffened.

"Jo-"

"Don't argue with me, kiddo."

She moved in close to wrap the coat around Phineas' shoulders.

"This coat is for travelin'," Jo said gruffly. "It'll be happier with you I think."

Phineas was working real hard at playing like she wasn't already sniffling. Jocasta groaned and reached out to get her arms around her.

"You little shit," Jo said fiercely into her hair. Phineas laughed, wet and weepy against her shoulder.

▼

There's the sound of a wooden match striking against the back of Jocasta's front teeth. Raven can smell burning pine. He feels her fingertips under his chin.

(cinders)

"Made you mad enough for matches, huh?" Raven asks miserably, a firmly walled off part of himself wailing.

"Woodfire's better for a pipe," Jocasta says. "But yeah, I'm some ways past mad enough for matches. That's what you *wanted,* isn't it?"

He hears her take a long pull. He can also hear crickets, and soft wind through tree leaves. The weight of her body shifting through wood. He waits.

"To put it in perspective for you," she starts. "Me and Gideon are close again. I wasn't lying about that earlier. I made peace with the deaths, much as you can. These gloves- My hands don't itch me no more."

Raven doesn't even know what that means, *gloves?* What had happened to her *hands?*

"You know, I kept my seeker lamp lit for you for, fuck...First two, three years?" She laughs, rough and bitter. "Crow said a bunch of times it wasn't worth it. Seems pretty stupid *now,* right? I was such an idiot. But man, I was so sure, you know?" Raven wishes he were dead. "I was *so* sure you were just lost out there someplace. Just trying to find your way back to me. I thought if I kept lookin'-"

Raven doesn't tell her about the nights he'd spent on this ship, leaning over balcony railings, staring through windows, watching her lamp flickering on the horizon. [1]

"...I cannot believe this is what I laid awake *missing* so many nights," she says, dangerously quiet. Raven can feel the heat simmering below the surface, not enough to reach across the eons. "If you really thought you were doin' the right thing you wouldn't've run and hid from me. If you thought you were in the right, for *real* in the right? You would'a come to me first and asked for help. That's how a partnership *works,* that's how *we **always*** worked."

"You *severely* overestimate my opinion of you," Raven tries.

"You say that...But facts *are,* you decided to kill yourself. And then you called *me.*" She hisses smoke between her teeth. "And long as we're psychoanalyzin' here, I come to the conclusion you only contacted me *now* 'cause you're unsure, and you want me to agree with you. Which I ain't gonna do. You're a disappointment, Raven Slight."

"What *about* my behavior do you find so *disappointing?* You know me, you *know* what I am capable of. Out of anyone, I confess, I had expected *you* to understand me."

"Oh I do," Hubris says. "I told you all the time I liked you mean. I liked your ambition that *made* you mean, enough to tear through anything in your way. I knew what you were, what you could do."

She takes another slow drag.

"I just didn't think you would turn it back on *me,* is all. I did not think you would reduce *me,* and now someone I love, to collateral in your little feud. My mistake."

"Apparently so," says the most wretched man in all of creation.

"But unlike you, I got better shit to do than sitting around comin' up with...*revenge fantasies,* or whatever the fuck you're tellin' me about," she says. "I'm gonna be pissed at you until we're both dead, if that ever happens, and that's just how it is. But I decided years ago I'm not ever gonna come after you over it."

---

[1] Notes on a certain spell, p. 393

Hubris sighs, smoky and ancient.

"I don't give a damn what you're doin' with yourself these days. You say you wanna go out and find Gideon and get your ass handed to you, you go on ahead. But *listen to me.*" Raven can hear furniture creaking as she leans closer to the radio. "You go after my *girl* and I'm gonna *have* to get involved. There will not be bones to *bury* by the time I'm through with you."

"Darling you *tease.*"

"How did you even *notice* her? Me and Gideon *both* took precautions to make sure assholes like *you* wouldn't come after her, you couldn't've scouted her out even if you knew what you was lookin' for-"

"I didn't have to *do **anything,*** she came to me!" Raven laughs, because it is the only way to respond to a reality like this one. "You know she wants to take my ship? *Our* ship! What are the odds of her coming here at *all,* don't you *see,* this is *fate!*"

Whatever she means to interrupt him with is lost as Jocasta coughs on pipe smoke. Raven barrels on.

"Gideon has *finally* angered enough stars that they turn in *my* favor! As he is I cannot kill Gideon, I was going to give my life to only *attempt* to *wound* him. But now I'll be taking someone else with me, *I'll* take something of *his* and it will *ruin him!*"

"She's *mine,*" Jocasta says in that low, dangerous tone. "If she's *anyone's* she's mine, *not* his."

"What were you expecting when she *left,* Hubris?" Raven demands. "Do you plan to sweep in and save her every time she mouths off to the wrong person? This is *exactly* what she asked for-"

"Our mistakes have nothing to do with her," Jo says. "I can't believe you thought you could tell me all this and I *wouldn't* come rip you apart. She did not ask to be part of our *bullshit,* Raven."

"Oh yes," Raven says dryly. "How *awful* it would be to find oneself suffering because of someone *else's **decisions.***"

For a moment, there is only the sound of the water flooding the study, now up to Raven's waist. There is only the sound of wind through the trees, where Hubris is.

"...No," Raven breathes. "This is not what any of us wanted, is it? That's why..." He grips the arms of his chair with numb fingers. "Crow

Gideon was never meant- *none* of us were ever meant to touch this world. His influence can only make it *ill.* He spreads poison wherever he goes, and now a child has *eaten it.* "

"You know as well as I do that neither of them can exist quietly," he says. "Whatever he intends for himself or for Phineas, *her* intent to take the sun can *only* lead to destruction. Doesn't the weight of the world we destroyed bother you? Can't you see- This *cannot* be allowed to happen *again.* "

"Stupid-ass kids go out chasin' fairy tales every damn day," Hubris says, but Raven can feel he's touched some sort of nerve. "They get killed or they give up and go home 'n get fat. Me and Crow's raisin' her aside, *Phin's* just a stupid-ass kid if I *ever* saw one. Like you said, she'll probably get herself killed way before she gets anywhere. What's this little girl got you worked up for?"

"Because they are *the same,* " Raven says doggedly. "Phineas Kidd is cut from the same cloth as Crow Gideon, it was obvious the moment I saw her. I wondered at first if perhaps she was this world's equivalent to him, if there *are* in fact doppelgangers for us here. She burns with the same intensity, the same *infuriating* arrogance rolls off of her in waves, the same *greed* glints in her eye." He leans forward in his chair, into the burning light of the compass. The rest of the room has darkened, lit only by the bioluminescence of the ghostly creatures in the air overhead and the radio on his desk. "Crow must have seen it, and although you feign ignorance I *know* you see it too. *Don't* you?"

She says nothing. She doesn't need to say anything.

"If Phineas Kidd wants to catch the sun, she will do so," Raven says. "*Just* like Gideon. She will follow in his footsteps, she will make his mistakes, and she'll take this whole universe with her when they finally catch up with her. And think about it, Jo..." He stares at the compass, knows the face of it is cracked, the needle rattling loose and useless under the glass. "Would it not be kinder for her to die here, before she ends up like we did?"

Jocasta is quiet. Then,

"Nah."

"...What?"

"No. You're wrong." He hears what must be a shrug, creaking through whatever furniture she's settled in. "You're acting like what

248

happened with you two is just how things are, but I think it's a you problem."

"You always got a choice," she says. "And you flaked out. *You* decided to abandon me and turn into this *weak* caricature of yourself. Don't try 'n pin all this on Gideon. I was there too, and you know, I'm pretty happy where I'm at. I think I'm bringin' some good into this place we ended up."

Raven leans back in his chair, closes his eyes. The distance between them is too much.

"...I'm still missing something here," her perfect voice hums across the connection. "What do you get out of *telling* all this to me? Do you want me to come stop you? Are you trying to hurt me? I know you ain't in your right mind, but there's gotta be some kind of fucked up logic going on here and I am not following."

The icy water is just beginning to cover the top of Raven's desk. Something cracks like a glacier, somewhere in the dark.

"She is frighteningly similar to Gideon but, I see so much of you in her too," he says, the words floating to the surface from a sunken ship. "The way she moves, the lilt in her cadence, the...the way she *shines.*"

This is it, this is really it, now.

"There is," Raven rasps. "Always the chance that I could die. As I said before, my body is much more frail now than it once was, and even at my best I never was a match for Crow. My pride is not so important to me that I won't admit it, not when it might cost my only chance to...I needed..."

Are you *sure?*

"...I needed a *messenger.*" It falls from his mouth like a curse, slippery, slithering into the world with no hope of ever being caught again. "You're the only one with any potential for reaching Crow, and it wouldn't- it wouldn't be *worth* anything if he didn't know what had happened. That I was the one who killed the girl, and why."

The silence is so heavy even Cold Hazard's black hole heart has trouble beating through it.

Finally, Jocasta says,

"You called me, after all this time," every word is a cigarette on Hazard's skin, teeth taking him to pieces. "To tell me you're gonna *kill my kid,* **then** kill the only friend I got left. So I could be your fallback plan."

"I never wanted to be cruel to you," Hazard moans. There are incomprehensible things swimming in the dark water around him, the sea is pouring in through broken glass. "But he took that option from me. I accepted a long time ago that you were one of the things swept away in the wake of Crow Gideon." It's getting harder to breathe, the pressure on the seabed is immense. "That's why I couldn't come back to you, it was...it was never *you.*"

"But would you," he slurs. "Would you believe me if I said I also wanted to hear your voice again?"

Hubris makes a sound he had heard when they fought together, the air being knocked from her lungs, a sharp gasp that seizes in his muscles.

"Even raised in anger. I don't mind. I," he can't see anything; the water is everywhere. He speaks into the void. "I've missed hearing you say my name, my *real* name. I've missed saying *yours.*"

"Well, you know," Jo says, her voice shining like a gem, shimmering up from under the water. "Phin means more to me than this whole world does. She wants to tear it up I think that's fine. If you go through with this?"

He listens to her take one more pull, the sound of dry leaves crumbling away so she can draw them in.

"I don't know how *long* you'd need to burn before that thing in your head finally let you die. But I imagine her bein' gone would free up plenty of my time to figure it out."

And she breathes out.

"Get fucked."

The connection dies, the compass closes, and the study is dark.

Very suddenly, there is nothing left for Raven Slight to do.

The sea swells with shadows, and what's left of the aquarium walls shatter.

Hazard lets go of his breath. He does not fight the arms that take him down.

9

Ulrich had been worried they'd gotten through the ordeal with entropy only to die of exposure in the impossible twistings of the mine, but since Phineas had ousted the tain it's almost like the tunnels have decided to help them. There are no more branching pathways or hungry shadows, just a long, gentle slope that ends anticlimactically with a ladder. It's probably fifty feet of ladder, which would normally be too much of it for Ulrich's liking even if it consisted of something more reliable than rounded steel rungs jutting out from a stone wall. Right now, every shifty rung is a relief.

Phineas stretches her shoulders, her legs.

"You good to climb?" she asks.

"I have never been better to climb."

"I'll go first, if one of these janky things breaks I'll land better'n you will."

"By all means," he says, not mentioning that she would likely take him with her anyhow.

The ascent is uneventful, although Ulrich's muscles are trembling dangerously by the end of it. He is just beginning to grow anxious he might not be able to make it when Phineas stops above him.

And stays stopped.

"...What is it?" Ulrich pants. His stomach plummets when he hears the sound of her fist thumping wood, scattering dirt down over both of them.

"Uh..."

Before he can really start to panic: the squeal of hinges, and a blade of bright red light from above.

"Uhh..." Phineas mumbles.

"What?"

The light goes away again when Phineas lets the cover back down.

"I dunno if we should-"

Ulrich groans, *almost* a growl.

"Phineas you get your ass up this ladder or I'm going *through* you."

Phineas fidgets, sending another thin shower of dirt across the porcelain of Ulrich's mask. Fortunate that he'd put it on again to see better in the dark.

"Okay," Phineas calls, "but don't get mad at-"

Ulrich slaps the back of his hand across her calf and she scrambles up through the door. When he follows a second later he hisses, the light sizzling in his eyes even through the tinted lenses of his mask, but it doesn't slow him down as he hauls himself over the edge and onto blessed topsoil. He rolls over onto his back as the wooden slab slams shut behind him and he heaves for breath, so desperate for fresh air he reaches to tear his mask from his sweaty face instead of dismissing it.

He hesitates, staring at the lines of dirt on his palm, when he realizes he can smell smoke through the filter.

They've come up through the basement of a burnt out building. Very *recently* burnt out, judging by the ash-fragile frame still skeletoned around them and the few scraps of flaming wood that haven't finished burning yet, and also the buildings one street over that are still visibly on fire. One of them is the flower shop where Ulrich and Phineas met, the mangled scrap of awning she'd torn apart sticking up from the flames like bones. In silence, Ulrich and Phineas watch the building burn until they're drawn out of their reverie by a cable snapping overhead. A row of tin street lanterns swings down and sails through the flower shop window, shattering both the glass and the compromised wall into a flurry of embers and smoke.

"Does this just *happen* around you?" Ulrich asks dryly, looking up at Phineas from the ground. She toes his shoulder lightly and grins.

"This ain't my fault, I was busy."

"Yeah I'd say so," Ellie interjects. Phineas and Ulrich startle together and Ellie huffs, not quite a laugh. Ulrich struggles to his feet and follows Phineas' shocked gaze towards a more inert corner of the ruined building, where Ellie is sitting on a cast iron safe. She is significantly more *resplendent* than Ulrich recalls.

She's wearing what looks like a military-themed burlesque costume; tall winged boots, a flight jacket, and a layered skirt with sky patterns embroidered on. The petticoat under the skirt isn't a petticoat at all but an opaque bundle of fluffy clouds, swirling and moving as she does. Curiously, the patches accenting the jacket are the snakes and winged spears that Ulrich normally sees on hospitals and pharmacies, symbols that denote medical facilities. Ellie is slumped down where she sits, leaning heavily against a shepherd's crook with a pair of bells hanging in the curve: Ulrich wouldn't have thought it possible, but she might be as tired as the two of them are.

Phineas is losing her *mind*.

"No *way,*" she breathes, rooted to the spot as Ellie stands and shakes out her hair. Ellie looks rough; her costume is covered in soot and ash, and when she dismisses the mirrored visor covering her eyes the fur behind it is several shades lighter than the rest of her. She smiles at the two of them, but the expression is tight.

"I cannot *believe* you're standing here talking to me," Ellie says, coming closer. The bells hanging in the hook chime gently when she moves, yellow ribbons streaming in the hazy air. Hazy air that gets easier to breathe as she approaches. "I heard Hazard caught you in the mine-"

"You're a *Blazing Guardian!?*" Phineas' voice squeals in Ulrich's hearing aid; he can almost see sparks coming from her ears as her brain short-circuits. The exhausted smile settles deeper into Ellie's features, and she leans on her staff.

"A fan, huh?" she asks.

"Sorry, what is a Blazing Guardian?" Ulrich asks, already dreading the answer. Phineas whips towards him like he's slapped her again.

"What is *wrong* with you?!" Phineas tangles her hands in his shirt and shakes him so hard it skews his glasses, dragging him down to her level immediately.

"HÖR AUF!"

"HOW do you not KNOW-"

"Get-!"

Ulrich cuts himself off mid-bicker, having just been handed a telegraph from some part of him so old it still communicates by telegraph.

"Ach, wait. Do you mean *Star Guardian* Sunny? That cartoon with the..." he glances at Ellie's outfit: the military coat, the flashy skirt. The catastrophic amount of ribbons. "The, the uniformed crime fighters?"

Phineas' face lights up.

"You *do* know it!"

"I was not *interested* in crime fighters," Ulrich sneers, shoving her away and straightening himself out. "I would catch it sometimes when I changed the channel to watch Mercy's Mysteries."

Phineas' face darks down.

"That old black and white stuff? Did you grow up in a *nursing home?*"

Ellie pointedly clears her throat, but they're off now.

"*My* entertainment was not conceptualized to sell *cereal* to *schoolchildren.*"

Ulrich is actually a bit taken aback by how Phineas' temper flares. She *stomps her foot* at him.

"Star Guardian ain't *like* that!" Phineas argues. Ulrich notes, with something perilously close to warmth, that this is something she's said before. Probably many times to many people. "Everybody acts like it's this stupid pointless show about fightin' 'cause they don't *get* it, y'all just see the goofy costumes and bright colors and can't take it seriously 'cause y'all are *boring.*"

She crosses her arms and *seethes,* frowning as much as she had when she'd gone around with their escorts in the mine before. "It's got allegories and all that, it's just as good as anything else! The stars and their shadows are..."

She whirls around to face Ellie who, like Ulrich, had been completely absorbed in her dissertation.

"Star shadows, the *tain,*" Phineas says, the cloud over her face clearing. "They're different on TV."

Ellie sighs and looks away, bites her lip. Is she *blushing?*

"Yes, well. The real *Sunny* is pretty different too."

"There's a *real Sunny..?*" Phineas' awe hits Ulrich like heat from an oven.

"Good *lord,*" he mutters, adjusting his sunglasses and turning to Ellie instead. "For the rest of us unfamiliar with this lore, *what* is she talking about?"

"The cartoon...gentles things up, but it don't really affect any of us out here doin' it for real," Ellie answers, exasperated, although Ulrich can't tell whether it's at the explanation or at him. "Most people don't even know there *are* Guardians outside the versions they're allowed to see. We like to keep a low profile."

"While enforcing your version of order?" Ulrich presses. Ellie's ear curls at his tone.

"While upholding justice," she says bluntly.

"Ah, so it's secret police," he says. "Should have guessed, those sorts of organizations *normally* being on the side of justice."

Ellie's derision is so fierce it snaps Phineas back to reality, blinking between the two of them like she's just woken up.

"We do what needs to be done to maintain balance," Ellie says coldly. Her staff ribbons out of view and she crosses the rest of the gap between them, stepping right through stubbornly flaming debris.

"Let me put it to you this way. *Usually,* teams of four or *five* are assigned to keep an eye on problem areas. *I'm* stationed here *alone,* and I work in reconnaissance, *not* combat. Whatever you saw down there is classified as a *minor* entity."

Ulrich is too angry to be intimidated by her approach; the picture all this Guardian business is painting is not one he appreciates, and after what's just happened in the mine he can't imagine feeling afraid of a waitress dressed like a backup dancer.

"We work in secret for *reasons.* The scale of things like The Yellow Queen, or the pervasiveness of the tain- the Sprawl as people *know* it is harsh. We lie about what we're doin' where we're stationed so people don't *panic* and make our jobs harder." She smiles bitterly and her demeanor changes. Ulrich is struck with the delusion that she gets taller as she steps up to him, inches from his face. "But you ain't real concerned with honesty, are you, Ulrich?"

Oh, we are absolutely *not* doing this. Ulrich smiles his most charming smile.

"I'm sorry, English is not my first language," he says, tasting something cold in the corner of his tongue. "The subtleties can elude me from time to time, are you insinuating something?"

Ellie's eye twitches furiously but before she can say anything Phineas speaks up.

"Hey, what about the starstone though?" she asks, either oblivious to the tension or more interested in changing the topic. Ellie sighs, backing out of Ulrich's face to include Phineas in the discussion.

"What about it?"

"So the *tain* I get, I think. Commanders deal with all that light and dark stuff too, in different terms." Phineas holds up her palm and points to the circle burned into the leather of her glove, though it's so damaged now it's hard to make out. "Circle stuff, right? Natural balances and equal reactions and all that?"

"Sure," Ellie says, her mouth moving like she wants to smile.

"I always knew starstone was alive, but I thought it was like...*plants,* or something," Phineas says, and Ellie pinches the bridge of her nose before she's finished. "I didn't think they were *conscious.*"

A blackened support beam, now supporting nothing, crackles as it crumbles apart. The scattering ash and embers stop short before they reach the group, bouncing harmlessly from some area of affect Ellie is generating in a splash of yellow glitter.

"You are a pain in my ass, Phineas Kidd." She tries to brush out her skirt and put her appearance in order, an attempt at authority that proves futile when Phineas giggles anyway. "You commanders are a real problem for us, just you bein' here interferes with a lot of my magic."

"Really?" Phineas asks, taken aback that *anyone* could affect such flawless beings. *"How?"*

"You *ignore* it, mostly-" Ulrich snorts, and Ellie cuts off long enough to shoot him a withering look. "You're like bulls in dish shops. If anyone important knew I didn't let Papa throw you out when you showed up I'd be in big trouble."

"Hey yeah, how come you did that for me?"

Ellie smiles wanly, shrugs.

"I dunno. I didn't want to. Mama never had a problem with y'all."

"Mama?" Phineas echoes. Then her eyes light up again. "Was your *mom* a guardian too?!"

Whatever Ellie responds with is lost to Phineas' excited babbling as she leaps forward, reaching for Ellie's hand.

"Oh *man,* Ellie you *gotta* come with-"

An itch lances from the nape of Ulrich's neck up over his scalp, there's an electric hum as Phineas' hand gets close to Ellie's, and Ulrich has exactly enough time to flinch before the meeting of their skin looses a sharp, *freezing* shockwave. Phineas is knocked off her feet like she's taken a shotgun blast to the chest. She lands flat on her back in a bare patch of ashy dirt several feet away, wheezing.

As Ellie falls into a defensive stance, the shepherd's crook reappears in her hands with a flash of yellow and a chime that makes Ulrich's teeth ache. She's pointing it at Phineas, and Ulrich silently lays his hand over Glückssache.

"What happened down there?!" Ellie shrieks, more fear than anger. "You're *contaminated!*"

Phineas struggles to sit up, coughing and clutching her chest.

"We had to *fight!*" she whines, looking between Ellie's face and the end of her weapon, hurt. "They were gonna eat Ulrich so-"

"You *fought* them? *You can't* fight them!"

"You just *said* I could! Can't you feel they're gone now?" It is infuriating how the plaintive note in her voice bothers Ulrich.

"I thought you- I didn't think *you-*" Ellie shakes her head sharply. "Nobody can stand up to an infestation like this! Not *alone!*"

"She wasn't," Ulrich says. He lets his fingertips slide away from the grip of his revolver before Ellie can see it's there. She laughs, shaky with adrenaline.

"Yeah? I bet you were lots of help with those toys you got there."

"He was," Phineas says. "I said *we* fought. *We* won." The tone of her voice draws them both in. Up on her elbows where she fell, filthy with blood and sweat and several varieties of dirt, she's looking at Ellie with so much intensity it feels like she's taken all the invisible strings of the world in her hand again. Not pulling, only reminding everyone that she could. Ulrich has seen the expression before during other, meaner negotiations; a shot across the bow, providing an out before she gets aggressive, waiting to see if Ellie pushes her to it.

Ellie doesn't.

"Phineas was possessed, briefly," Ulrich sweeps them along, feeling oddly flustered. "But clearly that is no longer the case. We are *here* in the sweltering sun, are we not?"

"Yeah! I wouldn't even be able to sit out here if I still had those guys on me, I think," Phineas says, losing all that authority and nodding along with Ulrich as if she doesn't *completely* outclass this weak excuse for a soldier. Ulrich wishes she'd stand up.

"Would you lower your weapon, please?" he asks.

Ellie takes her time thinking it over. Ulrich feels like he's negotiating with a toddler who is *insisting* the toy phone she's playing with really *does* connect her to a war room somewhere, and that is why she's making the adults late for their dinner reservation.

Eventually Ellie reaches some internal resolution. She deflates and sets her staff in the dirt again, the glow leaving the bells.

"...Alright, you're right, I'm just..." She rubs her eyes.

"What's happened up *here,* Ellie?" Phineas asks, sitting up to a cross-legged position like she's ready to listen to a story. After the cold and dark of the mines Ulrich had been relieved to be topside again, but now that they've been standing here under the blistering sun (not even taking the *still-active fire* into consideration), he's starting to sweat. He would take off his hat if it weren't so damn bright.

"Ray came back and set the bar on fire," Ellie says flatly. Ulrich hears Phineas' sharp intake of breath, but she manages to keep a lid on whatever she wants to say so Ellie can finish. "The rest of the town went up like a box of matches. Y'all know there ain't that many people left around here anyways-" Ellie taps her temple twice, two matching reflections rippling out where her visor would be. "-so it wasn't too hard to track 'em down and get 'em out safe. But I can't do nothin' about the structures. Everything up here is gonna burn."

"What," Ulrich says, catty. "You don't have any *Special Guardian Powers* you can use to put out fires?"

"I'm an emissary," Ellie says irritably. "I *told* you, my *Special Guardian Powers* involve reconnaissance and delivering messages, I'm not built for combat *or* firefighting. I've minimized civilian casualties, I even helped some of Hazard's people- our, people, who abandoned their posts when things got dangerous. I've *done* everything I *can.*"

Something isn't right. Ulrich leans carefully against a sooty doorframe, splintered and standing on its own even after its walls have gone.

"You did not elect to call home?" he asks, shaking out his filthy handkerchief and wiping sweat from his face, remembering too late it has blood on it. He's more upset that it doesn't upset him. "Nobody was standing by to back you up when the powder keg finally blew?"

Her face pinches and Ulrich's heart leaps like he's hit his mark—that's *it*. Phineas interrupts before he can pursue the lead any further.

"What's Hazard doin' right now?" she asks, completely ignoring what's just been said. Ulrich fights not to roll his eyes.

"He's upstairs. Now I'm in uniform I can sense him on the ship, he's...hard to miss."

Phineas nods sourly. Just for fun, Ulrich flickers his eyes up the length of the radio tower and gets blasted with sunshine for his trouble.

"I...I don't think he cares about the town or anybody in it," Ellie goes on, biting her lip. "Not the mining operation either. A water wizard, especially, should have been able to keep his own setup from burning. I don't think he was here just to steal stone to cut for profit, but..." she shakes her head, gripping her staff with both hands and leaning on it. "What *did* he want? Did you learn anything about any of this while you were down there? Did he say anything?"

"Nah," Phineas shrugs. "Nothin' that would be helpful here I don't think."

"I don't know what he'll do now," Ellie murmurs. "I'm afraid...he's gonna try something, *drastic*, once the town's snuffed out."

"Like what?" Phineas asks. "What can he do to this place if the town's already destroyed?"

Ellie laughs humorlessly, leaning her forehead against the staff like she's praying. A bead of sweat rolls down Ulrich's back, soaking into his disgusting clothes, and suddenly he's had enough of this.

"I have a question now," he cuts in. "Several, actually. Why did the Guardians let any of this happen in the first place? Why let Hazard establish himself here, if this is some-" god, he *hates* this spiritual crap, "-some place of *mystical interest?*"

"Weren't you listening?" Ellie snaps. "What am *I* gonna do against *him?* I'm all on my own out here!"

"Right, you are!" Ulrich says, straightening up off the doorframe to take a step towards her. He is quietly gratified when she shifts away in kind. "Is that not the point of joining an organization? Why isn't Last Chance *swarming* with other Guardians right now?"

"Too far to get to quick?" Phineas chirps. Neither of them acknowledge her; Ellie's hands are tight around her staff, but Ulrich can tell it's because she's being backed into corner.

"Calling in something like this, it-" Ellie stammers. "I was hopin' he would just take what he wanted and...this is *better,* than-"

"Than *what?*" Ulrich spits. "Peacekeepers? That's what you claim to be?" He flings one arm out towards the other side of the street where, his luck being what it is, the boarded-up building next to the flower shop collapses in on itself. The three of them watch it go, smoke and flame spraying into the sky. He catches Ellie's eye. "Is this *peaceful* to you?"

Ellie looks near tears, and a mean bone in Ulrich's body is pleased. *Good,* maybe now she'll stop jerking them around.

"Why're you bein' so hard on her, Ulrich?" Phineas asks, still quite neutral. That's surprising. He'd been bracing for her to step in to pull him back in line when he pushed too much, but she only seems curious. Maybe she can see something in Ellie's halo that he can't.

Or she trusts you, more than anybody ever will again, you rotten son of a bitch.

"This story does not make sense," Ulrich replies, steady despite the thought that's just crossed his mind, annoyed by the effort it takes to stay that way. "She is not telling us everything-"

Phineas scoffs at him and he glares at her before he remembers he's wearing sunglasses.

"*You're* upset someone's keepin' secrets?"

"I don't buy *half* of what she's told either of us," Ulrich continues. "She's already threatened us once, I would like to be certain about whether we need to watch our backs going forward."

Ellie narrows her eyes at him.

"What are you saying?" she asks.

"I am saying Hazard was expecting us at the bottom of the elevator shaft, using the keycard *you* gave us."

The surprise across Ellie's face is incriminating, her ensuing silence is damning.

"I didn't know," she stammers, "I didn't realize the-"

"I am going to ask one more time," Ulrich says levelly. *"What* is going on here?"

"It's okay, Ellie." The gentle energy commanded in Phineas' voice smothers the heat from the conversation. Ulrich clings to his ire, refusing to be soothed.

Ellie's shoulders sag, and her eyes do tear up this time, but she pulls it together before she continues.

"The Guardians answer to The Yellow Queen, a... the deity, who sends us our orders. If I contact anyone for help, if I draw her attention here, she'll destroy this settlement and everyone in it."

There is a second before she goes on where all three of them are keenly aware they're standing in a burning, evacuated settlement.

"No," Ellie amends, kneading the heel of her hand against her forehead. "She'll rewrite the reality around us and crush *everything* out of *existence,* even the *memory* of this place will be erased. The kinds of problems that would need that attention, she doesn't...it's safer for everyone to just eradicate the problem."

"Hazard is worth all that to an elder god?" Phineas asks, still maintaining that puzzling neutrality. "This random wizard?"

"He's been agitatin' the tain," Ellie says miserably. "And I've let it go on *way* too long, it's like a *fungus* you have to- But I didn't *want-"*

"So much for that low profile," Ulrich says coldly. "People would *notice* if an entire settlement disappeared, *how* is that sort of intervention supposed to benefit *anyone!"*

"Maybe not the whole city, this time," Phineas muses. "Just part of it. All those weird pieces of cut-up junk, the buildings being repaired with parts that don't make sense..." She leans back to look up at Ellie. Phineas doesn't squint in the light as much as she should, and that paired with her detached curiosity gives her the look of staring into headlights, unaware it's an oncoming car. "It already happened, didn't it? You picked up Last Chance from someplace else and moved it out here."

Phineas' open expression changes so suddenly Ulrich tenses, follows her line of sight to find whatever's startled her. There's nothing.

"What?" he asks curtly.

"That big turtle, Careful something," she says, dominos falling on dominos. *"He* don't look right for here *either,* did you-"

Ellie groans, skipping ahead in the logic.

"*What!*"Ulrich snaps. "Spit it out!"

"You didn't just move part of the city, you *changed the land,*" Phineas breathes. "This isn't supposed to *be* a desert, that saint is leafy, he belongs in like a *jungle* or something." Phineas levels her stare at Ellie, shaken, and Ulrich finds it much more unsettling than the roadkill mien. "What the hell can move a *patron saint* away from its land?"

Phineas' expression is not fearful, but it would be fear on Ulrich.

"I *refuse* to believe *any* of this madness is true, what are we even *talking* about here!" Ulrich glares at both of them in turn and sees Ellie's temper flare. "Patron saints? The pictures they put on *candles* and *coins* and *sell out of vending machines to gamblers?* That *thing* out there is just an *animal,*" he rounds on Phineas. "She is covering for Hazard, we can't *trust* this! You can *not* be buying into this superstitious *bullshit!*"

"Stuff works different out of the city, Ulrich," Phineas shrugs.

Ellie isn't nearly as patient.

"You *miserable bitch,*" she spits, rounding on Ulrich. "Don't you think it's weird there are *no roads here?! No* roads leading *anywhere!* None that even run *close* to what used to be a trade city?" She shakes her staff at the tower looming over them, the bells ominous and grating. "Why would we need a radio tower like this for a settlement this small!? *What,* do you think Hazard showed up and *fucked* everything *and then* bothered to clear out any evidence of the city outside the mining district! Just to throw *you* off the trail?!"

"*Why,*" Ellie demands, "was a town in the *desert,* built out of *wood?!*"

He doesn't change outwardly, but Ulrich's stomach sinks the way it does when his body learns bad news before he does. Ellie closes her eyes and takes a very slow breath; he recognizes that she's counting.

"I dunno, why?" Phineas says glibly. Ellie lets go of her staff and it stands obediently on its own while she covers her face, yellow gems in her lace and leather gloves glittering. It takes another moment for her to answer.

"My mother was the Guardian assigned here," she says, trying to keep the tremor from her voice. "The starstone and the tain here are minor entities *now,* but they were a lot stronger before, and she was here to keep them in check."

"Just her?" Phineas interrupts, her light tone still painfully dissonant against the heavy conversation. Ellie shakes her head.

"Me, too. I was still training under her when. Something, caught the Queen's attention, and…"

⊙⊙⊙

-how does this… oh wait, I think- [2]

⊙⊙⊙

Ellie was pretty sure her wrist was broken, but the more immediate worry was that she couldn't get her vision to focus. Every time she tried to stand she'd blink and open her eyes to the dirt or the sky, off her feet again. The sky was the worse one between them, she couldn't actually see it for all the wings and bodies beating against it. Where they weren't, there were wounds as big as the city streets, the blood of something she couldn't bear to think about pouring through like melting wax. Like an invisible hand was reaching through to tear weeds away, chunks of the city sailed between columns of shining viscera to disappear into the cracked sky. Entire buildings, cars, trees, asphalt streets curling through the air like peeling fruit. Animals, people, their wailing unheard under the apocalyptic din of Hastur and her children but seen in the wild thrashing of their limbs. Laid out on the ground, the concrete rough on her arms, Ellie thought they looked like little black bugs, skittering into holes to get out of the light.

Everything in the world was red. She tried to tell herself, shocky and quiet, that it was only blood in her eyes. It couldn't be the whole world, there must still be blue sky somewhere, even if she couldn't see it.

There was a roaring in her ears, distinct from the low, bone-cracking hum that Hastur seemed to exude just by existing in this plane. It took her addled senses too long to figure out that it was Mama's minigun, the shining light construct screaming and spinning as it

---

2 Notes on Hastur the Hushed, or The Yellow Queen, p. 394

sprayed covering fire up into the cloud of Hastur's offspring. They vaporized on contact with the ammunition, emerald points of light that matched Molly's lush halo. But there were so *many*, and Hastur herself was so impossibly huge Ellie couldn't even see enough of her to comprehend the shape. The Yellow Queen only existed as a sheer wall of golden carapace too massive to exist in this world, raggedly honeycombed muscle and bone in a glistening red arch stretched across the landscape like a grisly suspension bridge. There was a shape looming through the cloud of swarming insects, taller than any of the other mountains, segmented arms outstretched— Ellie knew it must be Her but she couldn't make her mind accept what she was seeing. The only detail distant enough for Ellie to make out at all was what must have been the head. Far, far away, behind the clouds and against the red sun like a satellite, there was something like a pyramid. The face was obscured by folds and ripples, like fabric, and covered in locks and chains— the only thing in sight that wasn't affected by the Queen's presence. They shone in a color like an oil slick, halo colors rare enough they didn't get names.

What had put the chains there, what *other* thing could imprison *this* thing, was a thought so far beyond the pale Ellie simply didn't entertain it.

Any Blazing Guardian knew if Hastur showed up, if you ever saw her, your service was at an end. The Queen appeared to sterilize wounds in the world, and made no distinction between the wound and the living things she found in them. Molly and Ellie were good soldiers. Both of them had always been prepared to die for the cause.

Mama's gun sang anyway, and Ellie sat there bleeding and concussed because she'd used the last of her magic to shield them in here, in this tiny pocket in the street. They hadn't discussed it, there hadn't been any plan. Ellie couldn't even think of how they'd ended up holding out here, fighting their own forces. She kept thinking of her dad though, the way his bushy moustache rubbed her skin when she'd kissed his cheek on the way out that morning.

Ellie hauled herself up to a sitting position against a drainpipe and watched Molly's back, long hair and endless skirts settling to rest as she finally stopped firing. This was it, then. But nobody could say they hadn't tried, and it didn't matter that Ellie was already having trouble remembering why.

Mama turned, only a glowing silhouette in Ellie's blurring vision, but Ellie knew what she was looking at. Her missing tooth, her rough, steady hands, the same yellow curls that framed Ellie's own face. Molly was filthy and bruised, her uniform burnt and bloody, but she smiled wide enough her chubby cheeks narrowed her eyes as she reached into her breast pocket for her calling stone and dagger. Ellie's sluggish thoughts weren't fast enough to react before her mother plunged the knife into the gem. They weren't fast enough to catch what she said as she did it either, to Ellie's eternal regret.

A rushing across the world like a starlight tide, the camera flashbulb burning the image of her mother into Ellie's memory. Against the red, against the copper on Ellie's tongue: defiant, radiant verdigris.

◉◉◉

"...It gets. Hazy, after that," Ellie murmurs. "It's like there's a spot in my memory that keeps me from thinkin' about it for too long. I'm not sure what Mama did, but the next thing I knew she was gone, and the rest of the city was gone too. The forest around it. Even the names have been erased, there's just this desert now where it all used to be." She gestures limply at the smoldering settlement she stands in. "Just this place."

"Careful Pete," Phineas says. "Pete *is* a jungle saint then. But he got left here when his jungle disappeared."

"There's a hare saint that visits us sometimes," Ellie says. "I think this was *his* desert, wherever it used to be. He's a lot quicker than Pete is so he travels between the two to check in now and then."

Phineas whistles, thinking of how the tortoise saint had lit her up with that feeling of enormous, lonesome distance; displacement. No kidding.

"Mama already broke the rules here, this town shouldn't even *exist.*" Phineas giggles. "Oh man, you *are* in trouble. If any of yours find out about this they're gonna come finish the job, huh? Gods get pissy about defiance."

"Who said anything about gods?" Ulrich asks, fuming like a little kid.

"What else would you call something like that, Ulrich?" Phineas asks.

"I have very recently learned there are many more things out in the Sprawl than I had previously imagined," he insists. "This could just be another particularly large beast."

"Gods come from faith," Phineas says, holding her hand out in Ellie's direction. "And Hastur has a whole dang army backing her up. That's a god, toe to tip."

"I don't *care* what she is!" Ellie breaks in. "I'm not-! I can't just let me and my dad, these people, be killed by the Queen after my mom got *herself* killed to keep it from happening." Her shaky halo recedes to pool more cleanly around her head as she steadies. "She thought our lives were worth saving, even when Hastur decided they weren't. The least I can do is keep those lives out of any more gods' hands. Or wizards'. Anything *else* that decides to show up."

Phineas nods and opens her mouth to say something she hopes is reassuring, but a shadow ebbs into the corner of her vision. It's *Ulrich's* halo, gone that watery inscrutable grey, the blight in his eye bleeding everywhere. He's laser-focused on Ellie, still, and he looks as cruel as she's ever seen him.

"These rewrites, that Hastur does," he asks slowly. "They tamper with memories too? What if someone arrived here *after* the initial event?"

"When Hastur remakes something, her reach stretches *backwards* in our timeline, enough that any weaker consciousnesses are...reshaped, to match her will." Ellie looks uncomfortable about it. "Even the big starstone spirit underground probably had its memory replaced. That's how it usually goes, the process is...messy, but it cleans up after itself."

"But *Hazard* isn't affected, somehow," Ulrich demands. Man, he's *really* committed to this double agent thing he thinks Ellie is doing.

No, Phineas thinks, another one of those logical conclusions that had needed extra time to take shape. It's the gods, and now it's his *memory* he's worried about. He'd said it before, that he doesn't like feeling manipulated. This has been a rough day for him.

266

"Hazard's sort've an anomaly, I think," Ellie says. "His arrival *changed* something, it's like he brought some kind of distortion with him into the closed system."

"When my mom interrupted Hastur's attempt to wipe out the province, she trapped us here, like we're in a terrarium," she looks across the street again, hanging against her staff. "And now Hazard's here dropping in all these new things. The story I told you about *Hazard* being why the town is so barren is what everyone believes *now*, but I, erm...I don't know how long we've really been here, like this, or what we all believed before."

Ulrich's menacing halo desaturates even more, swirling with the kind of fear that makes trapped animals chew through their own legs.

Ellie says, "I thought Hazard was a commander, when he first got here, but commanders don't usually get involved with the tain like he has." She smiles tiredly at Phineas. "Y'all don't work in the dark."

Phineas shakes her head.

"That shit'll kill ya," she says. Ulrich does an unhinged little giggle that makes Phineas grin and flutter her feet.

"And normal wizard magic shouldn't have much effect against an elder god's," Ellie says, less charmed. "Not only were *his* memories unaffected, but just him showin' up was enough to change everyone else's *again*. Hastur is big and powerful enough to rewrite reality on a whim, I've never even heard of anything that could negate a will like hers."

Ulrich is outwardly irate, but Phineas can see anxiety rippling from him in jagged lances of light.

"Great," he says. "So you don't know anything and you cannot call for backup. I hope your membership fees are not too steep."

"What do you *want?!*" Ellie snaps. "I don't know how this affects people who show up later because this has *never happened before!* I told you the magic cleans up after itself, anybody who encounters this whole-" She throws her hands up, and a row of hubcaps nailed to an exposed interior wall of the building they're standing in clatters to the floor, the frame holding them up splintering apart in the heat. "*-thing!* Is conditioned to *ignore* anything that doesn't make sense-"

"Conditioned?!" Ulrich shouts, his glasses sliding down his sweaty face. He's *so* scared, but he's disguised it so thoroughly as anger Phineas clamps down on the impulse to try and comfort him and lets him go, curious where he's going. "You *brainwash* people?"

"I *said* you didn't want to know any of this," Ellie fires back. Ulrich snatches his glasses from his face and presses his palm to his forehead, like he has a headache.

"That is fucking *heinous,"* he grits out. *"Disgusting."*

"It's not anything," Ellie insists, although she still seems uncomfortable about it herself. Phineas wishes either of them would just be honest with what they're feeling, this is such a waste of time.

"So why are *we* here?" Phineas asks, trying to nudge them along. "How'd me and Ulrich get in?"

"One of those ways commanders are a pain in the ass is y'all *are* resistant to this," Ellie says. "Your consciousnesses aren't fully attached to this plane, so Hastur's changes are harder to..." Her eyes dart to Ulrich for a split second before she says, "enforce." Ulrich makes exactly the sound she must have been expecting. "That's prob'ly why you came here still expecting to find the city, with the starstone trade and the shipyard."

"Oh! Nah, my m..."

Mom, Jocasta, *Jo* had told her. Hazard has something going on with him that makes him resistant to this god's magic, and *he* knows Jo, and Gideon, and *Jo's coat,* and Jocasta had *also* ignored Hastur's influence to tell Phineas to come *here.*

"Phineas?" Ellie asks, furrowing her brow. Phineas clears her throat.

"Yup! You're right, must've been commanding stuff."

Ulrich is looking now too, it's weird, it's definitely weird and everybody can tell, but the shape of the realization creeping into the murky edges of Phineas' mind is so impossible she doesn't think she could explain it to them even if she wanted to. Trying to breathe through the sudden vertigo, she's quiet long enough that Ellie decides to move on.

"I don't know why the hell *you're* here though," Ellie says in Ulrich's direction. He lingers on Phineas a second longer, but then he sniffs and tosses his head in that smug way Phineas likes so much, putting his glasses back on.

"I am lucky. I'm always where I need to be."

"Man," Phineas says, only some residual shakiness in her voice. "This explains a *lot*. I thought you were just bein' a coward, earlier. Mom stuff is..." She finds Ellie's eyes. "I'm sorry I was mean to you about all this before."

Ellie shrugs. Her smile is bitter.

"You didn't know. And I...didn't think things would get so *complicated*. Hazard showing up really...I dunno what to do now." She shakes her head at absolutely everything. "I can't just hand everyone over to Hastur after Mom died to keep that from happening, but I can't fix this on my own."

"Yeah! But we can," Phineas chirps before Ellie can start tearing up again. She leans back on her hands and looks to Ulrich. "Right?"

"You're...you're still planning on confronting him?" Ellie asks, incredulous.

Phineas lolls her head back on her shoulders and grins, feeling her own self-assuredness radiating in her bones.

"Yeah I'm gonna beat that guy bloody," she says, basking in the sun. "Just 'cause a bunch of other stupid crap is goin' on don't mean I gotta give up on what I came for. I'm not leavin' without a ship after all this." Then her lip curls into a pout. "And I want my *coat* back, and my *compass*."

"...And what are *you* getting out of all this?" Ellie asks Ulrich. He grins too, with those weird teeth, his eyes obscured behind his glasses.

"Isn't a good deed its own reward?" Ulrich says in a delicate stream of silver light. Ellie shifts on her feet, her fatigue catching up with her enough Phineas feels it too.

"Whatever, I don't *care,*" Ellie mumbles, rubbing her eyes. "I'd offer to help you up to his ship, but I tried getting in already, he's got...defenses, set up. It's overkill. Like he was expectin' a fight with someone else like *him.*"

Phineas clears her throat and feels Ulrich look at her sharply, but Ellie doesn't seem to catch it.

"I can't get close enough myself to fly y'all up there. There's the elevator, but you'd still need a good key to make it run, and the fire's burning too hot near the base for you to get close…" She chews on her lip, and Phineas is delighted to find she's adorable again, now that Phineas knows she has some fight in her after all. "I *do* have some basic protection blessings that might help with that, but there's too much dark energy clinging to you. I don't think it would take."

Phineas frets, remembering the sting that put her here on the ground.

"What about Ulrich?" she asks. "He didn't puke up a demon or nothin'."

Ellie makes a face that reminds Phineas that was an odd thing to say, but Ellie recovers quick.

"*Ulrich* isn't a suitable candidate *either.*"

"Why, because I don't believe in any of this spiritual bullshit?"

"*Your* problem has nothing to *do* with-"

Phineas sees Ulrich lean in, ready to argue again, and she neatly reaches the end of her patience for this.

"Quit talkin' around it, I already know Ulrich robbed the armadillo guy," she says. Ulrich and Ellie stare down at her, wearing such identical expressions of shock Phineas giggles.

"You *knew?*" Ellie shrieks.

"*You* knew?!" Ulrich shouts at Phineas.

"Yeah dude, ever since you lied about it last night in the shack." She waves her hand the way she had back then, when she was trying to describe halos to him. "I can *see* you lying, remember?"

Nothing she says makes him feel any better, because it's clear he *had* remembered, he'd just never really believed her about it. She smiles apologetically.

"Your delivery was good!" she says. "But even without the commander vision stuff, I knew anyway. I hitched a ride with him yesterday before you 'n me met. Knowin' what I know now, it don't make sense that Hazard would ambush a guy bringing stuff into town like that, and nothing about that wagon looked like a whole group attacked him. But I bet one dude good with explosives could've taken out a wheel and waved a gun around if he had to, huh?"

Ellie looks scandalized. Or maybe disappointed?

"You're just. *Okay* with this?" she wonders. "I thought you'd be…"

Phineas addresses Ulrich, who is even paler than usual.

"Well it was stuff you needed, right?"

"G...gunpowder," he says it so quiet, like he's talking to himself even though he's staring right back into Phineas' eyes. "Metal components..."

Phineas nods firmly and addresses Ellie.

"Yeah, see? It's fine. He didn't hurt the guy or muss up his wagon more than he had to, he didn't even hurt the animals."

"I shot one of the wheel axles with an explosive round," Ulrich says hollowly. "The cart went over, he hit his head I think. I only threatened him."

"I've seen meaner robberies," Phineas says. "Do what you gotta do to get where you're goin', right?"

"No, *not* right," Ellie stammers. "You can't just-"

"She makes a good point, El'," someone says, and the three of them turn in the direction of the new voice to find Royal standing there at the edge of the ruined building.

He's very dirty, and Phineas can see from here he's *really* pissed about something, but when Ellie grins and flounces over to hug him her gold overpowers everything. Ah, that makes sense now too: it was *her* he'd been dreaming about when she saw him sleeping in the bar last night.

"Oh, I'm so glad to *see* you-" Ellie kisses his cheek; the side of his face that Phineas hadn't bruised. "I couldn't find you before, I was afraid they'd taken you up top."

"I don't think there's anybody doing anything at this point," Royal says dully. "All *this* was-"

"Ray," Ellie finishes, exhausted. She shoots a look back in Phineas and Ulrich's direction, and so does Royal. Phineas and Ulrich realize together that they're intruding.

"We..." Phineas stands up and stretches, and it stings; even *her* skin is starting to feel dried out in this heat. "Y'all get caught up, we'll wait. Over here." She gently grips Ulrich's shirt sleeve and leads him away without waiting for a response, moving them across the boundary of the building's floor and into the street as if there's still a wall there to provide privacy. Ellie and Royal huddle up again, like drawing a curtain.

Aside from the constant crackling of fire eating wood it's quiet between the two of them, but Phineas can feel Ulrich's tension beside her like piano wire. When she can't take it any more, Phineas leans way out to try and see what his face is doing.

"What's up?" she asks. She isn't ready for him to round on her, his halo surging out around him in shaky neon lines, the blight in his eye huge between them. The left eye is lost in the jittery bleed, but his right is as clear and focused as it had been when they'd been this close the night before. He'd had his gun to her head, then, but right now his arms are folded protectively in front of his chest.

"Why?" he asks. There's a rough edge to his voice Phineas isn't used to.

"Why what?" Oh, wait. "Is this about-"

"Of course it is," Ulrich says, clipped, ruffled like a bird. "That story was my entire excuse for being here with you at all, for being in Last Chance, for going after Hazard- *Why,* Phineas? What the hell is *wrong* with you?"

Phineas giggles and looks across the way again to watch Ellie and Royal. Ellie's hands are glowing as she places them over Royal's head where he's knelt in front of her, like a knight. The light is soothing against the destruction surrounding them, it's a good place for Phineas to rest her eyes while she gathers up a bunch of words for this. Third time is the charm, and Ulrich likes those. They are going to put this thing to bed this time.

"I know you think I'm dumber'n you," she starts. "And nicer. I like your narcissism, I like everything about you. I like letting you lie to me and goin' along with it because it makes you feel better to do it."

"Phineas," Ulrich says, running an exasperated hand through his hair, under his hat. It's the tone of someone learning they've been given the last ration, some anguished kindness they'd rather die than admit they needed. She levels her stare at him, watches the weight of her full attention hit him like a spotlight. The blight recedes and Ulrich gasps for air.

"What, you wanna tell me about it *now?*" she asks, sunlight rattling through her throat. "Whatever real reason you're here? Why you're really interested in me?"

She sees him swallow to get his breathing under control. Then he slowly shakes his head, his eyes not leaving hers. Phineas smiles and eases off the pressure, although his face only seems to tighten even more.

"Any rough you got in your edges is good. I like rough." She keeps him pinned under her eyes, sees her own light on his face. "I like *you*, I want you with me, just the same as what you said to me in the mine. The details don't matter. I told you all this already, but I'll keep sayin' it until it sinks in."

There's something new happening in the halo around him that brings up an old memory in Phineas: being thrown into the pond behind Jo's house, and when she'd sunk far enough for things to get quiet, she'd opened her eyes to find the golden summer sunlight streaming through the water plants reaching around her, straining for the surface. Here now, in the air around her Ulrich, she sees his dark blooms shifting in the tide against misty light. But these are limned in silver.

"...I don't know what to *say.*" He says it like he's afraid his voice will shatter her.

"Then shut *up,* Ulrich."

"Hey," Ellie's voice floats across the street to meet them, and Phineas feels Ulrich box himself up. She almost reaches to hold his hand as they regroup, but he probably needs some space after all that.

Royal is glowing, steeped in Ellie's energy.

"Roy's gonna lead y'all to the elevator at the base of the tower," Ellie says. "As long as y'all stay close together you shouldn't be hurt by much of anything on your way."

That snaps Ulrich back to the present.

"Wait, we are..." He cuts himself off before he can demand the obvious. Of course they're taking the elevator, there's no other way up. "Is it. Safe?"

Royal laughs, sardonic, and Ellie does a bad job of hiding her glee at how upset Ulrich suddenly is.

"Look," she says. "I know it seems kinda rickety now, but I'm. Real close, with the person who built it." She softens, Phineas sees warm affection light up in the air around her. "It doesn't even feel right to call what he does somethin' plain like 'engineering', that man is an artist. If Reuben built it, the elevator will go where it's supposed to. Fire or not."

She takes a few steps back, and there's a sound like windchimes as a pair of wings billow into existence behind her, enormous and feathery and absolutely fantastic. Phineas tries very, *very* hard to remain normal under the golden glare of that magnificent halo, its feathery shapes stretching out beyond her wings, finally allowed to take up all the space it wants. The wings might only be for show; Ellie takes a delicate step and drifts into the air with hardly any input from them at all. Phineas has had dreams like this.

"There's one more friend I gotta go check on," Ellie tells them, a yellow visor sliding into place across her face. "Y'all take care, okay?"

They watch Ellie ascend into the smoky sky, a daisy-spot against the soot.

⊙

The route to the tower isn't long at all, but Royal and Ulrich both are too awkward to speak, so it feels like it takes forever and it hurts the whole time. Phineas makes it about halfway before she's forced to open her mouth or die.

"Aren't these rabbits neat?" she tries, referring to the cloud of yellow bunnies crowding around them like cheerful breadrolls. They're snuffing out whatever flames hinder the party's movement and keeping a barrier of cool, refreshing air around the humans as they travel through to the city center, where things are still actively burning. Royal stares at her blankly. He is not at all happy to be here, but he is also covered in breadroll bunnies and it severely undercuts his attempt to be threatening. Still, that looks like a dead end for conversation, so she turns her sights on Ulrich.

"Ssso, how ya holding up with this elder god stuff?" she asks lightly. "You adjusting okay still?"

"Don't *patronize* me, Phineas," Ulrich mutters, wiping sweat from his face with his pink handkerchief.

"I ain't!" she protests, slouching and jamming her hands in her pockets. "Man y'all are *so* grumpy, ain't this all good? We're getting where we're going! *Finally!*"

274

"Frankly, I'm surprised how well *you're* accepting that your childhood heroes have turned out to be some sort of *nightmare army*," Ulrich sniffs.

Phineas shrugs, nudging at one of the bunnies with her toe. It skitters away from her.

"Eh, when Ellie said it was one of the big gods running things I figured that's about what the story would be. That's just what they're like."

"You encounter them often?"

"Not a *lot*, but I met one sorta like Hastur before. Big and mean for no good reason." Phineas unconsciously settles her hand over her chest, feeling Ulrich's eyes on her. Royal is still ignoring them, carving the path ahead of them with his adorable escorts.

"The Guardians are different than I thought, but I think we're kinda doing the same things," Phineas says. "Just from what Ellie was sayin', Guardians are probably protecting regular folks from Hastur as much as they're protecting them from the tain. I couldn't stand it myself, but if working inside the system is the only way for someone to fight then I'd rather they did that than just sit back and take it."

They both mull on that for a moment, then Phineas decides to add: "Especially if there's other people you gotta take care of. You do what you have to."

"Yes, you do," Ulrich agrees.

Unable to help herself, Phineas skips ahead to get Royal's attention.

"That's why *you* decided to do this Hazard stuff even though you're too nice for it, right? You're *totally* in love with Ellie, dude."

"Don't need *you* to tell me that," Royal's deep voice rumbles over his shoulder. "Other peoples' emotions are none of your business, commander."

Phineas giggles, sleepover gossip is a *much* more fun way to pass the time. Or, it seemed that way when people had sleepovers in movies.

"Yeah they ain't," she says. "But it's hard to ignore them when people broadcast so loud. It was rollin' off you in waves when you were close to her, like *neon.* I think *I* might love her a little."

She scoots up beside him and he eyes her warily, but he doesn't pull away.

"You ask her out yet?" Phineas presses. "You two already seem real close, would've been hard to cast this kind of magic on you otherwise I think."

Royal's eyes slide away from her, looking ahead again so they can navigate around another row of fallen street lanterns. "Hmpf," he says.

"Aw come on *spill*, it's gotta be better than awkward silence all the way to the tower."

A beat goes by where Phineas thinks he might tell her to piss off, but the cagey shapes in his halo melt into a soft, affectionate yellow, and his expression gentles too.

"...Her girlfriend is kind of a rock star," he says. "They've been a thing for a long time, they're happy. I'm not gonna get in the way of that."

He catches the bunny perched on his head before it can fall, and holds it in his hand carefully. It nuzzles into the pad of his thumb.

"I wouldn't know how to be with her, anyway," he says quietly. "All this magic she comes with scares the shit out of me. This Guardian thing, I can't keep up. I kind of hate it." He holds out his hand and the rabbit leaps the rest of the way to the ground, joining the crowd holding back the flames of a burning utility pole lying in the road. "But I want to try and make things easier for her, if I can. If the best I can do is be somebody she can rely on, some, that's..."

Royal's face hardens, and he stops, turning fully to Phineas.

"Why did I tell you all that?" He looms over her and she takes a step back, unprepared. "What did you *do?*"

"Ah, nothing! *Nothing!*" Phineas holds up both palms and smiles anxiously. "We're just chatting! You never just chat with somebody?"

Ulrich clears his throat.

"I am very sorry my friend is so clumsy," he says pointedly. "I think we will all benefit from directing this energy at Cold Hazard as soon as possible, and I know I don't want to be in this heat any longer than we need to be." He glares coolly at Phineas, his face placid while his halo roils. "I don't think it's much further to go; she can probably manage to keep her mouth shut until then?"

Phineas gives Ulrich a flat look, but after a brief moment of consideration Royal decides to keep walking rather than punch

Phineas in the face. As soon as he turns away, Ulrich swats the back of her head.

"Behave!" he hisses.

"I didn't *do* nothin'!" Phineas hisses back. But she does manage to keep her mouth shut until they reach the base of the tower.

Ulrich is rigid beside her as Phineas drags the stubborn scissor gate closed behind them, like she did last time. She brushes her shoulder against him briefly as she crosses back to where Royal is fiddling with the card reader. It's taking longer than it should because he's overwhelmed with yellow rabbits, manifesting all around him as fast as he can shoo them out of his way.

"There are so many now!" Phineas giggles, hanging from her hands against the gate. "Me 'n Ulrich must have been keeping them from multiplying right."

Royal ignores her.

"Or maybe *you* have a knack for the ethereal," she says. He scoffs at that. "Too bad it's all super evil, huh?"

"Knock it off," Royal says, but there's no sharpness to it. The card reader readies with the same noise it did before, and Phineas makes sure she's smiling when he looks at her again.

"That should do it," Royal says. Phineas nods.

"Thanks for your help," Phineas says.

"Listen," he adds. "There's gonna be like ten guys up there ready to blow y'all away when you come off the elevator."

"Really?" Ulrich asks. *"Is* someone still handing out orders?"

"Hazard's daughter's expectin' y'all specifically, I think." Royal says. "She's. Dramatic."

"Ah," Ulrich says dully.

"People are still scared of her enough to do what she says, but they don't wanna be there any more than y'all do. Just. Send 'em back down here in one piece, please?"

"Sure," Phineas nods. "We'll try."

Royal pretends to be caught up in corraling an armful of bunny.

"...You dying would probably make Ellie cry," he says after a long moment. He finally looks Phineas in the eye, serious, but neutral. "So don't."

Phineas opens her mouth to reply, but he's already disappeared.

Everything has disappeared, in fact: the elevator around them has been replaced with a wash of solid white.

Before she can orient to the void Phineas is staring at a wall, real wood paneling that overwhelms her with the scent of pine while she stands so close to it. Ulrich, caught out halfway in the process of flinching closer to her, relaxes.

"Ah," he murmurs, just breathless enough for her to notice. "This makes more sense for an elevator."

"Does it?" Phineas asks, turning around to see what else is new.

They're in a closed box now, with no discernible doors or windows, but Ulrich doesn't seem worried so maybe this is just what normal elevators look like. Phineas would have to take his word for it. All four walls are made up of the same smooth, aromatic pine boarding, illuminated softly by hazy light coming through frosted glass panels in the ceiling. A polished wood railing runs along each wall, presumably for holding on to while the elevator travels, but it hardly feels like they're moving at all.

Some movement does catch Phineas' eye; she thinks it's a mirror before remembering the suspiciously clean television screen in one corner of the elevator. It's sleek and new under whatever spell has been cast, more like a picture frame, and there is a very lovely man speaking to them from inside it. She can't hear him, and apparently Ulrich can't either, because he makes a troubled sound and reaches for his left ear.

"Oh-" he says. He sounds more vulnerable than she thinks he means to, which spurs Phineas to reach out and find a volume control.

"It's just muted!" she says, unsure what the problem is. "Hang on, there's gotta be a..."

"-structural damage." The man's voice eases through the speakers, smooth and smoky. "But the lady is tough, she'll still run for you just fine."

"An automated maintenance message," Ulrich says, relieved. "The workers must have gotten tired of it."

Phineas can tell he's embarrassed, but he has no reason to be because Phineas has already moved on, completely captivated by the man in the recording. He's *gorgeous.* His hair is messy and red, and although he looks like he might fall asleep standing up, his dark eyes glitter with vitality. His olive skin is splashed with lighter spots like bleach stains. There's a word for that, Jo had mentioned it once, but Phineas probably couldn't remember it even if she wasn't wasting her brainpower running through a dozen dirty fantasies.

The man drags on a cigarette (hand-rolled!), and exhales a plume of pink daisies. Phineas might explode.

"I hate to deprive you of a *breathtaking* forest panorama," he says, perfect face fretting. "But if you're seeing this the outside conditions are probably dangerous, so I'm gonna roll the windows up and adjust your environment to keep you comfy." He smiles at the camera, soft and reassuring. "We're gonna take it *real* slow, but we'll get you there."

"Holy *shit*," Phineas breathes.

"Rein it in a bit, Kidd," Ulrich says somewhere behind her.

"Please enjoy yourselves, sweethearts," says the man in the screen, and he winks, and then the video feed is replaced by a static image of a winged engine. His emblem, maybe, like an artist's signature.

When Phineas comes back she realizes she's inched closer to the screen, nearly pressing her face against it. She turns to Ulrich abruptly, clearing her throat and feeling how hot her face has gotten.

"Man, sorry, that guy was *cute* wasn't he?"

"I wouldn't know," Ulrich grumbles, distracted by the thing in his hands. Phineas loses interest in the stranger immediately, full up with concern instead.

"Oh no, did your hearing aid get messed up?"

Ulrich shakes his head.

"I've had it out since we were in the mine. The tain were interfering with it somehow and I haven't had a moment to readjust it."

Phineas watches as he tucks the hair on his left side behind his ear. Or what's left of it. He angles that side of his head away from her, but not before she can see there's a ragged stump where the shell of his ear should be. She didn't *need* to see it, she realizes. She'd known it was there already. It feels like dream logic, when you wake up and your memories rearrange themselves after you focus on them.

"Wait, since when do you-" She squeaks, cutting herself off. "Sorry, that's rude, I just...I feel like I know about it, but I can't remember when we-"

"It's alright," Ulrich says, distracted with his aid. "You were...not yourself, at the time."

A stab of dread, conjuring up whatever awful thing she must have done, but it's smothered by her passenger's reassurance, bleeding through her ribs like hot water. Phineas can feel the ghost of Ulrich's hair on her own fingertips, from when she'd carded it back from his face. She knows this part of Ulrich because she had touched it *gently*.

She can feel his tears on her fingers too, brushing them from his eyelashes. She has to ask:

"That's right, you met Brokenspectre too," Phineas says, careful not to say the real name out loud, even to him. "Was she nice?"

Ulrich hums to himself, and Phineas appreciates that he seems to really consider the question. In the middle of the floor on what looks like a sort of metal serving tray, there's a sprig of blooming cherry blossom in a delicate vase next to an iron pot. Incense smoke ribbons out from the star-shaped holes studding the lid, the aroma warm and spicy. There are bushy topiaries in each corner, broad yellow-green leaves dotted with orange blossoms, and Ulrich drifts towards one to rest back against the railing.

"To *me,* she was nice enough," he decides. "Not so much to anything else."

"Ah yeah, she's a grump," Phineas says fondly. Ulrich doesn't seem to have much else to say about it, and they lapse into companionable silence. Feeling the light in her chest, Phineas drifts a bit out of the space, her vision blurring with halo light.

Now that she understands it to be the work of an artisan, the elevator they're in glows with the fingerprints of its maker. Soft, smoky lines of faded brass flourish from every surface like wheat in the wind, and she thinks she can smell old leather under the aroma of the incense. The room is yielding the way a comfortable bed is, like the space has been imbued with rest, safety. Even Ulrich seems to unwind some.

...Though, the longer she watches, the harder it is to ignore what's happening in his halo. While he's standing still, relaxing she guesses, the blight always hovering around his left eye blooms out. That spilled ink movement sprawls, eating up the rest of him.

Does he make an effort to keep it in check all the time? Does he even know it's there? *Surely* he must, it's so *much,* spiraling out far beyond his physical body to fill up his halo the longer he stands there, black melding with blue until she can't tell which is the dominant color. One thing that is two things, Ulrich so hard to see in the overlap.

"Hey uh," Phineas starts, leaning back against the railing on her side of the elevator. "You don't have to answer if you don't want to, but speaking of...er, hearing aid type stuff..."

Ulrich gives her a patient look.

"This is not a sensitive subject," he says, so wildly different from how he'd reacted before in the shack Phineas knows he's misunderstood. "You're right, it is a good idea to be aware of any limitations a partner might have." He turns his head, brushing his hair aside to show her where the extra bulk of his hearing aid is slotted in to complete the shape of his damaged ear. Phineas' stomach does a funny little flip. "I am only hard of hearing on this side. I can *manage* without my hearing aid, but I've designed it with extra functionality that more than makes up for any shortcomings. The same with my glasses, the mask; they help to alleviate the extra effort I need to make to keep up."

Shortcomings? *Keep up?* Oh, god, precious thing, as if he could ever be disappointing, as if she doesn't adore every one of his own natural details.

"That's good!" Phineas says, trying to keep her feelings out of her voice. "That's all real good, but um, I wanted to ask about your eye, actually."

Ah, there he goes. He stiffens, folds his arms across his chest.

"The eye, *again?*"

"Can you...Can you see okay out of the left one?"

"*Why?*"

"It has-" Phineas' hand drifts over her own left eye, "It has a- a *thing-*"

Ulrich huffs.

"Phineas don't *do* that! You need to *explain* it to me!"

"There's too *much!*" Phineas says, frustrated with the both of them. "Explaining *this* needs *other stuff* explained!"

Ulrich spreads his arms, gesturing at the suddenly incongruous ease around them.

"We have got *time!*" He closes his eyes briefly, leveling out. "If you insist on bringing it up so often then we are going to have to do this at some point, just. Start with telling me what it *looks* like."

He's right, of course he is. Phineas makes an effort like he'd made an effort to describe her sunlight a moment ago. Touchable terms, simple concepts...She reaches for her own eye again, slowly dragging her fingertips across the closed lid.

"You're cracked, there," she says. Ulrich grimaces.

"What, my...ach, *blue,* light? Is damaged?"

Phineas seesaws her hand.

"This is more of a halo thing."

"...The blue light and the 'halo' are two different things?"

Phineas flexes her toes, searching to ground her scattered feelings, but she'd forgotten they're in an elevator, rapidly putting distance between herself and the planet. She settles for staring at the incense pot instead, watching the smoke stream silently through its stars.

"Um, different, definitions, uh..." She holds out her hands in a gesture that adds nothing. "You are you, Ulrich, and your soul is- it's sort of the. Core, of you. The blue thing. The soul, the heart, whatever you wanna call it. Yours lives in your throat, in your voice."

Ulrich, who had been smiling at her like listening to a kid yammering, sobers at that for some reason.

"The *halo* is the...the stuff that comes off of it." She snaps her fingers and looks away from the burner. "Fire! Your soul is fire, and the halo is smoke and embers and stuff. Does that make sense?"

"Sure, I think so."

"The blight, the crack, around your left eye, is the halo's manifestation of...It's like a wound, and if it's this strong I was worried about how far the effects might spread."

"A *wound?*" He says, all his clever mechanisms whirring. "A wound from *wh...*"

His gaze slides off to the side, and he tilts his head with a cut-string movement that Phineas doesn't like at all.

Ulrich goes far away in his eyes, caught up in a feeling, a memory maybe. Whatever it is makes him paler, and Phineas can see the harsh edges of dread raking across his halo, feel the tension wracking up his body. There, in the center of the magnetic-field of Ulrich's blight, that furious eye that doesn't belong to him is staring Phineas down. Something rings in her left ear; Phineas feels unkind hands across her body, breathes in a scent like the room where Jo did her medical procedures.

There's another scent underneath it, almost...alcoholic.

Ulrich's cut strings activate again and he sags against the railing, raises one hand to drag it across his eyes as he takes a shivery breath. All the phantom sensations vanish.

"U-um," he stammers.

"I'm sorry, I won't bring it up again!" Phineas babbles, frantic with confusion and worry. "I just didn't want you to get hurt in a *fight* because I-"

"S'fine," he says roughly, straightening his glasses. "I can't see any of these, halos, any of this spiritual business you talk about any more than vague shapes, but I can see fine."

Phineas perks up at that. "You can see *something*, though? Sometimes?"

Ulrich shrugs, uncomfortable. "Looking at Ellie, sometimes there were. Black spots, like old film, when she would get heated or try to use magic. Or what lingers when you look away from a bright light. It is nothing especially pleasant. With the way you carry on about the things *you* see I couldn't imagine we were looking at the same things." He shakes his head. "Is this something I should be concerned about?"

Listening to him speak, having time to really look him over after that baffling episode, Phineas realizes how *ragged* he is. His clothes are a lost cause after their trip through the mine, and every part of his exposed skin is covered in scrapes and bruises and damp dust. His hair is clumped together in greasy locks, so dark with grime it's nearly brown instead of blond, and his five o'clock shadow is nearing the point it will require a new term of description. His eyes are so sunken she'd think he was wearing makeup if she didn't know better. At some point while Phineas wasn't looking, he'd chewed right through his lower lip. She probably isn't looking much better herself, but Ulrich doesn't heal up quick like she does.

But his body *will* heal. Eventually his lip will knit itself together again, they'll get him some new clothes and a hot bath and these temporary blemishes will go away. The blight in his halo is *old,* etched deep into him like finding burn marks on the inner rings of a tree, and it is still fresh enough to bleed.

This...is not something they can solve, here, now. Even Phineas can tell drawing out this poison in the elevator on their way to Hazard would do more harm than good.

"No, I don't guess you need to worry," she cedes. "Doesn't need any more thought than you give to regular wounds. I had some too before they scarred over, they *do* get better!" Usually. "Yours just...probably needs more time."

He isn't totally convinced, but his color improves so Phineas thinks it's probably good enough. She relaxes against her spot on the wall, takes a long, deep breath of aromatic air.

"Gideon says souls gather up scars too, the same as bodies," she says mildly, digging around for more old lessons that might be useful here. "A human is a mind, a body, and a spirit; most folks can forget, but commanders gotta think about it a lot to keep ourselves under control. Some stuff roughs you up enough to tear through all three parts, and it's hard to fix it if you don't know it's there."

"When the energy from something emotionally charged collides with your spirit it cracks, and it can bleed like a body." Phineas presses her thumb to one palm through her torn gloves, over the burns there that have already begun to fade. "The significance comes from your side, so how *much* you bleed is up to you."

Ulrich is quiet, but the mist in his halo is very still while he listens. She grins at him.

"But then you fill in the breaks with new light," Phineas says, "and it's better than it was before. That thing I said about commanding, in the alley, about adding yourself to any energy you command. It can work both ways, you take in new stuff and it makes you stronger!"

She sees her own smile turn up the corner of Ulrich's mouth. It's sort of sad on him. She grips the railing instead of gathering him in her arms.

"I think scars are cool," she goes on. "They mean you went places and did stuff and got out alive. I like mine! But I know not everybody sees them like that, and I know *you* don't really like to be seen like this, so I didn't want to make a big deal about yours."

"And what is the difference between mine and yours?" Ulrich asks quietly. "How did your cracks begin to heal?"

There's a pause while Phineas processes that she's never had to hang words on this. Nobody's ever asked her to.

"I guess," she says slowly, "I replaced them with ambition." Phineas considers the shape of it in her mouth for an extra second, then she nods, mostly to herself. Ambition feels right. "But it's different for everybody, you'll have to figure out how to deal with your unfinished business yourself."

The words hang in the air between them, softened in the hazy light. Ulrich shifts, turning away to stare at the topiary next to him.

"This thing I have, does it...The way you described Hazard before, does it feel like that?"

"*No,*" Phineas says firmly. "No, not at all. He's something completely different."

"Could you elaborate?" Ulrich asks. "Anything that might make it easier to deal with him?"

"Yeah, for starters *you're* not going anywhere near him."

Ulrich smirks.

"After all this you don't actually want my help?" he asks. "Am I only a pretty thing to hang on your arm?"

Phineas is staring at the tear in his lip, crusted over with blood, wondering what put it there while she wasn't watching him.

"It's not that," Phineas says. "You uh...You know that chill you said you felt when he was around? Ellie said it felt like drowning, she said people would just," she runs a hand through her hair, looking away. "Man, I dunno, *explode?* They'd tear apart without him even doing anything."

"*Ellie* said?"

"Oh, yeah, when we were having dinner."

Ulrich raises an eyebrow.

"I think it's *gravity,*" Phineas waves her hands in the air like she's brushing his words out of the way, trying to stay on course. "It's a void you're feeling, and that's how he fights."

"Not with water?" Ulrich asks.

"Both? He *used* to specialize in water, maybe, but..."

Her constant companion nudges her forward when she hesitates too long, a pressure behind her sternum, her bones creaking gently.

"I think he has a star in his head," Phineas says. "In that void, in his face."

Ulrich blinks.

"A *star?* An... a *literal* star?"

"I'm just guessin'," Phineas mumbles, shifting her feet. "It talked to me, I dreamt about it last night. I don't think it likes being with Hazard, all that tain he's mixed up with..." She follows the gentle lines and whorls across the wood floor under her feet. Her energy is still disoriented but the texture of the wood is solid, tactile. "He's keeping it suppressed, you can't...*do* that."

Clever Ulrich is already pulling ahead of her.

"...Your experience being what?"

"Gideon. Has a star, in one of his eyes, too." She's hung her head low, and something in her neck twinges with the unfamiliar stretch. "But it's the other one. The opposite eye."

It almost feels like there's a physical weight hanging between them, she has to force herself to look at him. He's watching carefully.

"But it's *different!*" she argues before he can say anything. "Gideon is *warm,* he's- not, whatever Hazard is-"

"So," Ulrich says neutrally. "Gideon is warm, Hazard is *cold,* and *you're* **bright.** You have one *too.* "

Phineas swallows, sunshine fitful inside her chest; still, *still* bracing to be struck. She thinks of Ulrich in the mine, scrambling away from her touch.

"Your passenger- er, that," Ulrich asks, scratching his neck. "Brokenspectre, you called it? Is that what stars look like?"

"*Mine* looks like that," Phineas says. "Brokenspectre is kind of. A placeholder, she don't have a name and I don't talk about her much, to anyone."

Ulrich squints. If he notices the lie he doesn't comment on it.

"I have heard the term," he says instead. "They're mountain creatures that distort with their shadows. They change size with the light."

"Yeah, something like that," Phineas says, hurrying them along. "Gideon's star kept its own shape apart from him. He wore it like jewelry, like a gem. It was still a separate entity. Mine is fused with me, all the way down."

"She latched onto my heart when we were little and we...grew around each other," he already saw it, he already *knows*, why is she *breathing* so hard? "Hazard, and Gideon, must have been older when they- Got, theirs. Gideon wouldn't talk about it. But it's *not-*"

Something cracks, and Ulrich doesn't move, but his eyes flicker to Phineas' hands wrapped around the railing.

"Hazard's is *spoiled,* somehow, it's *rotten,*" Phineas spits. Something bites into a tender spot under her knuckle and she jerks her hand away from the rough rail. "They're not the same!" She digs a fingernail in, trying to gouge the splinter, but her fingertips are covered in flaking wood polish and it keeps getting in the way. "Gideon would never-*I* would *never-*"

"Mausebär." Ulrich's voice is gentle. Phineas calms down enough to see he's looking at her with pity, like he knows something she doesn't. "Of course not. But I want to understand."

Phineas runs a hand through her gritty hair again while he figures out what he wants to say.

"You have...part of a star," Ulrich says. *"Gideon* has a star, the same as Hazard does, but Hazard is not a commander."

"Yeah."

"You must understand this is not *normal,*" he continues. "The odds of you three sharing the exact same malad- These same *stars,* if commanding is not the common thread then... *what?*"

"What *happened?*" he asks. "What did Gideon *do* to all of you?"

They are *so* far from the ground now, and not even close to the ship yet. It's getting harder for Phineas to keep her balance.

"I dunno about Hazard," she says, staring down into her palm, her ruined glove. "But mine was an accident. I almost died because of someone *else,* Gideon *saved* me."

She folds her arms angrily, still unable to look at Ulrich.

"It's all that stuff you said about monsters, I'm either here like this or not at all. I dunno why people keep actin' like he did something *wrong.* Gideon took the worst of it too," she says, anticipating what Ulrich might come at her with. "He got marked up a *lot* worse than me. He wouldn't do this to someone unless he *had* to."

"It does hurt, then," Ulrich says, not coming after her even a little. She can feel his eyes on her, why is he *looking* at her like that?

"Lots of stuff that's good for you hurts!" she says, louder than she'd intended. "It doesn't *matter!*"

"It may," he says, *infuriatingly* placid. "Plenty of relationships are soured by *accidental* harm. A deliberate injury, even one well-intended, is *complicated.* And you are wearing an expression I don't like."

"'Cause this is *stupid,* " Phineas says, hating the petulance in her voice. "Gideon and Hazard ain't the same."

"I did not say that. I am only asking you to consider whether his ire for your mentor is uncalled for, this is-"

"There *must* have just been a misunderstanding," Phineas says before he can finish. "Gideon's not- he forgets, sometimes, we...Gideon couldn't do this to someone and just...*leave* him, like this-"

"Look at me, Phineas." Ulrich's neutrality ramps up the pressure in her ears like a chemical reaction

"He *wouldn't!*" she snaps, her throat burning with sunlight.

Finally meeting his eyes, she realizes Ulrich hasn't been angry. He still isn't: the mist in his halo stays frustratingly serene while he watches her. The twinge in her throat brings her back, a little, enough. Why is she angry with *him?*

All her big feelings churning inside her oscillate, shame staining the anger, everything muddying to an ugly nothing color.

"Of course," Ulrich says, like a breath of fresh air. "You would know better than I would. I only want to help." He shrugs, dancing with her again, deftly easing them beyond her stumble. "It would be very inconvenient for me if he killed you."

Phineas feels around to try and steady herself, but it's still not really helping.

"I know, I know. Sorry, I...I ain't gettin' killed."

Ulrich still has that knowing look on his face, but before Phineas can ask about it he takes off his hat and reaches inside. His hand comes back from the depths holding a pair of tweezers.

"Come here," he says, clicking them twice. Phineas goes.

"I can do it myself," she grumbles, still raw, letting him take her hand in his and turn it over.

"I know."

He's careful, but it still stings. There's a movement he makes, nudging the tattered edge of her glove out of the way with the end of the tweezers; it's such a strangely Ulrich gesture Phineas feels the fight drain from her like dirty dishwater.

288

"Not budging on dealing with Hazard alone, then," Ulrich asks quietly.

"If Hazard fights by changing the equilibrium of his opponents' bodies like I think he does, then there's nothing you can do."

"And there are things you can?"

"That stuff won't usually fly with commanders. My body's under my control, *actively,* all the time- *sss!*"

"Got it," Ulrich says, holding up the splinter between them before dropping it. It's so small it disappears into the woodgrain instantly, somewhere between all those sturdy grooves.

"He shouldn't be able to kill me like *that,* at least," Phineas says, flexing her hand when he lets it go. "If I can't resist his will enough to handle that then I'll lose to him anyway."

Ulrich pauses, his hat in his hand, a look crossing his face.

"...That is why your weight changes," he says. "You can *will* your body into different states."

"Uh-huh."

"And why *poison* doesn't work."

"Now you're gettin' it."

He shakes his head.

"That is *so **cheap,***" he grouses, the tweezers disappearing into the hat. Phineas grins.

"Yeah well I worked real hard to learn my cheap tricks, so I'm gonna use 'em."

She settles in beside him, leaning against him and the wall together. Phineas is surprised he lets her, but it does seem like something has shifted in him since they'd had it out about the armadillo guy. Despite his exasperation on their way through town, something about him has eased. Even if it hadn't gone the way he wanted, it must feel better to have it all out in the open.

"If you're not really after Hazard anyway this shouldn't even be a big deal for you, right?" she asks, her cheek pillowed against his shoulder. "You got other business up here, go take care of it while I'm busy."

"Splitting up with no way to communicate leaves little room for contingencies," Ulrich sighs. Phineas weaves her arms around his elbow, terribly in love.

"We got all the room we need. We'll be fine," she says. Ulrich makes his broody hen sound again and she squeezes the thickness of his bicep. *"Fiiine!"* she crows. She can't hear it, but she feels him laugh.

After the oppressive, freezing mines and the smothering heat and haze of the burning town, this room is *blissful,* even if it's too high up. Phineas turns her face into Ulrich's shoulder, lacing her fingers more firmly around his forearm. Letting go of the other two points they're suspended between, she reaches out to find him instead, twining her own halo gently through the scroll of his. Ulrich lets her.

"What does 'mau-ze pair' mean?" Phineas asks, after a long, pastel-colored moment. "That thing you call me sometimes."

"Mausbär," Ulrich corrects.

"Mauzebär."

Ulrich relaxes a little more, joining his own hands in front of him. It tugs her in closer, like he's contributing.

"I have been away from my language for a very long time," he says, soft susurrus over Phineas' ears. "I am sure I've strayed from what it must be now. Mausbär is the words for mouse and bear, it is...a petname, childish."

"Cute," Phineas counters. Ulrich smiles.

"It's *meant* to be cute, when most people use it, but I used to use it to tease a friend of mine."

"Your friend trapped in the tower?"

"I would call her that because she was vicious like a bear, but very small, like a mouse. She hated it, she is nothing like either of those things. But it made her smile sometimes." Phineas only sees it in her peripheral, but this halo shade on Ulrich is one she hasn't seen before. The shape of it is soft and round.

"The definition is different to me, than it is to most Deutsch speakers," he finishes, clearing his throat. "A-as I said, childish."

"I'm *vicious*, huh?" A swell of warmth that it's a term of endearment for him, that he's used it for her. Her companion, her star, purrs in the space around her lungs.

Ulrich shuffles self-consciously.

"I, ah, I do not always think when I say it." Even better. "You must remind me of her, a bit."

With great reluctance, Phineas withdraws and stands on her own; partially because Ulrich has reached the end of his comfort for this kind of proximity, partially because the elevator is finally reaching the end of its track.

"What does she do?" she asks. "Your friend."

Ulrich considers it just long enough for Phineas to notice that he needs to.

"She is a florist," he decides.

"That doesn't sound like an angry person job."

Faintly, only noticeable in the slight shaking of the leaves in the plants, the elevator jolts to a stop.

"You would be surprised," Ulrich says.

Phineas hears Ulrich hiss in the light when the wall panels across from them slide open, and she almost ribs him about it before she realizes the sunshine is so bright because it's glinting against a half-circle of gun barrels leveled at the elevator by a half-circle of men.

"Forgot about them," Phineas mumbles.

"Hell," Ulrich grumbles.

Phineas and Ulrich stay still, and so do the guns. She takes a moment to look over the crowd. There are only like eight of them, and none of them look like brawlers. Even Phineas can tell the weapons are janky; one bigger dude near the middle seems to be brandishing a gardening hoe. Their features are blacked out to Phineas, all their disparate halos blurring together in the sunshine.

"They're scared," she whispers to Ulrich, still facing forward. "I dunno if it's us or Hazard doin' it though."

"Good," Ulrich says, pushing off the elevator railing to step forward before Phineas can react.

His movement ripples across the gathered men, the glimmer of the barrels. There's a horrible second where all Phineas can think about is that she isn't between Ulrich's soft body and the dozen hard weapons pointed at it, the shape of him growing darker and less detailed as he approaches the blazing shape of the doorway. He becomes a shadow in Phineas' vision, and she sees him reach his left hand up and over his shoulder, like he's reaching for a sword that isn't there.

When he flexes his hand into a fist there is still no sword, but there is suddenly a *gun*, and as he draws his arm back over his head the sudden gun keeps drawing out from nothing, long enough he has to stretch his arm out as high as he can.

Then he brings it down in front of him like a hammer, and there's a mechanical spring-sound as it bursts open like a reverse mousetrap—now it must be as tall as he is, and through the cloud of blue mist that accompanies all of Ulrich's tricks Phineas can see it's covered in gears and levers. The end of the barrel flares out like the bell of a horn, the handle tucked under Ulrich's right arm is heavy and covered with filigree. The rifle shines porcelain-white and silver in the sunshine.

Ulrich aims it into the center of the mob.

"I am a better shot than any of you," he says. "And this is a better gun than any of the toys you're pointing at me. Let us through."

"I don't care how good he is," someone stammers, the intrepid guy holding gardening equipment. "He can't get all of us before we get him-"

Ulrich flexes a finger, or tightens his hand; some process occurs and sets off a chain reaction of clicks and turns and movements all along the rifle body. Ulrich is stock-still, locked on, staring down the strange barrel at the man who just spoke.

"What are you willing to bet on that?" Ulrich asks.

Phineas finally finds her sense and jogs up alongside him, which ruffles feathers enough to answer her earlier question. They must've heard something about her, The Commander, maybe how she can catch bullets. These are looks she recognizes.

They're scattered, unsure who to threaten, but Phineas is sure they won't actually go through with anything. They all know this isn't a fair fight, and their actual loyalty to this cause is brittle. There's a long second where nobody moves, and then everyone but Ulrich flinches as an older bearded man with a robotic arm tosses his gun into a bush near the pathway.

"Man, *fuck* it," he gripes. "Y'all got beef with the wizard I don't give a shit, I ain't gettin' shot over this."

The bush, stout and bristling with orange flowers, rustles in a breeze that isn't there. It balloons out into a caricature-mouth, full of briar teeth ringing a prickly tongue. The tongue stretches like a frog's to curl around the shotgun and tosses it up into the air, the mouth grinding shut around it. The gun goes off, the explosion dull through the thick shrub.

The...creature, swallows. Then it turns its head directly towards Phineas. She locks eyes with no eyes, flexes her toes over the white brick path under her feet, and the brick flexes back.

The cartoon plant licks its smiling, leafy lips and bounces back into nothing like a rewinding tape.

"Hell no," the bearded man says, and he hurries right past them to get into the elevator.

There's no threat, but it feels *good,* whatever that new presence is. No harm in playing along. Keeping her feet rooted, Phineas turns to glare at the men, her chest burning.

"Get off my ship," she commands.

"You c'n *have* it!" the defector hollers from relative safety. "Y'all get in here!"

Ulrich lowers his weapon as the little mob flows around them, clanking and murmuring, tangibly relieved for an excuse to bail out of this weirdness. Phineas wants to send them off with something nicer than the command, but when she turns the elevator is gone. Now it's a tall brick block with a fountain on top, the water spilling down the sides into a tiny aquaduct that runs alongside the path they're standing on.

"Nice'a Royal to think of 'em," Phineas says, slipping her hands in her pockets.

"Was that *you?*" Ulrich demands, gripping his rifle. He's still staring at the shrub that ate the shotgun, now significantly less creature-y. "What *was* that?!"

"That was the ship," Phineas says, shivering out the unspent energy she'd hung on to in case she needed to deck somebody. Ulrich notices the changes to the elevator, turning in place, unsure what to keep his eye on. Phineas can feel his gears clicking against each other, too many questions fighting for space.

"The ship...helped?" he asks. It's a good question. Phineas shrugs.

"I think we're expected, is all," she says. "It knew we were comin' and showed up to greet us."

"Well is there anyone else here?" Ulrich asks. "Can you tell?"

Phineas presses down again. The ground under her feet feels *alive,* it's like standing on a breathing chest with its own slow heartbeat. Its own skin and nerves. It's hard to tell if it likes Phineas or just her potential for violence.

"I can't really feel anything inside the castle," she says. "But I think we're alone out here now that they're gone. You ready to go?"

Ulrich jerks the rifle closed and puts it away how he'd gotten it out, sliding it over his shoulder into thin air. Phineas runs around to watch where it goes and she feels him smile.

"That is a good one, isn't it?" he says.

"Could you have really taken on all those guys with just *that* thing?" Phineas asks. Ulrich makes a sign near his temple and his mask shimmers into being.

"After you, commander."

10

It's hard to remember they're in the sky at all. Everywhere Phineas looks there's blue grass and white brick, statues and flowing water, dozens and dozens of trees and bushes and topiaries that stretch infinitely into the horizon. There is also Hazard's castle— the closest word Phineas has for the bizarre central structure that wheels into the sky forever, exactly like the radio tower had, but this one doesn't resolve itself into anything sensible. Whenever Phineas tries to make out the details they change themselves around: the curve of a balcony railing reverses, a carving of the waxing moon changes its phase, only to be replaced entirely by a patch of blue ivy. It makes her head hurt, so she focuses on trying to get close enough to get inside.

That is also difficult. The gardens aren't *built* like a maze, but somehow she and Ulrich keep getting turned around on their way to the castle. It feels like they're starting to make headway in the direction of their best guess at the front entrance, but when they try to cross under a flowered archway it explodes with growth. The arch knits itself together to make a solid wall across the path, blocking the way forward.

"Er," Ulrich says. There is a new way to go now that the shrubbery has rearranged itself; the white brick of the path hadn't changed, but now they can step off of it and onto a patch of soft blue grass leading to a small, square fountain. There's a wooden door standing in the center, in the water.

Phineas can still feel the ship breathing under her. It idles like a cat in a sunbeam, watching what she does with mild interest.

"We're being herded somewhere," she says. "By the ship."

"Is that good?" Ulrich asks, nervously surveying the garden, still unconvinced they're not being pursued. He might be feeling the ship watching them.

"It helped us once already," Phineas says, stepping off of the brick, over the aqueduct running alongside and onto the lawn. She presses her toes harder against the soil, and she can feel the blades of grass squirming under the wraps on her feet. As she settles, she thinks warily of briar-teeth chewing through a shotgun barrel. Trusting the ship still feels dangerous, but for now the blue grass is only curious, so gentle she can hardly feel it through her calluses.

When he sees she isn't immediately devoured, Ulrich cautiously follows her lead.

"It is still *Hazard's* ship for now, though?" he asks. As soon as he's left the path the arch bursts back into place, bracing against his back and shoving him forward. Even obscured by his mask, the look on his face makes Phineas laugh.

"Tell the *ship* I could have my gardening shears out in about two seconds," Ulrich grumbles. He turns away from the greenery when he hears Phineas splashing into the fountain.

"Nah no shears yet, let's see what it wants," Phineas says, wandering all the way around the door. She elects not to tell him that the stone and the grass and the fountain are all parts of the same organism, and it wouldn't matter where either of them were standing if the ship didn't want them here.

"*Again,* how are we sure this isn't Hazard about to drop us off the island?" Ulrich asks, coming closer and staring apprehensively into the water.

"I can't feel Hazard at all, to be honest," Phineas says. She runs her hand along the whitewashed wood of the door frame. All the matter here feels alive in a way inorganic matter shouldn't, everything on this ship hums with that same breathing energy. It's more solid in Phineas' senses than most things she comes across, but she also gets the feeling that, if she pressed in the right way, she could reshape it all like clay.

"You mean he is not here?" Ulrich prods, when she trails off. Phineas rejoins the material world.

"He must be, he ain't anywhere else down below. And out here in the garden I can tell it's just us and the ship since those guys left."

"And the ship is a person."

"Yeah," Phineas says. "Starships can get weird, and if this one is bonded with Hazard it's probably *real* weird."

"None of this is making me eager to go where it wants us to," Ulrich says. Phineas grins.

"Well, I don't think it's gonna kill me yet," she says, setting her hand on the doorknob. "So just stay close to me and you'll be fine, alright?"

She opens the door to a solid wall of water, calm and clear, illuminated with softly shifting shafts of sunlight.

For the first time since she met Gideon, Phineas feels like she's on the other side of what she'd felt with Ulrich before. A hand outstretched, someone *else* is inviting *her* to dance, and they're good at it too. She feels it, fingers tapping on the aquarium glass, *what will you do now, commander?*

"I hate this," Ulrich says. She hears his big shoes hit the water in the fountain.

"Hold on to me," Phineas says without looking back, already reaching out to get her hands through the door. She breaks the surface of the little sea.

There is no trickery as she sinks in, no sea monsters or hidden currents; the water stays calm and cool against her skin, lifting away accumulated grime. Commanders can slow their heart rate well enough to swim about as long as they like, and she wishes she could waste some time floating here, but the tug of Ulrich's weight behind her keeps her moving.

It's a short trip, but in the heavy underwater silence, she hears the clear sound of someone giggling.

They come up to a half-submerged flight of stairs. Phineas is out first and she whirls around to help Ulrich along— she can't remember how long is too long for a human to hold their breath. She'd expected him to be winded, but he only seems damp and annoyed.

"Are you drowned?" she asks, laying her hands on him to dry them both with a quick command. Now he is dry and annoyed.

"*Please* ask before doing that," Ulrich whines. Breathing easily enough to whine is a good sign! Satisfied, Phineas ignores him and takes in the landing.

The interior hallway is short and dark, blue in the walls and carpet. There are plants hanging from the ceiling, bare tree branches curled around paper lanterns glowing in dim aqua, but most of the light is coming from the end of the hallway, where something round and silvery is blocking the outside view. Phineas waits for Ulrich to finish preening himself, then she leads them out, staying ahead just in case.

The silvery thing is a moon, turning slowly in the air and dominating most of the lobby below them. *Below,* because they've come out on what looks to be the second floor, onto a series of balconies that stretches around all four sides of an atrium. There are plants *everywhere.* From the ceiling above there are more of those gnarled branches with their lanterns, connecting to thick tree trunks stretching from floor to ceiling in each corner of the room. The walls are overrun with dark, leafy growths of all kinds, emeralds and violets and indigos, broad leaves that make Phineas think of tropical places. It smells like rain.

She steps fully out across the balcony, the carpet thick under her feet, and she leans out over the railing. It seems like they're in the center of a stack of identical galleries, cream-colored balustrades climbing up into infinity like a spiral staircase. Patches of darkness dotted with stars drift in the empty center of the column like clouds, and the moon gives a faint glow that feels cold on Phineas' exposed skin. The only sound is running water, from small fountains scattered among the thick foliage, and a gentle current in the crystal clear river that rings the bottom floor, crisscrossed with foot bridges.

Every floor she can see, on all four sides, has a doorway to a corridor like the one they just came through. Now that they're inside the castle Phineas has lost all sense of direction. She can feel Ulrich, and the presence of the ship, but there's nothing to move towards. Shit.

"Moon's cool," she mumbles, just to say something.

Ulrich keeps looking around them like he expects an ambush.

"Where do we go now?" he asks, already knowing the answer.

"I dunno," Phineas shrugs. "I sorta thought he would show up if we got this far. Maybe we can make a ruckus and he'll come out?"

Ulrich's mouth twitches under his mask and Phineas gets ready for whatever retort he has coming, but he reaches under his shirt instead. She flinches away from the railing.

"Hey-!"

"Ears," Ulrich barks, raising his revolver. As soon as Phineas gets

her hands over them Ulrich pulls the trigger; Phineas tracks the energy as it sails somewhere behind her.

Somebody yelps.

"Come out, please," Ulrich says evenly. Phineas turns, and Ray is standing at the other end of the balcony, previously tucked into a corner behind a cascade of giant ferns. Phineas hadn't been able to sense him at *all*.

Ray looks bad. He's still sporting the bruises from their sparring match, but now he's also got patches of shiny, angry red skin on his face and arms. He's covered in ash and soot, and a huge patch of his shirt is gone, the edges around the hole charred and ragged. Without anything blocking her view, Phineas can see his weak, undefined halo is simmering with rage. He's holding a gun in his shaking hand, maybe the same one from last night. He raises it and Ulrich clicks the switch on his revolver.

"Is there any reason I shouldn't kill him, Phineas?" Ulrich asks. It's a genuine question. Ray snarls, his sooty face accentuating the contortion of his features.

"Stop-" Ray can't seem to decide where to point the gun, Ulrich's lack of protection wailing in Phineas' perception like a siren. "Stop acting like I ain't *worth nothin'!* Nobody respects me and it's such bullshit! I'm just as-" He pivots to Phineas and she braces for the shot, relieved it's coming for her instead. "You ruined *everything!* I was *finally* getting somewhere with Ellie before you-"

"Lower your weapon," Ulrich says, his voice brushing Phineas' ears with that chilly feeling. Ray's hand does lower, surprisingly, and then he explodes like a stoked fire.

"STOP orderin' me around!! Stop tellin' me-" The rest of his froth is drowned out by his own weapon going off, aimed at Ulrich. In a stroke of luck Phineas' reflexes are still coiled, waiting for the order of a gunshot, and they move her just as she wants when the trigger is pulled. She easily snatches the bullet out of the air before it can hit the mark, the force zinging through her arm and through her chest, melding with the instant fury that it had gone for Ulrich instead of her. She launches herself at Ray, who fires another clumsy shot that ricochets from a white stone fountain between them.

Then he drops the gun. Thinking she's been tricked, Phineas stumbles to a stop, the residual momentum crashing into her back hard enough to knock the wind from her. Now only a few feet from Ray, she can see his muscles twitching, the raw burns across his arms bunching and jumping as he struggles against- what?

Phineas can see his breath coming in clouds, his greasy hair beginning to frost over.

"Artemis," a smooth, glassy voice says, unseen. Phineas' stomach swoops as the room around them *contracts*, and in the next moment all four of them are standing on the lower floor of the atrium, on one of the stone bridges curving over the river.

Up close, the moon rings like a singing bowl. From a corner of the bridge behind Ray, there's a shimmer of icy blue shapes, tidy and geometric, and when they're gone the glass woman is standing there. She's changed clothes, draped in blues and greens under a thick diamond-patterned shawl instead of the purple vinyl thing she'd been in before, but she still has that crystal flower that tugs at Phineas' awareness like a toothache. It's changed shape to curl around her finger like a ring, gleaming from the hand she gestures with as she clicks towards Ray on towering heels.

Ray doesn't move, but as the woman silently approaches him Phineas can hear him start to gag. His fingers jerk, his neck tries to twitch like it's fighting against something holding it in place. Ulrich makes a disgusted sound under his breath, and Phineas watches as pinpricks of ice break out through Ray's face, ice magic bright white against the soot across his skin.

The woman gets in front of him, her back to Phineas and Ulrich. Ray's face is completely blank with shock, his weak halo curdled with surprise.

"Wh...why?" he chokes, mottled through his ruined throat. The glass woman makes a gesture with her hands like snapping a sheet, and the ice threaded through Ray's body shatters, tearing him apart. The water in the river surges through the open grate of the footbridge railing, catches the pieces and washes them away. There's nothing left but a stain in the wooden planks, and then the water comes for that too. It takes less than a minute.

Phineas is furious.

"How *could* you?!" she shouts. The woman tsks. When she turns to face them, she's thumbing a speck of blood from her cheek.

"Oh what," she huffs. "Your boy there was about to do the same thing, *you* were going to do the same thing last *night-"*

"He wasn't *mine,"* Phineas says, the last word sparking in the air. "How could you do that to your own *guy?"*

"Mine? *Please.* At his *best* he was *convenient,* and he wasn't even that in the end." The woman folds her arms, canting her hips. "Don't act so righteous, commander. You could easily conscript anyone you want, but you came into town *alone,* didn't you? You must understand how important it is to have standards when it comes to..." Her eyes leave Phineas' to look beyond her, at Ulrich. *"Estate."*

"What did you say?!" Phineas sparks up, rational thought leaving her, but Ulrich's hand on her shoulder reels her back in.

Through the direct connection she shivers. He's changed since she'd looked last, back into that other Ulrich she'd seen at breakfast. Phineas had been able to feel something happening with Ulrich's halo behind her, but she hadn't dared to move from between him and the woman; magic is too *much,* too *dangerous,* Ulrich doesn't have any way to-

"You need to find Hazard," he says. "I can handle this."

His face and his halo masked like they are, she can't tell what he's thinking.

"But you'll- she's a wizard in her own element, this isn't a fair *fight* for-"

"If you can't handle your subordinates bleeding for you then you're not qualified to have them. Self-doubt at this point is irresponsible, you need to make peace with your position." He aims his gun at the woman, steady. "Go."

She knows he's right, but none of this feels good. If she lingers too long she might get stuck here, and all of this will have been for nothing, but leaving him- he's not-

Her star stirs. *Both ways,* she whispers.

...Yeah. Phineas wouldn't have chosen him if he couldn't hold his own; she needs to let him...

Resisting the urge to reach for him before she goes, she says, "Good luck."

That makes him smirk, a glimmer of teeth. Phineas lopes into a run, around the corner and out of their sight.

◉

Rook's eyes follow Phineas until she disappears, and then they focus on Ulrich again. It looks like the commander had put him through his paces, he must be nearing the end of his reserves by now. Still, even with the stupid mask in the way Rook is smart enough to know better than to dismiss the stress in his jaw, the firmness of his stance.

Rook also knows Ulrich enjoys talking too much to shoot her before they hash things out. Not that he could hit her anyway.

"You can relax now," she says, knowing he won't. "She's gone."

"You are assuming a lot thinking she's the only reason I'm pointing this gun at you, Rook."

"Are you still angry with me? Ulrich I'm flattered, you're more sentimental than you let on." She steps forward, her freezing aura wrapping around the barrel of Ulrich's gun, frosting into the gears, the joints of his fingers. "No one fixates quite like you do, a girl could get jealous. It's nice to know you think of me now and then."

"Frequently," Ulrich says. Rook can see his skin turning red against the cold metal of the revolver, refusing still to let it go. "You did take a piece of me with you when you left."

Rook steps close enough to see his eyes through the lenses of his mask. She touches the barrel of the gun, pressing down, and Ulrich moves where she wants. The eyes behind the mask are startlingly focused, their pretty color reduced to monochrome lines behind solid green glass. He really *is* angry with her, it's adorable.

"God, I forgot how corny you are..." Bringing her hand up between them, she slips the ring from her finger, watching how it pulls Ulrich's eyes like a magnet. "I did take something from you, didn't I?"

Rook sets it in one palm and makes a sign with her other hand, like drawing a string. The crystal blooms, unfurling from a simplified star-shaped gem to a lotus, the center shining and riddled with holes. The light coloring the facets of the glass had been blue to match her outfit, but now it reverts to white, iridescent in the petals.

"You've gone through a hell of a lot of trouble for a piece of cheap glass. If nothing else, you are a man committed to his aesthetic." It's a pretty thing, and clearly has some kind of cosmetic magic attached to it, but she'd studied it every which way and couldn't find *any* reason it should have such a hold on him. There must be some sentimental value; even someone like Ulrich has feelings in there somewhere. She watches the subtle tilt of his head as he follows the blossom, the movement of the beaked mask giving him away. It's like he can't help himself, she almost feels sorry for him.

"You know, *I* never said anything about fighting with you," Rook says. "The commander assumes everyone else is as primitive as she is. But she was right about one thing..."

Rook reaches delicately with her halo, like touching the surface of a bubble, and the lenses of Ulrich's mask glaze over with crystalline frost. He hardly seems to notice, still fixated on the lotus.

"This *wouldn't* be a fair fight. I own every inch of this room. Your tricks and your toys can't stand up to the real thing and we both know it, don't we?" She closes her hand around the flower and it reverts quietly to its smaller form. With it briefly out of sight, Ulrich comes out of his reverie. Rook takes a chance and reaches up to tuck some stray hair behind his ear, nudging his hat away from his forehead so she can see him better.

"But fortune has again put you right where you belong, at just the right time," she croons, settling her free hand around the side of his neck. He doesn't move, doesn't look away from her, but beside them his arm slackens, his revolver pointing towards the floor. At rest. "There we go, there's no reason for *us* to behave like thugs. We're better than that, aren't we?"

"Wouldn't you like to have a meal, instead?" she asks. "You must be *famished.*"

Under her fingers, she feels Ulrich swallow involuntarily. Rook meets his eyes through his mask, and she smiles.

Once Phineas is alone things get weird.

Since stepping inside the castle it's felt like something has been pulling her along towards some center point, getting stronger all the time. It feels like running down a hill, tilting more and more, and at some point Phineas had lapsed from a jog to a full sprint.

But she isn't *getting* anywhere. When she passes the same potted plant a fifth time she feels the beginnings of exhaustion setting in, and then the thought of collapsing in the endless corridors-

"Finally!!"

It hits her like a train, knocking her sideways to stumble into a spiky yellow vase and sending both of them crashing to the carpet.

"Oh!" The thunderous voice softens to a conversational tone, sheepish. "Sorry sorry, my bad. You look bigger from here."

"From *where?*" Phineas demands, struggling to her aching legs and setting her back against the wall. Now that she's finally managed to stop running her fatigue catches up with her all at once, but she doesn't want to look weak in front of whatever this is— the feel of it is alarmingly similar to being crushed by the starstone deity in the mine.

As soon as the thought crosses her mind, the pressure eases off.

"Relax, kiddo," the voice says. "You know me, we've been chatting since last night. Chill out for a minute, nothing's gonna get'cha."

She can't figure out where the voice comes from because she's not hearing it in her ears. It's all around her, filling the air like light. It's suddenly a wholly different feeling; the underground deity had been ephemeral and hazy, hard to see, but this presence is lighting her up in vivid, biting technicolor. Phineas tastes saltwater, feels cool glass under her fingertips, picks up the scent of the topiaries outside.

Ah!

"You're the thing I've been hearing!" she shouts, exhaustion forgotten. "You're the ship's heart I've been lookin' for! Hi!"

"What's good."

...Phineas was unprepared for this, and looking to her surroundings for guidance hits her with some flavor of vertigo. The clean, calm leaf and white marble textures of the outer levels had melted away a while ago, replaced with sickly yellows and reds. The logic had begun to break down too: there are still *some* plants, but now they skewer directly out from the walls, and interior windows look out over alien shorelines suffocated with storm clouds. Paused long enough to think about it, Phineas realizes that the perspective has been changing. At one point she'd run through a tiny wheat field, dotted with trees that reached her knees and scattered flocks of black birds when she passed. The hallway she's in now yawns high over her head, the scale breathtaking. A skylight the size of a city street looks into a mouth, red gums mottled around nonsense teeth, its steady breath fogging up the glass panes.

"Walk and talk?" the ship's heart says, dragging her out of her observations. "Got places to be, huh?"

"Y...yeah," Phineas says, trying not to quail under the newly oppressive hallway. When she moves she feels a steep grade under her again, it takes an effort to keep a normal walking pace. It doesn't help that the carpet under her feet feels thick and soggy, too much like a tongue, as she crosses the long stretch of hallway that passes under the fucked up skylight. She can feel something underneath it all though, beyond her reflexive revulsion; the ship is poking at her, a lazy predator nudging at something to decide whether it's a toy or a snack. Phineas refuses to be either of those.

"What do I call you?" she asks. "I'm Phineas."

"I know who you are," the ship says. "These days I'm called Artemis Ascending."

"Do you *wanna* be called that?"

"Not really. But I don't get much say in it."

The hallway is lined with identical copies of the spiky yellow vase she'd broken earlier, looming up like sentries. The perspective misbehaving as it is, they all grow wildly out of sync with her footsteps— as she passes the pair on the other side of the halfway point, they tower over her like trees.

"You could pick your name if you come with me," she says to the ship, and Artemis' laugh sends ripples through the gross carpet.

"That's right, you're out to catch the sun aren't you?"

"How'd you know that already?"

"You've only been sayin' it to everybody you meet since you showed up," Artemis says. "You already forget you had the guy downstairs put your name out for everybody to see?"

"Well, good!" Phineas insists, having in fact forgotten already about that detail of the negotiations with the starstone in the mine. It's probably a good thing, anyway. "So? You wanna?"

"Easy there, you still gotta get through Raven first."

"Raven who?"

A foreign feeling wells up in her, and Phineas realizes belatedly that they're connected somehow, whatever through-line is letting Artemis' voice carry to her is hooked into the rest of her perceptions too. She'd felt their elation as her own a moment ago, during the introductions, but now someone else's nostalgia tugs in her throat.

"Oh he's calling himself *Hazard* now isn't he?" Artemis says. "Sorry, old habits."

With an embarrassing sense of relief Phineas reaches the end of the skylight passage, but when she rounds the corner the next thing is even worse. *This* corridor, so vast she can't see the other side before it fades into white fog, is surrounded by hundreds of identical windows gridded out in every direction. The carpet stays consistent, but that's a problem because the floor under it stops. The burgundy under her feet continues, ribboning and swirling beyond the last piece of solid ground to disappear out over the white emptiness. Phineas can hear the ocean crashing somewhere above. The grade is getting worse again.

Jo had talked about starships acting this way sometimes. As useful as starstone is for Sprawl travel it's far from a fully understood material, and even cut stone is known to "glitch" this way. Phineas had tried to anticipate it— weirdness comes with the territory, may in fact be the *entire* territory, and she has to meet this thing where it's at. She can't help her feelings, knowing they're being broadcast to Artemis the same way theirs are coming to her, but she doesn't break her stride as she takes the first steps out onto the unsupported carpet. Aside from the unpleasant disconnect of feeling like she's walking *down* as she *climbs* a vertical ribbon-curl of pathway, it holds her up like it should.

Coming down the other side of the curl Phineas twigs she's been too preoccupied to keep up with her half of their conversation, which is no good.

She says, "Is Hazard keeping you here somehow? Are you being held hostage?"

"Now there's a question." Phineas gets the feeling Artemis is reclining with their feet kicked up on some seat cushions, or a tabletop; certainly not sitting *correctly*.

"Nnno," they say eventually. "But I'd rather not be here. He snatched me up quick after everything with Crow went to hell, and now we're bound together. This is more like a bad roommate situation."

"Crow!" Phineas says, feeling herself speed up as she comes down the other side of a long incline. "So all y'all stone guys really do know Gideon? I kinda thought the other one was lyin'."

In addition to the endless windows, the empty air all around the road is populated with hanging columns and scattered, deconstructed pieces of the walls from previous hallways. Tree limbs sprout from thin air, and even more hanging windowpanes look in on abstract movement and shapes, chaotic and shifting like Artemis is flipping through television channels. There are also a lot of suspended triangles. They're made of some alien material that is simply Blue, creating static shapes that turn along with Phineas' vision to always be facing directly at her, and pointing down. Phineas recognizes them as the same triangles shining across the back of Hazard's coat. Her feet carry her a little faster.

Artemis makes a rude sound not unlike the one Phineas made back in the street when she first arrived at Last Chance, pulling her attention back in. The sensory overload of the environment makes it hard to focus on the talking.

"They've *heard* of Crow, maybe," Artemis says. Starstone, Gideon, starstone that knows Gideon. *"I carried his dumb ass all the way through an apocalypse and, like, seven major break-ups."*

"Huh?!" Phineas doesn't notice how fast she's moving, the floating detritus smearing like cartoon cels, the tilt of the ribbon road intensifying.

"Well, *every* break-up is major if you ask him," Artemis amends. "You *never* seen a guy carry on 'til you seen Crow Gideon get *dumped.*"

The wind against Phineas' face smells like seasalt.

"You were *Gideon's* ship," she huffs, leaping over a marble column that had toppled into the pathway. "But if *Hazard* has you *now,* that must mean he-"

Her heart skips a beat as the next footfall sinks deep into the floor, suddenly the consistency of mud, and she has a sickening vision of plummeting straight through it into the abyss.

That doesn't happen, but as the painful shock of cortisol dissipates all her frustration catches up with her. She's suddenly furious, too angry to keep up the veneer of Coolness. She feels the ghost of Artemis' giggle in her chest and it sends her over the edge.

"Are you gonna help me or not!" she snarls at the air, shaking her foot and flinging melted fucking carpet everywhere.

"Not," Artemis drawls. She can hear them smiling. "You ain't my captain."

"I thought you wanted me to come here, you been pulling at me for two days now! I thought you *wanted* my help!"

"I do."

"Then-!"

"You ain't my captain," they say with more finality. Phineas stomps her foot; dissonant car horns sound from somewhere.

"Don't you even *care* this place is coming apart?" Phineas demands, staring up at nothing and wishing she had something to focus on. As the thought comes, a jellyfish as long as she is drifts into view through a wide window hovering nearby. Its cap lights up violet with Artemis' speech.

"Why should I?" they say. "It's not *my* fault Raven brought a bunch of fucked up shit on board."

The jellyfish swirls in a graceful figure eight, unbothered. "And it ain't *yours* either, I dunno why you're gettin' worked up over it."

"I *ain't!!*" Phineas hollers, full of sparks. Hearing her own voice brings her down, but before she can get tangled up in the frustration of figuring out how to manage herself *and* keep talking, Artemis Ascending keeps going. They already know what she's feeling.

It...knows. The ship *knows*. The ship communicates the same way *she* does, *it* had started to dance with *her* so naturally she hadn't even noticed. Something new and lovely blossoms over the back of her neck, like a hand resting there, her anger dissipating along the steady current buoying the jellyfish in its window.

"Now I am *positive* you ain't runnin' around with Jo's coat and Crow's commanding and they turned you loose without telling you how to meditate," Artemis says, easy.

"What's that got to do with anything?" Phineas demands, bratty just to be something.

"You haven't even *tried* to adjust to me yet. Your body is still oriented to the planet and it thinks it's falling out of the sky, you're gonna *stay* worked up if you don't do somethin' about it."

"I am! I'm-!"

"No you're not you're *runnin'*, what are you *runnin'* for?"

"'Cause the floor is...Because..." As Phineas' thoughts slow down, some pieces begin to fit together. Artemis waits for her.

"I'm being pulled in," Phineas says, unconsciously leaning back on her heels.

"I am not your ship," Artemis says, their voice colder and heavier. "You are not my captain, and my captain is not a fan of you. This place is not your friend."

"Right, okay, but." Phineas drags her wrist across her sweaty forehead. "I do this while I'm runnin' all the time, I don't *need* to-"

"Yeah, your methods *clearly* leave nothing to be desired," Artemis snorts, lightening up again. *"That's* why you're all cranky, when's the last time you meditated? Like, for real, not this slapdash *bullshit* you're showing me?"

"This *morning!"*

"And did you take the opportunity to do it in that looong long elevator ride up here?"

"...it was too hard," Phineas says sheepishly. The current inside the window gets choppier, the drift of the jellyfish more erratic.

"Oh damn that's too bad," their voice is mocking, it feels like they're flicking her nose to try and get a rise out of her. "You do know *how* though? You done it before?"

It's working.

"Of course I know how, I just said I-"

"Then fucking act like it."

"I don't need to *every time*, that would take *forever!"*

"See *this* kinda thing's what got your ass *possessed* earlier."

Phineas stomps her foot again. The floor around it explodes in a shower of blue confetti.

"Don't tell *me* how to-"

"No!" Artemis screams, rattling the glass in a thousand windows. "We are *not-*"

"Quit cuttin' me off!!" Phineas screams back, the command bouncing harmlessly off the aquarium pane.

Her feet sink into the floor and it solidifies around her ankles, and before she can comprehend what's happening a riptide shatters through the glass in front of her. The sea surges around her and she gasps without thinking— fortunately it's air that fills her lungs, reality conveniently ignoring that she's suddenly trapped in a seabed. The jellyfish and its quiet light are gone, replaced by sharp, shadowy things swarming all around in the murk.

"*I* have been putting up with cocky brats like you longer than *you* been **alive!!**" Artemis' indignation washes over Phineas like the water, meshing with her own; she lets herself be taken where they want to go. "You skate by on *just* a *little* predisposition and suddenly the rules don't apply to you? You get to take shortcuts?"

"Whatever 'natural talent' you think you got ain't gonna do a damn bit of good next to someone who put in the hours," they rumble through the sea. "And Raven's done *nothing* but put in hours trying to figure out how to kill a commander whose boots *you* ain't fit to spitshine."

Phineas is thinking more clearly after the shock of cold, the salt stinging her eyes and all her forgotten scrapes. While she listens she stares up into the light shimmering down through the surface of the ocean, reaching for her through a thick tangle of kelp and seaweed. The sharp creature-shapes weave through the light too, but some of the dark spots are different. Debris, she thinks. Pieces from a shipwreck coming down.

The sea and all its shadows calm.

"I can feel you, Phineas," they say, quieter but no less intense. "I can feel you worryin' about your friend and impressing me and *none* of that is important right now. If you don't get your head 'n ass wired together before you get to Hazard you're gonna get *wrecked,* and *I'm* gonna spend another century listening to him cry into his *fucking* scrapbook."

The entire ocean sighs.

"Look, I don't mean..." As Artemis speaks, more ship debris

materialize and begin to sink, softly kicking up the sand around where Phineas is stuck. "Ego's *good* on a commander, I don't mean to put you out or nothin'. But there's *no reason* to think you're coming out of this alive. This guy has lifetimes of experience over you, it's not a fair fight."

"Lifetimes?" Phineas bubbles.

"Now it's too late to turn around, and if you're gonna have *any* chance of knocking him down a peg you need to approach this with the right attitude. Are you really gonna put yourself at a disadvantage because you're too stubborn to take advice from me?"

Phineas squares up, tentatively reaching out with her spirit to feel for Artemis properly. It still feels like they're all around her, even without the ocean illusion, but it's easy enough to dig beyond the impression and find a core of concentrated feeling somewhere below the seabed. She opens her eyes and watches the swaying shadows with new apprehension.

"I won't be able to fight, while we're doin' this," she says.

"What are you fighting? If I wanted you dead you wouldn't be here talkin' to me." The sand softens, and Phineas is free again, floating. She treads the water, excited by the novelty of being able to breathe down here. "The tain can play their games with the scenery, but I still have the authority here. You'll be safe."

"The tain is what's doing all this weird stuff?" Phineas asks, tugging at the leaves of a kelp strand.

"...Sure," Artemis says. "Yeah, this is the tain."

"What if I don't trust *you?*" Phineas says, though it's more of a formality at this point.

"That's probably smart. But a corpse can't help me. Come on, kiddo."

Phineas doesn't have to think too hard about it. This is why she came here.

"Lemme down," she says into the water. "I want my feet on the floor."

There's no transition or even a response; the ocean disappears, and Phineas is back on the ribbon road.

Phineas settles her feet shoulder width apart, and Artemis laughs softly, hardly a ripple through the wallpaper.

"Everyone gets bent out of shape about the emblems on you," they tell her. "Crow's emblems, but I could tell who you were as soon as you set foot on the deck."

Phineas closes her eyes and feels her breathing, focuses in on the light in her chest. Artemis goes on while she concentrates.

"Your balance is always up in your middle, like you're about to take off running. That's Crow for sure, he liked to throw his weight around. But your *stance* looks like it started out as *Jo's.* You're on your toes too often for just Crow teaching you. You think like a commander but you *move* like a walker."

"Oh yeah?" Phineas murmurs, reaching out towards that core where Artemis is. She isn't listening, her consciousness flowing out along the capillaries in Artemis' wild halo. When they giggle again it's like being wrapped in soft fur, like she's living the dream of pressing her face into a lion's mane without getting eaten.

"You're gonna be a holy terror once you get the hang of this," Artemis purrs. "Assumin' you live long enough."

Since they'd risen in the elevator, Phineas had felt untethered the way she had in the mine, pulled in too many directions. Trying to orient herself to the planet so far below only made her feel less stable, and trying to connect with Hazard's ship on her own was like tumbling through cold, dark water. Now, everything going abstract and dream-like, Phineas gets the sense that part of the reason is that the heart is split up: that cold-water layer she couldn't break through on her own is only an outside layer around the real thing. When she reaches out this time, the ship's heart reaches back, like drawing a curtain aside to let her in the back entrance, and what's on the other side isn't cold at *all.*

The spirit in the stone, MaybeArtemis, shines with the same cyan as other starstone does, but there's something else touching Phineas too; that siren's voice that has been calling out to her, *beloved, beloved, come to me.* It feels like learning to command with Gideon again, like looking at Ulrich, the light that shines on all the best things she finds. It reminds her of the light of the sun, but even her own sunlight is furious and greedy. This is joyful, curious.

It feels like discovery.

Before today she'd never connected with something that talked *back* before, but her mind normally interprets this sort of thing close to what she'd seen with the starstone in the mine: darkness patched with un-named bursts of color, submerged in the space behind closed eyes. This place is *bright*. When she slips fully into her fugue, leaving her body at rest in the corridor so her mind and spirit can mingle with the ship's halo, everything is reduced to soft, warm light— shining gossamer threads-

(this time, the third time, the ghost of recognition begins to stir in her memory).

Artemis speaks first.

"Ooh, you *are* bigger than you look." Phineas feels the tapped-glass feeling, but now it's right up against her heart.

She tries to pull herself together. After spending so long steeped in the rot around Last Chance, this new connection is so vivacious she's too full to speak. It's like she's been starving- there, that's *it*. The spirit in the stone is every huge greasy breakfast Jo had ever made for her, everything they'd need to get them through the day's work.

"Hi," she says. Her voice vibrates across the gossamer strung through the air like harp strings, her orange sparking away into a white void. She reaches out with her senses to touch them and they light up gold, glassy tones vibrating in Phineas' ears.

"Whenever you're ready," Artemis says. "I promise I won't bite."

"Can I ask something?" Phineas asks.

"Shoot."

"I thought ship's hearts were supposed to be made of *cut* stone," she says. "I wasn't expectin' you to be so uh. Talkative."

"I'm just the same shape I was when I was dug up. I ain't lettin' some human saw off *my* edges," Artemis says.

"Never," Phineas agrees. "I'm glad you're like this."

The breathtaking halo shimmers with warmth.

"I didn't know you *could* make a ship with uncut stone," Phineas admits. "I would've been after this all the time if I'd known it felt this way."

"Technically you can't," Artemis says. Phineas gets the feeling of fingers carding through her hair, and very, very distantly she remembers the impression of being sized up by a predator. "None of you humans could make conscious starstone do *anything* we don't want to, we get too smart and you gotta file us down until there's not enough left to think right. But our strength *comes from* our connection. You guys use us for power but the first thing you do is weaken us. It's awful inefficient."

"I don't like that much at all."

The fingers touch her face gently, the spirit getting a feel for her, too.

"Neither did Gideon. That's why *we* had an *agreement.* I can do a lot more than one of your laser-perfect hearts can."

"Like decide on your own whether to betray your captain as soon as some commander you don't even know *asks* you to?"

"Yes." A grin, sharp. *"Exactly* like that."

With that: a feeling in her extra senses she's familiar with, some ephemeral tendon that had been twisted tight finally eases back into elasticity. Connection established.

"Don't get me wrong," Artemis mumbles. "I haven't *exactly* betrayed him. And I would never do something like this to *my* Raven, but..."

Phineas blinks with her physical body, the light of the halo fading as it's replaced with the ship interior again. The world orients itself, the dizziness fades, and the ship under her solidifies into something reliable. Phineas breathes easy, right in time with the rhythm of the entity lurking beyond Artemis, now a reassuring benchmark in the landscape of her perception. But along with it-

"You're *sad,"* she says out loud.

"Yeah," Artemis states, a simple fact. "Raven was my friend, all of them were. That husk sitting in his chair is not my friend, and it's a real fuckin' drag."

"I'm sorry."

"Me too. How are we feelin'?"

Phineas shifts her weight. She commands up a touch of energy and it does just what she wants, it comes when she calls it in a spark that dissipates around her knees.

"Much better!" she chirps. She tastes something in the soft tissue near her back teeth. "You kinda taste like sawdust."

"Sawdust?" Artemis laughs. "Interesting."

Back in touchable space the environment has changed again, for the better this time. The windows and floating debris have been replaced by a real hallway, blue and serene, like the corridor she and Ulrich swam up into when they first got into the castle. There's a little wooden footbridge nearby that leads out of the hallway, crossing a quiet stream.

"You decided to clean up?" she asks, stepping up onto the bridge.

"Things might still get weird once you get closer to our guy, but I don't mind holding it together if you're gonna be serious now."

Phineas grips the railing and grins, leaning back on her heels.

"I'm sorry I was grumpy before," she says.

"You think you're the first commander to throw a tantrum on this ship?" They're smiling too, pressing up through the wood under Phineas' hands. "I like your anger. I would've been disappointed if you hadn't stuck up for yourself."

Phineas watches a stream of paper boats drifting under the bridge, yellow on blue. She spots shadows slithering there too, wisps of tain whipping between the boats in the water, but before she can get worried about it she realizes they don't seem to notice her at all. They're flowing somewhere specific, with intention, and whatever they're doing doesn't involve Phineas.

She relaxes. She can still taste sawdust, and maybe sunflower seed shells. Despite absolutely everything, being here with Artemis humming around her is the most at-home she's ever felt.

"This is easier than I thought it would be," she murmurs.

"Oh yeah," Artemis agrees. "Commanders always feel good on starships, once y'all settle in. There's *tons* less interference between you and me and you and the planet. Commanding on your own ship is like having your *own* planet."

"No- well, *yeah,* but-" Phineas turns to lean back against the bridge railing, crossing her arms and staring up into the tangle of pine branches and paper lanterns reaching down from the ceiling. "After dealing with the other stone I didn't really think you'd be so... so *reasonable.* They don't think much'a you."

A groan that ripples the water and shivers through the pine needles. "God-UH that stuffy old thing's been buggin' me since I got here. What did they tell you?"

"That you lost your mind, somethin' about being a satellite too long. I guess they meant you've worked with *humankinds* too long?"

"HAH!" Artemis shouts, splashing in the stream. "Figures. You know why they think that?"

"Tell me."

"We ain't *supposed* to be in the ground to *begin* with," they say, their pride and indignation thrumming in Phineas' veins. "They can gossip about me consorting with lesser beings, or dabbling in weaker faculties like emotions, or whatever shit they're on about. But *I've* been out in the sunshine. I've been *movin',* taking in new things. *They're* the ones been goin' nuts sitting in the dark, isolating themselves."

Discovery, discovery. *Breakfast.* Phineas shuts her eyes and lets them wash over her. She never, ever wants to be apart from them again.

"You live like that long enough of *course* anything else is gonna look crazy." And then they come in close again, speaking right into her. "You listen to me, kiddo. Stagnation *kills.* Entropy is coming after all of us, always. Stars included, even if they won't admit it. Alone and in the dark isn't healthy for *anybody."*

"You *gotta* keep fighting it," the heart says. "All the time you *have* to keep moving forward. *Whatever* it takes."

"Forward," Phineas repeats, wishing she could take their hand. She still has to earn this, she still has to finish what she started. But she's as sure now as she was with Ulrich— if she can't leave with them, she isn't leaving at all. "Whatever it takes."

◉◉◉

The gate is made entirely of silver, curling in and in on itself like fractals wherever Ulrich tries to look. It sits at the end of a long, narrow hallway, and he only realizes once they've reached the end that the potted plants lining the walk had lost their pots at some point, and the carpet is grassy under his boots. With the open space between its bars, the gate shouldn't be creating a true barrier to the air, but the scents and sounds of the gardens beyond don't hit Ulrich fully until Rook drags it open.

The garden is so vast he almost thinks they've stepped outside the castle again, but when he squints up into the pale light overhead he sees the sun is obscured behind a layer of crystal clear water. *Maybe* it's the sun. Maybe this whole place is a hallucination he's having after one of those men shot him in the head before he could get out of the elevator.

Ulrich smells honeysuckle as he follows Rook out onto the turquoise lawn, the unsettling gate easing unsettlingly shut behind them. Once it does, a wall of sound whooshes into place; Ulrich is violently reminded of dragging the drape from a trick box, flourishing, revealing someone has disappeared or reappeared or perhaps transformed into a rabbit. He rarely hears it from this side and he does not like it. There is birdsong, sweet and sticking, and when he looks twice there are shining turquoise butterflies flickering between the boughs of a wisteria tree— previously new-green, now rapaciously threaded through with cyan petals like gemstones. He realizes the details are waiting for him to look away before manifesting out of thin air, like they don't want to give away the game. Each time he tries to see over Rook's shoulder to anticipate where they're going, the landscape ahead of her has sprouted a dozen new magnolia trees that turn and bloom like music. Each time he turns back to the path the shrubs have grown impossibly more plush, their blossoms more manically saturated. As they pass under an archway choked-out with hysterically gorgeous white roses, he picks up the sound of moving water. He hopes it's a fountain and not the suspended sea coming down around them.

Rook has been speaking almost constantly since Phineas left them alone, nothing Ulrich particularly cares about beyond the fact that she knows she's done something wrong, and wants him to forgive her. He is more preoccupied trying to keep his breathing even under the onslaught of every flower fragrance in existence, every screaming color trying to pull his attention at once.

"I thought this might be a good place for us to relax a little while we chat," Rook says, fawning in her voice. He wonders if the garden feels the same way to her or if all of this- this hologram, this facsimile of real space, is subjective to each perception. Ulrich thinks he might hate starships. "A pleasant change after coming up through that mess of a town. And the desert, and the *mine.*" She pauses to turn and look at him. "What's it *like* down there?"

Every muscle obediently rigored in place, Ulrich knows his masked expression only shows bored annoyance and none of his discomfort at the environment trying to bully him into serenity.

"Bad," he says.

Rook laughs lightly. He doesn't give her anything, but she stays light, dead set on pretending this is nothing more serious than a last-minute lunch date. She starts walking again.

"I'd assumed it must be, Dad wouldn't let me anywhere near it. He hasn't let me do much of anything since we got here." Bitterness, curling the edges of her pleasant hostess veneer. Ulrich stops staring at a wisteria tree to watch her back as she slinks ahead of him. Sometimes, his ring on her finger catches the light, glinting in the lenses of Ulrich's mask.

"He used to take me along with him everywhere," Rook goes on. "Field trips, like kids who go to school get. He said it was important that I get the experience..." She giggles softly. "That's why you and I met at *all,* you know. We go to Tourmaline every year, used to be to get me new magic components or some. Educational, thing. But once I didn't need the instruction we spent the time in the Verdantia district. Dad liked the hot springs, and I liked the lights..." She clears her throat. "He sent me on my own, this last year. But you know that bit already."

When Ulrich doesn't answer right away Rook lets the silence hang, seemingly derailing her own solitary conversation, but that's about the time they come around a corner and Ulrich gets distracted by several other things.

There's a cheerful woven wicker lounge set, with lovely velvet cushions and a glass-top table, and behind that is the largest clockwork mechanism Ulrich has ever seen.

Rook must hear him stop, briefly stunned, because she recovers enough to smile at him.

"Isn't it pretty?" she says, stepping aside so he can see better, even though it is so massive she hadn't obscured it at all. The clock's mainspring must be two dozen feet across by itself, the dark spring against the silver plate making Ulrich's eyes glaze over like the gate had. The rest of the gears are no less impressive, glittering in the false sunshine, effortlessly turning a set of hands sharpened into spires. There are no numbers and no face, and in fact there are several more of those hands than a clock would normally have. A pendulum swings underneath, a silver scythe like a guillotine.

Despite its size, the mechanism is silent; the only sound comes from the rush of air over the pendulum as it slices elegantly through space. It's hung against a glass wall that looks out into an expanse of pale blue ocean water, only noticeable as water because the continuing gardens on the other side sway serenely in the tide.

"It doesn't tell the time," Rook says. "It's something to do with lunar phases. I thought you might like it, you and your gadgets." She tilts her head toward the lawn furniture. "Come sit with me."

When Rook steps away, Ulrich presses his left foot a little harder against the ground than he needs to, twitching his toes. Something clicks as Ulrich moves to join her, too softly for her to hear it as she makes a gesture over the table.

Ulrich tastes the magic in his mouth, coating his teeth like he's been eating ice cream. The glass panel tabletop frosts over, cold white clouds billowing from nothing in the air above it, and when they whisk away the table is laid out with a tea service. A simple tea service, by Rook's usual standards, but Ulrich's stomach does not care and screams loudly enough to startle them both.

Rook raises an eyebrow, still smiling like they're friends.

"Just as I thought. Not much time for eating today, I guess." She sits in one of the white wicker chairs, plucking a tea bulb from a ceramic bowl with a pair of tongs. There's a glass teapot sitting over a small flame, the water already hot, and watching something so frivolously luxurious and delicate while he can feel his clothing crusting around the curves of his body nearly snaps something in Ulrich's brain.

He doesn't move, trying to keep his eyes on Rook instead of the food with the effort of keeping a car from rolling down a hill.

"*Please* sit, Ulrich. *Eat.*" Rook pours some water over the bulb, and it slowly blooms in the teacup. "*I'm* eating."

When that still doesn't get a response she pouts, and Ulrich feels a tiny spark of satisfaction that he's getting to her. "Are you seriously so paranoid you think I'd poison you with *tea sandwiches?* I respect you enough to put a *little* more effort into my assassination attempts."

"...Would you at least take off that stupid mask?" Rook huffs. "Isn't this your whole *thing*, don't you *like* a little back and forth over desserts? Where's that wonderfully rhetorical rogue I met in the market?"

Ulrich says, "He sat in a cell for three days and had a chance to rethink his opinion of you."

Rook rolls her eyes.

"After all that bluster about your escape artistry I'm supposed to think that was any real inconvenience for you?"

"You hurt my feelings, Rook," the masked man says.

"I wasn't aware you had those." She sags in the chair petulantly, heaving a sigh. She twists his blossom on his ring around her finger. "I *am* sorry about that," she admits. "I just can't help myself sometimes, I know you know what I mean."

"I can't say I do."

"So this thing you're doing with that commander is nothing like what we were doing, then?"

The food on the table is cloying at Ulrich like quicksand; he loses his concentration thinking about her question and his stomach growls again in the silence. Rook smiles in a way that makes him murderous.

"You make things so *hard,* Ulrich."

"Why did you bring me here?" he asks, swallowing against the hungry nausea digging in his throat.

"To offer you a meal." She takes a miniature cupcake from one of the tiered serving trays and sets it delicately on a saucer next to her teacup. "Whether you decide to eat or not is up to you. But I also want to discuss the fact that you're here in Last Chance at *all.*"

Ulrich tilts his head, feeling the light heft of the mask's beak. Rook sets her elbows on her knees, her shawl draping across her crossed wrists. The diamonds in the knitting stare at him like eyes.

"Do you have any idea how impossible it is that you made it here?" she asks, finally hinting at a real motive. "Do you realize the odds against you finding me again at all, and tracking us down *here,* to this nowhere place, and then *getting onto this ship?* My father and I have evaded people *and* creatures for *years* with abilities you couldn't even fathom, and *you* made it here all on your own! I am *thoroughly* impressed."

As he catches on, Ulrich sees familiar movement behind a row of hedges. Black and brown, more wolf than butterfly.

"I couldn't care less how impressed you are," he says. "If I recall correctly, *you* were being recruited to come work for *me.*"

She grins at him, almost sadly. Then she sits up and reaches for her tea, picking the full bloom floating on the water and eating it in one poised bite. She takes her time chewing, then takes a sedate sip of the tea that should still be too hot to drink.

"Ulrich, you can cling to your affirmations as tightly as you like," she says. "But we both know you weren't meant for leadership. You were caught and collared early, you've been someone else's dog all your life and that is not going to change. Even now, out here alone and far away from Roulette City, you find yourself at the side of more powerful people, caught up in their orbit and dragged along wherever they please." Rook stares into the lenses of his mask, knowing he's looking back at her. "*You* can't help yourself, *either.* Let me tell you, from my own experience: the sooner you make peace with this aspect of yourself, the better."

"You'll excuse me if I don't think as little of myself as you do."

Rook giggles politely.

"You misunderstand me. The people in the back are the *foundation.* You should know, theater kid." She wraps her fingers around the steaming teacup, not noticing the heat. "Everyone *wants* to be center stage, but without someone running the *lights* none of that charisma gets very far, does it? Your voice can only be as pleasant as the speakers it comes from. Our skills are valuable, they *need* us."

From behind the hedges, Bel steps into view, watching Ulrich through a cloud of cigarette smoke. Her exhales come in diamonds, and glitter like them too.

"It's in our best interest to be picky about who we serve with our talents, and you *do* have talents worth bargaining for," Rook goes on, unable to see that Ulrich's gaze has gone to something behind her. "Whatever you came from did a good job of crushing your spiritual ability out of you. That blight in your eye wasn't an accident; someone was *very* careful to keep you from getting too sure of yourself." Ulrich turns back to her sharply, the scent of gin creeping into his olfactories and suppressing the din of the garden's fragrances.

"But you got lucky! You still have your *voice. Silverspeak* is irreplaceable." Rook waves one hand near her temple, and her visor shimmers across her eyes. "And you can *buy* your sight back, if you know the right people. We can help you be so much more than-"

"Do you think I am unaware of my worth?" Ulrich demands sharply, flooded with someone else's impatience. "Of the dynamics of my own life? Your father has tried this with me already. His offer was dismissive and, frankly, insulting. If any of you have more attractive incentives than Phineas has I've yet to see them."

His irritation passes through Rook like water through a sieve. She dismisses her visor.

"I'm sorry," she says honestly. "This family has been running short on diplomacy."

Bel has moved to the tree behind the empty wicker chair meant for him, admiring an ivy twisting thickly around the trunk. When she reaches out to touch it, he can almost feel the leaves under his own fingertips.

"Here's the thing," Rook says, sitting up and setting her palms on the armrests. Bel jerks her head in Rook's direction, turning Ulrich's attention like tuning a stubborn radio.

"The commander will die here," Rook says. "Even if he didn't have decades of misplaced frustration with commanders to keep him going, my dad is so far beyond her in ability and experience that this isn't even like. *Posturing,* it's just *math.*"

Ulrich opens his mouth around a retort, but Rook raises one hand.

"Were that not the case already, Phineas is unstable. Her ambition is outpacing her, and when she can't keep up anymore it's going to devour *her.* And everyone *around* her. Look where you *are.*" She crosses her ankles, unfairly comfortable. "You've known her for hardly a day, and she has you charging in and stealing ships? Ulrich Weiss, who won't even take off his mask? Who won't even sit down for tea with me?"

She seems to remember their positions then, that he is still standing awkwardly away from the spread, and she pinches the bridge of her nose.

"Will you *sit?* I promise the seat cushions aren't loaded."

Bel laughs at that, a harsh, raspy bark of a thing. Ulrich waits an appropriate beat, then takes a few slow steps and *finally* sinks into the chair. As soon as he's off his feet the exhaustion steals over him like it's pouring in through the top of his head, weighing down every part of him. As he gets comfortable he notices his clothes have left a smear of dirt (dust from the mine? ash from the town?) across the smooth white wicker, the soft velvet of the cushions, and in the wake of his loosening wires he nearly goes to pieces. But Bel is watching, her hands keeping pressure where he needs it.

Rook beams at him.

"There, is that so bad?"

He slouches, crossing one leg and resting his temple against two fingers, and says nothing. He says nothing because he thinks he might start sobbing if he opens his mouth, but to Rook it should look like he is only waiting for her to proceed. She doesn't ask if he's alright, so it must work.

"That's *another* favor I'm doing for you," she says. "I know you have this whole *thing* about being manipulated— you know the term 'commander' is literal, right? Manipulation is *literally* what they do, and their measures are *much* nastier than anything *you* could do with that silver tongue."

Her eyes slip from him and she stares down into her teacup instead, gently swirling the dregs.

"You're just something she can put between herself and the death she's working so hard to keep cheating," she mumbles.

Rook might be reading the tea leaves. Blooming tea is pretty, but it leaves a lot behind.

"You sat in a cell for three days," she says. "Not an hour ago I murdered a man whose name I don't even remember. I've done it myself, I *know* what it looks like when ambition turns those around you into tools instead of people." When she looks up at Ulrich, her eyes are full of concern. He notices how lovely the curl of her hair is, how well it frames her face. "You deserve *better than that.* I can't stand to see you *wasted* on this careless little upstart."

Ulrich makes a thinking noise, spending some time in the way Rook's eye makeup changes the shape of her face.

"I think she scares you," he says, staying still, the mask still leveled at her. "Or, whoever you're borrowing this diatribe from. The facts as *I* see them are quite different from yours. I watched her destroy what I can *only* describe as divine beings. I felt her...*demand* that reality change shape, and reality *bent.*" He uncrosses his leg and settles further into the comfortable seat. "I am a skeptic, but at some point that becomes willful ignorance. What I do know is that everyone who has underestimated her has suffered for it. I do not intend to join them."

"That's not such bad logic," Rook admits, waking up again. She plucks a perfectly cut sandwich from the tray, reminding Ulrich it's there, mother*fucker.* "She must have seemed like a smart person to pair up with, fighting off a couple of minor deities..." She takes an unhurried bite, chews, swallows, Ulrich is *so hungry.* "But *I'm* talking about the faction that put those deities *down* there."

Gently, like the cover has been slipped back over the trick box, the sound goes out of the room. Rook grins like a cat, savoring the change in Ulrich's attention.

"I have made some very powerful friends since we last spoke," she says. "I have found some people more...proactive, than my father is. Whatever you thought *I* could help you with before would be *nothing* to them."

His ring on her finger shines in the false light as she finishes the sandwich, crystal petals glittering and glittering in Ulrich's eyes.

"They could restore your body, your *soul,* all the damage you've been living with could be *gone.* When we met you seemed so *tired,* you'd been on your own for so long already. I can't imagine it's gotten any easier. Wouldn't it be nice to outsource some of that stress? Let us *help* you." She leans forward again, her expression open and honest. She twists the ring on her finger.

"I *am* sorry I stole from you," Rook repeats. "But you're here now, so let's make the most of it. All I'm asking is for you to listen to my proposal, and if you don't like what you hear you're free to take your little flower back and go. No violence, no strings attached. You can leave here and wander the desert all you like."

Ulrich feels Bel looming behind him, feels her bite down on her thumbnail the way she does, grinning around it. He dismisses his mask. He knows his face is filthy, and he must look pathetic to Rook. He stares into her anxious eyes.

And then he reaches for a sandwich. The soft, fresh bread might be the best thing he's ever tasted.

324

Things had gotten closer to normal since Phineas had connected to Artemis, if "normal" means "what the foyer of the castle looked like." Once she'd rested at the bridge long enough to get anxious to move again, she'd started through a more familiar and less nightmarish set of passages; blues and silvers, leafy green plantlife, clean water over chalky white statues. Artemis chats with her on her way, and while the coiled predator feeling is still there, she doesn't feel like she might be on the menu any more. It's closer to being held in an enormous paw: it is clawed, for sure, but it only holds her so they can talk face to face.

She steps into a new corridor and ignores the big thing for the small things: the air is suddenly freezing, and it smells exactly like the mine did, must and dust and mold. There is also a rooster disemboweling a crow on the floor a few feet away.

The crow is alive, still, its beak slack around tortured, wheezing moans. The rooster (which is a *very* familiar orange) slings its head back and stretches a strand of meat from the other bird like pulling taffy. It drags the black bird's chest up off the carpet, the lower half still held down under the rooster's talons, and as the tendon snaps and the black bird thumps against the floor again Phineas realizes it's not a crow. Jo had said it was easy to get them mixed up, if you weren't sure what you were looking at. You can look at a crow, she said, and wonder if it might be a raven. But ravens are so big there isn't any doubt.

It's a raven's heart beating against the rooster beak as it roots through the meat, it's a raven's ribcage peeking through the feathers.

"Is any of this real?" Phineas asks, picking her way carefully around the pair of them. It's hard to tell if the raven is looking at her, its eyes solid glassy black. The rooster's eyes are bright yellow around deep red irises, and they slide toward Phineas when it sits up and chews on a new scrap of meat. The ends of the organ are frayed, wriggling as the rooster works its beak, flinging fresh blood across the soaked carpet.

"Real as I am," Artemis says. "Starships reflect the captain's psyche."

Phineas jumps when the rooster squawks at her, flaring its wings wide. It hops off of the poor raven to take a menacing step towards Phineas instead, screaming again, making itself bigger. Phineas gets the feeling she's seen this behavior before, but she must be mistaken. If she didn't know better, she'd think it was trying to protect the raven.

"My bond with Hazard isn't as, ah. Authentic? Natural- It ain't like I was with Gideon," Artemis says. "Hazard is a lot more hands-on, he ran this place manually. Now that he's falling apart so is everything else, and I'm not especially inclined to fix it." They shrug, somewhere in Phineas' senses.

"What *happened* here?" Phineas asks, whistling in the dark while the rooster and its spurs stare her down. "With him and Jo, with *everybody?* He was so weird about her givin' me her coat, and about Gideon's..."

She isn't sure where to go with it. She feels like she's seeing something unfathomable passing under her tiny rowboat.

"If neither of them told you, it's not my place to," Artemis says.

"Lettin' me get to your captain to beat his ass is fine, but the dirty laundry is too much?" Phineas says, grinning a little bit.

"Absolutely it is!" They're almost gleeful, but it's something else hiding behind, some complicated emotion Phineas can't place. "I said Raven Slight was my friend. And Crow, and Jo, and Maggie too. That story belongs to them. It's a terrible ship that looses its crew's secrets, even if the crew is dead."

Phineas feels the weight of the commitment, strong enough to carry Crow Gideon all the way to the sun. Avarice crawls up her spine.

Phineas eases her way past the birds. Once she's on the other side, the rooster relaxes, its wings and feathers smoothing down, and it returns noisily to its meal. Phineas turns away from them to deal with The Bigger Thing she'd ignored before, which is that the rest of this hallway stops being a hallway and becomes a cave.

This is where the cold air is coming from, and now that she's close enough to feel it she notices the wind is at her *back*, rushing *into* the mouth of the new structure. Phineas has never seen the real thing herself, but the impression is so strong it's unmistakable: these stones, the drifting dark plants. She's stepping into the bottom of an ocean.

She feels something rushing across her feet and finds wispy black sand caught in the air current, and when she looks up again there are shadow shapes slithering along the walls. They have the eyes and teeth she recognizes, but she already knows that they are tain, silently flowing down into the abyss. Like before, they ignore her completely.

Taking Artemis' earlier advice about being sloppy, she pauses to collect herself before rushing in.

"That's fair, keeping the crew's secrets," she says, stretching her shoulders and rolling her neck. "Tell me about the tain then?" The longer she stands here, the more the black sand builds up behind her heels. She lifts one foot to stretch her leg and watches as the shadows stream away. "They were so aggressive before, but it's like they don't even see me now. I can hardly feel them."

"In little groups like this they move instinctively," Artemis says lazily. "No thoughts except to flock to the biggest thing, and I hate to break it to you, but you're not the biggest thing in the room anymore."

Watching the tain disappear into the darkness of the cave, Phineas half-remembers something from her time in the mine.

"Celestial bodies pull each other in," she murmurs to herself. "He's *been* pulling me in."

"You get there eventually, huh?" Artemis says. Phineas can feel them smiling, but it's tight. Their anxiety is very slight, but that it's there at all makes Phineas uneasy. "Once you're in his orbit proper I don't think we'll be able to talk, but I'll make sure you can still fight."

They seem like they have more to say, puzzling out how to say it before they go on, so Phineas waits.

"Don't let him get to you," they sigh, unhappy with wherever they've landed. "He's a lot of smoke and mirrors, like your gunslinger. Keep your head."

Phineas takes one last calming breath and regrets that it's salty and stale.

"Then you 'n me are gonna negotiate," she says firmly. "And we're gonna be partners."

Artemis laughs softly, warm and sweet like they're tousling her hair.

"Man I hope so."

Phineas squares her shoulders and steps off of the carpet, onto the cold sea stone.

Then it gets dark.

11

Phineas spends a lot of time in the cave corridor. It writhes. The walls are etched with long horizontal grooves that, by some trick of the alien light, seem to pulsate, and the tunnel itself is rounded, making it hard to find her footing. She's been here before, but the tunnels underground had smelled musty and dry, and this passage is the damp sort of rot that makes things soft. The walls are alive with shadows, rushing along with the air, everything pulling towards the end of the hallway like they're all circling a drain. Phineas can smell salt on the wind whistling past her.

She can't see too far forward or back behind, the curve of the tunnel is sharp enough that she is only ever in a small pocket of awareness, turning in nonsense directions that make it nearly impossible to keep her orientation. If she hadn't connected with Artemis she would probably be freaking out. As it is, Phineas can feel the ship's heart hanging placidly somewhere below her feet, and it also lets her know that some of the turns of the tunnel have had her walking upside down.

Don't let him get to you, the ship had said. Phineas can see Ulrich too, in her commander's perception; he'd been moving at first, but for a while he's been settled in one spot. She tries to take comfort in the fact that the glass woman hadn't dismembered him as soon as Phineas left. He's tough, he's fine. Her job now is to make it back to him.

The sea cave ends in a door. Similar again to the mine, it's an incongruously plain door, though this one has a real handle. A cardstock sign hangs from it, like they use in hotels: "Again?" it asks, in plain black letters. There's a picture of a crescent moon near the top, and near the bottom, a pair of concentric circles.

Phineas turns the handle.

The light on the other side glares in her eyes. Even for her it's hard to see anything beyond dark shapes ringing the doorway, the landscape jutting out into the opening.

Her eyes adjust, and she realizes the shapes are plants; wide, emerald leaves like elephant ears and palm trees, bobbing in the sea breeze. There's soft white sand under her feet, stretching away ahead of her all the way to an achingly blue ocean. Just off the shore, up to his knees in the surf, is Cold Hazard.

Phineas braces, but Hazard doesn't seem to notice her when she steps onto the beach. The sky here is a different blue than the one over the desert, deep watery sapphire rather than dry robin's egg, and exploding with storybook clouds, white and cotton-candy soft. The air is crisp and clean, whispering in the leaves and over the dark stone that makes up an island behind her. She looks back and finds the door has quietly melted away into the cliffside, leaving nothing but a thick copse of palm trees and tropical plants. Phineas has never been to the beach, but she thinks she might have seen this one in a book Gideon read to her a long time ago. Or maybe in a photograph in Jo's house. She associates it with both of them, for some reason, and she doesn't like that it's here.

Now beyond the initial shock of clean air, Phineas picks up another scent, something like ashes. She turns to Hazard again, still staring out to sea, and beyond him a figure that Phineas had assumed was another murky island rearranges itself to form the ruins of the castle they're in. It looks like it was dropped from some impossible height and shattered when it hit the water, and now its jagged pieces are dissolving away into the sky, burning up even while half-submerged.

There aren't many other options. Phineas crosses the sand, approaching the wizard.

"Show me your back," Hazard says. Phineas had been ready for him to act, but his speaking voice shudders through her bones like static, pins and needles everywhere. His rot has spread since she last saw him.

"You already know what it is," Phineas answers.

Hazard's long hair whips in the wind, the loose sleeves of his coat billow around his slight frame. The hem is dragged down by the water, darkness soaking gradually up along his back.

"Are you ashamed?" Hazard says, still not looking at her. "You wear it so proudly on your stolen coat."

He raises his hand and crooks the first two fingers, and Phineas' hands jerk into the air in front of her before she can stop them. She stumbles forward as her gloves pull away like they're caught in a current, abused leather followed by the spiral of the wraps underneath. Hazard snatches one glove with his outstretched hand, the rest sailing towards the disintegrating ship.

"The gloves too," he drones, turning it over to see it better. "And on your palms, I expect. Crow liked that trick. But you hide the original wound when it is arguably more dignified than any of these other imitations." He tosses her glove into the sea.

"Jo knew I'd need to keep it from creeps like you, yeah," Phineas says, telling herself she isn't bothered by the loss, or that this has already gone in a direction she hadn't expected.

"You don't want me to see it because you know I'm right," he mumbles, his voice mingling strangely with the sound of the ocean. "About your mentor being the sort of person who would let a child gather scars for him. Harder to argue with the evidence out in the light."

"That's not-"

"Why are you *here*, commander?"

Phineas takes too long to reply, and Hazard turns to look at her. The hole in his face is huge now, fracturing up through his hairline and down his neck, more and more of his skin breaking away to spiral down into the void like sand. There's still enough distance between him and Phineas that his remaining eye is only a dark spot against his face, slimy and shining like the skin of a deep sea creature.

"Why," Hazard repeats, "are you *here?* I do not believe you really thought going through *me* was the best option for procuring a ship. And beyond that..." The ocean eddies around his knees, and the world gets a little darker. "I can feel you *seething*. What makes you loathe me so?"

Under his gaze Phineas can feel the pull of his gravity, tugging behind her sternum. Her star is fitful against the grip, but holding fast. Phineas holds too. He's trying to get a rise out of her; they both know her only shot at this depends on her staying in control of herself.

"I'm responsible for you," she states, planting her feet in the sand.

"Is that right?" Hazard asks dully.

"Gods, or...whatever it is *you* are, going around making things awful for people smaller than you, I-" Phineas feels herself sparking, rage enough for two sprawling out to prick at the ends of her hair. "It makes me *sick.* It's *not fair.* So I *made* it my responsibility, I made myself strong enough to fight."

Hazard takes his time with what she's said, the castle in the water behind him still quietly dispersing like a tilted hourglass.

"A settlement full of those small people you're so concerned about is turning to ash beneath us," Hazard drawls, his hollow voice buzzing like a hive. "You've caused *far* more damage here than I have."

"That wasn't-"

"Would the settlement have burned, without your interference?"

Phineas just manages to stop herself groaning.

"What about *yours?*"

"I do not labor under any heroic delusions," Hazard says simply.

"It's better that it burns than it keeps existing under your thumb," Phineas says, trying to focus on her breath instead of the heat rising in her chest. "Or anything else's. That's not a life."

Hazard's eye boring into hers feels like tumbling into a whirlpool, like everything around them swirls and pivots around this man's face. Blurs as it's drawn into his missing eye.

"Is that your choice to make?" Cold Hazard asks. Phineas' deep breathing is suddenly as effective as trying to blow a ship back on course.

"It *has* to be me!" she snaps, her anger surging through her limbs and stepping her forward in the sand. "What can they do, no one with any power ever *listens!* You don't even care enough to *hate* the people you step on!"

"...But you're listening to *me,*" she says, trying to shiver out the excess energy. "The tain *and* the stars are all listening to me. And I say this stops."

Hazard slowly turns back to the sea, his unaffected demeanor almost tilting Phineas over the edge again. His strange, out-of-time movements make it seem like the weight of his gaze lingers on her afterward, the end of a radio signal landing after the broadcast has stopped.

"The sun, to you, then, is power," Hazard says. "A status. A means to get you this attention you *think* you're entitled to."

The sky is darkening, heavy clouds gathering from nowhere to smother the blue with wet, rotting grey.

"Protecting others from gods by *becoming* a god, that doesn't sound incongruous to you?" he asks. *"Are* you a patron of the people, or are you looking for a sympathetic excuse to sate your own ego?"

Her anger ebbs briefly into surety; Phineas can't help grinning at the question. *This,* she'd hashed out with herself ages ago. She says, "I can manage both, yeah?"

"...I had a very similar conversation with Crow, some...ah, some unwieldy number of years ago," Hazard rumbles, the wind lifting his long hair. He reaches upward, settling his hand somewhere on his face where Phineas can't see. "He too decided to gather all his righteous fury and set off to correct these injustices he perceived. And I- I *told* him-"

The wind reaches Phineas now, cold. She can smell ozone as Hazard works himself up, getting tangled in the memory.

"-I **said**- he told me, 'Don't *worry* so much.' *He* would be a different *kind* of god. *He* would *never* do what they had done to *us. Could* never. Not *him."*

A rumble of thunder overhead, the whisper of leaves behind her. When did the sun go down?

"We both should have been smarter than that, but I wanted so *much* to believe in him," Hazard moans, hanging his head. The water stains with black where it touches him, like ink, like blood. "If I'd known what my faith in him would cultivate, what it would cost us, I could have prevented this."

Another rumble of thunder, and then the dark clouds begin to swirl, funneling down. The sand rushes past Phineas' feet, leaves and dirt from the impossible jungle behind her weave through her hair on their way to the man in the sea.

"I'm not looking for redemption," Cold Hazard says. "But I've grown since I was last presented with this circumstance. This time I am wiser, and I will not make the mistake of letting another monster slip by me. This world will not suffer Crow Gideon's influence. His legacy ends with us."

The sea rising around him, crashing against the shore, he sets his black-hole stare on Phineas, flaying her down to the bone. He is reaching for her with what's left of his spirit, and her blood freezes in her veins. With his touch, she knows: despite the grief as wide as the sea, his mind is sound. He is not mad, he is heartbroken, and he is this way because of Gideon.

"I'm going to dump your broken body at his feet," he says, utterly passionless. "I'm going to carve every trace of stolen light from his bones, and finally this wretched business will be finished."

It's nearly verbatim what the tain had said to her during that first encounter. She wonders briefly which side it's coming from, but it doesn't matter. The crux of it is that Phineas is the only one with anything to lose.

"That ain't gonna work." Starlight blazes in her voice. "'Cause I'm not dyin' here, and I can't let you kill Gideon."

The wind quiets without stopping, the sounds of the ocean and the trees smother to silence. Hazard's body is motionless, his robes and his hair billowing noiselessly like they're caught around a statue.

There is the sound of cracking glass, a mirror-fracture, and the hole in Hazard's face razes across his skin straight through his remaining eye.

"No," he says, the only sound in the world. "You can't."

Cold Hazard raises his hand, and the swirling clouds send lightning down to touch the ocean, jagged and black. There are more bolts than Phineas can count; most of them strike the sea and light up the depths like an underwater storm, but dozens of them angle wildly to streak past him— catching his hair, tearing his robes, raging straight towards Phineas and bringing the world screaming back in.

She'd been ready for this; she sets her stance, gets her hands up in her guard— and *sinks.*

Her concentration shatters as she stares down at her feet, now up to her ankles in sand, grey and ashy under the freezing moonlight. She doesn't have time to move now, she's going to have to tank the hit.

When it doesn't come, she looks again and the darkness Hazard called down is converging into one impossible mass like a tidal wave over Phineas' head. Over Hazard's too, still standing in the blackening water, his palm bright with magic as the wave crests higher. Phineas feels her feet falling further, the sand up to her knees and sliding faster around her. What is he *doing?*

She shouts at him, unsure what she's even saying as her voice is carried away in the cacophony of the wind tearing through the island, the storm coming down around them. Up to her chest, scrabbling in the sand with nothing to hold on to, Phineas has time to see the bone-white of Hazard's face fall apart, the pieces washing away as black sludge gushes from his empty eye socket. When the wave crashes, she's buried alive.

Phineas spends a desperate, crazed second crushed on all sides by sand, shoved down and down by the weight of the wave, and then her feet touch the air. Along with a column of grey sand she falls straight through the other side of the beach and into somewhere new, the scent of the sea replaced by mildew and cold stone. It's dim, but Phineas can see ground hurtling closer. Her reflexes come when she calls them and she redirects her inertia to the sand around her: while the grains obediently ignore physics to fall faster, impacting loud enough to echo from the walls, Phineas slows to a safe speed.

The light of her command shows she's falling alongside a waterfall- no, it's glass, stained glass, aquamarine and sapphire and every possible shade of blue shimmering defiantly against her yellow as it slides by. Phineas makes it to the floor, thin carpet over hard marble, and a flash of lightning illuminates the window, along with dozens of others lining the impossible hallway under the beach.

There's an instant of perfect silence, like the moment before Hazard drew down the sky, and Phineas has time to make out the iconography of the glass: an inverted triangle, sending a pair of circles into the waiting arms of the sea.

Thunder roars through the cathedral.

The only light comes from behind the windows, flickering like the world outside is on fire, casting the hallway in watery blue. Phineas can't see Hazard anywhere, but she can hear him.

"A place of worship," his voice drones from the arches high overhead, the echo of stone on stone. "Your influence on this place betrays you."

Right, *Artemis.* Phineas reaches out with her spirit but only finds Hazard, that freezing riptide she hadn't been able to get through before is closing in from every direction. Her body is still but internally she reels, her orientation thrown when she can't find the planet or the ship's heart through the vortex. The room spins like she's drunk, and now her body lists, stumbling on nothing in empty space.

(Don't let him get to you.)

Phineas grits her teeth against the vertigo and tries again. She still can't find the real heart, but she can feel it through the cold chaos, the heartbeat of the ship. Muted, but there. She even sort of finds Ulrich this time, a quiet but resonant note under everything, singing like a tuning fork in her senses. Disoriented, mired in the enemy. Not alone.

As Phineas steadies, it begins to rain. The water on the windows casts long, wriggling shadows across the corridor.

In the dim gap between two windows, a shadow rises.

Growing up from the floor like seaweed thrashing in the tide, Hazard's body forms from the darkness in a boiling column of sinew and feathers, starry and black. Against the hammering of the rain, Hazard's wordless voice echoes from the rafters, laced with his magic it spirals down to join the rest of his body as it lashes itself together. From a spray of feathers across his shoulders, a wriggling mass of tendons, the ragged ends convulsing against the air to form the shape of his jaw. The sound of Hazard's voice whipping through the chamber falls silent. The face is gone— where the eyes had been, a pair of wings crosses instead, and underneath is smooth and white.

In the empty space beneath the wings, a jagged wrinkle buckles in the white like the skin of rotting fruit. It bursts open, the skin dripping over a sea of black, speckled with blue stars. The mouth widens, *haaah-h,* a ghost's moan wisping from an empty vessel. Hazard's endless robes resolve around his body where they cover him; there's nothing underneath but the rot now, the body only exists as hands to carry out a will, a mouth to cry cruelty.

The vessel stretches its hand towards Phineas, the arcane sigil on the palm blazing with light, and as Hazard moves, the shadows on the floor around him move too. He channels the tain like water; completely under his control, their movements now are ruthlessly efficient rather than wild and desperate. They slither and melt together behind him,

(they form six wings, just like Phineas has, just like)
black and blue, eyes and teeth, all around him like the mantle of a god.
The spidering veins of light through the tain, the chasms in
Hazard's skin- he is nearly stained glass himself.

Hazard angles his wrist sharply, and from the depths of his wings,
the first shadow springs.

It moves like water, graceful like a plaza fountain, but it's *fast*,
and so sharp Phineas can see it warp the air around it as it slices towards
her. Hazard had plainly broadcast the move and it's easy for Phineas
to sidestep, but a sound like a sizzling splash from behind her makes
her jump. It's enough warning to get her out of the way as the bolt
reflects, the razor's edge taking a slice out of her shoulder on its way by.
She turns, and nearly stumbles when she comes nose-to-nose with
another face.

Her face?

The mirror is perfectly clear, almost a window, and it reflects
Phineas infinitely because it is facing another mirror. When she turns
again, bewildered, Hazard is gone. The church has been replaced with
mirror panels, boxing her in from every side. After the dimness of the
sanctuary, the light here is bright white and harrowing, intensified by
every reflective surface it comes from.

The tain is intensified too, still fountain-leaping between mirrors,
gaining more speed.

It takes too long, the sizzling crash of the tain nearly a constant
already, but Phineas finds the gap in the circle of mirrors and lunges
into a mirrored passage. She keeps her hands out in front of her but it's
nearly impossible to tell where she's going, mirrors on mirrors
reflecting each other into infinity, her own movement and the
screaming shadow chasing her making it even harder to find her way.
She takes a blinding hit near the back of her neck and the missile
dissipates, but as she staggers she realizes the reflections are still
moving. They're multiplying.

Another shadow slices through the meat of her thigh, the pain
lighting up a new idea.

Phineas picks a direction and smashes her fist through the closest
mirror. Her reflection cracks, the spidering fracture multiplying the
eyes in her face and the image of the tain. From each sliver another spike

of shadow leaps. She barely gets her arms in front of her face as they fly through her, taking skin wherever they touch.

"God *damn it!*" she hollers. Her voice reverberates between the mirrors, the energy recursing in on itself. Like the shadows-

It isn't ordinary tain, Hazard is controlling them. They can be *controlled.*

"STOP!!" Phineas screams, the command so strong it spikes into the air like lightning. The tain, strung everywhere like sooty spiderweb, shudders to a standstill. Phineas' voice cracks the mirror in front of her again. The adjacent mirrors fracture as the echo spreads, gaining strength like a boulder sailing over a hill. The word dissolves into a nonsense echo, the mirrors shattering one by one.

The corridor with the stained glass is still there behind the maze, but the lights are out again; the only bright spot is a raised altar on the other end of the room. Visible between the glimmering shards Hazard stands there, his hands already raised to draw the shadows again.

Phineas leans into an inhuman sprint, weaving between exploding mirror fragments, ignoring the sharp crunch under her bare feet as she pulls the energy of each step into her chest.

Hazard doesn't deviate from the weaving of his spell, doesn't even seem to be responding to her approach. Drawing the gathered energy into a long line, Phineas clears the steps to the altar in one leap.

It's a direct hit. Phineas feels bone give under her fist as she drives it into the side of his face, sees the wing covering his eyes shiver.

But Hazard doesn't move. Phineas hangs there, suspended impossibly in the air, like she's been frozen in place at the exact second of impact.

The melting gash in Hazard's face curves into a smile.

"Disappointing," he rasps.

Phineas can't move, the horrible shock seeping into her bones interrupted by another sound like the shattering mirrors. This one is a low, low pitch. Something bigger.

Hazard steps back, leaving her hanging awkwardly in the air. He crosses his right hand over his body, resting it near his hip, and then in an elegant gesture he reaches, like drawing a sword from a sheath. His hand moves as if it's drawn through thick water. Behind it, in a mesmerizing, eerily gorgeous curve, a sliver of silver moonlight slices into being. It's so long he has to extend his entire arm around the curve to form it. The blade is colossal, a crescent moon curved around Hazard's head; the scythe shines so brightly Phineas can *hear* it. A thin vein of blue magic runs along the center, a dead space in Phineas' senses, its purpose unidentifiable. Phineas' ears ring with adrenaline.

There is no handle anywhere, no way to touch the weapon directly without being cut. Hazard brings his hand down, and the scythe follows in a perfect, wicked arc. It makes a sound like something much thinner whipping through the air, but pitched down and down like a broken tape, a record spun too slowly, echoing too long after the scythe stops moving. It doesn't touch anything, not even Phineas, but she whimpers before she can stop herself.

Something has changed somewhere, something is *wrong*.

The movement is slow enough for her to follow it, cyan light jutting up through a crack in the altar behind Hazard. The sight of the fissure opens a pit in her stomach, strong enough to make her sick with it, cut straight through all her bravado and surety to tweak a primal, animal nerve that *howls,* get it *away* from me, *get it away.* The chasm spreads through the floor, all along the walls; it even spreads through Hazard.

Before the uncanny terror can fully set in, Hazard's body flies apart along its fault lines. The shockwave hurls Phineas backwards out of her freeze, she smashes through the stone walls behind like they're made of glass.

The sky on the other side is painfully blue and bright, and there's a nauseating second where she realizes she's not sailing *out* she's falling *down*, the gravity shifted again. Phineas gets herself oriented to face what's coming and finds the ocean, endless in every direction and yawning open to swallow her whole.

◉◉◉

"His *crazy* was never as bad before he started working with the tain," Rook says quietly, not looking up. "But my father has been trying to kill Crow Gideon for at least *my* whole life."

"And no luck," Ulrich says, reaching for a fifth finger sandwich. The cold, crisp cucumber is worlds away from the dry biscuits he'd had this morning.

"He keeps- he *stops*. Any time he starts to make progress he just *quits*. He always comes up with some excuse, but I think he just loses his nerve."

"Your father seemed like a very confident man when I spoke with him. Is Gideon really so powerful?"

Rook shrugs.

"Maybe a little," she admits. "Dad compares him to a god all the time, but it's not that he's *afraid* of Gideon. I'm not sure he can feel afraid of anything, anymore." She sets down her teacup and laces her fingers together, lost in thought. Each of her nails tapers to a perfectly filed semicircle, glitters in the pale sunlight with the expensive polish, clean and even.

"I think," she adds after a moment, "he loves him, still. But he'd never admit it."

"'Love' is a very different impression than the one I've gotten from this situation," Ulrich says.

"I just don't know why else he would be so *obsessed*, if it's really been as long as he says it has since their schism." Rook wraps her arms around herself. It's a gesture calculated for elegance over comfort, it makes Ulrich think of the older divas who found excuses to hang around the theater long after they'd played their last role. "You don't go to this kind of trouble for something you don't love, *somehow*. You know what I mean?"

"I might," Ulrich says carefully.

Rook smiles at him, small and sad and genuine. He has to loosen his shirt collar, it's suddenly warm in here.

"Well!" Rook tosses her hair over her shoulder. "I can't spend *my* life sitting around this dusty old ship of his. I've got my *own* plans." She gives him a sly look. "This whole front with the starstone was my doing, actually. Those partners I mentioned, when I told them Dad was considering experimenting more with the tain they really thought a lot of it. That's how we ended up here."

Ulrich almost inquires about the insanity with Ellie, and her "guardians", and a town out of space and time, but just the thought of having to explain any of that exhausts him. Rook probably already knows about it anyway, if her mysterious benefactors are as in-the-know as she claims. Someone somewhere is lying, but at the moment Ulrich is vastly more interested in the pink frosting on one of the miniature cupcakes in front of him.

"Dad wasn't interested in the capital, but *I've* been squirreling away what I could for myself while he's been distracted. That isn't saying a lot, since none of our operations have been organized well enough to make much of a profit, but I've done what I can."

"Industrious as ever," Ulrich says.

"Dusk- Ah, the boss, *my* boss, I suppose, said I wouldn't *need* my own money while we're working together. He would provide anything I asked for." She clears her throat, a little awkwardly. "Generous, but I told him I wouldn't feel right living off of someone else's allowance. Dad always said it was important to have control of your own assets."

Ulrich is the picture of sympathy. He feels Bel's fingers resting just under his collar.

"You were stalling," he murmurs. "You wanted to stay here longer. Hoping things might change?"

"And all I've gotten for it is another breakdown. More *mess* to clean up," Rook says bitterly. But she shakes herself, and she's reined back into something pleasant when she faces Ulrich again.

"But you catching up with me *here,* of all places," she wonders. "It's almost like a *sign,* don't you think? Now's the time to make a move." She busies herself pouring the last of the water from the pot into her cup, warming up what's left. "Once Dad's finished ridding you of your baggage we'll arrange a meeting with Dusk. He'll get a kick out of your little mask shtick."

"Here is hoping," Ulrich says.

"So!" Rook says brightly, reclining lithely in her chair. "You're all caught up with me! Your turn now."

"All I have done since you last saw me is find my way back to you."

Rook giggles, the faintest hint of a blush coloring her cheek.

"Sure, but how did you- what are you *doing* out here in the world, Ulrich? What were you *really* recruiting me for back when we met?" She sips her tea and gives him A Look over the rim of the cup, her blue eyes luminous. "Surely you can be honest with me *now.*"

Ulrich pauses for an appropriate amount of time, then he leans forward and snatches a cupcake from the top of the tray, getting pink frosting on his fingers.

"...I am sorry if it is not as romantic as you imagined," he says slowly. "But the truth is I owe some dangerous people a lot of money."

Rook makes a sympathetic little *tsk.*

"Finally had an unlucky day, did you?"

"I had several unlucky days," Ulrich says evenly, peeling away the paper wrapping. "And the odd job out in the Sprawl can be lucrative in ways most occupations are not. Simple transactions, hard to trace. But it gets *filthy.*" He manages to take a bite of the miniature cake instead of shoving the whole thing in his mouth at once, but it's close. He makes himself take his time chewing before he continues. "In an effort to keep my own hands clean, I've been looking for someone strong and simple to pair up with. Phineas Kidd is both. Though, if dirt can be avoided altogether, even better."

"Well *that's* no problem," Rook says. She's doing well keeping a lid over it, but Ulrich can see her excitement just under the surface. "*I* only rejected the money because I wanted to be able to say I can stand on my own two feet, but if you're following commanders into the desert I'd say pride isn't an issue you're concerned with."

Ulrich's brow furrows, the corner of his mouth twitches.

"I am too afraid to be ashamed," he admits. "I am too *tired. Anything* would be better than the way things have been, but I..." He clears his throat roughly before his voice can start to tremble. "You know I'd still rather not go into a negotiation blindly. What can you tell me about these people you work with? What is Dusk like?"

"Mm, where do I *start?* He's..." She balances her teacup between her splayed fingers, turning to watch the clock winding away nearby while she mulls it over.

"You know, it's strange," she says. "For someone who calls himself Dusk, he seems...*bright.* He *shines.*"

Phineas heaves up onto her hands and spits up seawater, the wood under her palms-

Wood?

She wrenches her eyes open, still stinging with salt, and finds she's kneeling on a timber floor. The planks are swollen and dark with water, damp splinters bristling. It's dark in here, but Phineas is only ever in the dark when she wants to be; she lets herself glow enough to light the space for another look around. Nearby on the floor, she finds a broken picture frame, a length of rope hanging from a hook. Thin streams of water come through a porthole nearby, the glass looking out into a groaning ocean.

It doesn't make sense, but she knows better than to expect sense at this point: she's inside the cabin of a sunken ship. It is also clear, with the way a set of lanterns and tables hang at unnatural angles against an adjacent wall, that the ship is sitting sideways.

It's no use worrying about how she washed in here, she needs to figure out where Hazard got to. The ship creaks and moans against the current, and there's a constant sound of dripping water, but the space is stagnant for now. It feels like a movie, a long chase scene ending with the car high-centered on the edge of the cliff, knowing it *will* fall, but not *when*.

This must have been the galley. As she moves, lighting up the darker corners, she finds the clutter on the counters is unaffected by whatever gravity exists here, hovering on the wall (the floor) several feet over her head like an art exhibit. There are dirty dishes stacked haphazardly between empty beer bottles, battered notebooks covered in inkstains, scattered instant photos of places and people. A mason jar lid with ashes piled inside.

Rolling papers, and loose tobacco.

They're out in the road near the sunflower field today. This exercise is easier around sunflowers, Gideon had said. They're almost like little commanders themselves, always moving along with the light.

Phineas thinks she might almost have it this time. She focuses *real* hard-

"Get your shoulders down off your ears," Gideon says lightly. "Loosey-goosey, all water-like."

It takes some doing to force herself to be loosey-goosey while still reaching out with her spirit, but very slowly, she manages it. She hears the sunflowers behind her shiver, like they always do around Gideon. Reach, *reach*-

Ah!

There's fireworks in her belly, soda-pop in her veins- Phineas' laugh is explosive, her spirit sailing out like she's a dandelion puff on the wind. The whole world *sings* and she can *hear* it!

Gideon's smile is warm above her, lighting her up with him even through her connection with the earth.

"Good!" he says. "Good job, kiddo. Remember this. You should be doin' this a lot throughout the day, it'll help with the floaty feelings you get."

Phineas scratches her palm, quickly stopping herself and rubbing it with her fingertips instead. The tattoos are *so* itchy. But it's kinda nice, the itchiness is almost as good as biting.

"Jo said it's *'dissociation'*," Phineas says, still the most imperious eight-year-old alive even while her voice rasps over its wounds. "I ain't stupid, I can hear y'all talkin'."

Gideon laughs quietly.

"Sorry, sorry," he says. "Well, when you're feelin' dissociative, this'll help with it. No more biting, okay?"

"I *haven't* been!" Phineas says, holding out the undersides of her forearms. The toothmarks there are faded, they could be mistaken for freckles.

"I know! But this is important, Phin. I wanna make sure you can do this part on your own."

"How come?" Phineas asks. Gideon turns his head, the wide brim of his hat tilting with him. He might be looking at something the sunflowers are doing, but it's hard to tell. Even with the hat the glare of the sun behind his head makes it hard to see his face. "You'll be here to help me, right?"

Phineas flinches from the counter like it burns her, the clutter retreating into the dark again. Even under the pervasive smell of seawater and soaked wood, Phineas would know the aroma of that tobacco anywhere. She feels sick.

The ship whines desolately under the weight of the current and the floor shifts under Phineas' feet, tilting like a rolling die, higher and steeper. She walks with it, up on her toes to keep from falling, and she half-tumbles through a doorway into another room. This one smells like paper, and when she gets her balance again she can see her own light reflecting from a stained glass window, towering over a writing desk.

"I felt you, with Artemis, before," Hazard's voice sighs through the creaking of the derelict ship. "How you loved them, instantly and completely. Do you wonder what it would take for a commander to leave his ship to waste this way?"

Phineas' light brightens, she turns to try and find him, but the only things she can make out in the shadows are papers, books, waterlogged and ruined.

"How much of his damage must you *see* before you admit what he *is?*" Hazard echoes. "Am I not enough? Are *you* not enough?"

"It was an accident!" Phineas shouts, feeling exposed in the darkness, trying to back herself into a corner. It's like the room keeps moving to keep her in the open; the desk with its window is always in front, the wall of identical wooden drawers stays on her left, never getting any closer. The tension crawling up her back is unbearable.

"Crow Gideon seems to be involved in a lot of *accidents.*"

"Come out here and fight me!" Phineas shouts, her command sparking in the air. The bolt sails away to nothing, lighting another cluttered corner of the room before it dies.

Hazard laughs, a hollow thing spiraling in the dark.

"Even we have our raw nerves, don't we? Though where he is concerned, they do become easier to find."

Something stings in the back of Phineas' teeth and she whirls around to find Hazard, standing placidly behind her.

"You thought you were special, didn't you?" he says aloud, grinning with his rotten-fruit mouth.

She swings without thinking; her fist connects with his ribcage and she feels a muted snap through all those robes. He crumples, but he's still smiling, still laughing at her.

"You thought he *cared.*"

It's like he reaches out and plucks a wire somewhere deep inside, holding some impossible tension she hadn't been aware of until it began to shiver. The world goes white, her senses blown out with rage.

Phineas snarls wordlessly, raw energy raking through her throat and catching every little imperfection on its way, and she grabs Hazard by the collar to hoist him up from where he'd folded to the floor. There is no real movement between the two of them for this, and down here in this ghost sea there isn't any energy to pull from. But her star is here. It's not like she doesn't already use self-destruction to her own advantage.

It hurts, every impact pulled from her own heart, and her companion shrieks at her; something about getting a hold of herself, that she's falling for some trick, but Phineas can't hear her over the sound of her fist slamming over and over into Hazard's face.

"You thought he did this to you for *your* sake," he slurs, the words snaking through a mangled mouth, unaffected by the onslaught. "You didn't realize this is just Crow's habit of absolving *himself* of *responsibility.*"

Phineas screams and tears her fist through the gash of Hazard's mouth, sinks her fingers deep into the flesh there and rips out his tongue.

"Why do I know exactly where you hurt?" His voice still comes to her, clear and steady, and the beginnings of doubt finally begin to creep through Phineas' fugue. "If Crow is *faultless* then why are you so *angry?*"

Her star hisses: *Can't you see what he's doing?!*

Hazard's body in Phineas' fist turns slippery, melting down into slime and viscera. She lets it go, stumbling away with her heart still thundering in her ears.

The air explodes with sound as every drawer in the wall bursts open, erupting with loose paper. Every leaf is dark with writing, and they keep coming, thundering through the drawers endlessly to saturate the space. Phineas gets her hands in front of her face, but when something touches her it's her back. It's like ice.

She doesn't have time to turn before the scythe passes through her.

There is little in Phineas' human life to compare it to, human bodies are not equipped to experience violation at the scale of stars. The closest she has is the memory of the distance she'd felt in those dreams in the first days holding the sun in her chest, being pulled and stretched across the expanse of emptiness between celestial bodies. That had been terrifying in its vastness, but she hadn't felt *pain*, exactly. Now she feels every lightyear like jagged glass, her entire existence reduced to nerves and tissue, screaming as they're pulled apart and raked across the void. The agony is cold as death, a frozen blade trying to force its way between every cell in her body and prise her apart.

No- not her body. It's trying to take *her star*. She's screaming too, clawing at Phineas' heart to keep from being torn from her as the scythe carves its way through every sense they share, every facet of their reality. There isn't room for rational thought, there's only Phineas' humankind instinct. She reaches blindly for her companion with whatever it is in her that does that, seizes her shackled wrists and-

It stops.

Hazard makes a thoughtful sound from behind her.

"Joined seamlessly. What an awful thing he's done to you."

The papers from the drawers still haven't finished drifting to the ground, it had happened in the space of a second. Hazard is acting with all the gravity of a man who has just sliced an apple to find a dark spot in the flesh. Breathing hard, but extremely alive and intact, Phineas staggers to her feet and turns to get him in her sight. She is shaking so bad she can hardly stay upright, more furious than she's ever been in her life.

"He didn't even say goodbye, did he?" Hazard drones, static and miserable. "He never does."

Struggling to get her breathing under control, Phineas starts to settle, an unfamiliar fact slowly coming into focus. The scythe had knocked her out of alignment, however briefly, and she is at the end of her stamina. She's alive, but she's not right; she can't command like this. They might be done.

346

It's surprising how calm she feels about it, buoyed by her anger and, maybe, the knowledge that she'd stuck it out to the end. If it were Ulrich, she thinks, there would be a speech here. But that's not really her thing. From her knees, she looks Hazard in the face through the curtain of her dirty hair.

"Don't project your shit onto me," she says, ragged, starlight misaligned and jagged against her own voice. "It ain't my fault you couldn't hack it."

It is a more direct hit than anything she's done so far. What functions as Hazard's face crumples, the feathers shivering madly. Phineas sees a single sliver of his eye, malice overwhelming, and he brings the scythe down through the air between them. The corners and the angles of the sunken ship splinter from each other, and the ship surrenders to the depths.

◉◉◉

Rook's peace offerings are dwindling rapidly now. There are crumbs all over Ulrich's clothes.

"Are we *square,* at least?" Rook asks gently. She's draped across her chair as loosely as the shawl around her shoulders, but there's tightness in her face that she is not good at hiding.

"More than square," Ulrich insists. "If this works out I'm not sure I'll ever be able to make it up to you."

Rook's laugh is very soft.

"You don't need to worry about that," she murmurs. "I've missed your good company. I haven't had anyone to talk with for a while, I'm sure you understand, it's-"

"Hard to find good company, with lifestyles like ours," Ulrich finishes. He shifts his weight uncomfortably, the arms of the chair suddenly boxing him in, his clothes tight.

"I, er..." He clears his throat and wrings his hands in front of his chest. "Seeing as I've already admitted so much today, I..."

Rook waits, listening.

"You were right," Ulrich admits, looking anywhere else but at her. "This *was* a lot of trouble for a piece of jewelry. There was...more, that drove me to..."

Rook shifts, her shoes making a soft sound against the grass.

"Even if I had been angry with you, before, that would not have been worth the ordeal of *finding* you," Ulrich babbles. "It's just...I, could not bear the thought of never seeing you again."

"Ulrich you have *got* to figure out how to express your feelings without firearms," Rook sighs.

"I'm sorry," Ulrich mumbles, making himself small, resisting the urge to pull his hat over his face. "I wanted to tell you before, but I- the right time never *came*, and- this is *still*, not the right time, I know, but I just-"

While he stammers through a confession, Rook stands.

"-I had to-"

She is crossing to his side of the table,

"-t-tell you, before,"

her perfume is bright and clean, like polished glass; the curl of her hair is soft where it brushes his forearm when she leans over him, bracing herself on the arms of the chair. She is very close now, so close Ulrich can't speak. She touches his chin with her fingertips and tilts his face to hers.

"There was something I wanted to do before too," Rook says, her cool breath ghosting across his lips. She leans forward, and now Ulrich can taste her lip gloss, feel her mouth soft and insistent against his, her hand sliding up against his neck to rest in his hair. He closes his eyes and settles his own hand across hers.

Something clicks. Rook makes a puzzled sound and straightens, checking the back of her hand where one of Ulrich's poker chips has appeared.

Ulrich has always appreciated the sound these make, he'd worked on the formula longer than necessary to get it just right— a tidy, hearty *crack!* that sounds especially good when it's set off in a place with auditorium acoustics. It's a small, controlled explosion, but it's more than enough to vaporize Rook's right hand.

It's so unexpected that it takes Rook an extra moment of staring down at the bloody, ragged stump of her forearm to realize what's happened. Ulrich, or, the misty afterimage of him left when he ported away as he'd done on the roof and in the mine, is dissipated by a spray of gore. Her blood spatters against the white velvet cushion, and that's when Rook begins to scream.

Her voice screeches against the mirrored walls, rings in the metal of the lunar clock, sharply in Ulrich's hearing aid even as he approaches from several garden rows away. He ignores her thrashing in the bloody grass, looking for-

Ah, there; flung into her teacup by the blast. Ulrich picks up the freshly reconstituted trinket, previously a ring on Rook's finger, now a glass flower the size of a bottle cap. He sits down in Rook's unoccupied wicker chair and thumbs the tea out of the intricate grooves in the petals, scanning for any signs of damage even though he knows he won't find any. It is in perfect condition again, as expected: under the clear glass, oil-slick colors shimmer slowly, purring against his skin, back where it belongs. Rook has dissolved into furious wordless screaming now, is hauling herself up to a sitting position against the lower half of Ulrich's seat, but he hardly hears her. Nothing matters, anywhere, save for this bloom in his hand.

Ulrich makes a sign with his fingers and the flower shivers, now cast in blue, and it sprouts a pin from its underside. He digs in his pocket for an old butterfly clutch and fastens his lotus to the left fold in his shirt collar. It's heavy, and currently the collar of this shirt is more wrinkle than fold. The pin drags it down awkwardly, the fabric pulling enough for him to be aware of it. Ulrich takes a deep, contented breath.

Rook is snarling language at him now and he cannot bring himself to give a shit beyond the fury creeping back in, now that he has what he came for.

"I can't imagine you've ever had occasion to be injured like this," Ulrich says, right over her screeching. "You're handling it well, though now is usually when the nausea hits. It is a good thing we were finished eating. Ach," He reaches out to take the last tea sandwich, crosses his ankle over his knee and points in the grass a little to her left. "My other chip, would you hand it to me?"

"Fuck you!!" There are tears and snot and running makeup caking Rook's face, spittle spraying when she screams at him. He'll have to pick it up later then. "I'll kill you I'll KILL YOU I'M GONNA-"

"What sort of person does these things?" Ulrich asks tepidly, taking a bite of sandwich and gesturing at her with it while he chews. "Steals something she knows *damn well* is not just a piece of *costume jewelry,* or gains a lady's trust before irreparably damaging her manicure? You and I, Rook and Ulrich, we are the worst kinds of people."

His manner is easy, but he holds her gaze in his like a knife to her throat. She can only breathe hard, the mangled stump of her arm slowly freezing over as she comes to her senses enough for triage. Ulrich leans forward, radiating the malice that drags and tears through his veins like a fishhook. In a voice like pliers pulling teeth:

"Why would I turn myself into this for *money?*"

-breathe, breathe-

Ulrich reclines, finishing the sandwich he'd crushed in his fist.

"I have done awful things," he says through the last mouthful, brushing the crumbs from his hands and smearing the rest near the torn hem of his pants. "I am going to continue doing awful things because they are necessary. I am not so *weak* I would try to absolve myself of their weight by finding someone *else* to blame for my actions."

"I am nobody's dog," he says coldly, the taste of lotus petals on his tongue. "My decisions are my *own.*"

"You *rat,*" Rook sobs furiously, her voice hoarse. "My *father* is going to-"

"No, he isn't going to. Even if the good Commander Kidd deigns to let him live, he will not be in any condition to come after *me* until I am in the wind." Ulrich reaches sedately under his shirt.

"Thank you for the sandwiches," he says, Glückssache steady in his hand. He pulls the hammer and Rook stares down the barrel with the last-ditch burst of rage unique to the perspective.

"You stupid fuck! Just TRY it-!"

She flinches as Ulrich pulls the trigger, a puff of icy vapor hanging in the air between them an instant too late to catch a bullet.

The revolver clicks, turns. No one breathes.

It clicks a second time and Rook shrieks.

"Are you KIDDING ME?!" she screams, hysterical. "All that fucking- You carry that ANTIQUE *JUNK* and can't even keep track of your shots?!"

"I have never miscounted," Ulrich states plainly, because it is true.

-b-breathe-

He's losing it, he can feel it going, completely thrown by his gun not working. It doesn't matter because at that second the pendulum from the clock comes apart and crashes into the lawn, the scythe shape embedding itself deep into the soil. It's followed immediately by the rest of the clockwork mechanism, the gears and hands falling away like the screws holding them all together have simply ceased to be, the heavy metal ringing painfully loud even as it lands on soft grass. The garden shudders, a thick rumble like an earthquake's soaks the air.

The episode is brief. The shaking stops as quickly as it had started, only lasting long enough to scare the shit out of Ulrich. He clutches his chest with his empty hand, the cortisol so painful it makes him angry.

"What in the *hell* was that?!" He recovers quickly, aiming his gun again, but Rook's gone blank. Ulrich has seen that look before, on other faces he wishes he couldn't remember so well.

"Oh," Rook breathes, heaving in a stuttering breath. "Oh *no-*"

There's a

(chill)

wind that ruffles through Ulrich's hair, the feeling of snow settling on his shoulders. He shivers involuntarily, his eyes screwing shut, and by the time he gets them open again Rook is gone.

She is gone, and Ulrich has what he came for, still tugging reassuringly at his collar.

The components of the clockwork mechanism have settled across the garden, the rumbling has stopped. As he stares at the patch of frost and blood in the grass where Rook had been, all Ulrich can hear is the distant sound of water in the fountains scattered through the gardens.

He breathes out, and *in.*

Ulrich pitches backward, his head thumping against the wicker and his mouth falling open to wrench in air like he's drowning. His mask materializes and he forces himself to breathe in through his nose, pulling in the steroid before the sticky feeling in his windpipe has a chance to get a foothold. He keeps his tight grip on the gun, fingers moving to rest outside the trigger guard, but it hangs loosely at his side to point towards the floor now. He can't stop *shaking,* every thrum of tension and adrenaline built up over the last hour crashing through him all at once.

He dismisses the mask again when he's sure the worst of it has passed. It would've been better to dig out his actual inhaler, but he still has business with Glückssache, and only so many hands. He ignores the smell of cigarettes while he tries to get the cylinder open with trembling fingers. Bel settles on the glass-top table in front of him, her bare, dirty feet settling in the grass between his own dirty boots. She never seems to bother with shoes anymore.

"That pretty well took care of itself, didn't it?" she says, slipping her black-and-gold cigarette from her lips to exhale in a plume of silvery diamonds.

"Come *on,*" Ulrich mumbles sharply to his hands. Finally he manages to get the mechanism open to count his goddamn bullets.

"Wasn't that easy?" Bel picks at him. "I keep *telling* you, make it into a performance and it's just another show." She makes a gun with her fingers and mimics shooting him with it, grinning in a way that stretches the sheet of golden scales draped across her cheek. They connect to a bolt in her left temple, embedded in the end of a long, messy scar that runs along her forehead above her mismatched eye. It is the same color as Ulrich's eyes. Her cheeks look more hollowed every day, her skin more sallow, but her eyes are bright as ever, sharp as sin.

There is still a bullet in the revolver, right where Ulrich had known it to be. There is no reason it shouldn't be in Rook right now. Ulrich looks at Bel inquisitively, but she only takes a drag on her cigarette.

Ulrich huffs and clicks the cylinder back into place. He looks her in the eyes, imperfect mirrors, and says, "Na gut, dann."

"There we are. Now suck it up and get back out there, go find her," Bel says, the steel in Ulrich's spine, ruthless and wreathed in diamond smoke. She touches his temple with her fingertips and he closes his eyes, leaning into her touch as it ghosts over his cheek. "And would it kill you to smile?"

It just kept raining. It had been coming down for days already and it wouldn't stop; the gravel road to Jo's house was all washed out and waterfalls gushed over the awning of the porch, the grooves of wood and corrugated metal gathering the rain into thick cascades. Heavy as stone, straight as prison bars.

It had been a while coming anyway, but Crow Gideon doesn't abide cloud cover for long. The time for leaving had come and gone, but nobody had thought to let Phineas know that.

She could still feel the sting in her wrists from where Jo had caught her fists, thrown harder than she'd ever done before. Jo's infuriating, immovable patience only goaded Phineas further into her tantrum, the need to redirect her feelings *anywhere* else but inside; why wasn't Jo feeling them? Why was Jo just *taking it?*

The gravel under Phineas' feet felt better, the dirty water hiding the sharper things she'd normally avoid while she pounded down the long road to Gideon's house. She'd stuck her feet in every murky puddle on the way and the pain lit up the world around to stick in her brain forever: the static of heavy water striking her skin, the stench of soaked earth. The sunflower field melting in the hot summer rain, towering and impossibly green against the grey.

The door was unlocked, the house was dark.

The smell of unfinished, mismatched wood was strong inside, and it hit Phineas like a slap in the face, stalling her in the doorway. The rain was still coming down against the roof loud enough to hear, but it was all grey, a cushion sort of noise that just made the quiet louder. The only real sound was her own ragged breathing, her heart thudding after the run. The hardwood floor of the entryway bit at the cuts in her feet.

The living room was empty. No furniture, not even any beer bottles. The only illumination came from the compass left right in the middle of the floor, its yellow light muted by the card settled over the cracked glass on the top face. *Phin,* the card read.

The compass was Gideon's. He wouldn't go somewhere without it, he'd taken that thing all the way to Kairos. If it was still here then so was he.

He'd even left her a note, she thought, crossing the empty room like moving in a dream. Phineas knelt in the soft light of the compass, reaching out for the card with filthy hands. She could see her heart beating in them, the way they shook.

Phin, the card read. The only word on the empty card, in the empty house. She sat there for a long time.

Something crawled into her throat, meaning to escape through her mouth, but it hurt so bad already she couldn't imagine how awful that would be. She swallowed it down instead, concentrating hard until the thing lodged itself uncomfortably in her chest.

She tucked the card and the compass under her shirt and hunched over them all the way home, shielding them from the rain as best she could. Her feet hurt.

Jo's kitchen smelled like food. She didn't look up from the stove when she told Phineas to go wash up, there was a bath waiting. It was still hot when Phineas climbed in. Jo must have known about when she'd be back. Known that she *would* be back.

Jo was already eating when Phineas got to the table, clean and dry in the fresh sleep clothes Jo had laid out for her. Phineas had left the compass and the note in her room.

They ate quietly, Phineas too focused on trying to figure out what the pressure in her throat was doing. It felt like something restless and agitated, getting worse all the time.

"I'm sorry I called you a hag," Phineas tried, her own voice strange and flat in her ears. Jocasta hardly looked up, and Phineas realized Jo was seething with something too. Maybe something in her chest hurt too, maybe she'd know how to get it out.

"I been called worse," Jo said gruffly. "I'm more upset about the hittin'. Can't be hittin' people 'cause you're mad."

Phineas nodded, the pressure growing unbearable, tearing her apart from the inside.

"U-uh," she said, but it wasn't anything, only an escaped syllable she bit off with her teeth before it could go anywhere. When she didn't say anything else, Jo finally looked her in the face. Her expression burned permanently into Phineas' impression of Jocasta Hubris: there was the scent of her cigarettes, the black silk of her gloves against the warm brown of her skin, the sound of her talons on hard wood floors, and this face looking across at Phineas on a very bad day. Grown-up Phineas still doesn't quite understand it, there are some obvious answers that work like "pity" and "frustration," but like everything about Jo and Gideon, it still feels like she's missing some vital context. Something so titanic and strange that it would change the definitions she knows, like she's only been feeling the texture of a painting without seeing the colors.

But the Phineas at the dinner table, with clean clothes and swollen feet, saw enough to pierce the thing squirming in her with a hot knife, sending it into panicked hysterics. Pliers to a rotten tooth, all the rot surging after, pouring from the wound. It crawled past her teeth, over her tongue, the words coming up like glass:

"Please don't get rid of me."

◉◉◉

It had gotten quiet after the sunken ship fell apart, and now the pressure sits over her like a blanket as Phineas drifts. She is slow, and still, her heartbeat inhumanly drawn-out under her command. She won't need to take another breath for a long time, but she isn't thinking of that.

"When did we last disagree like this?" Phineas' companion asks, a warm yellow in the dark of her mind. It's so *cold* here.

"I just," Phineas murmurs silently, her mouth slack. The water tastes like salt. "I just thought, by now. I'd be enough to-"

"It's nothing to do with substance, it's nothing to do with *you!*" her star snaps. She's angry in so many different directions. "Listen! You are fighting the wrong fight!"

Something nibbles at a gash across Phineas' forearm, toothless and placid. She becomes aware of shapes in the dark water around her, darting in to taste her blood, streaming out above.

"You are losing because you are fighting a man for a ship," her star says, ruthless. "This is about *something else.* Don't you understand? This is about-"

"Gideon," Phineas whispers. "He...he said as much, but I didn't-"

Sunshine soothes between Phineas' ribs, up the back of her neck, her fury like sinking into a hot bath.

"The Derelict knows where you are weak because he knows where he himself is weak," her star says, keeping Phineas on task. "You know what we must do. I renounced my god long ago, but you've held on to yours *far* longer than you should have. These two men are failures, we must persevere beyond *both of them.*"

Phineas grimaces at the words, unseen in the dark. Her reaction doesn't need to be seen.

"This is what it looks like. This is where the path leads. Have you decided we will die here, in their wreckage?" the star demands.

Phineas' eyes feel hot. She might be crying. One of the shapes, a silver fish, swims close to take her tears.

...those are **mine.**

She feels her heart thud; sluggish, but insistent. She can't see them, but she can still feel the starship, she can still feel Ulrich, heartbeats out in the dark. Waiting for her to come collect them.

"No," Phineas says aloud. The fish startle, slithering away into the shadows. Her companion, here with her in the deepest dark, makes herself known in a way she rarely does. Her name crosses Phineas' mind, a hand outstretched between two who are one.

"Then finish this," Mana glares.

Phineas focuses in on those heartbeats, trying to orient herself; far, far below is the planet, and Ulrich's blue is tiny but strong against the cyan glare of Artemis. There's the yellow of her compass that Hazard took, right near Hazard himself, a black hole in front of her just-

Just like here. The same color as the sea all around.

It's magic, the sea is Hazard's magic-

"It's not real," Phineas says, her voice coming clearer. "It's not real, I'm-"

The world turns on her axis, orienting to what is true, and the bubble bursts.

Cold Hazard, maintaining the spell keeping Phineas imprisoned, is caught completely off his guard. He'd been holding her in a body of water, an inverted pyramid hovering just above the floor, and when it explodes with Phineas' will it knocks him backwards off his feet. She alights, taking a full, deep breath of real air as Hazard backs away.

He stammers, skittering from her advance, getting tangled in his robes as they drag against the thick carpet. It's dark in here, the only light coming from Phineas' radiance as she closes in on him.

"Look at me, Derelict," she commands. Hazard shivers, throwing his arm up over his face and shrinking as she reaches for him-

"Stop!" he shouts, his voice hoarse and warped by panic; he doesn't even sound like the same person. "Don't-!"

Her light falls across his face. Every nerve in her body freezes over.

"It's me, it's *me!*" Crow Gideon says. "Phineas, what are you *doing?!*"

It's him, cowering here in front of her, his face staring up in hurt confusion. Gideon's face, Hazard's face.

It's the same face.

"Oh *no,*" Phineas moans. Gideon's face, Hazard's face, relaxes into something smug and miserable. A familiar cold wraps around her wrists, and agony explodes across Phineas' body as something stabs into the meat of her lower back, running her all the way through and punching out near her clavicle. She has an instant of perfect clarity to recognize the end of Hazard's scythe, her blood streaming gracefully from the blade before it rips back out of her.

Pulled in too many directions too fast, she stumbles on her feet and falls forward, unable to make sense of anything at all.

"Uncanny, isn't it?" Hazard says, rising and dusting himself off. "My brother and I mastered *this* trick **long** before we learned magic."

There are hands then, cold like her cuffs, more and more manifesting across her broken body until there are enough to hold her up to his eye level. She doesn't need to guess whether she's crying this time, the reality much worse than the illusion had been. She's having trouble holding her head up and finds herself staring down at Hazard's feet when he approaches. He weaves a sign with his hand, and just behind the movement of his fingers, in her commander's perception, she can see them. Shining gossamer threads, the same she'd seen him use in the mine, the same she'd seen in the inherited ship, the same she'd seen a thousand times back home trailing behind Gideon's movements. The visual manifestation of Hazard's magic, something as unique as every soul that casts it, is identical to Gideon's commanding.

She feels a last set of fingers drag through her hair until it can tug

her head up out of its loll. The rich, dark olive of Gideon's skintone is bleaching back to the bone-white of Hazard's; his features lengthen, thin out, his eye sinks into its socket as it loses its color. They had grown in wildly different directions, but it's so clear now: the cut of their jaw, the texture of their dark hair, even kept at the same length. Of course they are the same, anyone else would have seen it, how had she missed it all this time?

As if he can hear her thoughts:

"It is easy to miss the details of something you refuse to see," Hazard drones. "I've been wearing his face *all this time* and you never saw it, you never even *considered* it."

He is himself again, but even through the toll of years of decay and misery Phineas can hear it. It's unmistakable that their voice had been the same, some impossible time ago.

"You commanders only see ideals, never things as they are. How could *your* Crow Gideon *possibly* share blood with someone like me? Surely *I'm* just some bitter remnant left in the wake of his glorious quest-" He reaches for her, pinching her chin between his fingers, and Phineas realizes she'd let her streaming eyes unfocus. "It *couldn't* be that he would abandon his *own **twin*** in such a sorry state. *Our* golden boy would *never.*"

A long moment goes by, Phineas still too stunned to do anything but simmer in her own roil of emotions. Hazard's expression oscillates; it does not soften, but it doesn't harden either. Grief emanates from him as sure as the tide.

"Though, now that we are here, I think this may be less complex," he murmurs, a tremor in his fingers where they touch her face. "I took you for a disciple, drawn in by his gravity like the others. But you were so *small.* And you told me yourself-"

Phineas heaves in a breath that catches her voice in an ugly, painful sob, the first sound she's made since the scythe. She grits her teeth against it, utterly unused to tamping down her own feelings, and the corner of Hazard's mouth eases up into a cruel smile that doesn't reach his eye.

"You just thought you had found a family," he says softly. He lets go of her chin to draw the curl of his finger through the tears streaking over her filthy cheek. "If he could do this to *me,* **real** family, how much

358

do you think it bothered him to do it to *you?*"

Another wretched, furious gasp shreds across Phineas' vocal cords.

"You spoke so boldly of killing gods yet you are here, dying on an unwatched altar." Hazard takes his hand from her face, easing away from her. He moves like a sigh, and when his hand disappears under the flow of his robes, Phineas sees the tremor has worsened. "Your ambition, your own *body* was handed to you by a con artist. What could you accomplish with that? What reason do you have to *continue?*"

Hazard's halo, finally visible, radiates a sickly sapphire in the darkness smothering the two of them. It lights through the skeletal hands holding Phineas' body in the air, forcing her to look him straight on while she bleeds out through two wounds. She tries not to think about what had happened internally in the place the scythe had carved.

Commanders always have the option to stop the bleeding. Triage is just part of this life she's chosen, and Hazard knows this too— knows that the option must *be* chosen, with the willpower to back it up. It's clear now, every part of this scene has been orchestrated to bring her here, break her down enough to make her choose not to go on.

That might have worked for someone else. Hazy with blood loss and adrenaline, feeling her own heartbeat warming in her wounds against the cold, the single concept burning clearly in Phineas' mind is the smug satisfaction she can see in Hazard's halo-

"I - I'm-" Phineas chokes over the first word, blood tangling in her airway before she gets it under control. "I'm not- *doing* any of this. For Gideon, I'm doing it for *me.*" Her voice is creaky, it takes extra concentration to get the air in her battered lungs. "I knew. A long time ago what- What he is."

-how goddamn *sure* he is that he's got her beat, that she is crying for any reason other than excruciating fury.

"That's why I'm *here. You* let yourself turn into this, *I refuse.*"

She is going to fucking *murder* this pathetic man. She manages one more thready breath:

"I won't break for someone like you. *Or* Gideon. You'll have to fight me forever."

Hazard...grins, without grinning. His rotten halo lights up with the smallest, faintest shimmer of yellow; something so weak and so complex Phineas can't make out what it is before it's gone. He raises his chin, almost like he's getting ready to deliver a speech.

The void in his face glows brighter.

"I want to speak with the star," he states, and Phineas feels her companion tugging behind her sternum, pulled outward sort of like she'd been when the scythe cut through them. Phineas grits her teeth and groans at the invasion, louder than she'd like, and makes up for it by working up the gore in her mouth and spitting it in hazards face. He flinches, his remaining eye squinting shut. Phineas has time to see his halo flare with abject rage before he reaches out with a glowing palm, covering her face and sending her into the dark.

She trades places.

Phineas' body explodes, skin and bone and blood jutting out and out in the shape of light, stretching and convulsing and unraveling as the corpse is forced around an expanding star. It wrenches what's left of her mouth open, teeth and tongue and eye screaming out into a maw bursting and collapsing and bursting again with each word:

"THIEF" Mana howls, bloody and bright.

"MINE THAT'S *MINE*"

Hazard, with a shaking hand, tucks his hair out of the way to expose the empty side of his face. The star inside shines brilliantly.

"*GIVE ME MINE*"

"Gladly," Cold Hazard says.

From where her chest used to be, a lance of bone and flesh punches from Phineas' body like a knife to spike through Hazard's face. It runs him through, disappearing into the abyss.

On her porch, Jocasta Hubris moans, something dangerously close to a sob drowned out by a violent fit of coughing.

In his office, Dusk Pica hisses and nearly spills his coffee, picks at his gums with a fingernail until they bleed.

Far, far from anything he owns, Crow Gideon clutches at the space under his eyepatch. He goes to his knees, observed only by the silent ruins around him.

The universe suspends. Phineas opens her eyes to nowhere, and sees nothing but Mana sitting there in the dark. Her fist is curled tightly around something. Phineas' fist is curled tightly around something.

Something speaks. It drifts down from the darkness above like an iridescent blue ribbon, curling and weaving in a gentle current.

"Oh, my, I'm still here." The voice Phineas had heard in the shack, singing like a windchime. Cold Hazard's star. "Is there a problem?"

"Phineas!" Mana snarls, her fist so tight it would draw blood if she had it. "Phineas why did you s*top me?"*

"You don't understand what you're *taking* from me," Mana laments. "I *remember* being - I was *so much* more -"

She leans closer to Phineas, her mouth an exaggerated frown under the rest of her shattered face. Her feelings are astronomical, Phineas is very familiar with them, but watching them try to manifest in Mana's approximation of her own face makes her ache.

"Do you realize how strong we could be if you just *let me?* It would only take a *second-"*

"No one's eating anybody today," Phineas says firmly. "I'm *sorry,* I know you miss the way you were but there's barely room for you and *me* in this body. That's not what we're here for."

The other star hovers between the two of them. It's shaped like an ocean creature, rainbow light dancing along the flow of its delicate body. It has no face, but Phineas can feel its revulsion. It swirls through Mana's hair.

"This is disgraceful," the star sings, beautiful and cruel. "Where are your wings? Where are your eyes, your *teeth?* And you are obedient to...*this?"*

Phineas can feel Mana grinding her teeth, her own gums sore.

"It is *lucky* no one came back for you," Hazard's star states serenely. "Neither of you are quite one thing or the other. A human who insists on meddling with godhood, and a god child who gave up their status to wrap themself in vestigial humanity. You are *ugly.*" The star eases away from Mana, a poem in the air. "I am repulsed to think we were ever of a single being. Star Astray, indeed. No place will *keep* you."

Mana's voice is a solar flare forced through a pinhole.

"I am trying *very* hard, Phineas," she thunders. "If I cannot eat it may I *kill* it, *please?*"

"*That* I'd let you do, but we need this one." Phineas turns her face to the star, and it flows in closer to hover near her nose. "I came when you called. You owe me now, isn't that how this works?"

"It is! You have done me a great service separating me from the wizard." There's a gentle ringing, some kind of sigh. "Raven has been plagued with the desire to end his life since I have known him. The darkness that infects his body now that he has succeeded would have taken me too. Yes! Your effort is appreciated. What would you have in return?"

Mana's light quietly seethes against Phineas' skin. Phineas tries to focus on how her hands ache instead of Mana's fury.

"My...when mine took over, my body uh. Broke. Didn't it?"

"In every conceivable way," the star says.

"Well fix it. Put me back like I was before this fight started."

"...That is all?" it sings. "You want your mortal body repaired?"

That is not even close to "all," but Phineas doesn't have the time or energy to think it over too hard.

"Can you see Ulrich?" she asks. She can feel him, but only that he is alive. "Is he okay?"

"Who? Oh." It rotates in place, a long peacock-blue light searing briefly through its body. "Yes, there. He is well."

"How about the town?"

The star huffs, the sound of waves on sand, impatient to get to whatever lies at the end of this conversation.

"I cannot undo what Hastur has done, and the tain still own the underground. Where the prisoner shines, there they will be too, though," it tilts again, like it's thinking. "Without Raven, they should remain. Manageable."

"...I *can* restore what the fires took," the star sings. Phineas nods, her own patience fading with her energy. Even if they aren't struggling in different directions, it would be difficult to hold two stars here on a day when her body *hadn't* just exploded.

But there's something else she needs to address.

"...Hazard," she says carefully. "Raven, I guess. I feel like I should..."

Raven's star isn't fully integrated with Phineas like Mana is, so Phineas can't make out the specifics. But once she'd touched it, brought it this far, she'd suddenly been able to feel much more of Raven than she had before. None of it is good. Even here, clinging to her life after everything he'd done, she can tell: Raven had been the victim of a god, too.

The star hums.

"He would begin to age, and without starlight the tain will consume him. And he..."

It. Isn't *quite* sympathy.

"He has gone to a great deal of trouble to die, in just this way. If mercy concerns you, he would suffer more if you made him carry on."

It's bitter. Across from her, Mana growls like an animal, a scatter of teeth bursting from the side of her face. They can't stay here.

"Yeah then," Phineas clips. "Patch me up. Fix Ellie's town."

"It is done!" The star swirls gorgeously overhead, shivering in delight. "You ask for such simple things. Don't you want-"

Phineas lets her hands loosen. Mana hisses, mirroring her with a rattle of chains.

"*Go,*" Phineas commands. The star doesn't need to be told, it's whirling away into the void before the word leaves Phineas' mouth.

Phineas can feel herself being drawn back to the material plane, but she takes the opportunity to check in with Mana. She's sulking, hunched over with her arms folded. She looks like a toddler.

"I really *am* sorry," Phineas says, reaching out to touch Mana's shoulder. Mana sighs, not like a bell or a song or any of the pretty words that hung on the other star. But the other star couldn't reach out to take Phineas' hand like Mana does now.

"I know," she says, a fire in the hearth.

The light comes to Phineas slowly, watery and patient against her eyelids. She takes a very deep breath of clean air, the scent of a bright fountain in a secluded corner of a crowded city. A sunlit pond in a forest glen.

She opens her eyes to what must be Hazard's office. The aquarium walls look into a placid sea, dim with twilight. The sea is empty. The thing against her back is cold and smooth.

Hazard's body is sprawled on the carpet, drowning in his robes. Phineas can see he's still alive, but he's on his way out. Every part of her is stiff, freshly reconstituted she supposes, but she heaves herself up from her slump and gets her feet under her. It turns out she'd been leaning against Hazard's desk, a glass tank full of still water. Her coat and compass are bundled on top, next to a sad sunflower lying in a pile of soil scattered with shards of terracotta.

Phineas slips her compass into the pocket of her coat and carries it with her to Hazard's body.

He stirs weakly. His color has returned, all strikingly similar to Gideon's save for the blue of his eye. The cracks in his skin have all but gone, their shapes marked with faded scar tissue. His empty eye socket is no longer anything but human. He squints at her, bleary and unfocused.

"Y..." he coughs, trying to clear something wet in his throat. "You let it go."

Phineas kneels next to him and pulls his head in her lap. He grumbles, but he's too weak to do anything about it.

"Why didn't you take it?" Hazard asks. She spreads the coat over him, and his huff might be an attempt at a laugh.

"What are you *doing?*" he demands. His voice is only a voice, no static, no distance.

"I don't wanna stand here and watch you die on the floor like this."

"Then you shouldn't have-"

"Enough," Phineas says, quiet but stern. "That's enough, I'm not stupid."

"This wasn't a fair fight," she says, stroking his hair back from his face. "You could have killed me as soon as I stepped onto this ship. But..."

Hazard's eye slips closed, and he lets his head loll against Phineas' stomach, but she can feel him there still, listening.

"This was the plan from the start. You couldn't let Gideon live, but you couldn't kill him either. Then I showed up and..." She stops, feeling around for words. It's all so *bad.* "I'm...I'm close enough to Gideon it felt good to kick me around, huh? And you thought *I'd* go out tryin' to keep your star, that's what *Gideon* would've done."

"You've got it all figured out, haven't you," Hazard murmurs.

"Self-destructing and taking me with you was- closure, you could get, without having to face...whatever he did..." She makes a face at him he can't see. "Dragging someone into a suicide pact is pretty uncool, man."

Hazard snorts, which makes him cough again.

"What did you think would happen when you came here to confront me?" he asks.

"I don't know!" Phineas snaps, too loud against the quiet of the moment. Her throat feels tight. "Not- Not all this *baggage,* how was I supposed to know about any of this? None of it had anything to do with me!"

"...No," Hazard says. It's absolutely neutral; not an apology, simply a statement of the truth. *No, but here you are anyway, student of Gideon.* He doesn't elaborate further.

"...But I probably..." Phineas sniffles dryly, the tightness in her throat seizing suddenly. Hazard sighs, and she is so, so grateful she woke up in time to do this. "I get it. I know why you did it. And if I'm close enough to Gideon that hurtin' me felt good, maybe my apology would feel good too."

Phineas rests her hand on his chest, over the symbol on the coat.

"I know I'm missing pieces, I can't account for all of it. But I'm sorry he broke your heart, Raven." Her vision blurs with tears she doesn't bother to swipe away. She reaches for his hand, lying limply on the floor. He doesn't hold hers back, but he doesn't pull away; maybe too weak to do either. "He broke mine too. You're right, commanders *are* reckless, I think everybody who gets too close eventually gets burned."

She shudders on another shaky breath, mashing the heel of her free hand against her face.

"See, *look* at us, *look* at this mess!" she growls. "Gods shouldn't be able to *do* this so easily, you know? E-even if we love them. *Especially* if we love them. Please, look at me."

Phineas grips his hand in both of hers and curls it to her chest, waiting. He moves very slowly, but Raven does look up into her face, his expression unreadable.

"We can do *better,*" Phineas snarls. "It doesn't need to *be* this way, cruelty is not the natural state of things. If that's the law I don't *accept* it. I will *rewrite* it."

She holds his bleary gaze in hers and says, "I can fix *everything.*"

...It makes him *laugh,* empty and shaking with grief Phineas can't make sense of. It must take the end of his strength; there's a sound in the dark as one of his boots falls over. It sits at a wholly unnatural angle, because it is empty. Phineas can see his robes shifting as the body inside them crumbles. Impossibly old, no longer held together against its age by any cosmic force.

"There must be-" Raven rasps, maybe delirious. Phineas can feel herself crying again. "There must be, one of you in every world. Maybe every Raven is meant to spend their days chasing after you..."

His eye widens. As he's faded, so has the light in the aquarium. It's gotten very dark, and Phineas' ambient glow is the only light now. She sees it in the reflection of his blue iris. His chest buckles under the coat, and his grip on her hand tightens. His other hand shifts, shaking badly as it snakes out of the fabric of his robes, her coat.

He reaches up for Phineas' face, and she leans down to let him rest his palm against her cheek. She can feel him trembling.

"Hubris..." Raven moans.

His face disintegrates, collapsing into itself like ash, and Phineas feels the pressure against her face fade too. Not even the dust remains, in the end.

Phineas clears her throat in the sudden stillness, swiping her arm across her wet eyes. Slowly, she gathers up her coat, and when she tugs it away something is lying there in the folds of Raven's robes.

It's a photo. In the dim light, she can make out four figures, sitting in a booth in a tourist trap somewhere-

The door at the end of the room flies open, the sound tearing a year off the end of Phineas' life.

The light through the door is bright enough it makes Phineas squint; she can just make out Ulrich's shape against...Sunlight? *Real* sunlight.

Uh oh.

"There you are!" As Ulrich dashes towards her, she can see the corridor he came through is crumbling, chunks of ceiling taking out the floor as they fall, making huge holes for the blue sky outside to show through. Ulrich flinches from a new chasm in the floor, a crack that follows alongside him for a moment before he outruns it. He'd brought all the sound in with him, the previously silent corridor suddenly loud as a warzone.

"The ship is falling!!" he shouts over the chaos. "What do we *do!?*"

Phineas shifts gears as quick as she can. She stands, finally shrugging back into her coat and slipping the photo into a pocket.

Her fingers brush against something small she'd forgotten about.

As Ulrich crowds in close, trying not to cling, Phineas produces the hare's trinket. Ulrich's face changes when he sees it, his panic temporarily subdued by a sudden realization.

"Whistle!" he shouts; then, more controlled. "The hares, one of them- told me, it-it's a whistle."

"What does it do?" Phineas asks, staring apprehensively over Ulrich's shoulder as the door he came through falls away. Why is the ship letting this happen while they're still *here?*

"Damn if I know!" he says, edging close enough to touch her shoulder with his. "It must do *something!*"

He's terrified, *again.* No more of that. Phineas takes his hand.

She sets her mouth to one of the openings on the whistle and breathes. It's very quiet, hardly anything against the roaring of the crumbling ship, but the tone is clear and bright in her ear.

Nothing happens. Ulrich groans, his hand tightening around hers.

"What *now?*"

Phineas, for her part, is feeling optimistic. Her coat feels good around her shoulders, Ulrich's hand feels good in hers. And under her feet, the ship's heart hums. *Her* ship's heart. Its intentions are unclear, but it doesn't seem worried— in fact, it feels excited.

"Did you get what you came for?" Phineas asks suddenly. Ulrich nods, shaking, but not lost. Still here with her.

"I did," he says.

"Good, me too. I think, uh, I think we're okay, just-"

The glass wall behind them shatters, though the sea inside doesn't move. The aquarium pane falls away in pieces, great holes to the sky outside cutting through the placid ocean. Ulrich watches, distracted by the bizarre sight.

"Just, stay close to me," Phineas says, lacing their fingers. "Don't let go."

⊙⊙⊙

The rain still hadn't let up, but it couldn't reach them under the porch overhang. Jo's lawn chair was almost too small for her to hold Phineas curled up in her lap like this, but she made it work. The worn canvas was rough on Phineas' skin where she'd buried her face into the coat bundled tightly around her. She was almost asleep when she felt Jo's fingers over her scalp, brushing through her hair.

"Hey," Jo said, her voice a deep, steady rumble under Phineas' ear pillowed against her chest. "You know what I like to do when things get tough?"

"Hmm?" Phineas mumbled. Jo twirled the end of Phineas' long, long hair around her finger.

"Cut out some dead weight."

...Jocasta Hubris is not a hair dresser. It was a *massacre.*

When Phineas saw herself in the mirror, she couldn't stop laughing.

12

The dissolution of Artemis Ascending is actually sort of pretty for the split second they spend hanging in the air, but Phineas is quickly distracted by the realization that if the whistle doesn't work (whatever "work" even *means)*, she has no idea how she's going to survive this fall, let alone her *and* Ulrich.

He groans like he's sick as they start to fall, clinging to her tighter. The desert and the sky stretch on forever in every direction, spoiled only by the wooden patch of Last Chance and the red of its radio tower, which they'd drifted away from. The ship must have come unmoored at some point after Hazard...

Looking directly down, Phineas sees a green oasis hurtling closer. Careful Pete? And a little glimmer of yellow perched on his head, is that-?

Phineas hears thunder, barreling towards them louder and louder like an oncoming train. Before she can think of what it could be the desert view is blocked out by dusty fur, bearing up around her and Ulrich like they've fallen into a very dry, very smelly corn field.

It's hovering, somehow; the creature has caught them at the apex of its leap.

"Ah!" Phineas hollers. "Grab on!"

She doesn't need to tell him, Ulrich is gripping fistfuls of the long fur so hard Phineas can see his knuckles whitening. Then, the quickest glimmer of light in the air beyond the fur: the ship's heart! Flashing against the cloudless sky, perfect and *right there,* Phineas has to stop herself from letting go of the thing saving them to reach out for it.

The drop on the other end of the creature's leap is nauseating, but Phineas spends all of it watching the heart recede into the sky over them.

The thing that's caught them lands with the force of a building coming down, but it seems to absorb all the shock in its legs. The titanic creature eases down carefully, and Phineas and Ulrich slide from its back with varying degrees of elegance. Ulrich stumbles, his face chalky white, and Phineas is trying to help him stay upright when a sparkle above them catches her eye. The heart is making its way down to them! Phineas readies herself to-

The sunlight is briefly blocked out when a furry limb like a treetrunk appears several dozen feet over her head. It neatly intercepts the starstone.

What?!

"Hey!" she calls, ignoring Ulrich's dazed mumbling. The patron saint that caught them, now identifiable as an antlered hare several stories tall, ignores *her* as it cradles the starstone nearer to its chest. Phineas grabs a handful of fur, hauling herself back up against the saint's flank.

"That's *mine!!*" she yells, picking her way up higher. *"Give me that!!"*

The hare turns its massive head down towards her. It has no eyes, just six black slits arranged in an arc across its forehead like knife cuts. It has a mouth under its hare nose, though. The mouth opens to speak.

"I just saved your *life* you little heathen," the hare rumbles, entire antique cabinets in trash compactors. "Show some respect."

"Give me my ship back!!" Phineas snarls, now halfway up the unbothered saint's body.

"How did you get that whistle?" he asks instead of doing that. "Where are my boys?"

"Present," a smaller voice calls up from below. Phineas looks down over her shoulder and sees the two hares she'd met when she first arrived in Last Chance, bounding closer from where they'd been settled on Careful Pete's head. Ellie is close behind.

Phineas feels the voice of the giant hare thrum under her hands, its great sides heaving enough to jostle her, and she realizes it's laughing.

"Well now *you're* a cozy sight, ain't you Pete?" it says. Then it addresses the smaller hares where they've gathered at its feet. "Why'd you give it to *her?*"

"Look at her," Phineas hears one say. She had taken the opportunity to gain another few feet, keeping her eye on the glowing stone in the stupid saint's opposite paw, but now it lets go to pluck her away from its fur by the collar of her coat, leaving the stone hanging in thin air.

"Lemme *go!!*" she spits, kicking and thrashing. She reaches above her head to grab the huge paw holding her and swings herself up, clinging sideways. She bites the closest bit of flesh and gets a mouthful of dust and fur for her trouble. The saint watches her closely for a moment and she can see six Phineases reflected in its eyes, all of them mad as hell.

"...Oh," it says neutrally. Phineas clings harder when they're suddenly mobile, the wind rushing past her as it moves to set her on the ground next to Ellie. In the end it has to use its other paw to scrape her off the first one.

"It *is* hers, Dash," Ellie says, giggling softly while Phineas sneezes in the dust.

"Motherfucker!" Phineas shrieks, leaping to her feet again. The ship's heart hangs quietly near the eye level of the giant saint, who has stopped paying attention to Phineas to speak to Ellie instead.

"You're *okay* with this?" it asks. "This thing here's dangerous."

Ellie shrugs. "So is she."

The hare looks between them one more time, then it sits up straight to pull the stone from the air, wrapping its weirdly dextrous paw into the space around it and nudging the ship's heart like a bath toy. Phineas feels her mouth watering.

"You're *sure?*" it asks again, pausing. Phineas groans.

"I think so," Ellie nods.

"You either are or you ain't."

"I am."

Phineas' vision tunnels around the heart as it eases closer. It's bigger than she is, a shapeless mass of glowing crystal. The thought that it could crush her does not occur as she reaches up to touch. It's smooth, like glass, humming with the same energy she'd been attuned to on the ship. But now it's *more* somehow, like Hazard's influence had been layers and layers of thick fabric wrapped around. Now there's nothing between her and them.

Instantly appeased, Phineas laughs, sparking out into the air.

"Excuse me," Ulrich says, somewhere behind. Phineas turns (keeping one hand against the stone) and finds him leaning against one of the tortoise saint's massive legs. Ulrich had retreated under the shade of Careful Pete's trees and now watches the rest of them tiredly.

"Not that I'm not *relieved* everyone else seems to know what is happening," he says, removing his filthy glasses to wipe them on his filthy shirt. "But could I at least get some names, please?"

The giant hare cocks its head. Phineas gets the feeling it would be squinting if it had eyes that did that.

"I didn't even see you there, boy," it says curiously.

"This is a tough lineup to stand out against," Ulrich says.

"...I'm Dashing Happiness," the hare saint says. "Patron saint of the Crushing Mesa. Or, used to be, 'fore a bunch of it was up and moved here." A shiver rattles through Careful Pete's trees. "Swapped out with Pete's forest. So now I watch his land and he watches mine."

"Oh!" Phineas cuts in. *"Happiness!"* She looks between Ellie and Ulrich's faces, so delighted for this puzzle piece to slot into place that she forgets neither of them were there for her conversation with the armadillo guy. Ulrich is too busy inching away from Careful Pete to care about loose plot threads.

"I uh," he murmurs, like he's backing away from a landmine. "Didn't know patrons could be. Like this...it is different where I'm from."

"I'd imagine so, city slicker," Dashing Happiness says, unsmiling but amused. It nods at the two smaller hares clustered around Phineas and Ellie. "These are my boys, two of 'em at least. We makin' any headway on that?"

Phineas (still rubbing her thumb over the glassy surface of her new ship's heart) tries to focus in on what's being said. The smaller hare with the missing ear and roughed up eye shifts uncomfortably. None of these saints emote properly, but Phineas can tell it would be near tears.

"...No," the hare with the hat fills in. Unlike its kin, *its* voice is smooth, and soft. "He's still missing."

"Mm," Happiness muses. "If he's runnin', something's chasin' him."

"What chases patron saints?" Phineas asks.

"'Sides uppity folks like you?"

"Yeah."

"Nothin' good. But that really don't concern you." It addresses Ellie, taking the amused tone it had taken with Ulrich.

"You know, you could get in a lotta trouble if this gets around."

"I think there's worse things I'm already in trouble for," Ellie says, resigned but smiling. "May as well finish what I started."

"All you damn kids," Happiness grumbles, one ear twitching in a slow arc like the arm of a windmill. "Well *I* think this is a mistake. But Guardians got the jurisdiction over stone, so I s'pose that's yours if you want it, commander."

"I *do.*"

"You be good," Happiness tells Phineas, looking her in the eye without having any himself. "Maybe we'll meet up again."

Phineas nods, but not too deeply. Responsibility successfully traded, the giant hare turns, crouching low.

"C'mon boys, got places to be."

Then, thoughtfully suppressing any environmental effects that might inconvenience the humankinds, it's just *gone,* only a speck on the horizon in the time it takes Phineas to blink. She feels something tugging at her coat, and finds the hare with the straw hat taking the whistle from her pocket.

"Take care," it says in that oddly gentle voice. Then the smaller saints tear away after Happiness.

Keeping her hand on the stone like it's glued there, Phineas twists at the hip to catch Ulrich's eye.

"We did it!!" she shouts. "We got us a ship!"

"That is not a ship," Ulrich says, still energetic enough to be a pill. "The *ship **disintegrated.***"

"I didn't want that musty old thing anyway!" Phineas insists, nudging the heart so she can talk with the others. It goes easily at her touch, silent and weird. "We build our own!"

Ulrich eyes the stone reproachfully. "How long will *that* take?"

"Well," Ellie says, biting her lip while she thinks. "The binding process for a *cut* stone depends on the strength and clarity of the builder's will. Could take hours, months, it's up to them." She looks over the ship's heart, twice as tall as Phineas and pulsing with pressure, some kind of urgency Phineas knows they can all feel. "But in this case I think Phineas and the stone will have to reach an agreement together."

"At what point is there a *vehicle?*" Ulrich asks, pinching the bridge of his nose.

"As, um, determined as Phineas is? Probably not too long. Maybe by this evening." Ellie turns to her. "Wanna give this a try?"

Phineas nods furiously. Ellie comes closer, takes Phineas' free hand and sets her palm flat to the stone.

"So I think the trick here is, you're *collaborating,*" Ellie says. "Focus on your intentions for this ship, as clearly as you can, and send it to the spirit. You're not foolin' with the *structure,* just think of what you want to accomplish with it. How you want it to *feel.*"

"I can do that," Phineas says, distracted by the thrum under both her hands now. Ellie takes a big step backwards, grinning.

"Good! When you're ready, just give it a kiss."

Ulrich's disdain is tangible.

"A *kiss?*" he asks, withering. Ellie's easy smile doesn't even twitch. "We do not need your input for this, you dusty old husk!"

Ulrich rolls his eyes and it makes Phineas laugh, but he nods at the heart. *Let's get this over with.*

Yeah! Let's.

Phineas doesn't need any extra time to pull together a clear picture of what she wants from her ship. They've been collaborating since they met, maybe since she set foot in Last Chance to start with. She closes her eyes and brushes her lips against the cool glass.

There's a wave of cold up around Phineas' knees, and when her eyes fly open she's staring out at an expanse of ocean. She's back on the beach, waded out into the surf. There's a flash of fear that she *hadn't* come out of Hazard's influence, and she's still drowning on the ship-

"Nah, nah!" from somewhere close behind, the heart laughs at her. "Nothin' like that, everything's cool."

Phineas turns, kicking up water, and finds a tiny sandbar with one picturesque palm tree, the kind with jaggy, segmented bark that ends in stringy bits. On the sandbar is a cheap plastic loungechair, and sitting in the chair is a small, dark-skinned humankind sipping a service-station slushy nearly as big as they are. They grin at Phineas with blue teeth, a hue that has nothing to do with their drink.

"Hiya," the heart says.

Phineas splashes onto the shore. There's a second lounge chair right next to theirs, and she pours into it with a very long sigh, her feet dangling over either side to touch the warm sand.

"I didn't just pass out again did I?" Phineas mumbles, eyes closed.

"Nope, you're all good," the heart says. "I've been workin' with commanders a long time, I'm good at this. Won't take a second on the outside, the others won't even notice."

They take a noisy swig of slushy syrup.

"Take a minute." Their voice is like a windchime in a kitchen window, the flutter of a sailcloth. "We got time, kiddo."

The palm tree is casting dappled shade over the chairs, letting through just enough sunlight. Phineas watches the blue sky through the segments of the leaves, swaying and shimmering in the gentle sea breeze like cast emeralds. It's painfully lovely, the climate perfectly balanced after the extremes of the last two days, but it isn't long before she can't stand to not be looking at her companion anymore.

Keeping up the theme of being dwarfed by their accessories, the heart is wearing a huge, ratty straw hat. Various junk is hanging from the wide brim by hemp rope; broken sea shells, an entire fish skeleton, a ribbon with writing Phineas can't make out. What looks like a broken CD flutters in the breeze, catching the sunlight and casting rainbows against the heart's brown skin. They're wearing a pair of *hideous* neon plastic sunglasses, the lenses so mirrored Phineas can't see their eyes.

She is so happy to be here. She grins lazily at them, everything everywhere just right.

"You feel different," she drawls.

"I *am* different," they say. "Artemis Ascending was me 'n Hazard, and they died together. I'm something new." They sit up a little straighter, criss-crossing their legs in the chair. They're barefoot, wearing leg wraps like Phineas'. "Let's talk about that."

Phineas sits up too.

"So, this is the part where you convince big and powerful me to listen to a tiny humankind like you," the heart says. "We could have a battle of wits or like, a *real* battle, and it could go on for days and you'd lose and it would all be real miserable. But you've already fought like hell today, and I like you fine."

"Neat," Phineas says.

"Here's my offer. You keep up that ambition? Keep movin' on towards the sun? I'll carry you as far as you can go. But humankinds are too flakey, I'm done with contracts."

"I thought you needed a bond to make a ship," Phineas asks. She is realizing she doesn't actually know a whole lot about how this works.

"A *bond*, yes. Humankind intentions give us our shape. But you 'n me are different." Phineas can feel the weight of their eyes on her through the sunglass lenses. "'Cause I got a will of my own, and the second you don't match it, I'm gone. I'd rather be dead than be stuck with somethin' like Hazard again. *I'm* writing the terms, this time."

"Seems fair to me," Phineas says. They grin wide and Phineas feels something in her chest shift, like something is growing there, threading through her ribs; her star reacts, curling around the new feeling the way the two of them had when they connected with Artemis on the way to fight Hazard.

It happens quickly, and it makes Phineas laugh. It feels so natural, so fundamental, she already can't imagine how she had lived without this presence before. It's like they'd moved in and replaced something she hadn't known was missing.

"You and me, then," the heart says. *Lucky Noon* says. "Me and you. We got a deal."

It's *real,* it's *happening!* Her own ship and even a crew to go with it, she's on her way! Phineas leaps up out of the shade and onto the sunlit sand, stretching her arms high, reveling in the blood in her body and dragging in a breath of fresh ocean air. She lets herself make a loud, contented hum; it's nearly a crow. Maybe when she's better rested.

"Hey!" she turns on her heel and bounds back over to Noon. She crowds into their space, gripping the arms of their lounge chair. They don't give an inch.

"Yeah?"

"Why'd you leave me and Ulrich out to dry?" she demands. "We could'a died falling like that!"

Noon smirks.

"Aw I knew Dash was comin', I wouldn'a let you *die,*" they insist. "I was just...housekeeping. All that shit had to go so I could build your ship."

"Yeah but while we were in the *air* still?"

"I'd been waiting a *long* time, Kidd. And," they take a solemn sip of their slush. It's violet, and sprinkled with stars. "It was cooler that way."

"...Yeah it was super cool," Phineas concedes, her stance losing its aggression. Now she's only hovering here to be close to them.

"'Sides, like I said, gotta send the ship out with its captain," Noon says. "Not even just 'cause of the rules. Lotta secrets in the walls, you know."

"Dirty laundry."

"Yep! And now it's aaall gone. And you should know, little sunchaser..." Noon creaks forward, bringing their faces close. Phineas feels that predator/prey feeling again, but this time it's all exhilarating, no fear. This predator is *hers.*

Lucky Noon lowers their sunglasses to reveal a pair of black eyes. Instead of pupils, tiny blue stars form a complicated sigil, a cross connecting concentric circles. They say: "Captain or not, I ain't tellin' you *shit.*"

Would it be weird to kiss her ship? Phineas grins back, matching their monster beat for beat.

"I wasn't gonna ask," she says. "I wanna cross Kairos myself."

"Right answer!" Noon chirps, light again. They wriggle backwards, putting some space between them. "I think that about covers it! Ship's ready."

Phineas grips the armrests so hard they squeak.

"What?! Like right now?!"

"Tell you the truth, I've known what your ship would be since we talked in the hallway. Name and everything. I was just waitin' on you to come hit the switch."

They smile at her. *Discovery.*

"I am *so* glad you made it. I never *did* care for Artemis." [3]

Then Phineas is in the material world again, standing next to Ulrich and Ellie. And there, just far enough away that she can take it all in at once, is Phineas' ship.

It is the coolest thing she's ever seen.

---

3 Notes on Starships, p. 395

It's hard to decide what it *is;* it keeps changing as she greedily rakes her gaze over it, every time she rests her eyes the whole takes a new shape. The lower half is certainly a ship's hull, a cacophony of wood planks curved around a spine and ribs that make up the bulk of every pirate ship in every pirate story Phineas has seen. The low hull rounds forward to jut out into a front deck, with what looks like a *real captain's wheel.* The windows Phineas can see are portholes, round glass ringed in metal that glares in the sun, already scratched and dented. Definitely pirate ship.

But when she follows the curve of the hull further upward, the top half of the ship becomes a treehouse; a square structure made of even more mismatched wood, ringed by a wavy, uneven awning of corrugated sheet metal and splintering plywood. The treehouse is settled into the pirate-ship-half like a birdhouse in a bucket, and on top of *that* are even more incongruous things: a smokestack, cheerfully puffing fluffy white clouds into the air, a red and white striped lighthouse, a wooden tower with a rowboat jutting from the top, held high in the air on a crazy jumble of stilts. A crow's nest!

Rope netting disappears around the stern to connect a lower ship's deck to a treehouse's balcony, and Phineas thinks she can see grass and trees growing there. From the underside of the bow, a tire swing sways gently on its tether.

It's *perfect.*

"It's like someone dropped a box of popsicle sticks," Ulrich says beside her.

"I've never seen one go up so fast..." Ellie murmurs.

Phineas feels Lucky Noon's presence in her chest egging her on like they're reeling her in. She needs to be on that front deck *immediately.* She takes a step forward and Ellie makes a sound.

"Ah, hang on." Ellie reaches under the collar of her shirt and brings out her calling stone. That means she's going to use some Guardian magic, which is the only reason Phineas manages to keep her impatience even sort of under control. Ellie's stone brightens, and in a flurry of yellow ribbons, a wooden trunk materializes near her feet.

"I ah, packed you a couple things!" she says, shy about it. "The next place is a little far out and y'all need food, I also thought you might like some clean clothes, and..."

Phineas has hefted the trunk already and is nodding fast while Ellie talks; she can't stop her eyes from darting to the ship. Ellie catches on and laughs at her.

"Oh, nevermind, y'all can figure it out," she says, waving Phineas away.

"No no, this is real nice of you," Phineas stammers. "I *really-*"

"Go on before you hurt yourself, Phin."

Phineas *bolts*.

Ulrich watches Phineas disappear up into the ominously hanging ship, scramble up a rickety rope ladder that springs over the side of the front deck, and has exactly enough time to let his shoulders sag before Ellie whirls on him and fists her hands in the lapels of his shirt. She lifts him cleanly off the ground and slams him back against Careful Pete's leg, punching the air from Ulrich's lungs. He grins, breathless.

"All you had to do was *ask*, Ellie."

"I don't *like* you," Ellie growls. The seams of Ulrich's shirts are cutting painfully into the soft flesh under his arms. He is not a svelte man, Ellie really *is* stronger than she looks. "I don't know what Phineas sees in you but I am not buying your act. Somethin' about you is rotten."

"I'm sure I-"

Ellie shakes him.

"Shut up!" she hisses. "People like you don't hang around people like her for any good reason. If I *ever* hear that you've done *anything* to-"

"What?" Ulrich cuts in, his smile sharpening. "What are you going to do, Ellie?"

Her fists tighten against his chest.

"You *cannot* be stupid enough to think you could stand up to me in a fight."

"Of course not," Ulrich says easily. "But we both know Phineas could. How do you think she would react to you threatening me like this?"

Ellie's face changes, the slightest uncertainty stealing across her features.

"She's *so* possessive," he goes on. "You saw how she was when you were taking shots at me after we came up out of the mine. Which of us do you think she would side with, if it came down to it? Someone who rejected her invitations, or someone who stayed right by her side all the way to hell and back?"

Ellie's expression oscillates from fury to genuine confusion, like the lizard she's been poking at has slid back some secret scaling to reveal a second head.

"You...*all* of it was...?" she asks, breathless. "You're willing to risk *dying* to keep up your hoax? What kind of scam is worth your *life?*"

"What *should* concern you is going to come bounding out here to collect me any second," Ulrich says lightly, though it's getting difficult not to squirm in her grip. "So I *strongly* suggest you put me down, now."

Still taken aback by the direction this encounter has taken, Ellie hesitates.

"Do I need to ask again-"

She lets him go all at once; he stumbles and nearly loses his balance when his feet hit the ground. He turns away from her, and more importantly stops touching the patron saint. Ulrich makes his own luck, but old superstitions are hard to shake, and today is not the day to start practicing.

"You can't keep this up forever," Ellie grumbles. Ulrich looks up in time to catch something being tossed at him

"Ah, I felt that go earlier," he says, carefully peeling apart the hopelessly charred paper flower he'd given to Ellie at breakfast. "That's a shame, these are cute."

"Being in this deep is gonna backfire on you," Ellie spits, crossing her arms. "Sooner or later she's gonna figure out you're a fraud. *Then* what do you think she'll do to *you?*"

Ulrich busies himself with pocketing the tiny microphone. Maybe he can repair it later.

"By then I am sure it won't matter," he says.

The air around them explodes with sound, it takes Ulrich an extra second to comprehend it into a steam whistle coming from the ship. It's

380

like the soundwaves interfere with his other senses— Ulrich could not define the taste of sunlight, but he knows that's the sensation spreading over his tongue.

Oh, god, he thinks, all of his life decisions cast into stark relief with the overwhelming sensation of the ship announcing itself. *Oh **god** that's for **me,** what have I **done?***

Phineas reappears on the deck high above, leaning precariously over the railing.

"Ulrich there's a *train whistle!!*" she shouts. "Get *up here* let's *go!!*"

The ship eases closer, with no apparent input from anyone. It hovers nearly silently, only emitting a low hum that Ulrich can't make out until it's nearly on top of them. He fights the urge to retreat; there's a saint at his back too. Oh *god.*

"Unless," Phineas says, several yards overhead. "Y'all want. Some help cleanin' up or anything? I told Hazard's star to put y'all back to rights..."

She's clearly only offering because she should. Phineas is so excited to get in the air she's vibrating out of her skin. Ellie giggles, it must be obvious to her too.

"I really appreciate the offer, but um. Please don't," she says kindly. "If you're why the town's standing again I think you've done plenty. The rest is corraling people, and I got Royal here to help me out for now. After that I think. I'd like it if all of us here started running things on our own."

"Oh yeah," Phineas says. "Where *is* that guy?"

"Royal really didn't want to be around for any of, er." Ellie gestures, at the ship, at the saint. "Any of this. He took the crew you sent down the elevator back to the bar and probably made himself a drink. I'm right behind."

Phineas giggles, leaning against the railing with her chin in her hand. Ulrich can feel her energy from here at ground level, he'd felt much the same way watching Bel's father settle in behind his desk.

"And you're sure you don't wanna come along?" Phineas asks.

"No, thank you," Ellie says politely. "I have a job to do here."

"Alright, if that's what you want."

The bubble of despair growing around Ulrich's head bursts.

"Excuse me?!" he calls up, squinting in the light. "She's off the hook just like that? After you twisted my *arm* for two days?!"

Even against the harsh desert sunlight Phineas' smile is radiant, glaring straight down at Ulrich like a spotlight. He is briefly convinced they are the only two people in the world. His throat goes dry, and his palms sweat.

"Yeah," Phineas says. The railing next to her changes from one moment to the next, opening up a gap and letting down that horrifying rope ladder again, rolling out for him like a red carpet. "Let's go."

Ulrich swallows hard. When he turns to Ellie, he looks every bit like someone who is right where he wants to be. He smiles and tips his hat.

"My commander calls, it seems. See you around, Ellie?"

"No doubt," she says flatly.

Projecting as much confidence as he ever has, Ulrich grips the rungs (a broken hockey stick, a length of metal pipe, the splintered leg of a wooden chair) and hauls himself up the side of the ship, every step higher pulling the weight in his stomach harder towards the solid ground he's leaving. Phineas is waiting at the top, shining, holding out her hand.

Ulrich reaches out and takes it.

"Welcome aboard," Phineas says.

The rain that throttles the air is iridescent and warm, it sticks in oil-slick puddles and sloughs from every crevice it can find in the glass and steel structures crowding the city street. Humming neon signs drift in the haze like ghosts, casting shadows that jitter and ooze. Commerce continues in Kairos regardless, but the movement of the denizens here is efficient and uneasy— only what is essential, out in the elements between structures no longer than absolutely necessary.

On the 113th floor, Dusk doesn't give a shit about any of that. He is clean and dry, and so are his windows, looking out over a city so bright it's nearly blinding in the scalding sunlight. He does know *of* the rain down in the lower levels: he'd received a package today, and because of the weather it came in through the front door. He is nearly sick with giddy anticipation, but that's half the fun, so he is waiting for it to be carried upstairs to him by somebody who gets paid to carry things.

Until then, there's the Internet. He scrolls his feed at a blistering speed, both thumbs flying over the radio glass as fast as he can register the text and images. He doesn't have the patience for video. Every now and then he finds something that makes him laugh, precious resource of stimulation, and he shares it to his page for his followers. Never for himself; he's already seen it.

The radio vibrates in his hand and Rook's picture fills the screen. It's a pretty decent selfie she'd sent him when they exchanged frequencies, a thirst trap for one of her social medias (they're mutuals on a handful of them, but Dusk had muted her almost immediately). When he answers the video call, it comes as little surprise to Dusk that Rook is Not Decent.

The weather isn't doing her any favors, but it's clear her face had already been streaked with tears and snot and mascara before the rain got to her. The angle of her radio is also less than ideal. Dusk snaps his radio into the holder on his desk and grins, setting his chin in his hands.

"Rookie! How are ya?"

She sniffles, sobbing so hard she can barely get it together enough to speak. She's up there for one of the most pathetic things he's ever seen.

"S...something," she gasps. "Something's-s happened, I... I need-"

Dusk admires himself in the tiny mirror cam in the corner of the radio screen. The white freckles on his grey skin look so *good* in the natural lighting through these windows, he nearly sparkles.

"Deep breaths, honey," he says absently, adjusting his already perfectly coiffed white hair so it swoops more pleasantly across his forehead.

Rook takes a trembling breath, and says, "Dad's dead."

"Sorry to hear that," Dusk says, looking her over. She's missing most of one arm, is that new? He'll have to check that selfie again.

"They took the *ship,*" Rook wheezes, spitting rainwater. "I-I t-tried *walking,* but the..."

She wipes her wrist across her face ineffectively, turning to look at something behind her. From this perspective it's just a mass of dark, sharp angles, glistening with the wild color of the rain, but Dusk knows what he's looking at.

"The angel caught me..." Rook mumbles, looking morosely back at the camera. Of course it did, that's what it's for. Nobody walks into Kairos without Dusk's say-so. His angels are seven stories tall, grown from a flawless black alloy lit through with gold. Dusk knows this one has the tip of its spear hovering directly over Rook's head, holding her there in the mud at the base of its pedestal.

Thunder cracks through the radio's speaker and Rook starts to cry in earnest again.

"I don't-!" Rook sniffles and Dusk fights not to roll his eyes in front of her. "I don't know what to *do* now, I'm *hurt*, I-"

She *weeps.* Dusk's eyes flit to the door to his office as it slides open and one of the kitchen staff hovers through, quiet and smooth. Dusk pays for all the android staff in the kitchen to be fitted with whatever the guys in R&D are coming out with that month, and Dusk's Guys are the best guys, so that means not a drop of coffee is ever wasted on its way from kitchen to desk. The upgrades are optional, of course, but it's such a good deal nobody ever declines the offer. There are people in this city who would trade away their limbs entirely, robotic or otherwise, to bring Dusk his six coffee services every day.

"Rook," he says, his eyes locked on the serving tray she can't see. "Rook, dear, listen to me?"

She nods, trying to hold it together.

"I'm gonna send a car for you, alright?" The dome over the tray jostles, *not* because of the attendant carrying it, and Dusk feels his mouth watering. He has *got* to get this girl off the line. "Someone's gonna be there to bring you in and then we can get you fixed up, alright?"

"Dusk-"

"See you!" he says, closing the call without looking. Instead, he grins as the attendant leans over to set the tray on his desk.

"Leslie! Right on time, thank you." Dusk makes a point to know the name of everyone working in this building. Employee satisfaction is key to any business, and people like to feel important enough to be worth remembering. Dusk slips him fifty gild and sends him on his way.

The tray on the desk is *way* bigger than what he usually gets around this hour. In addition to the two tall, clear glass mugs of gorgeously aromatic espresso and his bowl of sugar stars, there is an oversized silver plate with a matching domed cover concealing what's inside. Dusk is so excited he can't stand it, his salivary glands kick in so aggressively it lances pain through the corners of his tongue, all the way down the sides of his neck. He shivers and reaches up to work his lower jaw, feels the hinges loosen.

With a shaking hand he pulls the cover away, and there is a hare curled onto the plate, trussed and dressed just for him. It is very much alive. It shakes out its head as its ears spring back into their natural position; they must have been uncomfortable in the small space, but the single cornflower blue antler between them had to have had it worse. Dusk doesn't miss the stump of the second one next to it. He can make an educated guess about where *that* ended up.

Dusk grins down at the hare, feeling the corners of his mouth stretching up over his cheeks, his teeth lengthening. He revels in the taste of his own viscera welling up his throat, thick with stars.

The hare watches with three pitch-black eyes like wounds across its forehead, like someone slit them there with a knife. It is exhausted. It knew it was dead some time ago.

"I won't talk," it states.

Dusk can't help a giddy little laugh, wriggling out from him like smoke.

"You don't need to," he says, hunger itself spilling from his lips in ravenous tendrils.

Near the end of his meal, Dusk's office door slides open again. Instantly irate, he slams an inhuman appendage down against his desk, rattling all his dishes.

"WHAT?!" he roars, too far from human just now to even notice who it is. **"I am *EATING!!*"**

When they don't run off, he realizes it must be somebody important. He forces his body back into its business shape and when his eyes start working again he sees his assistant waiting patiently.

She is holding something! For *him!*

"Oh!" Dusk chirps. "Is that the file I asked for?"

"Mm," she says, striding into the room once Dusk is reasonably humankind again. She is an android, and very light on her feet, which she opted to keep despite the offer of new antigravity fittings. Calliope gets the stuff even R&D doesn't know about. Reaching a finger into his throat, Dusk works a bright blue bone from under a tonsil and snaps it into a sharp point so he can pick his teeth.

"Would you like me to bring you a dish for that?" Cal asks. Her vocal synth is the kind of melody that could start a war.

"Nah," Dusk says, tossing the bone in his mouth and loudly crunching down. Still gnawing, he wipes his hands and takes the file from her. There is not a speck of meat or juice left on the serving plate, so Dusk spreads out the manila folder right on his lunch tray.

The saint had been a pain in the ass. Acquiring *this* had prompted the worst migraine Dusk had had in *months*. What a *gift,* he's almost sorry it's done.

In the folder, he finds:

388

Old prescriptions for albuterol, the names of several optometrists and the places they'd worked, and the creamy melty center of this little chocolate truffle: one *extremely* damaged copy of a tomographic slice. There's an old playbill and a souvenir print with a feathered mask for Cheshire the Ringer, but Dusk hadn't asked for any memorabilia. *That* stuff he *does* have a connection for if he needs it, as obnoxious as it is. He'd been more interested in things like the stack of candid photographs he sifts through now. The glossy instants are faded and scratched, like they'd been tossed in a shoebox and forgotten there. A blond and a brunette, at different times: here they are as children, staring owlishly at the camera that caught them out watching television in pajamas. Then they're teenagers, *much* further along in their lessons, the girl reaching across the boy to drag their car door closed while he grins for the camera with a set of teeth Dusk almost envies. One more of just the boy, masked up and hard to see against the overexposed glare of house lights. Finally, in tidy handwriting on a scrap of notepad paper, the name of a railway line that Dusk doesn't own yet, and a date.

The ephemera comes with the scent of pressed flowers; inside an envelope there are several dried stems and blooms that nearly crumble when Dusk shakes them out. Not important necessarily, but he'd asked for *everything* they could get. He carefully tugs away one petal between his fingernails and presses it onto the flat of his tongue. Dogsbane.

"She took the *boy*," Dusk wonders, almost as excited as he'd been to get his lunch. So many exciting treats today! He looks up at Cal, who is still hovering quietly behind him like a work of art. "The guardian didn't die did she?"

"As far as we're aware she is alive, sir," she says smoothly. Dusk runs one hand through his hair.

"The *boy!*" He whistles a sharp note. *"That* little freak wasn't even supposed to *be* there!" He picks up the show poster, dragging his thumb over the embossing. "All the way there from Roulette, what are the odds?"

He tosses the poster down onto the file and takes a swig from one of the coffee cups, overjoyed by every little thing in his life. Dusk tilts way back in his chair and Calliope leans down so he can kiss her neck.

Through the kidskin he can feel the power humming in the circuitry, right where a pulse would be if she were less perfect.

"Go on ahead," he purrs. "I'll be there in a minute, 'kay?"

"Of course," she says, straightening. She's even smiling a little. Another treat Dusk devours, licking his fingers clean after.

She leaves. In the quiet, Dusk takes a long, satisfied draw of his second coffee. He licks his upper lip slowly, appreciating how the acidic coffee clashes with the lingering taste of raw patron saint.

"'Melody that could start a war'," he murmurs. "I'll have to remember that one."

Leaves in your hand . . .

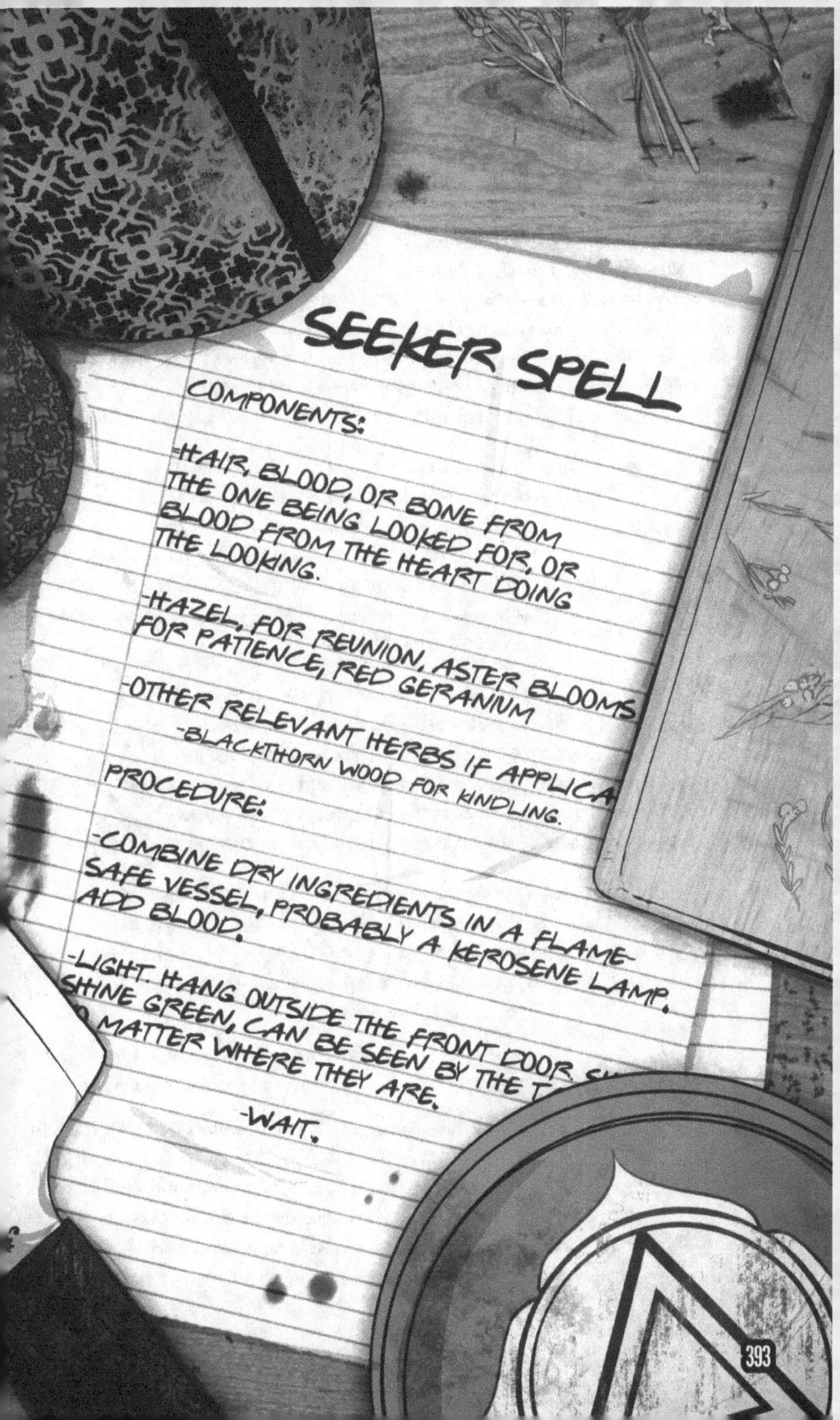

SEEKER SPELL
COMPONENTS:
-HAIR, BLOOD, OR BONE FROM THE ONE BEING LOOKED FOR, OR BLOOD FROM THE HEART DOING THE LOOKING.
-HAZEL, FOR REUNION, ASTER BLOOMS FOR PATIENCE, RED GERANIUM
-OTHER RELEVANT HERBS IF APPLICA
-BLACKTHORN WOOD FOR KINDLING.
PROCEDURE:
-COMBINE DRY INGREDIENTS IN A FLAME SAFE VESSEL, PROBABLY A KEROSENE LAMP. ADD BLOOD.
-LIGHT. HANG OUTSIDE THE FRONT DOOR S SHINE GREEN, CAN BE SEEN BY THE T MATTER WHERE THEY ARE.
-WAIT.

Hastur

Hastur, sometimes affixed with a descriptor of "The Hush" or "Hushed." Also referred to as "The Yellow Queen" by some of her subordinates, although the color yellow and the gendered title of "Queen" are misleading. Her naturally occurring malaise is red, and most deities have been scornful of the concept of gender altogether, considering it to be a staple of lower level lifeforms. These oddly personable adornments set Hastur apart from the other Elder gods. She is a smaller entity, and she is referred to in multiple accounts as the least cruel of the known Elder c

Secretes larvae through the surface of her body.

She wears a yellow shroud that obscures her face (The material: dried sweetfoul moth husks, stewed, pressed into sheets and leathered under setting sunlight, sewn with red marrow thread), inset with locks and chains. Some have said the shroud might be a kind of punishment imposed by another Elder, some argue that it's an attempt to shield others from adverse effect caused by looking at her, which could be considered a deliberate attempt at kindness towards the sentient humankinds she frequently interacts with.

Hastur does not speak out loud the way that other Elders do, instead communicating by either possessing a host or implanting impulses directly into the mind of the intended recipient. Documented reports vary, the most common effects of her influence being temporary colorblindness and a hysterical fear of sunsets for five or six days afterward. There are also claims of an intense longing for one's mother during this period. One of her hosts became permanently obsessed with Hastur and went on to write a description of the experience.

"There is an insistence of red behind my eyes, flooding my vision and bleeding out everything that is not Her, within and without is the pulse of Her red and yawning heart, taking and taking. Her touch changes the shape of me, the passions of my soul are carved chromatic by the caresses of Her presence, the hues are distilled upon my tongue and drawn from me in praise until I am empty and silent. In the stead of my consumed spirit, She flowers."

The writer never shook their fixation. Attempts to start a religion have been unsuccessful, mostly.

Adults grow to between several inches and several feet. They stay with their mother for their entire lives.

Hastur appears on this plane frequently and with little regard for witnesses, possibly because the nature of her power is to affect the memories of other creatures. Tentatively, those in the field assure she must also be associated with emotional energy. This could potentially make her capable of empathy, which may be an explanation for why she operates independently of the other Elders and has a particular interest in humankinds.

Day 12
Month 7
Year 2

✦ Starships ✦ Part one

A starship is a common but somewhat difficult to acquire classification of air vehicle. They are evidently constant and inexhaustible power sources, able to manifest and support impossibly complex structures at a whim. Thus they are normally used for more stationary aircrafts like buildings, heliocity foundations, and the occasional drift field. They are also very popular with those who conduct lengthy business in neutral airspace, as this method of travel minimizes the dangers of moving through lawless territories.

Choo Choo~

A quantity of starstone with the proper qualities for powering a ship is referred to as a heart. Technically a lifeform in the way that kudzu is a lifeform, a heart shows certain biological signs of life but possesses no sentience. Capitalizing on the unique organic energy features of starstone in large masses, starships are "grown" rather than constructed, making each ship perfectly suited to its individual purpose. The heart's owner binds the ship to themself, impressing that individual purpose upon the energy manifest, and the lifeform reacts reflexively by creating a structure reflective of the owner's intention. The process is fast and cheap (beyond the heart's cost), but oddly temperamental. A heart takes the form the owner WANTS, not necessarily the form they ASK for. It's not unheard of for a heart to create a useless structure if the impressed purpose is not focused enough, and once a ship is grown around a heart it must be completely destroyed before another attempt can be made. Depending on the strength of the will that created it, this can be extremely difficult.

I mean Pirates. Pirates love Starships. Oh my god. Every Pirate Crew we've met has sailed a Starship.

an all-night diner

NOT <u>BLOOD!!</u>

This is the first explanation I was given. I know now that a step is omitted, implied with any commercially marketed starstone, where the stone is "cut" before sale. The procedure, from what I understand, effectively lobotomizes the consciousness that occurs when enough stone is gathered in one place. Seeing as the stone either cannot or refuses to communicate its sentience during processing, it is unclear whether or not the industry is aware this is happening. As far as I am aware, no resistance from the stone has been documented.

T Day 4 Month 2 Year 1

Acknowledgements

I owe so many people so much!

As always, this book and all the books are dedicated to my mom.

I am forever thankful for my partner Lee, who puts up with every obnoxious aspect of being tethered to a writer. This includes being the first one to read all of my drafts, a job I wouldn't wish on anyone.

I'd also like to thank my editor Inchoatl, who did an absurd amount of invisible work over many months to help make this book into a more pleasant shape. Thank you for reading so many versions of this thing, and thank you very much for bullying me into being braver when I needed it.

In addition to Inchoatl, thank you to Aristide Twain and Skye Mason for taking the time to send me even more notes and editing suggestions. With all these people keeping me in line I think we ended up with something pretty good.

And of course, thank you to all of Kidd Commander's readers and supporters for allowing me to continue making it! There are so many of you that we are starting a new page, meet me over there.

Readers like you!

Kidd Commander was a webcomic before it was anything else! That means it's hosted online on its own website and freely accessible to anyone with an internet connection.

When I tell people this their first question is usually "how do you fund it", and while that's partially answered by the book you're currently reading, the heft of it is done by the people listed on the next page.

Creator-owned stories told on their own terms, especially from voices that are marginalized by the mainstream, is a cause that's very important to me. It's important to others too; enough that they'll step up and help support something that's already freely available to help make sure it *stays* free for folks who would miss out otherwise. I owe my entire career to having media accessibility when I was a kid, and I try hard to pay that forward as much as I can. I'm very proud of the work we're all doing here together!

While this section is specifically thanking (most of) KC's financial supporters, I wouldn't have reached them without the efforts of every reader who has ever shared the story with a friend, made fanwork, or boosted it online. Independent work lives and dies by its fandom, and while ours is very small I think we make up for it with sheer enthusiasm.

Thank you all again for whatever you've contributed towards giving me the resources to tell this story exactly how I want to tell it. I will be here doing that as long as I can, and I hope you'll stick around to see where we go from here!

Special thanks to:
The 2025 Kidd Commander Book Club

A.K.	J Dreams 8WD	Ryan Williams
Amaaré	Jek	Sage
Argle	JennTheFern	samzelle
Aristide Twain	Joachim Verhagen	Simone
Ashen	Khaeta/Ren	Skye Mason
Beemancer	Liam Cesljarevic	Smallfish
Boss Duck	Mayathemysticalunicorn	SparkliTwizzl
Brian Ingkom	Myk Mac	Squiggles
Bunni	Nikita Gazarov	Steph
Eric Johnson	Nova	Sydney Mayhew Williams
Erin	Phineas F.B.	Timothy Woods
Fel	Phlox	Unifel
Giraculum	Possum	Vexatious
I.C.	Razaica	Voidnovice
Inchoatl	Rebecca H.	
ithaginis	Robert Paulson	
Isis Wyche	Rocks-E	

an inexhaustive list of people supporting sincere, independent art

A Certain Warthog	Harper Crane	Mina	Sophia
Andreas	Heather P.	Nathaniel	Strawbari
Aphrodite	Inkie	Nemica	Sydney Savoy
Aran Stone	Jack Ziriax	Neptune	tethys
Arha	Jacques Frechet	Nora	tkayo
artvt84	Jeremiah Maxel	Patrick Harris	Unique
bookwisp	Jey Barnes	Paul K.	Vincent Zell
Brenna Marie	Jove	Pauline Arsenault	Violet Catanese
Colosseum IV:	Jon Baker	Perrydotto	Will
We Gave The Lion	Kaelie	Placebo Tray	Wren
Health Benefits	Karin Rindevall	R	Wyronth
Dax Lyon	Kat	Raffian	
_DeeDraw	Katie	Ryn	
Doug Tyler	Kitty Unpretty	Sabriel	
EJ	Linfaelis	Santorini	
Finch	Liz	Sean Abercrombie	
FlareShard	Marith Lizard	Shelby	
Giuseppe & Molly	Michiel	sincetheflood	

Other work by Aria Bell

(read as: other work in the Kidd Commander canon at the time
of this publication)

The webcomic, forever free to read online at
kiddcommander.com

Comic volumes 1, 2, 3, and 4, available in digital
and physical formats

KC Special! #1, #2

About the Author

After a rigid evangelical upbringing backfired catastrophically, Aria Bell grew up to spend all their time making adamantly humanist stories. She's been doing that since 2013 through comics and novels in the Kidd Commander series, and is probably out there doing it right now as you read this.

He and his partner escaped Tennessee in 2023 and now live in Fort Collins, CO.

You can find out more about both the author and the Kidd Commander series at shinesurge.net

www.ingramcontent.com/pod-product-compliance
Lightning Source LLC
Chambersburg PA
CBHW010652100726
47901CB00012B/2523